T0363633

Romantic Suspense

Danger. Passion. Drama.

Search And Detect
Terri Reed

Sniffing Out Justice
Carol J. Post

MILLS & BOON

Terri Reed is acknowledged as the author of this work
SEARCH AND DETECT
© 2024 by Harlequin Enterprises ULC
Philippine Copyright 2024
Australian Copyright 2024
New Zealand Copyright 2024

First Published 2024
First Australian Paperback Edition 2024
ISBN 978 1 038 93529 8

SNIFFING OUT JUSTICE
© 2024 by Carol J. Post
Philippine Copyright 2024
Australian Copyright 2024
New Zealand Copyright 2024

First Published 2024
First Australian Paperback Edition 2024
ISBN 978 1 038 93529 8

MIX
Paper | Supporting
responsible forestry
FSC® C001695
www.fsc.org

Published by
Harlequin Mills & Boon
An imprint of Harlequin Enterprises (Australia) Pty Limited
(ABN 47 001 180 918), a subsidiary of HarperCollins
Publishers Australia Pty Limited
(ABN 36 009 913 517)
Level 19, 201 Elizabeth Street
SYDNEY NSW 2000 AUSTRALIA

Cover art used by arrangement with Harlequin Books S.A.. All rights reserved.

Printed and bound in Australia by McPherson's Printing Group

Search And Detect
Terri Reed

MILLS & BOON

Terri Reed's romance and romantic suspense novels have appeared on the *Publishers Weekly* top twenty-five and NPD BookScan top one hundred lists and have been featured in *USA TODAY*, *Christian Fiction* magazine and *RT Book Reviews*. Her books have been finalists for the Romance Writers of America RITA® Award and the National Readers' Choice Award and finalists three times for the American Christian Fiction Writers Carol Award. Contact Terri at terrireed.com or PO Box 19555, Portland, OR 97224.

Books by Terri Reed

Love Inspired Suspense

Buried Mountain Secrets
Secret Mountain Hideout
Christmas Protection Detail
Secret Sabotage
Forced to Flee
Forced to Hide
Undercover Christmas Escape
Shielding the Innocent Target

Rocky Mountain K-9 Unit

Detection Detail

Pacific Northwest K-9 Unit

Explosive Trail

Mountain Country K-9 Unit

Search and Detect

Visit the Author Profile page at LoveInspired.com for more titles.

And the Lord shall guide thee continually, and
satisfy thy soul in drought, and make fat thy bones:
and thou shalt be like a watered garden,
and like a spring of water, whose waters fail not.
—*Isaiah* 58:11

To the ladies of the Mountain Country K-9 Unit,
I appreciate all the brainstorming and support
as we brought the characters to life.
And a huge thank-you to the editorial team
at Love Inspired Suspense.
These continuities are a team effort.

Chapter One

Singing with gusto, Zoe Jenkins stood at her kitchen counter with a plethora of paleo-friendly ingredients spread out before her. The rhythmic banging of a plastic spoon against a plastic tray underscored Zoe's melody. Nine-month-old Kylie's chubby little legs and arms waved happily from her high chair, a vision in soft pink in the middle of the cheery yellow kitchen.

A sharp contrast to the weather outside.

The day was gray and chilly. Late fall in Wyoming could bring snowfall and freezing temperatures. So far, the weather had been holding at gloomy.

But life was good right now. Zoe's business was taking off, and she had Kylie. What more could she need?

The whisper of loneliness and quiet anxiety of raising a child alone stirred within her, but she wouldn't give them any ground, too afraid if she gave in, she'd end up weeping on the floor.

She wiped her brow with her forearm as she stifled a yawn. A glance at the clock confirmed it was nearly time to put Kylie down for her morning nap. Today Zoe would take advantage and rest, too.

Fatigue pulled at her. She was definitely burning the wick at both ends. In addition to being a single mom, she worked part-time at the Elk Valley Community Hospital as a registered dietitian helping patients with specific dietary needs. She also ran her own special dietary needs catering business out of her home. To top it off, she was spearheading the upcoming Elk Valley High School multi-generation reunion.

Raising her daughter alone meant juggling multiple responsibilities.

But it was better this way. There was freedom in being alone.

Again, a whisper of discontent knocked at her consciousness. She ignored the annoying sensation.

She'd learned not to rely on anyone except God. A familiar bubble of anger clogged her throat. She quickly took several calming breaths and forced the hurt and resentment back into its cage deep in her heart. Being dumped by her ex-husband five days after Kylie's birth had been a low blow.

Best to concentrate on the fact she had a growing clientele who kept her busy. She created delicious meals and delivered them to her clients' doorsteps, which allowed her to work mostly from home and be with Kylie.

As she handed Kylie a slice of banana, Zoe's gaze snagged on the stack of flyers for the upcoming reunion. There was still so much to do.

Her small committee had been working for months to put this event together. Despite the fact there were those in town who thought having a reunion with the Rocky Mountain Killer still on the loose wasn't a good idea.

But the town needed to heal.

She'd been mourning her brother's death for ten long years. Seth had been one of the RMK's first victims.

It was time to honor those they'd lost and bring the town back together.

Or maybe she just needed this event to heal from her own heartache.

Kylie fussed, her cherub face scrunching up, a clear signal she was ready to be released from the high chair.

"Okay, sweetie pea," Zoe said. "I just need to fill one more box and then it'll be naptime."

She wrapped the prepared meal she'd made in cellophane and placed it inside a white catering box. She shut the lid, smiling at the sight of her business logo. A bright green *Z* above the words The Au Courant Chef—Zoe Jenkins. She set the box in the refrigerator next to several others. Later today she would bag the boxes up and drive them over to her client, Mayor Singh.

The trill of her landline startled her. She stared at the instrument sitting on the other end of the counter. Who would be calling her on that phone?

On the advice of her pediatrician, she'd had a landline installed after Kylie was born. Dr. Webb had said he always recommended one to new parents. Cell phones could run out of battery and be unavailable in the case of an emergency. However, a landline would always provide 911 with a physical address of where to send emergency personnel. She didn't have an answering machine set up and didn't intend to. She wanted the landline for calls out, not in.

Probably spam.

She ignored the ringing.

The phone went silent but started up again a few seconds later.

The insistent noise hammered at Zoe, grating on her nerves.

She quickly washed her hands. By the time she turned the water off the phone had gone silent again. She breathed out a sigh of relief.

After packing the rest of the ingredients into the refrigerator, she moved to release Kylie from the high chair.

The ringing started up for a third time.

"Someone is sure persistent," Zoe said aloud. She stared at the phone. Unease slithered down her spine. Would they just keep calling until she answered? That would seriously mess with naptime.

With a growl of frustration, she grabbed the receiver. "Hello?" She couldn't keep the irritation from her voice.

There was a brief silence then a stream of distorted maniacal laughter, like from a creepy recording of a horror movie, filled her ear. Zoe held the phone away from her as the unnerving sound continued.

"Ugh!" Zoe slammed the receiver down.

Prank call.

The world had turned upside down, and someone thought it would be funny to harass her on the landline. Someone needed to get a life.

Unsettled and beyond annoyed, Zoe picked Kylie up from the high chair and hugged her close. Singing a soothing tune, hoping to keep them both calm enough to nap, she carried Kylie to the nursery at the other end of the long hallway on the opposite side of the house.

The nursery was filled with fanciful motifs in bright cheery colors. Framed castles and unicorns and fields of flowers covered the walls. A white crib with bright pink and yellow bedding, a changing table painted in teal blue and a comfy rocking chair in cream with a floral print pillow sat beneath the window. A comfy and cozy space. The room brought Zoe joy. As did her daughter.

At the changing table, she continued to sing as she prepped Kylie for a nap.

A loud boom, low and deep, ricocheted through the house, rocking Zoe back on her heels. The entire house violently shook. Shock and fear exploded within her. She clutched a wailing Kylie to her chest and dove to the floor, covering her baby with her body.

Oh, God, spare us.

"Where are we on locating—" The sound of a distant explosion rattled the windows and raised the fine hairs on the back of FBI Special Agent Chase Rawlston.

He stood at the head of the conference room table in the Elk Valley Police Department for a task force meeting. The space had become the headquarters of the Mountain Country K-9 Unit. Sitting around the table were several of the men and women from various law enforcement agencies that made up the team tasked with locating and stopping a serial killer they'd dubbed the Rocky Mountain Killer.

The reign of terror had begun right here ten years ago in Chase's hometown of Elk Valley, Wyoming. Three young men, all recent grads of the high school, members of the Young Rancher's Club, had been murdered on Valentine's Day. Lured to a barn and shot dead. After that, the case had gone cold and a decade passed. But several months ago, murders in nearby states had the mark of the same killer. The victims were men originally from Elk Valley and connected in some way to the Young Rancher's Club.

The door to the conference room banged open and an Elk Valley police officer filled the open space. "There's been an explosion at a residence downtown."

Chase started moving while he said to the team, "Grab your gear and your K-9s. We need to find out what happened."

Everyone scrambled from their chairs to head to their assigned desks. Heart hammering with dread at the thought of the possible loss of life, Chase hustled out of the conference room ahead of the team.

"Could this be the RMK?" Deputy US Marshal Meadow Ames asked. Tall and fit from running, Meadow hailed from Glacierville, Montana, but was in Elk Valley to help with the RMK case. She, like several of the other team members, was staying at the Elk Valley Château until they closed the case.

"Not his MO." Detective Bennett Ford replied. Before joining the task force, Bennett had been with the Denver Police Department and still resided in Colorado but was also in town to help with the case. He was now married to the sister of one of their prime suspects. Chase had no doubt the strain on Naomi

Carr-Ford was immense knowing that her brother, Evan Carr, was a wanted man.

But Evan wasn't their only suspect. The task force had discovered Ryan York had both means and motive. The man had a Glock 17 registered to him. A gun that could have fired the 9mm bullets used by the RMK. Matching slugs had been found at all the crime scenes, though investigators had never found the murder weapon. Chase had his sights set on Ryan as the culprit.

But both men had gone into hiding.

"He's changed his MO once already by stabbing a note into some victims' chests. Why not use a bomb?" Elk Valley Officer Rocco Manelli pointed out as he hustled by. The local police officer who had followed in his father's footsteps had been a big asset to the task force. Rocco's father had been in on the original investigation into the Rocky Mountain Killer before dying of a heart attack with the case unsolved. Rocco had a personal interest in helping to bring RMK to justice.

Chase grabbed his flak vest and sidearm. His K-9 partner, a seven-year-old golden retriever named Dash, jumped up from the bed in the corner of the office clearly eager for some action.

"You ready to work?" Chase asked the dog. They had been partners since Dash was two years old. And Dash was trained in explosives detection, apprehension and protection.

Chase quickly leashed the K-9 and they headed out of the police department. The wail of sirens assaulted his ears. Smoke rose in the air, a dark plume that signaled destruction and stirred memories Chase had fought to lock away.

A deep grief slammed into him, nearly making him stumble as he and Dash ran several blocks toward the scene. He pushed thoughts of his late wife and child aside. He needed to stay focused and on his feet. Main Street in Elk Valley was slippery on this wet and cold late October day.

The temptation to pray, to ask God for there to be no casualties was strong, but Chase couldn't bring himself to do it. The chasm was too wide between him and God. And filled with hurt and sorrow.

With the team close on his heels, Chase skidded to a halt and drew in a sharp breath. The air was tinged with acid smoke. The left side of a small Cape Cod–style house located on a tree-lined street just off the main drag running the length of Elk Valley had been destroyed. Dash pulled at his lead and Chase followed. Dash led him toward the back northwest corner to what would have once been the kitchen and alerted. Some kind of incendiary device had been used.

Chase reeled Dash's leash in. He didn't want the dog to get burned by the flames licking at the sides of the house.

Concerned that there might have been occupants inside at the time of the explosion with no opportunity to escape, Chase redirected Dash toward the front door. Locked. Chase stepped back and then planted his foot with enough force against the door to bust the lock and send the door swinging open.

"Search," Chase said to Dash.

The golden retriever darted to the end of the lead, pulling Chase toward the far end of the house. Keeping a hand on his weapon, Chase stayed close to Dash as the dog moved straight to a room at the end of the hall that was quickly filling with in-sidious, dark wisps of smoke. A nursery. His stomach clenched. He fought back a sharp stab of grief.

A young woman lay crumpled on the floor beneath a chunk of the ceiling that had fallen. He could hear a baby crying.

His heart contracted painfully in his chest. Was the mother dead? Swiftly, he pushed aside the piece of plaster. "Ma'am?"

The woman didn't move. The baby continued to cry, its piti-ful wails muffled by the mother, whose dark brown hair fanned out, shielding her face.

With his heart beating in his throat, Chase knelt to touch the woman, hoping to find a heartbeat. Dash sat and whined as if he too were worried.

The moment Chase's fingers made contact with the woman's throat, she screamed and scuttled away from him, taking her child with her.

On his haunches, Chase raised his hands and stared into the dark, panicked eyes of a beautiful woman, clutching a baby girl to her chest. "Whoa, easy now. I'm with the FBI. I'm here to help."

The woman blinked, seeming to come out of her frantic state. She stared at Dash then back at Chase. "What happened?"

"Your kitchen exploded," Chase told her. He held out his hand. "Let's get you and the baby out of here."

The woman tilted her head as she stared at Chase. "I know you."

Chase had the sensation that he knew her, too, only he couldn't put a name to the face. But in a small town, everybody seemed to know everybody.

"You can trust me," he said.

She cocked an eyebrow. He thought for a moment she was going to resist, but then she held out her hand and allowed him to pull her to her feet. The baby pointed at Dash, babbling something that sounded like doggy.

Tamping down the swell of emotions rising through him, Chase tugged the woman and her child out of the room. Placing a protective arm around her shoulders, he guided her out of the house the way he'd come in. The smoke was thickening as more of the house caught fire.

The woman gasped at the sight of the destruction to her home. But he hustled her away before she could ask questions. He didn't have answers, and they needed to let the fire department get in and investigate.

Two paramedics rushed forward.

"They were in the house," Chase told them.

"We'll take care of them," the female paramedic said as she took hold of the woman and child, guiding them toward the ambulance bay.

Protective instincts surged. Chase wanted to accompany

them, but he knew his place was not at their side. He turned his focus to the smoldering house.

"Do you know who that is?" Officer Ashley Hanson—now Officer McNeal—asked as she came to a halt next to him. Beside her stood her K-9 Ozzy, a black lab specializing in tracking.

Chase stared at the local cop who had been thrust onto his task force by her FBI honcho father. Chase hadn't been totally on board with the idea of a rookie being a part of the team, but she'd proven herself, and now Chase was thankful for her presence.

"I don't. But I should. Right?"

"Zoe Jenkins."

Chase's stomach dropped. The sister of Seth Jenkins. One of the three RMK victims from ten years ago. Along with his friends Aaron Anderson and Brad Kingsley.

It made sense that Zoe would recognize him considering he was the head of the task force created to uncover and capture the RMK. But he'd never met her; other members of the team had interviewed her as part of the investigation. She was familiar, though, whether because he'd seen her photo in the RMK file or that they'd both grown up in Elk Valley.

"Do you think the RMK is out to get her because of her brother?" Ian Carpenter asked. A former sheriff's deputy who'd spent time in the witness protection program, Ian had been recruited to join the task force, and he and Meadow were now engaged.

"We don't know that the RMK is in Elk Valley." Chase knew that the killer had traveled to Utah where one of his targets—the *main* target—lived now, but Trevor had eluded the RMK and was now in a safe house with his fiancée, a member of the task force. The RMK would not give up, though. That much Chase knew.

He saw the fire chief heading toward the house.

"Do a canvas of the area to see if anybody saw suspicious activity in the last day or so," Chase instructed the team.

He and Dash took off toward the fire chief.

"Heard you rescued a woman and child from the house," Fire Chief Fred Hawkins said.

"This wasn't an ordinary fire," Chase told the man. "Dash alerted. Northwest corner. I'm sure you'll find an incendiary device. I want it when you're done with your investigation."

"You got it."

"Good. I'll send my tech around to collect the evidence."

The fire chief nodded and went back to work. Chase gazed at the house, then turned slowly, searching the area for any sign of someone too interested in the results of his handiwork. Residents all up and down the street had come out of their homes. Who had it out for Zoe Jenkins? Was this the work of the RMK? But that would mean the killer was back in town.

His gaze zeroed in on Zoe and her child settling into the back of the ambulance. A rush of concern hit him square in the chest. He and Dash hustled over. He climbed into the back and sat next to the paramedic without preamble.

"What are you doing?" Zoe asked.

"I need answers." Chase wasn't about to let Zoe Jenkins out of his sight. If the Rocky Mountain Killer was after the sister of one of his early victims, this might be the break they needed.

Chapter Two

Sitting on the exam room table in the Elk Valley Hospital with Kylie in her arms, Zoe struggled to believe she and Kylie were alive. Her ears still rang with the phantom boom of the explosion that had destroyed most of her home. The feel of the ceiling falling on top of her as she shielded Kylie would haunt her nightmares.

Even though the paramedics had assured her that Kylie was unharmed, Zoe had insisted on seeing Kylie's pediatrician, Dr. Webb.

The fact that Chase Rawlston hadn't left her side except for a moment or two since he'd first found them in the nursery left Zoe feeling off-kilter.

Chase was a hometown hero and an FBI agent.

He'd been three years ahead of Zoe in high school, but she'd watched him play on the varsity football team alongside her now ex-husband, Garrett Watson.

Watching Chase pace across the room like a caged animal only ratcheted up Zoe's nerves. He was a big man with brown curly hair cut close, wide shoulders and long legs. He wore khaki pants and a dark jacket with the words FBI embossed on the back and the front pocket.

His dog, a beautiful golden retriever, was doing a much better job of being patient. The dog, too, wore an FBI vest, making him very official and adorable.

From the moment they'd entered the exam room, the dog had taken up a position by the door as if to make sure no one came or went without his knowing.

"Why are you here?" she finally asked when she couldn't take the silence any longer. "I'm sure you have more important stuff to be doing than waiting with me, right?"

Coming to a halt in front of her, he said, "I told you. I want answers."

Yes, he'd said as much when he'd unceremoniously jumped into the back of the ambulance. But then he'd stayed stoically silent. His dog had shown more interest in her and Kylie than the man who consumed too much space. His presence sucked up the oxygen in the bay of the ambulance and she'd found herself growing dizzy. Thankfully she was sitting now as she stared at him.

He had a commanding aura around him with his broad shoulders beneath his FBI jacket. His deep brown eyes held her gaze.

Did he blame her for the explosion?

An anxious flutter in her stomach had her wondering if she'd left a burner on. "I don't know what happened. I'm sure I turned the stove off when I was done cooking. But maybe I accidentally—"

Chase held up a hand, stopping her. "This was not your fault."

Zoe wanted to believe him. "But houses don't just blow up. I had to have done something to cause this."

Chase moved to sit beside her on the exam table, crowding her again, yet she didn't feel the need to move away. Odd.

He reached over to allow Kylie to grab a hold of his index finger. "May I call you Zoe?"

"Of course." She steeled herself for whatever he was about to say.

"Zoe, someone deliberately blew your house up."

She tucked in her chin, unsure she'd heard him correctly. "Say what?"

"My partner, Dash, is a trained bomb-sniffing dog."

Her gaze moved to the dog lying by the door. His big brown eyes watched her and Kylie.

She tried to wrap her mind around Chase's pronouncement. "You're saying your dog sniffed a bomb at my house."

"Exactly. Dash is very good at his job. He alerted the second we got close enough to the back northwest corner. Outside your kitchen."

The loss of her work, the meals prepped and ready to be delivered, stabbed through her and tears pricked the back of her eyes. "Why would someone do that?"

The dog rose to his feet and ambled over, putting his chin on Zoe's knee as if to comfort her. Kylie reached down her little chubby hands, grasping a handful of fur.

Afraid the dog would bite, Zoe quickly loosened Kylie's fingers. The dog just stared at them.

"He likes children," Chase said.

There was a wistful, sad note in his tone. Zoe searched his face, but he averted his gaze to his watch. "Where is this doctor?"

She remembered reading that Chase was the head of the task force searching for the Rocky Mountain Killer. There had been several articles in the local paper over the past eight months about the hunt for the murderer. A different sort of anxiety twisted in her chest "You're looking for my brother's killer. Do you really think you'll find him after all this time?"

"We're hopeful." Determination marched across his handsome face.

"Because he's active again," she said with a shudder of repulsion and fear.

"Yes. We're trying to figure out what triggered him to resurface," Chase said.

A shiver of fear slid down her arms. "You don't think it was the Rocky Mountain Killer who bombed my house, do you?"

"I can't rule out that possibility," he said.

Her breath hitched in stunned surprise. "But after all this time?"

"The mind of the killer is a mysterious and dark place," Chase said. "All we can do is try to stay ahead of him and attempt to anticipate his next move."

Distress squeezed her lungs, making her chest tight. "Did someone anticipate him coming after me?"

Chase gave a heavy sigh. "Unfortunately, no. You were not on our radar. But this opens the possibility that he'll go after the families of his victims."

Zoe tightened her hold on Kylie. She had to protect her child. "So, you're saying he's back in town."

"Not necessarily. The RMK's last known whereabouts was in Utah. I have a team still there searching for him. Until we know more about who might want to hurt you, I'm keeping an open mind and considering all prospects."

Zoe digested his words. If not the RMK, then someone else wanted her dead. "I can't think of anyone who would want to harm me and Kylie."

There was a soft knock at the door before it opened, and Dr. Webb, wearing blue scrubs, walked in. The older gentleman's concerned gaze took in Zoe and Kylie and Chase.

"Is it true someone tried to...?" He cut himself off with a shake of his head. "Zoe, the paramedics tell me they checked out Kylie and she's fine. But I'm glad you brought her in anyway. I'll do my own check."

Relieved, Zoe smiled. "Thank you, Dr. Webb. I dove on top of her. I just want to make sure she doesn't have any bumps or bruises that the paramedics missed."

Chase rose and moved toward the door. He made a clicking

noise into his cheek and Dash scrambled to his paws. "We'll be right outside."

He and his dog left the exam room. For some reason, Zoe wanted to ask him to stay. Which was ridiculous. She didn't need him. Her days of relying on a man for her well-being were long over.

Chase stopped outside the exam room door. His gaze scanned the area, taking in the nurses' station and the various medical personnel going about their jobs. There were no discernable threats. He let out a breath, easing the constriction in his chest.

Being at a hospital with Zoe and her little girl made his heart ache, stirring the grief that was never far from the surface.

What was he doing here?

He should be checking in with the team, learning if there were any updates on the serial killer they were tracking.

They'd had the RMK in their grasp last month in Utah, but he'd slipped through their fingers. And they'd hit a dead end with their two prime suspects, who couldn't be located.

Evan Carr's alibi for the night of the original three murders had fallen apart when his then-girlfriend confessed in a recent interview that Evan had not been with her the whole night as she'd originally claimed. Which meant he'd had the opportunity to commit the crimes. Evan's sister had been humiliated by the victims—though one of them had simply been part of the group of friends—at a Young Rancher's Club dance.

Then there was Ryan York. His sister, Shelly, had dated Seth Jenkins, one of the Rocky Mountain Killer's original victims. From all accounts, Ryan was furious with Seth and his friends because of Seth's treatment of Shelly. Shelly had committed suicide by taking sleeping pills not long after her breakup with Seth. A stronger motive than a supposed prank date that had gotten out of hand.

Chase firmly believed York was the killer. But he needed to prove it by capturing him.

Both suspects were tall and blond, which matched the description they had of the man who'd kidnapped the MCK9 task force's therapy dog Cowgirl, a labradoodle, who had been in training. They knew the RMK had the dog.

At least the killer had had the decency to leave Cowgirl's recent litter of puppies for the team to find and care for when they'd been searching for him in Utah. If only he would release Cowgirl. Chase worried about the labradoodle's well-being. But from the taunt-texts he'd received from the RMK, it appeared he was taking care of the dog.

The killer had taunted the task force on other occasions, too. He'd stabbed notes into the chests of two recent victims, Henry Mulder in Montana, and Peter Windham in Colorado.

Notes that warned of more deaths to come. Sure enough, he'd killed Luke Randall in Idaho. And now he was gunning for Trevor Gage, Elk Valley's golden boy.

Trevor was now secured in a safe house with his fiancée, task force member Hannah Scott, a Utah highway patrol officer, and her K-9 partner, a Newfoundland named Captain. Chase was sure the RMK didn't know where Trevor was located. He'd called the team back to Elk Valley after securing his protection last month.

He needed to focus on the RMK investigation.

Yet, he hesitated to leave the hospital.

Call it a gut instinct or hard-earned experience, but something compelled him to stay.

Could the RMK case and the bombing of Zoe's home be connected?

A question that kept running through his mind.

Until he had the answer, he had to provide protection to the innocent victim and her child.

He took out his phone and pressed the speed-dial number for his boss in Washington, DC.

On the second ring, Cara Haines answered. "Rawlston. Good news, I hope."

Chase winced. He'd worked for Cara back when he lived in DC. She was the reason he was heading the task force. And she knew him well enough to know he wouldn't call unless it was important. "No. But there's been a development."

"You have the whereabouts of the RMK?"

He shook his head with a grimace. "Still unknown. But the sister of one of the RMK's first victims was attacked today. Her house was rigged with an explosive. I can't say for certain there's a connection but—"

"But you want to pursue the investigation," Cara stated.

"I do, and I'll need the task force's help," he told her.

There was a moment of silence as she considered.

"All right. But I don't want the RMK case to lag," she said firmly.

"No, ma'am. It won't," he assured her.

"Good. Keep me informed," she said. "And Rawlston, I've alerted Deputy US Marshal Sully Briggs that we will utilize the marshal service when you capture the RMK."

Chase appreciated her confidence in the task force's success. "I'll keep Deputy Briggs updated."

"Anything else?" Cara asked.

"No, ma'am, that's it."

"In case I haven't said it lately, Chase, you're doing a good job. Elsie would be proud of you," Cara added, her voice softening.

Chase squeezed his eyes shut against the pain her words caused. Squaring his shoulders, he said. "Thank you."

"Okay, then," Cara said. "Back at it." Cara hung up.

Chase pocketed his phone just as the door behind him opened. He steeled himself against the onslaught of emotions battering him. He had to stay detached, in control and vigilant. Anything less could result in tragedy. An outcome he would avoid at all costs.

As the doctor examined Kylie, Zoe ran through possible culprits or reasons why somebody would go to such destructive lengths to hurt her and Kylie. She tried really hard to be a good person. She may not be the warmest of people, but she certainly had no complaints from her clients or her patients here at the hospital. The only person who was disgruntled with her was her ex-husband. But Garrett wouldn't resort to attempting to kill her and his child to get out of paying child support and alimony. Would he?

"You can get her dressed," Dr. Webb said with a gentle smile. "She's perfectly healthy and normal. Not even a scratch or any sign of trauma." Dr. Webb patted Zoe's shoulder. "Good job protecting your daughter. What about you? The paramedics said you might have some abrasions on your back from falling debris?"

Zoe barely felt an ache where the portion of the ceiling had fallen on top of her. She would probably have a bruise. But the paramedics assured her nothing was broken. "I'm fine. Now that I know Kylie's all right, we'll get out of your hair. I know you're busy."

"I am always here for my patients," Dr. Webb said.

He opened the door to the exam room revealing Chase and his dog standing guard. Zoe smiled at the sight of the two males. Did he really think somebody would break into the exam room and try to harm her?

The thought sent a shiver traipsing down her spine. She didn't like this feeling of vulnerability stealing over her. Would the person come after her and Kylie again?

With hands that shook, she quickly dressed Kylie and joined Chase and his dog in the hallway.

A nurse in scrubs rushed up.

Chase held up a hand to stop her from reaching Zoe. A protective move that made Zoe's heart bump.

"Zoe," Haley Newton said. Her strawberry-blonde hair was pulled back into a tight bun at the nape of her neck. Her bright blue eyes were wide with concern. "I just heard what happened. It's good to see you uninjured."

"Thanks," Zoe replied.

Haley gave Chase a thorough once-over. "You're Chase Rawlston. I remember you from high school."

Chase arched an eyebrow. "Good memory. And you are?"

There was a flash of disappointment in Haley's eyes that she masked with a smile. "Haley Newton. I was a grade behind you. Are you back in town for the reunion?"

Zoe refrained from scoffing. Apparently, Haley hadn't read the *Elk Valley Daily Gazette*, which kept a running article on the Rocky Mountain Killer investigation. More than once Chase's name had been in the paper along with his team, several of whom were local to the area.

"Not exactly," Chase told her.

Haley turned her focus back to Zoe. "Are you and Kylie okay? Have you let Garrett know?"

Zoe gritted her teeth against the mention of her ex-husband but managed to say, "Not yet. And we're fine."

Haley reached out to run a finger down Kylie's cheek. "One would think this little bundle of joy's father would want to know if she was okay."

"One would think," Zoe repeated. But she couldn't say Garrett would care considering he'd walked out of their lives without so much as a backward glance. "I appreciate the concern, Haley. But we really have to head out now."

Haley stepped back. "Of course. Let me know if there's anything I can do to help you."

"I will," Zoe said, grateful for her colleague's concern.

Haley gave Chase another curious glance before nodding and hurrying down the hallway.

Chase put his hand Zoe's shoulder. She reflexively stiffened at the contact.

He immediately lifted his hand. "Sorry."

"No, I'm sorry," Zoe said. "I'm just a little rattled from the explosion."

Chase gave her a measured look. "Garrett? As in Garrett Watson? He's your ex?"

Zoe winced. "Yes."

There was a speculative gleam in Chase's eyes. "Let's get out of here so we can talk."

They started walking toward the exit. Then Zoe came to a halt. "I have nowhere to go."

"Your parents?"

"They moved to Florida not long after Seth's murder," she said. "I have responsibilities here. I can't just head south."

Chase pushed open the exit door. "We'll think of something. But we can't do it on an empty stomach."

"I'll have to stop at the bank and see if I can withdraw some money," she said. "My purse with my ID and credit cards had been on the dining room table. They're now probably blown to bits. Along with the mayor's meal order. I'll have to contact him, too. I'll need to get a new cell phone. And clothes. Everything."

"We'll get you all situated in time," Chase told her. "But for now, let me treat you and Kylie to lunch."

A heaviness settled on Zoe's shoulders. It wouldn't hurt to accept his offer. She would pay him back as soon as she could. "The Rusty Spoke has sweet potato fries, which are Kylie's favorite."

"Then that's where we'll go."

The Rusty Spoke had a busy lunch crowd. The dim interior and booths lining the walls were perfect for some privacy. The low hum of conversation from the other patrons didn't drown out the soft country tunes playing from hidden speakers. Zoe waved to one of the waitresses, Jessie Baldwin. Their grandmothers had been friends before Zoe's grandma passed away.

Jessie was in her early twenties and wore jeans with a Western-style shirt. Her dark hair bobbed about her chin as she moved. "Hi, Zoe. Sit where you'd like." Jessie eyed Dash. "Cool, a working dog. Can I get him some water?"

"Please." Chase pointed to an empty booth. "Let's take that."

Zoe nodded and let him and Dash lead the way. They wound around the tables in the middle of the floor toward the last empty booth. She felt conspicuous, like everybody in the place was watching her. Did everyone in town know that somebody had just blown up her home?

She glanced around, tightening her hold on Kylie. Was one of these people the bomber? She recognized most of the local patrons. But why would anyone want to hurt her?

Blowing out a breath, she silently admonished herself. She was being paranoid and ridiculous. Chase had just told her that the RMK was last seen far away in Utah. He wouldn't come back to Elk Valley.

Yet unease prickled the skin on the nape of her neck.

Zoe slid into the booth and settled Kylie on her lap. Kylie's chubby little hands banged against the wooden tabletop. Dash sat beside the booth.

Jessie approached the table and set a bowl of water in front of the dog, he immediately lapped it up.

"Zoe, we heard what happened," Jessie said. "Are you okay? I know my grandma has already started a prayer chain."

Heart thumping with gratitude, Zoe smiled. "We're good. Thank you for asking. And tell your grandma thank you, as well. We could use all the prayers we can get."

Jessie gave her a sympathetic smile, took their drink and food orders and hustled away.

"I don't know what we're going to do," she said aloud. "If what you suspect is true, that someone deliberately tried to blow me and Kylie up, it's not safe for us to stay with anyone we know. And I can't afford a room at the Elk Valley Château for an extended period of time."

"No responsibility is worth your life. You could go to Florida."

Zoe heaved a sigh. "I guess that's what we'll have to do."

She frowned as concern darkened her thoughts. "But what if the person who wants to harm me follows me there? Then I'm just putting my parents in danger, too."

Chase rubbed his chin, drawing her gaze. He had a nice jawline with a hint of a beard. His brown eyes were warm like caramel sauce.

Somewhere in the back of her mind, she recalled someone saying he was a widower. She wanted to ask but thought that would be rude.

Besides, she shouldn't be curious about Chase. She didn't want to become attached to him in any way. But at the moment, she was having to rely on him, and that fact grated on her nerves. "I know God will provide. I need to be patient. This is all just so new and surreal."

Chase's hand dropped to the table. "Yes, patience would be good here. We'll need to come up with a plan. As for God providing—it's a nice sentiment but in my experience that doesn't really happen."

"In your experience?" She hated to think of him so jaded. Was he referring to his wife's death? Or to his job? "I would imagine as an FBI agent you've seen some horrible things."

He shrugged. "I have."

"This world can knock us down," she said. "But God is always reaching out to lift us back up."

A slight scoff lifted one corner of his mouth. "If you say so."

"I've experienced it," she told him. "When I was at my bleakest, I felt God's presence. He surrounded me with good people. And opened doors I hadn't even known were there."

Chase tilted his head. "Are you referring to Garrett and your divorce?"

Her stomach knotted. "I am."

"Tell me what happened," Chase said, his voice hard.

Zoe tucked in her chin. "I don't think rehashing my failed marriage will be productive."

"I'll be the judge of that," he said. "This incident today could very well be related to your ex-husband."

His words were a punch to the gut.

Chapter Three

"Unlikely," Zoe said aloud, answering her own question. The clang of utensils against dishes mixed with the murmur of conversations around the restaurant. Zoe angled her back toward the other diners while keeping a firm hold on Kylie, who squirmed to be set free from Zoe's lap. "Garrett is many things… I can give you a litany of faults. But I don't believe he would do this. He wouldn't have the know-how. Nor would he expend that much energy on learning to make a bomb."

"You'd be surprised what people can do given the right motivation," Chase replied, clearly unconvinced by her argument. "How did you and Garrett meet?"

She sighed. Chase wasn't going to drop the subject. "When I returned after college to take a job at the hospital, I bumped into Garrett one day at the hardware store. We got to talking and he asked me out. Of course, I knew who he was. He was in your class and on the football team. He had gone to work for his father and was in the process of taking over the business so his dad could retire. He was charming and good-looking." She shook her head. "I wanted to put down roots."

"How long were you married?"

"Just shy of seven years," she told him.

"What happened to break you up?"

Gritting her teeth against the spurt of anger tightening her throat, it was a moment before she could speak. She bounced Kylie on her knee and allowed the love for her baby to push back the resentment wanting to take hold.

"I became pregnant," she said. "I knew Garrett wasn't interested in starting a family while he was building up the business he'd taken over from his dad. He'd wanted to expand. In the beginning, I was fine with waiting. I had my own career to think of but then I ended up pregnant. I never imagined he'd abandon me."

She scoffed, remembering Garrett's reaction when she'd told him the news. "He was livid. Accused me of cheating." Hurt spread through her chest at the accusation.

Chase's expression didn't change, which helped her to continue.

"Garrett confessed that in high school he had an injury and the doctors told him he would most likely not be able to father children. He kept that from me. I might not have married him had I known. I can assure you, Kylie is his child. He even insisted on a paternity test, which only confirmed what I already knew."

Chase shook his head, his disdain clear. "He still didn't want to be a father?"

"No. He thought children would—oh, I don't know. Cramp his style. He liked being able to party whenever he wanted. To go on trips at the last moment. Usually without me. My job at the hospital wasn't as flexible then."

"He didn't deserve you or Kylie," Chase said in a tone full of certainty.

His words were a soothing balm that she quickly pushed away. She couldn't get sucked into Chase's charm. She'd fallen for a handsome man's charm once before and it had ended in disaster. Though she knew, logically, it wasn't fair to compare

Chase to Garrett. They were as opposite as night and day. Weren't they?

She really didn't know Chase. Of course, she'd known of him for years, just like she'd known about Garrett before they'd started dating. Ha! Look how that had turned out. Chase could be saying what she wanted to hear in an effort to pry information from her. He had a job to do, after all.

What did it say about her that she was suspicious of his kindness?

"I want you to think back over the last few days," Chase said. "Was there anything suspicious that stood out to you? People in your neighborhood whom you've never seen before? A car that drove by more than once that didn't belong there?"

"I can't think of anything out of the ordinary." She paused. "Wait, that's not true. A few minutes before the house exploded my landline rang. A prank call."

His eyebrows rose. "What did the caller say?"

"Nothing." Irritation laced her words. "It was just this weird laughter that totally wigged me out."

"Laughter?" He considered for a moment then asked, "Male or female?"

Zoe shook her head with a shrug. "I couldn't tell. I hung up." Apprehension squeezed her chest. "I took Kylie to the nursery. A few minutes later..."

She shuddered at the memory. They'd come close to dying today. If it wasn't for Chase... "Thank you, by the way. I don't think I said that earlier. If you hadn't found us, I don't know what would have happened."

Chase reached across the table and gently took her hand. "You're safe now."

Warmth engulfed her. She stared at their joined hands. His was so much bigger and tanned, compared to her smaller hand that very rarely saw the sunshine. Her heart gave a little jolt. She resisted the urge to curl her fingers around his calloused ones, to cling to him. Instead, she extracted her hand and brushed back Kylie's hair.

Jessie returned to the table with their food and beverages. Zoe was thankful for the distraction as she fed Kylie sweet potato fries and picked at her own garden salad.

Chase had no problem devouring his cheeseburger and fries. Then he said, "Let me hold her while you finish your salad."

Surprised and grateful, she handed Kylie over the table into his capable hands. He bounced Kylie on his knee while Zoe ate. The nine-month-old was content, her eyes wide taking in the room, clearly undisturbed by being held in the arms of a stranger.

Zoe found herself distracted watching this big man with her child. He did well with Kylie, holding her firmly but also giving her wiggle room. The way a parent would.

Giving herself a shake, Zoe finished eating and took Kylie back so that Chase could slide from the booth and pay the bill.

He held out his hand to Zoe. "Come on. I know a place where you'll be safe."

Appreciating his gentlemanly manner, she grasped his hand and attempted to awkwardly slide out of the booth with Kylie in her arms. Chase quickly plucked Kylie from her and settled her on his hip. He looked so natural holding her, like he'd been born to be a caregiver. A father.

For a moment, all Zoe could do was stare.

Kylie touched Chase's face and he kissed her little fingers as they skimmed over his lips. His chuckle resonated through Zoe as she slid out of the booth and reached to take Kylie back. "She likes you."

He made an affirmative noise in his throat and headed toward the exit. Zoe watched his back wondering about his life. Was he seeing someone? Or was he still grieving his wife?

Ack! She had no business contemplating such questions.

At the door, Jessie hustled over with a to-go bag that she thrust into Zoe's free hand. "A snack for Kylie."

Touched by the younger woman's kindness, Zoe said, "You didn't have to—"

Jessie waved away her protest. "I know. We all want to be there for you, Zoe. We look after our own." She lightly touched a fingertip to the end of Kylie's nose. "I'm looking forward to the reunion. I bought a new dress."

Glad to know Jessie was eager to attend, Zoe gave the younger woman a quick, one-arm hug. "Thank you."

Emotions surged and Zoe blinked back tears as she pushed through the door into the late October afternoon. The air was crisp and filled her lungs.

"You okay?"

Chase's softly asked question drew her gaze. The warmth in the depths of his eyes had her saying, "It's almost my brother's birthday, which is why I advocated for the reunion to be in October. Losing Seth to the RMK ripped my family apart. I was his sister. I should have protected him."

Chase shook his head. "Don't take on that type of guilt. The only one responsible is the killer."

She appreciated his words, appreciated his patience with her. "My parents couldn't stay here in Elk Valley. It was too painful, you know. Memories everywhere. But I returned after college. I didn't want to forget my brother."

"I'm sorry for your loss," Chase said. "The tribute reunion will honor Seth and the other victims. The committee hopes the community will be brought together and those who've lost a loved one will find some comfort.

"A commendable reason for the reunion," Chase stated.

His praise was unsettling. "Where to?"

After a barely discernible hesitation, Chase said, "A safe place."

Hugging Kylie close, Zoe had no choice but to follow and trust him.

How long would it take him to find the bomber?

* * *

After a stop at the Elk Valley police station to check in with the team, Chase drove Zoe and Kylie to his family home. He led them up the front walkway, noticing the grass needed to be mowed. The shrubs rimming the porch could stand a trimming. The rosebushes were bare but still thorny under the front window. They reached the varnished wood front door of the house he shared with his father. There was no safer place in Elk Valley that he could think of, beyond the police department, than here.

He wouldn't think about how hard it would be to have a mother and child underfoot, stirring up memories that he worked hard to suppress.

What would Zoe think of the place? Why did he care? "It's not lavish, but you'll be safe here."

"Whose house is this?" she asked, hitching Kylie higher on her hip.

"My dad's," he admitted with a bit of trepidation. "And mine, when I'm in Elk Valley."

She blinked up at him, her pretty eyes searching his face. "This is unexpected. Is this your childhood home?"

"It is."

Her mouth dropped open slightly. "Are you sure we won't be in the way?"

"Not at all." He infused assurance into his tone even though a bout of nerves ripped through him. "My father will be happy for the company."

His father had been ecstatic, actually, when Chase had called him from the police department to let him know he would be bringing Zoe and Kylie home. He'd been quick to impress on his father the scope of the situation. He didn't want Liam Rawlston to get the wrong idea and believe that Chase had a personal interest in Zoe and her baby girl.

Nothing could be further from the truth.

Yes, it was his job to keep Zoe and her baby safe, and he would. But his heart had been ripped out with the death of his wife, Elsie, and son, Tommy. Now there was a gaping hole he had no intention of filling. Forming an emotional attachment wasn't something he could allow. He couldn't ever go through that kind of pain again.

Zoe preceded him into the house with Kylie on her hip.

The sensation of being watched itched over Chase's flesh like hairy spider legs. He didn't like it. He paused and glanced back over his shoulder, taking in the modest homes lining both sides of the road. Several cars were parked at the curb or in driveways, but he couldn't discern any occupants. No window curtains fluttered with curious neighbors. Nothing seemed out of place on their quiet residential street. The police station wasn't far, an easy walk.

He glanced down at Dash who stared up at him waiting for the release signal for him to go inside the house. The dog wasn't alerting or showing any sign of distress that would indicate a threat close by. Chase trusted Dash implicitly. He may be a bomb-sniffing dog, but he was also well-versed in protection and apprehension. He'd made sure of that when Dash was younger.

"Release," Chase murmured, and they went inside.

Chase shut the door behind them and let his senses adjust. Everything was familiar and comforting. The same artwork on the walls, the same furniture, and the same beige carpeting from his boyhood. The only big difference was the large screen smart television in the corner. His gaze zeroed in on Zoe, who had moved to the worn brown leather couch and sat with Kylie on her knee. His father was nowhere to be seen.

"Dad," Chase called out.

His father emerged from the kitchen, wearing an apron over his customary chino pants and plaid button down, and wiping his hands on a towel. "I didn't hear you come in."

Liam undid the apron and set it and the towel over the back of a dining room chair. His father walked with a slight limp, left over from his days with the Elk Valley Fire Department.

Burn scars had ravished his flesh on both legs and his right hip. The last fire he'd worked had almost killed him.

"You must be Zoe," Liam Rawlston said, holding out his hand.

"I am." Zoe took his hand in her delicate one for a quick shake.

Liam moved to sit in his favorite chair. A striped recliner that was a throwback to the seventies. "Chase tells me you've had a bit of trouble. And you need a safe place to stay. I can promise you, we will protect you."

Zoe bounced Kylie on her knee. "I appreciate this. Really. It just feels like we're an imposition."

Chase came fully into the living room from the entryway. "Not at all. My father's former FD but he's also a decorated Marine."

"Go on now, Chase," Liam said with a grin. "You're going to make me blush."

Zoe laughed, a soft sound that curled around Chase's heart.

Abruptly, he turned and headed for the kitchen, saying over his shoulder, "Come on, Dash. Time to eat."

Contrary to what he'd told Zoe, this would be difficult for him. As he'd sat across from her and her little girl, he'd been charmed. Zoe was so attentive, and Kylie was adorable. His heart ached with tenderness when he'd held her. So tiny and perfect. So vulnerable. Having them in his home would be an adjustment. One he'd never expected to make. The need to see to their protection personally wouldn't be denied. They were in grave danger, and he couldn't think of a safer place in town to house them.

The house line rang, and he heard his father answer and then tell Zoe the call was for her. After dishing out Dash's food, Chase returned to the living room. Liam held Kylie while Zoe talked to someone on the phone. Who could possibly know she was here?

Wariness crimped the muscles in Chase's shoulders. "Who is she talking to?"

Was it the mysterious bomber? Had the person who called her right before the bomb went off discovered she was staying with Chase and his dad?

"It's Pastor Jerome from the Elk Valley Community Church," Liam told him.

Unexpected and unwanted. Chase had no use for God or faith. Not after the tragedy that had taken his wife and child from him. Even as the thought stampeded through his mind, guilt stomped in, reminding him the blame for Elsie and Tommy's death lay squarely on his shoulders.

"How does the pastor know she's here?" Chase asked his father.

Liam shrugged. "When I got the call for donations from Martha Baldwin, I mentioned you were bringing Zoe here. Was that not okay?"

Chase cringed. He supposed in a small town like Elk Valley word would spread quickly about Zoe and Kylie staying with the Rawlstons. He'd have to consider moving her out of town. Though he doubted she'd go. Hadn't he just told her she'd be safe here?

And she would. He'd make certain.

Focusing on Zoe, Chase could see whatever was being said on the other end of the line was making Zoe happy. She thanked Pastor Jerome and hung up.

"The church has gathered donations for Kylie and me," she said. "We need to head over there and pick up what they have so far. Neither Kylie nor I have clothes."

Liam hefted Kylie up on his shoulder. The little girl snuggled in close, sucking her thumb.

Meeting his father's gaze and seeing the understanding in Liam's eyes made Chase's heart pound. His father knew how hard having Kylie around was going to be for Chase. For them both. Chase had lost a son and Liam a grandson. The baby was a reminder of their sorrow.

Yet, Kylie was such a sweet little one. Her wispy brown hair sported a tiny pink bow that matched her pretty pink outfit smudged with dirt from the explosion.

Kylie held no resemblance to the towheaded bruiser of a boy Tommy had been. Nor did Zoe resemble Elsie.

Pretty, in a girl-next-door way, Zoe had a down-to-earth attraction that surprisingly appealed to Chase. She was as she appeared, there was no pretense with Zoe. Honest and earnest. A devoted mom. Charming. He shoved those thoughts aside. He didn't want to be charmed. He wanted to find out who had tried to kill her and her daughter.

"We'll be fine here," Liam said. "I can make a bed for Kylie on the floor with the couch cushions and a couple of blankets."

Zoe hesitated, the conflict of whether to leave Kylie or not was evident on her pretty face.

Chase didn't want to go. The idea of setting foot in a church sent ribbons of anxiety winding through him. After the loss of his family, he'd given up on God, angered that God had taken his family from him. "We can have the donations brought here."

He'd have one of the task force members head over to the church.

That he was willing to use government resources for his own agenda was a minor infraction, and he'd deal with whatever fallout came as long as it kept him from having to go.

"That won't be necessary," Zoe said, seeming to come to a decision. "I think Kylie will be just fine here with your dad. You and I can zip over and bring everything back. I'll need to go through it all to make sure I get the right sizes for us both. And we'll need to visit the bank so I can access my money and then stop at a store to get a few other things since I have to wait until the fire department releases my house. Though most everything will smell like smoke and be unsalvageable, not to mention the water damage." She shuddered and made a face. "At some point, I'll also need to go to the DMV since my purse with my ID was destroyed."

Zoe stood there with her expectant gaze holding his.

Chase's breath stalled. His heart jammed in his throat. He swallowed hard. She needed him to go with her. He couldn't deny her this. He didn't want to cause her more pain or disappointment because of his issues. He was going to have to suck it up and face God in His own house.

Zoe gripped the door handle of Chase's truck as he sped up. Blood pounded in her ears. "Is something wrong?"

"We're being followed," he said, his voice strained.

She twisted in her seat. Behind them, a white sedan drove so close she couldn't see the car's hood, let alone the license plate. Was the car trying to make them crash?

Without warning, Chase took a sharp turn, the truck tearing up the drive to the Elk Valley Community Church.

The sedan zoomed past the church parking lot entrance and raced down the street, turning left and disappearing out of sight.

"What was that about?" Zoe asked as Chase brought the truck to a halt in front of the church's main doors. Her heart rate was too fast, making her body shake.

"Not sure," Chase said. "But nothing good."

The grimness in his gaze had her on edge as they climbed from the vehicle and headed for the entrance to the church. The temperature was cool inside as Zoe stepped into the dark wood-paneled narthex. The smell of candle wax and furniture polish teased her nose. She realized Chase was literally dragging his feet behind her. Like an errant schoolboy unwilling to go to the principal's office.

Or was he still concerned about the sedan that had tailed them to the church?

He'd left Dash home to give Kylie and Liam extra protection. Plus, he'd called the Elk Valley Police Department to have a patrol car cruise the area. All in an effort to put her qualms at leaving Kylie behind at ease. Chase was a decent man who cared for her and Kylie. His thoughtfulness was appreciated.

Remembering how jaded he seemed, she was surprised he'd agreed to come with her to the church.

She pushed through the swinging doors to the sanctuary, letting the peace of God envelop her and settle her racing heart. She knew the church was just a building and God was with her always. But for some reason, she felt His presence more acutely when she was here. And she had to admit she also felt safe with Chase following behind her. There was no question in her mind, he wouldn't let anything happen to her. And she had to trust that Liam and Dash would protect Kylie.

Pastor Jerome came out of a room at the front of the sanctuary. A tall man with black curly hair and kind, dark eyes, he exuded a sense of well-being as he held out his hands for Zoe.

"Zoe, it's just terrible what happened," the pastor said, giving her hands a squeeze before releasing them. He turned his gaze to Chase, who came to stand beside Zoe. "Special Agent Rawlston. I didn't think we'd ever get you into our humble building."

"We're here about the donations for Zoe and Kylie." Chase said in a voice ripe with irritation.

Zoe frowned. She couldn't abide rudeness. "Yes, we are. And we are very grateful for the church's help." She gave Chase a pointed look.

Pastor Jerome's smile held understanding. "We have everything downstairs in our children's ministry room. This way." He turned and headed out a side door.

Chase moved to follow, and Zoe grabbed him by the elbow. "What is going on?"

She really wanted to understand him. Though she shouldn't give in to her curiosity. But there was something about him that tugged at her heart in a way no one else had. She needed to ignore it. Yet, the curiosity and the need to help him find peace were stronger than her need for self-preservation.

And that was nearly as terrifying as being in the crosshairs of a bomber.

Chapter Four

Chase pushed open the door leading to the staircase that would take them to the children's ministry area.

He stepped back to allow Zoe to enter first, grateful he had a reprieve from divulging the reasons behind his hesitation and his anger at God. He didn't want to discuss any of it. Especially not with Zoe.

His job was to keep Zoe safe. To do that he needed her to trust him. Knowing he'd failed to protect his own family wouldn't instill a lot of trust. He wouldn't be able to effectively protect her and little Kylie if she doubted him.

Guilt swamped Chase, making his chest tight. Rubbing at the spot over his heart where the pain lived, he took several breaths hoping to alleviate the pressure building inside of him.

Stay calm.

The image of the white sedan riding the truck's bumper had his fists clenching. It could have been nothing more than an over-aggressive driver. Or it could have been someone with a sinister agenda. If Chase hadn't turned into the church's drive, would the sedan have tried to run them off the road? Chase hadn't seen the license plate, but he made note of the make and model of the car.

As they descended the stairs to the basement area, Zoe said, "Please, know that you can talk to me. I'm a good listener."

"Sharing isn't part of the job," he said through clenched teeth.

They entered the area used for the children's ministries. The large space housed stacks of chairs in the corner. A drum set, guitar stand and piano sat in front of a picture window where light streamed into the room. In the center, several long tables had been set up. A mishmash of boxes and baby paraphernalia covered the tops and the floor. "Let's just get this done."

Zoe gave him a hard, censuring look before she pressed her lips together and focused her attention on the donations.

Chase stood by the exit doors, allowing Zoe and the pastor to pack several boxes with items she deemed appropriate.

"Thank you, Pastor Jerome," Zoe said as she stacked the boxes beside Chase. "These will be put to good use."

"I'm glad." Pastor Jerome smiled. "I'm sure more donations will be coming in over the next few days. Now that I know what you're needing, I'll take the liberty of putting those things aside and send the rest to a local charity."

"I'd appreciate it," Zoe said. She glanced at Chase and raised an eyebrow. "We can stop by again later this week, yes?"

Chase's smile was tight, the muscles of his face pulling as he said, "I'm sure we can make arrangements." He looked at the stack she'd made of boxes filled with clothes and toys and other baby paraphernalia. "Is this everything?"

"For now," she replied. "We'll have to make a couple of trips to your pickup."

"I'll bring the truck to this side entrance," Chase told her. "Pastor, can you stay with her for a few moments?"

Pastor Jerome nodded. "Of course."

Confident Zoe and the pastor would be safe for the time being, Chase hurried out of the building. He took a few deep breaths, easing the constricting band around his heart before heading to the front parking lot.

The hairs at his nape quivered. He paused, searching for the source of his sudden acute unease.

A white sedan, like the one that had trailed them to the church, idled at the end of the parking lot. The tinted windows kept him from seeing the driver. He headed for the car.

The sedan shot forward, the wheels squealing on the parking lot pavement and swerved, heading for the exit. Chase noted the plate number as the sedan drove out of the lot, turned the corner and disappeared from sight.

He'd run the plates when he returned to the station. He sent off a text to his team requesting they meet him in an hour.

Shaking off the disquiet and anger, he quickly drove his father's truck from the front parking lot to the rear side door. He, Zoe and the pastor loaded the boxes into the back bed in no time. Chase kept an alert eye out of any signs of the white sedan.

"Zoe, I understand you're heading up the reunion committee," the pastor said before they could climb into the vehicle.

Chase's gaze snapped to Zoe.

"I am," she affirmed.

Narrowing his gaze on the woman, Chase refrained from saying she'd neglected to tell him she was in charge of the reunion committee. A detail he needed to know.

"I hope the naysayers aren't getting you down," the pastor said. "This town needs some rejuvenation and healing. I plan to bring up the reunion at this coming Sunday's sermon. A last push to get people to sign up."

"I would appreciate that, Pastor," Zoe said. "Right now, we have a very sparse attendee list."

The pastor turned his gaze to Chase, "Will you be attending with Zoe for Sunday's service?"

Chase's heart thumped in his chest. Would Zoe insist on going? Probably. "Most likely." Would it be rude if he wore earplugs?

Zoe gave the pastor a hug. Chase held open the passenger door while Zoe climbed in.

Before he could start the engine, she put a hand on his arm. "Will you really come with me on Sunday?"

"I'm committed to protecting you," he said. "Where you go, I go."

She gave a satisfied smile. "Then we'll be going."

Biting back his reluctance, he started the engine and drove toward home, while staying alert for any trouble. Namely a white sedan. "You didn't mention you were heading up the reunion committee."

She shrugged. "Is it relevant?"

"Everything is relevant unless I say it's not," he barked.

"Sorry." She tilted her head. "You're in a mood."

He took a deep breath, reining in the swirling emotions going into the church building had stirred. "For me to protect you, I need to know everything about your life. Including your involvement in this multigenerational reunion. The pastor said there are naysayers. I've heard rumblings, but I didn't realize the seriousness of the objections."

He'd had more pressing issues with the RMK. They'd theorized that maybe the announcement of the reunion had prodded the RMK out from under whatever rock he'd been hibernating beneath. "I need you to make a list of those who've opposed the reunion."

"I can do that." She turned away, keeping her face toward the window. "Though many of the negative comments have been posted on the reunion's social media page for everyone to see."

Chase regretted the harshness of his tone, but she didn't understand. An anxious flutter started low in his belly and worked through his chest, compelling him to say, "Look, God and I have not been on speaking terms for a long time."

She faced him. Her curious stare was a palpable force.

He slanted her a glance, noting the empathy on her face.

"Something happened," she said softly.

Understatement. "You could say that." He didn't want to

talk about this. Not to her, not to anyone. But she would find out soon enough.

She'd see the pictures of Elsie and Tommy in the house. Zoe would wonder. Best to nip her curiosity in the bud now.

"I worked in DC as a field agent for the FBI for most of my career," he told her. "Three years ago, Dash and I thwarted a bomb meant to blow up the National Art Gallery. The bomber escaped. Then he targeted me. Only he ended up killing my wife and two-year-old son." Pain lanced through his heart. "It should have been me, not them."

"Oh, Chase," she said with a breathy sigh of sympathy. Her soothing hand lay warm against his arm. "That's horrible."

He waited for the platitudes. For her to say he shouldn't blame God. That everything happened for a reason. All the things everyone else had said to him at the time when he was in the throes of grieving. Now, he endured the pitying glances and stares.

Instead, Zoe stayed silent, sitting with him in his misery.

And he was nearly brought to tears.

Zoe's heart ached for Chase and the tragedy he'd experienced. No wonder he was mad at God.

And he blamed himself.

He carried guilt like an anvil around his neck, thinking he should have died instead of his family. None of them should've died. It was devastating that life could unfold in such horrible ways. That evil could operate unchecked at times. But deep in her heart, she knew the tragedies of the world didn't negate God's sovereignty or His goodness.

But the knowing didn't make the pain hurt any less.

She couldn't fathom losing Kylie. Fear, dark and ugly, twisted in her gut. She sent up a plea for protection for her and Kylie, and peace for Chase.

The urge to hug him and offer some sort of comfort filled her, but she wasn't sure any gesture would be welcomed. Or that she should even make the gesture. Stepping over personal boundaries wouldn't be smart. She needed to keep an emotional as well as physical distance. Because anything resembling more than friendship would leave her open to heartache. She'd given a man her heart only to have him stomp on it. Better for her to not risk that sort of hurt again.

She settled for saying, "Thank you for sharing your past with me."

He gave a sharp nod as he pulled into the back parking lot of the Elk Valley police station. "I need that list of naysayers as soon as possible."

Tears clogged her throat despite her best effort to keep them at bay. He was hurting and grieving. There was nothing she could do to help him besides pray.

She didn't want to take on his pain. She had enough of her own. But how would she stay immune when they would be living under the same roof?

Chase tucked Zoe into the Elk Valley police chief's office. It was a comfortable space with a leather captain's chair behind the neatly organized desk. Two leather armchairs faced the desk. Zoe sat in one. She had pen and paper in hand to make a list of those in town who had expressed their opposition to having a multigenerational reunion.

As he headed to the conference room, he forced his mind to stay on task as he mulled over what Zoe had told him about the phone call right before the house exploded. A prank and unrelated? Or was the bomber making sure she was home and reveling in what was to come?

Most likely the latter.

"I assume you and your task force will be taking over the investigation into the bombing of Zoe Jenkins's home?" Police Chief Nora Quan asked as she fell into step with him. She was an impressive woman in her mid-fifties.

"I think we should work together," he said. "I hope you don't mind that I put Zoe in your office. I need to update my team."

"Not at all," Nora said.

Even though he had his boss's approval to use task force resources, he didn't want to overstep with Nora. "Zoe's the sister of one of the first victims. Our investigations intersect."

"Hey, I'm not complaining," Nora said, slanting him a glance beneath her dark bangs. "Just want to know what the expectations are. After an arsonist terrorized the town during the summer, the last thing we need is a bomber on the loose."

He couldn't agree more. Elk Valley had seen its fair share of tragedy and violence lately. They'd caught serial arsonist Bobby Linton last summer, who'd burned a path through town seeking revenge on people who'd wronged him in some way.

Now this morning's incident. Was this someone who felt wronged by Zoe? Her ex-husband? Or the RMK targeting the sister of one of his victims?

"The sooner we close this case and determine if the bomber is someone disgruntled by the reunion, or the RMK, the better," Nora continued. "If the bomber isn't the RMK, the reunion could be a powder keg that could bring the Rocky Mountain Killer back to town."

"Agreed." Chase stopped at the door of the conference room, where he'd arranged to meet the task force. They'd responded to the group text he'd sent. "I'll need extra patrols to help protect Zoe and her little girl."

Nora nodded. "Whatever you need. Tell the desk sergeant and he'll make it happen."

"Perfect." He didn't mention he'd already made the request before he and Zoe left the house.

Nora gave him a nod and headed down the hall, leaving Chase at the conference room entrance. He pulled open the door and the scent of freshly brewed coffee had him making a beeline to the coffee carafe. Several team members already sat at the conference table. Some of the K-9 handlers had their dogs at their feet while others, like Chase normally did, kept their dogs at their desks. Though being at the station without Dash was odd for Chase. Like he'd left an important piece of himself behind.

After pouring himself a cup, he settled into a seat at the head of the table. "How did the canvass go?"

Ashley leaned forward. Her dog, a male black lab named Ozzy, rose to his haunches at her movement. She settled him with a hand to his neck. "We knocked on doors up and down the street. No one recalled seeing anything suspicious."

"We had several door camera videos sent to Isla," Rocco said, referring to the team's tech analyst, Isla Jimenez. Rocco's chocolate lab, who specialized in arson detection, lifted her head at the sound of her handler's voice.

"Good," Chase replied. "Hopefully, Isla will spot something we can use."

Isla was good at her job. And an asset to the team. One of his recruits. He hated that she had been hitting roadblocks in her attempt to adopt a toddler named Enzo. It wasn't right. He made a mental note to look into the situation personally. Things had escalated for Isla recently when an arsonist had set fire to her home—with her inside. Despite their initial thinking, it wasn't the work of the serial arsonist from last summer, but someone else. Someone who'd been messing with Isla and making life difficult for her over the last eight months. Now that Chase was back from Utah, he'd devote some time to investigating who had it out for her.

Turning his attention to the other important case the task force was working on, he asked the room at large, "Update on Evan Carr and Ryan York?"

Silence met his question. He raised an eyebrow.

Meadow, who'd left Grace, her female vizsla, kenneled at her desk, said, "We're still beating the bushes."

"Not the news I was hoping for," Chase said. "Any more sightings of Cowgirl?"

"Unfortunately, no," Bennett stated. He, too, had left his K-9 partner kenneled at his desk. "Thankfully, the puppies are healthy. Liana is working on potty training and is doing assessments to see if they will make good therapy dogs."

Liana Lightfoot, dog trainer extraordinaire, had been working with Cowgirl as a compassion K-9 before the dog's abduction. Chase had seen firsthand how devastated Liana had been when Cowgirl disappeared. He was confident in her ability to train Cowgirl's puppies.

Last month, while tracking the RMK in Utah, they'd discovered a crate full of puppies with a note from the killer. The words were etched in Chase's mind.

For the MCK9 Task Force. I can't easily elude you and care for them. But I'm keeping their mom, Killer. Oh, and Trevor Gage: you'll be dead soon enough.

Anger burned low in Chase's gut, tempered by the knowledge that the RMK held the lives of dogs in higher esteem than people. The RMK had renamed Cowgirl and had placed a pink sparkly collar on her according to the reports they'd received from witnesses.

Switching back to the new case, Chase said, "Regarding the bombing this morning, I've been given the green light for our team to take the lead on the investigation since Zoe Jenkins is in charge of the Elk Valley High reunion. We suspect that might have triggered the RMK to kill again. It's the tenth anniversary of the original murders." His gaze landed on each member of his team. "It's possible that the bombing isn't connected to the RMK. But I don't believe in coincidences. Zoe Jenkins was targeted for a reason."

"Are we operating with the thought that RMK is now targeting the families of the victims?" Meadow asked.

"It's a possibility. Until we know for sure, we should put the families on alert," Chase said. "But we have another possibility. Zoe is making a list of people who have expressed displeasure at the idea of the reunion. Ashley, Rocco, I want you to interview everyone on Zoe's list. And look at the reunion's social media. Apparently, there's been some negative comments. The incident today may have to do with the reunion and not the RMK."

"You think someone would be so against the reunion they'd try to kill Zoe and her kid?" Ian asked. "That's cold."

"People have done horrible things with less motive," Chase reminded them.

"Do you think the reunion committee members are in danger?" Rocco asked. "Sadie's on the committee." There was no mistaking the concern in his tone for his fiancée. Sadie Owens was a divorced mom with a three-year-old son named Myles. Rocco had been the one to protect Sadie and Myles when the serial arsonist—known locally as the Fire Man—had targeted them over the summer.

"I wouldn't think so unless they are connected to one of the victims in a crucial way," Chase assured him.

Rocco nodded, appearing deep in thought.

Chase was aware Sadie did have a connection to Aaron Anderson, one of the original victims. They'd dated briefly in high school, but Sadie's interviews with the task force last March, and her brevity of her time with Aaron, hadn't given the team the idea that she could be a suspect or a target.

Chase cleared his throat. "Zoe also received a phone call right before the explosion. Weird laughter. Sounded like a recording. No idea about gender." Chase looked at Meadow. "Can you have Isla run Zoe's phone records to see if we can find where the call originated?"

"Will do," Meadow said.

"Ian, would you do a deep dive into Zoe's ex-husband, Garrett Watson?" Chase asked. "Find out if he has an alibi for the time of the explosion."

"On it," Ian said.

Focusing on Bennett, Chase said, "Reach out to Ophelia and Kyle. See how quickly they can get here. I want Ophelia to take a look at the remnants of the bomb once the fire department releases the evidence."

Ophelia Clarke was a forensic specialist based in New Mexico. Recently, she helped on a case and Chase had been so impressed by her, he'd asked her to be on call with the task force and she'd happily agreed. Kyle West was a fellow FBI agent and K-9 handler from the New Mexico bureau. He was on the MCK9 task force and specialized in tracking serial killers with his partner, a male coonhound named Rocky who specialized in cadaver detection. Kyle and Ophelia, his fiancée, were operating from Santa Fe.

"Got it," Bennett said. "I can also coordinate with the Elk Valley Fire Department. If the bomb was homemade, the perpetrator might have bought supplies in town. I can check the stores."

"Good idea." Chase pulled the task force laptop in front of him. He quickly did a DMV search on the license plate number of the sedan he'd seen in the church parking lot. Surprised, he sat back. The car was registered to Doctor Tyson Webb, Kylie's pediatrician. What was the doctor doing trailing them and then showing up at the church when they'd only just left him at the clinic?

"Boss?" Rocco said.

Giving himself a mental shake, he brought up a video chat screen and then sent a message to Hannah Scott, their team member providing protection to Trevor Gage.

His mind wandered back to the doctor. There had to be a reasonable explanation as to why Tyson had been at the church in the middle of the day. Perhaps dropping off donations for Zoe and Kylie? But why follow them and then leave only to return? What was he playing at? "Bennett, could you check into the background of Doctor Tyson Webb?"

"Sure," Bennett said. "Something we should know?"

"Zoe and I stopped at the Elk Valley Community church on the way here. We were followed very closely by a white sedan." Chase told them. "Then later I saw the same car was in the parking lot. When I approached, the driver took off. It's probably nothing, but—"

"Better safe than sorry," Bennett finished.

A few minutes later, Hannah's face appeared on the laptop's video screen. Chase turned the computer so that Hannah had a view of the room while he sent the video stream to the large monitor attached to the conference room wall.

"Good morning, everyone," Hannah said, her bright green eyes sparkled.

A chorus of greetings followed. Chase cleared his throat, drawing everyone's attention. "Hannah, how are you and Trevor managing at the safe house?"

A man appeared over Hannah's shoulder. Trevor cocked an eyebrow. "We're fine."

Hannah made a face. "Antsy to get back to our lives."

Chase understood. Getting Trevor to go into hiding had taken Hannah almost being killed. But Chase would imagine sitting on the sidelines was hard for both of them. The idea that had surfaced earlier reared up again, half-formed. "Trevor, did you RSVP to the Elk Valley High multigenerational reunion?"

Trevor considered. "I might have. The invitation came last spring."

Chase's heart pounded. "I do think the reunion might have been the catalyst to prompt the RMK to kill again. The timing seems right."

"Makes sense," Rocco said. "The whole town has been buzzing about the reunion for months."

"And causing some friction," Chase commented. "I hadn't realized how high the emotional meter was running. And if the reunion was the trigger for the RMK, we need to keep a close eye on the town. The RMK will strike when he's ready. It won't be obvious, and he'll try to catch us off guard."

"Do you think the RMK believes Trevor will return to Elk Valley?" Ashley asked.

"Maybe." Chase could use the idea of Trevor returning to town to trap the beast they called the RMK. Hmm. Chase needed to keep mulling over exactly how to execute the plan forming in his brain.

"Then the RMK could be here already," Meadow said.

Chase shrugged. "Not necessarily. At least not yet." He glanced at his watch. The timepiece brought both comfort and sorrow. It had been a gift from his late wife on their third anniversary. "I need to wrap this up. I'll let the others fill you in on what's happened. Rocco, Ashley, with me. Zoe should be done with that list."

Chase left the conference room with Rocco and Ashley at his heels. They entered the police chief's office.

Zoe rose and came around the desk to hand him the list. "I wrote as many names as I could remember."

"I'll take that." Ashley took the list and with a nod, she and Rocco left with the list in hand.

Chase noticed the dark circles bruising the tender skin beneath Zoe's eyes. She had to be exhausted. "Going to the bank and the DMV can wait until tomorrow. Let's head home."

Home. The word echoed through his head and his heart and landed with a thud in his gut. What had he done?

Chase lay on his bed with his head resting on his hands. The glow from the clock on the bedside table revealed the late hour. In the room next to his, baby Kylie fussed. Zoe's soft, soothing voice sang a lullaby.

Grief and guilt lay heavy on his heart as he listened.

The ding of an incoming text provided welcome relief. Glad for the distraction, he grabbed his phone. The number on the screen was unknown and held an attachment.

Wary, he opened the text.

A photo of Cowgirl, the pink collar with the word KILLER, sparkled around her neck. A man's hand and forearm, with the knife tattoo that they knew was on the arm of the Rocky

Mountain Killer, held a copy of the *Elk Valley Daily Gazette* in the frame.

Chase sat up, the bed shifting beneath his weight. His heart pounded.

The local newspaper was from today.

Chapter Five

Unnerved by the image of the labradoodle, Cowgirl, with the local newspaper, Chase threw back the dark blue covers and sat on the edge of the bed just as another text came through from the same number.

Looking forward to the reunion and finishing what I started!

A coffin emoji followed the sentence.

Dread clamped around Chase's chest like a steel trap. He sent an alert to the team requesting a meeting first thing in the morning.

Having confirmation that the Rocky Mountain Killer was in Elk Valley caused anxiety to riot in Chase's gut.

Dash rose from his bed and came to sit beside Chase, resting his snout on his partner's knee.

"He's here," Chase whispered, placing a hand on his dog. Acid burned through his veins. It was time to end the serial killer's reign of terror once and for all.

Burying his fingers into the golden retriever's soft fur, Chase contemplated the killer's next move. What did he mean *finishing what I started*?

Was he referring to the bombing at Zoe's house?

There was no doubt the RMK was gunning for Trevor Gage. The killer had said as much in his previous messages. But Trevor was with Hannah, far away in a safe house, not here in Elk Valley.

Was there someone else the RMK planned to target? Who? When? Why?

The questions spun around his brain like a revolving door.

The inkling of the plan that had tickled Chase earlier blossomed. He would need to discuss with his team how best to orchestrate a trap for the Rocky Mountain Killer. But first, he needed his boss and the Elk Valley police chief to sign off on the concept that was bubbling inside his mind.

Since he wouldn't get any more sleep tonight, Chase dressed for the coming day and then leashed Dash. They paused outside Zoe and Kylie's room. The baby had finally settled down and all was quiet. Mother and daughter were safe and sound.

Chase intended to keep it that way.

Zoe awoke in the guestroom of Chase and Liam Rawlston's home. Kylie slept nearby in the donated crib. Morning sunlight flooded the room through the window that overlooked the well-groomed backyard.

The soft cream walls were decorated with seascape paintings and the soothing tones of the blue-and-green bed covering were comforting. She would never have imagined herself being here yesterday when she'd awakened at home.

So much had happened in a short time.

Her house had been blown up.

She and Kylie were now living in the Rawlston home for the foreseeable future, and she was grateful to the two men for their hospitality. She hoped Kylie's fussing in the middle of the night hadn't kept anyone else awake.

She couldn't stay here indefinitely. She needed to call her home insurance company and determine when she'd be able to rebuild her house. She mentally made a note to call the mayor and her other clients about their food orders, but she didn't have a plan yet. She'd have to figure out where she could resume working from. The stress of it all tightened the muscles in her shoulders.

While Kylie continued to sleep, Zoe took the opportunity to shower and change into a pair of jeans and a lightweight sweater she'd taken from the donation boxes.

She returned to a wide-awake baby. After changing Kylie's diaper, she dressed Kylie in a cute little pants and zip-up jacket ensemble in a peach color with a white onesie underneath. Socks with a ducky motif and a yellow bow for her hair completed the outfit.

Zoe carried Kylie out to the kitchen where she found Liam busy cooking pancakes and bacon. Chase was nowhere to be seen.

His dog, Dash, however, greeted her and Kylie with a wagging tail. The large plume swept through the air, stirring the scent of bacon and making Zoe's stomach rumble.

"I hope you're hungry," Liam said. "It's not often I get to make breakfast for more than just me."

"Chase doesn't eat breakfast?" she asked.

"Not often." Liam carried a stack of pancakes and a plate of bacon to the already set table. "He's usually up and gone before I'm awake."

A strange disappointment settled between her shoulders. "He's already gone?"

"He is," Liam said. He held up a sheet of paper. "He left a note."

From Liam's tone, Zoe guessed this was abnormal. She arched an eyebrow. "And?"

Liam grinned and read from the page. "Dad, watch over Zoe and Kylie. There's an officer stationed outside. I'll be back by lunch."

Even when absent, Chase was keeping her and Kylie safe. Warmth spread through Zoe. She glanced at the kitchen clock hanging over the sink. "I have to go to the bank and the DMV. Chase said we would do that today. I'd like to get it taken care of this morning. Kylie will need to go down for a nap around one."

Liam took his seat. "Dash and I will go with you. And we'll bring along Officer Eric Steve. I know his father."

"Great." She and Kylie should be safe with so much protection. "I also need to help the reunion committee pass out flyers." The stack that she'd had went up in flames. But she could get more from other committee members. She wouldn't let all the work fall on everyone else without doing her share.

"Then it's a plan." Liam forked a pancake and waved it in the air. "Will the baby eat one?"

"She loves pancakes," Zoe assured him. Her heart filled with gratitude for these kind people. But deep inside, she feared this lull wouldn't last. How much longer would she have to look over her shoulder to make sure no one was coming after her and Kylie again?

The early morning meeting with the team broke up just after eight o'clock. The shock of seeing Cowgirl and realizing that the Rocky Mountain Killer had indeed arrived back in Elk Valley had everyone on high alert.

"We don't want to cause a panic with the public," Chase told his team. "For now, keep the news to yourselves. We will continue investigating yesterday's bombing of the Jenkins house while working to locate the RMK. If you see anything suspicious, don't hesitate to call for backup. I'd rather we overreact than miss our opportunity to catch the RMK."

"I'll see if I can enhance this photo of Cowgirl and the newspaper to figure out where it was taken," tech analyst Isla Jimenez said.

Chase nodded. "Perfect."

"I've been combing through the nasty comments on the reunion's social media pages," Meadow said. "There are some very disgruntled people out there."

"Tell me about it," Ashley said. She gestured to Rocco. "We interviewed four names on Zoe's list yesterday. Each one gave us an earful about how they didn't approve of the event while the Rocky Mountain Killer was still on the loose. Most find the event in poor taste while some fear it will draw the RMK back. Which I have to say is a legit concern."

"Yes we've established the reunion's connection to the RMK," Chase said.

"A few of the real nasty social media comments are by one poster," Meadow said. "Isla and I are working to find the ISP and the name of the person behind it."

Rocco spread his hands on the conference room table. "Despite my misgivings, which I've expressed to Sadie, the committee members are moving forward with the reunion."

Which was exactly what Chase would need for his plan to work.

"Boss, I checked into Dr. Webb," Bennett said. "Squeaky clean. Not even a parking ticket. He was with a patient when I called. He hasn't called back yet. I'll follow up later today."

"Thank you," Chase said. "Let me know what you find out. Does anyone have an ETA on Ophelia and Kyle?"

"They should be here this afternoon," Ashley offered.

"Good." He needed the evidence from Zoe's house examined, and he wanted Ophelia's close eye on it. He'd arranged to have her come out with Kyle to work the case.

He considered bringing in Idaho Deputy Sheriff Selena Smith, but she was investigating in Utah and would jump in as backup for Hannah if need be should the RMK show up there looking for Trevor.

After dismissing the meeting, Chase headed to the police chief's office. An hour ago, he'd requested a meeting with Nora Quan, and his boss at the FBI Special Agent in Charge Cara Haines, who would call in from DC. Both were waiting when he arrived. He broke the news that the Rocky Mountain Killer was in Elk Valley.

Nora stared at the photo the RMK had texted him. "Unbelievable."

"Send me a copy," Cara said, her voice tinny over the speakerphone.

Taking his phone back from Nora, he forwarded the image to Cara. Then he ran his idea for trapping RMK by the two women.

"So let me get this straight," Cara said, the intensity of her tone clear through the speaker. "You intend to go around town telling everyone that Trevor Gage has returned for the reunion."

"Correct," Chase said. "I'll rent a vacation house in his name." Trevor's family ranch had long been sold and the family relocated after the first three murders. "And I'll drive a truck around with his company logo on the side."

"So, in other words, you're going to be the bait," Nora said. She stood behind her desk with her arms folded over her perfectly tailored pantsuit.

"Exactly." To Chase it made perfect sense. He would pose as Trevor and hope the RMK made a move on him. He needed their approval before he presented the plan to the team. "It'll lure one of our suspects out. My inclination is to say Ryan York is our culprit because he's the only one with a registered handgun that could match the bullets taken from the victims." They'd also never been able to pin York down for an interview. He'd moved out of state years ago and tracking his whereabouts had been impossible. Elusive like the RMK. Because they were one and the same?

"We all know, bad guys can get their hands on a weapon without going through the process of registering it," Nora pointed out.

"True," Chase conceded.

"And if the RMK comes after you while you're posing as

Trevor," Cara said, "you and the team will be ready to take him down? Whether the suspect turns out to be Ryan York or Evan Carr or someone else."

"Yes," Chase confirmed. "Once we get everything all situated, between the task force, Elk Valley PD and the US marshals service, we can't fail. The plan will work."

It had to.

"Assuming the RMK doesn't get wind of the plan," Nora said. "You forget, Chase, this is a small town. Gossip flows down Main Street like rainwater down a gutter."

"That's what I'm counting on," Chase said. "All we have to do is tell a couple of people that Trevor Gage RSVP'd and he's returning to Elk Valley for the reunion. The wagging tongues of this town will do the rest to lure the RMK into the trap."

"What about Zoe Jenkins and her baby?" Nora asked.

"We're working on figuring out who planted the bomb at her house and why," he told her.

"The RMK?" Cara asked.

"Maybe," Chase replied with doubt evident in his tone. "The only issue is that the use of an incendiary device deviates from the RMK's usual modus operandi."

"Criminals have been known to change tactics," Cara reminded him. "The RMK included."

"Agreed." The first three victims of the Rocky Mountain Killer had been shot in the chest. The last three more recent victims had also been shot in the chest, but the RMK had added a knife buried in two of his victims' chests with a note taunting the police. In Utah, when Trevor Gage had been within reach, the RMK had opened fire and given chase through the woods to hunt Gage down—a departure from his usual MO of killing his victims in a barn. Still, changing from shooting to bombing was a big shift. "The RMK has proven to be unpredictable."

"Everyone in town knows Ms. Jenkins is staying with you and your dad," Nora told him.

Chase sighed. "I'm aware. My dad, Dash and a patrolman are keeping watch over Zoe and Kylie. I will also have one of the task force members stay with her when I'm posing as Trevor." Though Chase knew none of his team would want to be sidelined from the action of taking down the Rocky Mountain Killer, it couldn't be helped. "Hopefully, long before this plan comes to fruition, we will have uncovered who targeted Zoe and her baby."

"Do you have any suspects besides the RMK?" Nora asked.

"We are looking into her ex-husband. Apparently, the divorce was not amicable," Chase told the women. "Also there have been many in town opposed to this upcoming reunion. We are looking into all those who have expressed a negative response."

Nora narrowed her gaze behind her glasses. "I don't like the idea of one of our townspeople trying to solve their problems so horrifically."

"Nor do I," Chase said. "Once our team's crime scene investigator arrives and can look at the evidence, we'll know more."

Nora rose from her desk. "Keep me informed. Cara, it was nice to meet you via the phone. We will have to get together in real life one day."

"Same here," Cara said. "Chase, keep me in the loop."

"One moment." Chase held up a hand. "Just so I have clarity, you both approve of my plan to trap the RMK?"

Nora gave a slow nod. "Yes. Let us know how we can help."

Cara's sigh came through the line. "You have permission. Keep Sully in the loop. If this goes sideways, Chase...it just better not." With that, his boss hung up.

Nora chuckled. "I like her." She made a shooing motion with her hand at Chase. "Go do what you need to do."

Chase saluted Nora and walked out of the conference room, satisfied to have a plan of action in place. Drawing out the Rocky Mountain Killer meant Chase needed to be prepared for a final showdown. One way or another, justice would prevail.

* * *

Zoe pushed Kylie in a donated stroller along the sidewalk of Elk Valley Park with Liam holding on to Dash's leash and a patrol officer, Eric Steve, following close behind. The park was located across the street from town hall. The reunion committee had voted to hold the reunion in the event ballroom of the town hall building.

With less than a week to go before the big event, pressure to get everything done built inside Zoe's chest. The committee needed to decorate the ballroom at least a few days ahead of time. Zoe and Sadie Owens had partnered to cater the event, with Sadie providing a mix of Italian fare and subs, while Zoe had planned some dishes for those with dietary restrictions. Though now, Zoe wondered where she was going to prepare the food. She really needed to find a place.

She'd lost not only her home and all her belongings, but her business would now suffer until she could make other arrangements. It wasn't fair. Why had someone done something so awful? What had they hoped to gain by killing her?

Glancing sideways at Liam, who'd moved up with Dash and now sauntered beside the stroller, Zoe contemplated asking if she could borrow the man's kitchen. But that would be a big ask. Liam was so kind and generous, and she appreciated all he and Chase were doing for her and Kylie. She didn't want to overstep and take advantage of their hospitality. Besides, she needed to think of a long-term solution until her house was fixed and livable again. No, it would be better to ask Sadie to use her catering company's kitchen.

With that thought in mind, she said, "Would you mind if we stop at Sadie's Subs?"

"I love their sandwiches," Liam said and shifted direction.

Zoe aimed the stroller toward the pink-flowered food truck parked at the end of the park's lot.

Sadie waved from inside the food truck window. A moment later, she exited the truck and hurried to hug Zoe.

Sadie's pale blonde hair was twisted up in a bun secured beneath a hairnet. Her big, luminous green eyes searched Zoe's. "I've been so worried about you," she said. "Rocco told me what happened. Is there anything I can do to help?"

"As a matter of fact, a couple of things," Zoe said. "Since I no longer have a kitchen...could I use yours for the reunion?"

Nodding eagerly, Sadie said, "Yes, of course."

Relieved to have that problem solved, Zoe said, "I was hoping you have some extra reunion flyers I could pass out."

"Don't worry about those," Sadie said. "The rest of the reunion committee can take care of it." Sadie winked. "I tuck one into every order."

Zoe laughed. "Well, that is one way to spread the word."

Sadie shifted her focus to the men with Zoe. "Can I get you folks anything to eat?"

Liam patted his stomach. "We had a good breakfast. But I might take an Italian sub for later?"

"You got it. I'll make enough for you all to have some." Sadie hurried back to her food truck.

"Oh, here comes trouble," Liam said, though there was a definite lift to his voice.

Zoe followed his gaze to an older woman with graying hair and a flowing outfit that made her look like she was floating rather than walking. Martha Baldwin, Jessie's grandmother, made a beeline for Zoe.

"Well, hello there," Martha said. "Jessie told me she saw you at the Rusty Spoke yesterday." Martha air-kissed Zoe and then bent down to place a kiss on Kylie's forehead. She straightened and smile at Liam. "Hello, Liam. Nice to see you out and about." She smiled at the officer.

"Nice to see you, Martha." Liam's smile was wide and genuine. "You're always a ray of sunshine."

Pink defined the contours of Martha's cheeks. "You're always the charmer."

"I say it like I see it," Liam retorted with a wink.

Martha shook her head as she moved away into the park.

Zoe had watched the exchange between the two and suppressed a giggle at their flirtation.

Sadie rejoined them and handed Liam a bag. "Italian subs for everyone. I threw in an extra one for Chase."

"What do I owe you?" Liam reached for his wallet.

"On the house," Sadie said with a wave of her hand. Turning her attention to Zoe, Sadie asked, "Are we still on for our reunion committee meeting later this week?"

"We sure are." Zoe was determined to make the reunion a success. Seth would have liked the idea of everyone gathering; he'd always been up for a party. He'd had a playful side that at times turned sour when he was trying to impress his friends. He'd craved attention. Any attention. Good or bad. Seth had had his issues, but he hadn't deserved being murdered. "I'm not going to let anybody prevent us from putting on this reunion."

"We'll see about that," a deep male voice said from behind Zoe. She startled and whirled around to find herself nose to chest with Chase.

"Excuse me?" Her knee-jerk reaction was a defensive outage. Garrett had been tyrannical, thinking he had the right to boss her around. She hadn't realized how deeply his autocratic behavior had eroded away her self-esteem until he had abandoned her and Kylie. She had vowed never again to be controlled by someone else.

"We need to find out who destroyed your home and why, first," Chase said. "And I would prefer if you weren't out roaming around town making a target of yourself."

Taking Dash's leash, Chase turned to glare at his father. "What part of my note did you not get?"

Zoe pushed Kylie's stroller in between Chase and his father. "Your father, Dash and Officer Steve accompanied me to the bank and the DMV. I hardly think that counts as making a target of myself."

Chase ran a hand through his hair. A mix of emotions

marched across his face. "Maybe not knowingly. I need you and Kylie to be safe."

Her heart fluttered as she recalled what had happened to his wife and child. She hadn't thought about how protecting her and Kylie would affect him. She'd only thought of her own agenda and not the pain he was carrying around. She didn't want to care, but she did. "I'm sorry we worried you."

Chase gave her a nod and then heaved out a heavy breath. "Are we ready to return to the house?"

Liam held up the bag Sadie had given him. "Lunch for us all." Liam and the patrol officer walked on ahead as Sadie said her goodbyes and returned to her truck.

Still holding on to Dash's leash, Chase placed his hands on the stroller's handle. "I've got this."

Surprised and oddly delighted, Zoe released her hold and let him escort them across the parking lot toward the street corner where they'd cross and head back to his house.

The rev of an engine cut through the air, the loud sound making Zoe wince. The screech of tires spinning on the asphalt made her shudder. She turned her head in time to see a white sedan bolt out of a parking space. The front end of the car was aimed straight at them.

Chapter Six

In the space of a heartbeat, Chase assessed the threat as the white sedan ate up the space between its front end and Zoe and Kylie. Clearly, the driver intended to mow them down.

Reacting with a jolt of adrenaline, Chase released his hold on Dash's leash, certain the dog would jump out of the way.

"Dad!" Chase gave the stroller a mighty shove, pushing it into his father's hands. As soon as Chase let go of the stroller, he hooked an arm around Zoe, drew her body up tight against his and dove out of the way. At the last second, he twisted to land on his right shoulder and hip, while Zoe's body landed on top of him, knocking the wind from his lungs.

The car zipped past them with only a few inches of clearance before making a sharp turn and gunning it out of the parking lot exit.

Thankfully, Chase had tucked his chin so his head hadn't bounced off the asphalt. But he hadn't been able to see the driver either.

Zoe curled into Chase's chest. Her body shook. No doubt from shock.

He tightened his hold, running a soothing hand down her back. People gathered around them.

Officer Steve crouched down next to Chase. "Are you okay, sir?"

"We will be," Chase told the man as he rolled onto his backside, lifting Zoe with him as he sat up. "Zoe, you're okay. I've got you."

She lifted her head, her brown hair shielding her face. "Kylie!"

"Safe. Over here," Liam called out. He snuggled Kylie to his chest.

Zoe melted against him. "That was close."

"Too close," Chase murmured and smoothed back her hair to reveal her fear-filled eyes.

"By the grace of God, you managed to save both Kylie and me," Zoe said.

Seething that he hadn't seen the threat, Chase grunted. He chose not to think too closely about God's hand in the situation. Right now, he just wanted to know who was driving that car. "Did anyone see the driver?"

"The tinting on the windows was too dark," the police officer said. "But I'll put a BOLO out on it."

Chase didn't need the "be on the lookout" for the sedan. "I know who it belongs to," Chase told the officer.

Zoe pushed away from his chest and scrambled out of his arms. She faced him in a crouch, her eyes wide and luminous. "Whose car is it?"

"Dr. Webb's."

Zoe frowned and shook her head. "That doesn't make any sense."

She rose to her feet and hurried over to where Kylie and Liam waited. Zoe took possession of her daughter, kissing her cheeks and hugging her close.

Getting to his feet, Chase ignored the pain sloshing through the various spots where he'd landed on his right side. He'd take an Epsom salt bath tonight. That was par for the course in law enforcement. You took your lumps. Figuratively and literally.

Sadie rushed forward to wrap her arms around Zoe. "Oh my! I nearly had a heart attack. Are you hurt?"

"Chase took the brunt of the landing," Zoe said, her gaze searching his.

Dash moved to lean against Chase's leg.

"Son, are you okay?" Liam put his hand on Chase's shoulder.

"I'm fine." Chase held up a hand, stalling anyone from further questions and commiseration. "We need to get back to the house now."

Picking up Dash's leash, Chase tried not to limp from the ache in his hip as he hustled Zoe, Kylie and his dad down Main Street with Officer Steve close on their heels. They quickly turn down the residential street where they lived. Chase kept an alert eye out for the white sedan. As soon as they reached the house and were safely inside, Chase called Bennett.

"Hey, boss," Bennett said by way of greeting.

"Bring Dr. Webb in for questioning," Chase said in a hard tone.

"Did something else happen?"

"He just tried to run down Zoe and Kylie," he said.

"On it," Bennett said and hung up without preamble.

Chase then dialed Ashley's number. When the officer answered, Chase said, "Is Dr. Tyson Webb on that list of names of people who don't think the reunion should happen?"

"Well, hello to you, too," Ashley said. "Let me look."

Chase winced. He didn't have time for pleasantries right now. He had to know who had just tried to run down Zoe and Kylie. It wasn't lost on him that he'd been in the path of the car, as well.

"Nope," Ashley said. "Is everything okay, boss?"

"Not really." He told her about the incident.

"Could it have been the RMK?" Concern ran through her tone.

Chase considered this. "The RMK likes to look his victims

in the eye when he shoots them. I can't see him using a car. It's too impersonal."

"So is a bombing."

Chase couldn't deny that fact. The RMK didn't want anyone to recognize him. Chase wished they had a bead on Ryan York. Evan Carr's place outside of town was being watched but so far he hadn't shown.

"I'll keep digging through the names Zoe gave, but so far, I can't point to a suspect among them," Ashley stated. "Everyone has been very cooperative though vocal in their displeasure."

"You can't discount anyone at this point," Chase told her. "Some of the most innocent appearing and friendly people are monsters in disguise."

"Yes, sir."

Chase hung up with Ashley and called Meadow. She answered on the second ring. "Boss, I was just going to call you."

"Tell me," Chase said.

"We uncovered our most malicious poster on the reunion's social media pages," Meadow said. "Garrett Watson. Zoe's ex-husband."

Chase gritted his teeth and anger let loose a sharp spear through him. "Have Rocco and Ian bring him in. I'll be at headquarters in an hour."

"Will do. But it will take more than an hour," Meadow said. "Garrett now lives in Jackson Hole."

Chase hung up and entered the kitchen where his dad was handing out the Italian sub sandwiches. Unsure he could eat, but also aware he needed to, Chase accepted a wrapped sandwich. Liam then walked outside to give Officer Steve a sub.

Being in pain on an empty stomach wasn't a good idea. The salt bath would have to wait. For now, Chase swallowed two over-the-counter pain relievers with a glass of water and then dug into his Italian sub.

Zoe reached over from her place at the table and laid her

small, delicate hand on his forearm. "Thank you, again. If you hadn't thought so quickly..."

He stared at her hand on his arm, liking the way warmth traveled through his system. Then he glanced up, meeting her equally warm gaze. "I'm just glad I was there to protect you."

Because he hadn't been there to protect his wife and son.

Deep in Zoe's brown eyes, he saw her understanding. She squeezed his arm. "I'm glad you were, too."

His heart contracted in his chest. Her words soothed the ache of grief and guilt biting through him. He jerked his gaze away from her and lifted the sandwich to his mouth, forcing her to release her hold on him. He couldn't let her become attached to him. Nor could he become attached to her.

He wouldn't be able to survive another loss.

Zoe pushed the sting of rejection away. There was no reason for her to feel slighted that Chase practically shook her hand off his arm. She shouldn't be touching him anyway. The last thing she wanted was for him to get the wrong idea and think she was looking for a deeper relationship.

He had to be so frustrated with her and the situation. She didn't understand why he didn't assign someone else to her protection. But she certainly wouldn't voice the thought, because she had no doubt that she and Kylie were safe with Chase and his father and the big, beautiful golden retriever.

Reaching over to give Kylie a piece of banana, Chase asked, "What's Garrett doing in Jackson Hole?"

The question jarred Zoe. "He moved there after the divorce and opened another Watson Motors."

"Does Garrett have any connection to Dr. Webb?"

Did Chase think Garrett had been driving the vehicle that had tried to run them over? Zoe shook her head. "Garrett was not behind the wheel of that car."

"We don't know that for sure," Chase said, his tone razor-sharp even as he let Kylie wrap her chubby fingers around his index finger. "What we do know is that Garrett Watson is one of the offensive posters on the reunion page's social media."

Zoe tucked in her chin as her mind grappled with this news. Kylie giggled as Chase blew a raspberry on her hand. "I looked through those posts. I didn't see his name or his email address."

"Of course, you didn't," Chase told her. "He has a separate email for his vitriol. But my tech analyst tracked down the ISP, and it belongs to your husband."

"Ex-husband," she clarified with her own growing irritation. "I can't imagine why he would be so negative. When I brought up the concept of a reunion before we found out I was pregnant, he thought it was a good idea. He agreed with me that the town needed to heal and a multigenerational reunion would be a perfect way for everyone to come together and remember we are all still alive."

Chase pierced her with his intense dark gaze over Kylie's head. "When was the last time you saw or heard from Evan Carr? Or Ryan York?"

Surprise washed over her. Of course, Zoe knew who the two men were. Though to be honest, she still thought of them as boys because the last time she'd seen either one had been when they'd graduated from high school a few years ahead of her. "I can tell you neither one has RSVP'd for the reunion. Other than that, it's been over a decade since I've seen either of them."

"Was Seth friends with Evan or Ryan?"

"I don't recall them being friends. Seth had dated Ryan's sister, Shelly," she said. Sadness camped out in her chest. "I know people, Ryan in particular, blamed Seth for Shelly's death."

"Did Ryan ever confront Seth?"

"Yes," she replied, remembering that day and the horrible scene. "Ryan came to the house, enraged, and yelled at Seth for pushing his sister into committing suicide. My parents had to threaten to call the police before Ryan would leave."

Chase's eyebrows shot up. "They didn't report the altercation?"

"Not that I know of." She shook her head. "Seth was wild

as a teen. Always getting into trouble. Seeking attention. My parents shielded me from his antics as best they could. My poor parents didn't have any idea how to handle my brother."

Why was he asking these questions?

A horrifying thought ran through her brain, sending a chill down her spine. "Do you think Ryan is the Rocky Mountain Killer?"

"I can't divulge information on an ongoing case," Chase said. "Was Ryan or Evan friends with Garrett?"

She had to think hard about that. "Honestly, I don't know," she said. "I don't know who Garrett's friends were in high school. You'd know better than me since you were closer to his age. He never mentioned Ryan or Evan while we were married."

Kylie fussed in the highchair, banging her hands on the tray, a clear indication she wanted out. Zoe balled up her sandwich wrapper.

"I'll take that," Chase said, holding out his hand.

With a grateful smile, she dropped the crumpled wrapper into his palm. "Kylie and I are going to take a nap. It's been a stressful twenty-four hours."

The tenderness on Chase's face squeezed her heart. "Dad and Dash will be here, along with Officer Steve. Please don't leave again without letting me know."

Her first instinct was to rebel and tell him she didn't need his permission to do anything, but then she reined in her ego and nodded her acquiescence. "We'll do that. Thank you again, Chase."

She lifted Kylie out of the high chair and turned to head toward the hallway just as Chase stood up, blocking her path.

He ran a knuckle down Kylie's cheek. "She's such a sweetie."

Kylie's little fingers wrapped around his finger again.

"She likes you," Zoe said. "You're good with her. You made her giggle. That's a sign she trusts you."

"My son, Tommy, had the best laugh," he said, his eyes misting as he lifted Kylie's hand and kissed her knuckles.

Empathy for his loss constricted her throat but she managed to say, "I'm sure you miss him."

Seeming to pull himself together, Chase said in a soft voice, "Rest well, little one."

Prying Kylie's fingers away from Chase, Zoe stared into his eyes. An unbidden thought ran through her brain.

Chase would have been—would be—a really good dad. She hated that he'd been robbed of his family by the senseless and destructive actions of someone else. She wanted to help him heal from the pain. But to do that she would have to open her heart. She couldn't let down her defenses around Chase. She wouldn't take the risk of being hurt again.

As soon as it was safe, they'd go their separate ways.

After giving instructions to his father and Officer Steve to make sure that Zoe and Kylie remained inside for the rest of the day, Chase walked from the house to the police station. He needed a few moments to catch his breath and clear his mind of a pair of sweet brown eyes and the soft soothing tone of Zoe singing to baby Kylie as she put the little girl down for a nap. He couldn't help but hear as he'd changed out of his dirt-smeared clothes into fresh slacks and a dark blue long-sleeve collared shirt with the MCK9 logo on the breast pocket.

Zoe was a good mom. There was no mistaking her love for Kylie. He saw her bristle a time or two whenever he had given her instructions. He wondered about that. Wondered what hurts she carried from her marriage. From the death of her brother. Chase had left town before Seth had entered high school. So he had no recollection of him. But from all accounts, Seth had been a troublemaker. Zoe had mentioned her parents had difficulties with their son. He could imagine it had been hard for Zoe living under the cloud of her brother's less-than-stellar behavior. His heart ached for her.

When Chase entered the police station, Ashley was bouncing on her heels, waiting for him. "You are not going to believe what I just found out."

Falling in step with her as they headed to the conference room, he said, "Lay it on me."

"Melissa, you know, my new sister-in-law?" Ashley said.

"I'm aware that you have a new sister-in-law," he told her. Ashley and Cade McNeal had married not long ago after a case where Cade's sister, Melissa, and her son were in jeopardy.

A flush stained Ashley's cheeks. "Right. Anyway, Melissa works at the Rusty Spoke with Jessie Baldwin—"

"Again, I'm aware." This time he couldn't keep the impatience from his tone.

Ashley grimaced. "Melissa and Jessie were talking with Jessie's grandma, Martha Baldwin, who heard from Teresa Newton that her granddaughter had been secretly engaged to Brad Kingsley before his death." She said the last part in a rush as if the excitement was too much to contain.

Chase stopped at the door to the conference room. He cocked his head as he digested her words. "Brad Kingsley was secretly engaged to someone? Why didn't we know this?" Brad was one of the RMK's initial victims. And his fiancée hadn't come up when they'd interviewed locals connected to the cold cases back in March.

"According to Martha, Teresa said that her granddaughter was distraught when Brad was killed, and her parents feared for her safety. They moved away a month later."

Chase's hand tightened on the conference room door handle. "And does this mysterious fiancée have a name?"

"Haley Newton."

The name conjured up a woman in scrubs. "She's a nurse at the Elk Valley Community Hospital."

Ashley nodded. "She is. She returned to Elk Valley a few years ago."

"Bring her in for questioning," Chase said, his tone sharper than he intended.

"Going to do that now," Ashley said and hurried away.

Chase frowned, not liking how he'd handle that situation. His blood was running too hot from the close call with Zoe and Kylie. He didn't need to be taking it out on his team.

He entered the conference room and found crime scene investigators Ophelia and Kyle, along with Meadow.

"Good to see you two," Chase said. "Ophelia, I need you to get over to the FD and sift through the bombing residue collected at Zoe's house. I want to know everything you can find out about the bomber."

"Sorry we couldn't get here sooner," Kyle said. "Ophelia needed to get permission from her boss to take a few days off to help the team and we had to arrange for childcare for my nephew."

He understood the childcare dilemmas of his team. "You're here now. That's all that matters," Chase said. He'd never ask the team to put duties before arranging childcare. Ashley and her fiancé, Cade, helped with their nephew's care. Bennett and Naomi had just welcomed a brand-new baby boy. Isla was trying to adopt a child. Now Chase had a baby living in his house, along with her beautiful mother. Why did his thoughts always return to Zoe?

He gave himself a mental shake. *Stay on task*, he admonished himself.

Bennett pushed open the door to the conference room, "I have Dr. Webb sitting in interrogation room one."

Chase followed Bennett to the interrogation room and walked inside. The doctor sat in a hard plastic chair at the lone table sitting in the middle of the room.

Dr. Webb smiled. "Special Agent Rawlston. How is Kylie? And Zoe?"

Interesting he'd asked about the pair so quickly. Taking the seat across from him, Chase said, "They're safe."

The doctor nodded. "Good to know. My wife and I've been praying for them."

Chase sent Bennett a questioning look. Bennett nodded, confirming the doctor was married.

Maybe they needed to investigate the doctor's wife, too. Was this a case of the doctor becoming too friendly with a patient and a jealous wife? Chase placed his hands on the table. "Tell me about your relationship with Zoe Jenkins?"

Dr. Webb cocked his head. "I'm her daughter's pediatrician."

"Is that all?" Chase persisted.

"I'm not sure what you're getting at here, Agent Rawlston, but I do not appreciate the insinuation that I would have less than a professional relationship with one of the parents of my patient."

His indignation rang true. "Where were you yesterday afternoon?"

"Seeing patients," the doctor said. "In fact, I saw Kylie and Zoe and you at the hospital."

"What about after seeing Zoe and Kylie? Were you at the Elk Valley Christian Church?"

Dr. Webb shook his head. "No, I had patients until well after six p.m. What is this all about?"

"Where were you this morning?"

The doctor heaved an exasperated sigh. "Seeing patients. I am a doctor. That is what I do."

"Why was your white sedan seen at the church yesterday afternoon?"

Frowning, Dr. Webb said, "That's what this is about? My car? Don't you people talk to each other? I reported my car stolen last evening when I was leaving the hospital."

Chase arched an eyebrow and glanced at Bennett. Bennett made a face and ducked out the door. Irritation swamped Chase. This was his fault. If he'd allowed Officer Steve to put the BOLO out on the sedan, he would have known it had been reported stolen. "While my colleague checks on that report, I'd like a list of the patients you've seen in the past twenty-four hours."

"You know I can't do that." Dr. Webb said. "HIPPA laws and all."

"Then I will get a court order asking for the records of everyone you've seen."

"Is this really necessary?" Dr. Webb said. "When your colleague comes back, he will tell you I did indeed report my car stolen. My wife drove me to work this morning. I've not left the hospital until your man there picked me up and brought me here."

"We'll check the hospital CCTV to confirm your statement," Chase said.

Bennett opened the door with a contrite pinch to his expression. "The white sedan was indeed reported stolen last night."

Chase stood, softening his expression. "We thank you for your cooperation, Dr. Webb. I'm sure the police department will find your car soon. We will verify that you were at the hospital, but you're free to leave for now."

Dr. Webb stood and held out his hand.

Surprised, Chase shook the man's hand.

"No hard feelings, Agent Rawlston," Dr. Webb said, releasing his hold on Chase. "I know you're just doing your job. Whatever you need to do to keep Zoe and Kylie safe, I approve of. Now, if your man could give me a ride back to the hospital?"

Bennett held the door wider. "This way, Doc."

Chase rubbed his temples. The over-the-counter pain meds were wearing off. His shoulder was throbbing and his hip protested after sitting on the hard chair.

He headed into the kitchen for an ice pack, a bottle of water and some more medication.

Rocco appeared around the corner of the hallway with Garrett Watson in tow. Chase pivoted away from the kitchen and followed Rocco and Garrett to the same interrogation room they had just occupied with Dr. Webb.

It was going to be a long day.

Chapter Seven

Chase watched as Rocco led Garrett Watson into the interrogation room. Tall with a wide chest, Zoe's ex-husband carried himself with an arrogant swagger that grated on Chase's nerves.

This was the man who'd won Zoe's heart and then tossed it away.

Rocco stepped out of the interrogation room, shutting Watson inside.

"I thought he was living in Jackson Hole," Chase commented.

"He is," Rocco said. "He was halfway to Elk Valley when I reached him by phone. I met him on the outskirts of town and escorted him here."

Interesting. Suspicious? To be determined. "Why was he coming to Elk Valley?"

"He'd heard about the explosion at his ex-wife's house," Rocco said. "Claims he was coming to make sure they were okay."

Chase wasn't sure what to think of that information. The man abandoned his family and now rushed to check on them? To make sure they were safe, or to finish what he'd started?

Carrying the file with the information Meadow and Isla had

gathered, he opened the door to the interrogation room and stepped inside with Rocco close behind him.

Garrett Watson sat at the table in the same place that Dr. Webb had just vacated.

Chase tried to view Garrett dispassionately, but all he could think about was that this man had deserted his wife and child, leaving them alone and unprotected. Garrett had had the most precious thing in life—a family—and he threw it away. It infuriated Chase to no end.

Corralling his thoughts, he grabbed the chair opposite Garrett and dragged it away from the table, letting the legs scrape along the concrete floor with an unnerving noise that visibly shuddered through Garrett.

Once he had the chair situated at a comfortable distance from the table, Chase sat. "Thank you, Garrett, for coming in. I understand you were headed to Elk Valley to check on Zoe and Kylie."

"Yes. I'd like to see my wife and daughter," Garrett said. "I don't understand why you wanted to see me."

"Ex-wife," Chase clarified much the way Zoe had clarified the status of her relationship to Garrett earlier that day. "You're here because I want to know what type of explosives you used to blow up your ex-wife's house."

Chase watched Garrett closely.

The man's eyes widened. His mouth opened as outrage crossed his expression. "You can't seriously think I had anything to do with that!"

"Where have you been the last few days?"

"In Jackson Hole. I opened a second Watson Motors garage there. You can ask my employees," Garrett said.

"Oh, we will," Chase said. "Tell me about the posts you made on the social media pages of the Elk Valley High reunion."

Garrett's face scrunched up in confusion. "Posts? I have no idea what you're talking about."

"Really?" Chase laid the file folder on the table, opened it, and spun the file around so Garrett could read the page. "These posts, which are quite vehemently opposed to the upcoming reunion, all trace back to your ISP address."

Garrett looked at the page. A frown marred his brow. "I didn't send those. Ask Zoe." He looked up at Chase. "She knows I was totally on board with the idea of the reunion."

Yes, she had said the same. But Garrett could have just been paying her lip service. "If that's so, who made these posts and sent them from your account?"

Garrett sat back and crossed his arms over his beefy chest. "You're the experts. Somebody must've hacked my computer or my email account. You hear about that happening all the time online."

Convenient excuse. "We need to see your computer and have access to your accounts," Chase said.

A smirk crossed his face. "Do you have a warrant?"

Garrett's smug tone grated on Chase's nerves.

"I can get a warrant," Chase told him, barely holding on to his annoyance. "That will take time." He shrugged. "But if you insist. You can wait here. It might not come through until tomorrow or the next day."

"You can't leave me in this room for days on end. That's illegal," Garrett said.

"True. But I can put you in a cell on a twenty-four-hour hold until we get that warrant."

All smugness left Garrett. He splayed his hands on the table. "You're arresting me?"

"I will if I have to," Chase told him, knowing full well he wouldn't go that far. Yet. But holding him as a person of interest wasn't out of bounds. "This would go a lot smoother if you cooperate."

For a long moment, Garrett remained silent. "Where's Zoe and Kylie?"

Chase raised an eyebrow at the change of topic. Did the man really expect anyone to believe he cared? "They're safe."

"I want to see them," Garrett said. "I want to make sure for myself."

"I think that can be arranged…if you cooperate." Chase wasn't above a trade-off. If Zoe agreed. But Chase kept that tidbit to himself.

Anger flashed in Garrett's eyes. "Fine. My computer is in my truck."

Chase glanced at Rocco and gave a nod. Rocco dipped out of the room in search of the computer.

"Were you friends with Evan Carr? Or Ryan York?"

Garrett shook his head. "No way. They were too good for the likes of me. Them and that club."

"You mean the Young Rancher's Club?" Neither Evan nor Ryan had been members, but Chase didn't feel the need to reveal that information.

"Yeah, that's the one," Garrett said. "I was the son of a mechanic. What did I know of ranching?"

"So you weren't invited to their shindigs?"

"Nope. Good thing, too, since it seems like all those golden boys have fallen victim to the Rocky Mountain Killer, eh?"

"So it seems." Chase made a mental note to go back through the Elk Valley high school yearbooks to see if there were pictures or places where Garrett intersected with Evan or Ryan or the other members of the Young Rancher's Club. Did the man have a knife tattoo on his right forearm? "Roll up your right sleeve."

"Excuse me?" Garrett scowled. "Why?"

"Is there a reason you won't?" Chase pressed.

Garrett's scowl deepened but he complied. He undid the button at his wrist and yanked the sleeve up to his elbow. No tattoo. "Satisfied?"

More like disappointed. Chase gave a nod. "Yes."

The door to the interrogation room opened and Rocco stepped back inside. "Isla's taking a look at the computer now."

Chase was a man of his word. He rose from the chair. "I'll

let Zoe know you're here. If she wants to see you, then so be it. But it's her choice."

Garrett frowned. His hands clenched into fists. "I deserve to see my daughter. After all, I have to pay child support. I don't care if I see Zoe."

It took all of Chase's restraint not to launch himself across the table at Garrett and throttle the man. Instead, he gave him a clenched-jaw nod and left the room, shutting the door with a hard click behind him.

Taking several deep breaths, Chase headed for his office. His gaze went to the bed usually occupied by Dash. He missed his dog. He missed Zoe.

Giving himself a mental head slap, he picked up the phone and dialed the house number.

His father picked up on the second ring. "Rawlston's."

"Hey, Dad," Chase said. "I need to talk to Zoe."

"Here she is."

In the background, Chase could hear Liam telling Zoe that Chase was on the line.

A moment later, Zoe's sweet voice came through to tickle Chase's ear. "Hi, Chase. Is everything okay?"

"Yes. There's been a development," he said carefully. "Garrett is here and wants to see Kylie. Officer Steve can bring you over."

The silence on the other end of the line reached out and grabbed Chase by the throat. He wished he were there with her right now, letting her know it would be okay.

"We'll be right there," Zoe said, her voice devoid of any inflection.

Long after Chase hung up, he stared out the window to the park visible down the street. In the distance, the Laramie Mountains rose like sentinels watching over the valley floor.

The overwhelming need to pray rose within Chase. He tried to fight it. But the more he did, the more agitation swarmed through his system like bees after their nest was disturbed.

Staring at those mountains, he gave over to the swelling in his soul. *"Okay, Lord. I've ignored You for a long time. You have my attention. Now I want Yours. We need this to wrap up. We need to find the person who wants Zoe dead. We need to find the RMK. I need these wins."*

A check in his internal conscience made him wince. He was making it all about him. With a heavy sigh, he said, *"Forgive me, Lord. But please, help me."*

Zoe mechanically went through the process of changing Kylie's diaper and putting on a fresh cute outfit. Her mind felt numb. Garrett wanted to see Kylie. After all this time. Why? Was he going to fight her for custody? Was he going to blame the explosion on her? Her hands shook as she reached for the donated diaper bag. Liam came up to her and put a soothing hand on her shoulder. Much like she'd seen him do with his son after that awful car tried to run them down.

"Take a breath," Liam said. "Tell me what's wrong."

Zoe clamped her mouth shut. She didn't want to burden Liam with her problems. But the more she tried to hold in the torment, the more pressure built in her chest. Finally, she just gushed out all the angst gathering inside her, telling Liam about her failed marriage. About Garrett abandoning her and Kylie five days after Kylie was born. Serving her divorce papers one month later. And now he wanted to see Kylie. "I'm afraid I'll lose her."

Liam's face hardened. Anger snapped in his eyes. Eyes like his son's. "Neither Chase nor I will let that happen. I'll go with you to the station."

Dash rose from where he'd sprawled out near the front door. After a good stretch, he came and leaned against Zoe. Comfort radiated off the dog. "Are you sure he's not a therapy dog?"

"Not technically," Liam said. "But he was with Chase during the dark days. I think Dash is the only reason Chase didn't spiral farther down into the abyss after Elsa and Tommy's death."

Her heart ached at Chase's loss. "That makes sense," Zoe said running her fingers through the fur behind Dash's ears. "He's a multipurpose dog. Bomb-sniffing, protection and therapy."

Liam smiled. "Yes, to all of that."

Liam leashed up Dash while she strapped Kylie into her stroller. Liam escorted Zoe and Kylie out the door. Liam explained to Officer Steve that they were headed to the police station. The tall officer fell into step with them. Zoe felt like a celebrity with two bodyguards walking on either side of her. Only there was nothing to celebrate in this gauntlet walk to the police station to see her ex-husband.

Zoe spied Garrett's silver four-by-four truck with the Watson Motors logo on the side door parked in the back lot at the police station. Her stomach cramped. She disliked that truck and everything it represented. When Garrett had insisted on buying the vehicle, he'd used the money they'd put aside to do renovations on the house. The house that, thankfully, Zoe had retained ownership of after the divorce proceedings. Though Garrett had tried to take it from her. He'd wanted to sell the place and split the proceeds. But the judge had sided with Zoe's lawyer, stating that Kylie needed a stable home. Besides, the house had been in Zoe's family long before she married Garrett.

More butterflies took flight in her stomach when she and Liam and Kylie entered the police station. Chase met them, giving her a sympathetic smile. She fought the urge to request a hug. Instead, she returned the smile.

"He's in the conference room," Chase said. "I thought that would be better than an interrogation room. For you and Kylie."

Her heart melted that he'd arranged for the meeting to be held in a less traumatic place, not for Garrett's sake, but for hers and her child's. She pushed the stroller and followed Chase through the police station. As they drew close to the conference room, she saw Garrett through the windowed wall. He was pacing, wearing jeans and a long-sleeve green shirt that brought out the green of his hazel eyes.

Oh, he was handsome. There was no denying it. He had a nice smile with nice teeth, thanks to orthodontia. He was tall and muscled from working on motors. But how had she ever thought him charming? Once she'd seen past the mask he wore, she'd realized he was the big bad wolf in disguise. And she had been his little red riding hood. She'd trusted him. Never again.

Chase's hand landed on the small of her back as he pushed open the door. A grab bag of emotions swirled through her. She was so grateful that Chase was by her side and she didn't have to face Garrett alone. Chase made her feel safe and cared for. An answering affection rose within her, making her aware she was letting her guard down with Chase. She needed to bolster the walls around her heart. She didn't want to fall for another charming and handsome man. Not when the wounds from her failed marriage were still so raw.

Garrett turned as she rolled the stroller into the room. Something flashed in his eyes, there and gone. But she had seen the anger plainly enough to send a shiver of unease down her spine. Then his gaze dropped to Kylie. She watched him closely. Hoping to see some softening, some sort of paternal emotion. His face was an impassive mask.

"So that's her," Garrett said.

Zoe didn't answer, but instead released Kylie from the stroller, picking her up and putting her on her hip. Stepping around the table, she intended to ask Garrett if he wanted to hold her. He stepped back, putting his hands up as if warding off an oncoming threat. She halted.

"Oh no. I just wanted to see for myself that she was safe."

Zoe's heart folded in on itself. The man really had no emotional depth. She could feel the wounds inside scabbing over. Soon they would heal. The failure of her marriage wasn't hers, it was his.

"As you can see, we are both unharmed," she said in a steady voice.

He flicked a glance at her. His gaze went back to Kylie. "I'm not going to help you rebuild the house. You got it fair and square in the divorce."

Really? He had to bring that up? She rolled her eyes and turned her back on him, heading back to the stroller. "Why are you here?"

"Ask him," Garrett's voice was rough with suppressed rage, a tone she'd heard plenty during their time together. It usually proceeded some sort of rant. One where he found fault with everything, including her.

She'd shared with Chase how Garrett had hurt her and abandoned them. Why had he summoned Garrett? Her gaze sought Chase's. "You brought him here?"

"As I told you, we discovered he is the nasty poster on the social media sites for the reunion," Chase said, in a tone that was both neutral and professional. "He's here because we needed to question him." His gaze bore into hers. "About the explosion at your home. Now that he's brought up said home—"

"Hey, I am not saying I did it!" Garrett practically yelled.

Chase turned his gaze to Garrett. "But you did bring it up, which will give us the impetus to get a warrant to search your residence and both of your businesses for any materials used in the bombing."

"Just because I discussed something with my wife—"

Zoe whirled on him. "Ex-wife."

At the same time, Chase said "Ex-wife."

Garrett waved away their words. "Yeah, yeah, whatever. Ex-wife." He pointed a finger at Kylie. "She's still my daughter. I'm not a monster just because I don't want to be a dad. I wouldn't do anything to hurt her."

No, not a monster. Just a jerk with narcissistic tendencies. She lifted a silent prayer to God for patience and understanding, because at the moment, she had little of either. "We're done here."

Garrett's gaze bounced away from her to something over her shoulder outside the conference room. He frowned and his face lost some color. "What's she doing here?"

Zoe turned at the same time as Chase to see Ashley with Haley Newton in tow. Haley's eyes widened when she saw the tableau inside the conference room.

"Unless you're arresting me, I'm leaving," Garrett said as he made a beeline for the door.

Chase stepped out of the way. "You may go, but stay in Elk Valley until we've executed our warrants."

"If you insist," Garrett said. "I'll be at the original Watson Motors," referring to the local mechanic shop his father started and he'd taken over before expanding.

He stormed out of the conference room, pausing briefly to look down the hallway where Haley had just disappeared, then he did an about-face and hurried out the exit of the police station.

"What was that all about?" Chase asked.

Zoe shook her head. "I don't know."

"They both seemed unnerved to see each other," Chase observed.

"It did seem like that." Zoe's blood turned to ice. "I didn't even know they knew each other." But apparently, they did. How well?

Chase's gaze searched hers, and she hoped the awful suspicions rising to poke at her weren't visible. "Are you and Kylie okay to wait here while I talk to Haley?"

She narrowed her gaze on him. "Why did you bring her here?"

He gave her a pointed look. "That is something I cannot discuss."

She hated being left in the dark. But he'd asked her to stay. The only way she might learn what was going on with Haley and Garrett was if she complied. "We can wait here."

Chapter Eight

Chase walked out of the conference room with his heart in his throat. He'd seen the suspicion in Zoe's eyes. And the hurt. That same suspicion was clambering within Chase. There was something between Haley Newton and Garrett Watson.

Just what, he didn't know, yet. A look had passed between them that led Chase to believe they weren't strangers. Friends? Lovers? Adversaries? Haley's eyes had definitely widened with recognition and a flash of panic, while Garrett had clearly been spooked to see the woman.

What a strange turn of events. They'd brought Haley in for a completely different reason—her connection to one of the RMK's first victims—and now Chase was wondering at the connection between Haley and Garrett. And did that connection have anything to do with the end of Zoe's marriage?

Inside the interrogation room, Haley sat at the table.

Ashley stood quietly near the door.

This was the third time on the same day that Chase had sat across from someone he was questioning. So why did he feel as if he wasn't making any progress?

He wasn't any closer to catching the RMK or the person who blew up Zoe's home.

Haley watched him with wary eyes. She wasn't dressed in scrubs as she had been when he'd met her at the hospital with Zoe and Kylie. Today Haley wore a gray cardigan over a white blouse and blue jeans. Her blond hair was held back by a clip. Apparently not a workday.

He decided to let the silence stretch.

She fidgeted in her seat. Finally, she asked in a voice laced with irritation, "Well? What am I doing here?"

Deciding to table Haley and Garrett's possible association and dive into the reason they'd asked her to come to the police station, Chase said, "What was your relationship to Brad Kingsley?"

Haley blanched. Her mouth dropped open. She slammed it shut. "I don't know what you mean."

From behind him, Ashley stirred. He turned to look at the rookie and motioned her forward. Chase stood and gestured for Ashley to sit. She gave him a curious look before she sat and turned her gaze on Haley. Chase hoped that because this was Ashley's intel, maybe she would make more inroads with the other woman.

"We understand that you were engaged to Brad Kingsley." Ashley's voice was friendly and gentle.

Apparent shock flashed across Haley's face then tears welled in her eyes. "Why are you asking me this? Brad died a long time ago."

"Is it true?" Ashley reached across the table to take the other woman's hand. "Were you and Brad in love? Planning to get married?"

Haley glanced at Chase and then back at Ashley. She sniffed, then said, "Yes. We were. His snobby parents didn't approve. They wanted some Ivy League debutante. Brad and I were going to run away after graduation."

"Why didn't you tell the police about this after Brad's murder?" Ashley probed.

Haley jerked her hand away from Ashley. "Because nobody

was supposed to know. I didn't want anyone gossiping about Brad. He was dead."

"You moved out of town not long after," Chase interjected.

Keeping her gaze on Ashley, Haley said, "My parents saw how distraught I was. They knew about me and Brad. I became very despondent. They were afraid I'd hurt myself. So we moved far away and I was checked into a—facility. The doctors there helped me through the grieving process. I've made a good life for myself since then. I became a nurse to help others."

"Yet, you came back to Elk Valley," Chase said. "Why?"

"Because I was once happy here," Haley told him. She looked at Ashley. "You have to understand. We were young and in love. Returning here, being in Elk Valley, helps me to feel closer to him. I miss him."

"Where were you the night the three victims were murdered?" Chase asked.

She reared back as if struck. "What? I didn't have anything to do with the murders."

"No one is saying you did. We just need to know where you were," Ashley stated in a gentle tone.

Haley heaved a sigh, clearly relieved by Ashley's words. "I was at home waiting for Brad to text me. He didn't. Then the next day…" Her shoulders slumped slightly as sadness crossed her face.

"Did you know where Brad was going that night?" Ashley asked.

"He said he had some business to take care of," Haley said. "He asked me not to go to bed. That he would come by after. He said he'd text when he was on his way. I waited up all night."

"Haley, do you have any ideas about who killed Brad and the others?" Ashley asked.

Haley's face crumbled and she shook her head. "The Rocky Mountain Killer. I wish I knew who it was. I'd tell you. Whoever did it has to pay."

"Do you know if Brad had any sort of beef with Evan Carr? Or Ryan York?"

Haley stilled. She glanced up. "Why do you ask?"

Something in her eyes had Chase leaning forward. He didn't like her answering a question with a question. In his experience, that usually meant the person was stalling as they tried to come up with an answer, usually a lie.

"Answer the question, Haley," Chase said.

"I know there was bad blood between all of them. Some things happened. The guys laughed and joked about the pranks they pulled."

"Pranks? Like the one they pulled on Naomi Carr?"

"Yeah," Haley grimaced. "Seth, Brad and Aaron Anderson thought it would be great fun to target Naomi. I don't know why they didn't like her. But they were so mean to her at the Valentine's Day dance. They'd convinced her Trevor Gage had only asked her to the dance as a joke. They threw spitballs at her and made fun of her. She ran out in tears." Haley shuddered. "I remember thinking that I hope they never turn on me."

"Did they turn on Shelly York?" Chase asked.

Haley's gaze dropped to the table. "Poor Shelly. She didn't deserve what happened to her."

"Do you mean the breakup with Seth Jenkins?" Ashley asked.

"Yes. Seth was so nasty. He only went out with her to try to get her to sleep with him. When she wouldn't, he broke up with her in front of the guys. Said horrible things to her and about her. The guys laughed about it for weeks," Haley said softly. "I told Brad it was cruel."

"And yet you kept his secret and stayed with him," Chase commented.

Haley's gaze snapped to his. "I was young and in love. What was I supposed to do? Blab and get my boyfriend in trouble?"

"If you'd told someone about the bullying, things might have ended differently for Shelly." Chase couldn't keep the anger from his tone. And Ryan York wouldn't be one of their prime suspects. The more Chase learned about Ryan and his beef with Seth and his friends, the more guilty Ryan appeared.

"Maybe." Haley spread her hands. "There's nothing I can do about the past now. I can only move forward. And try to be the best version of myself I can be. That's why I went into healthcare. To give back. Pay some kind of penitence for not protecting Naomi or Shelly."

"Those weren't the only pranks, though, were they?" Chase persisted. No way would they have not been up to more shenanigans. "What other things did the guys do that were funny to them?"

Haley shrugged. "There was something to do with the caves in the mountains."

This was interesting. And the first time anyone had mentioned caves. There were multiple caves and caverns in the mountains of Wyoming to explore. Most were open to the public. Some were not. "Which caves and which mountains are we talking about?"

"The guys never said," Haley replied. "I assume the Laramie Mountains. They are the closest."

Frustrated with the lack of information, he pressed. "Who was involved? What happened during these cave incidents?"

"I don't know," she said. "I don't know anything that's going to help you. Can I go now?"

He wasn't sure she was telling him everything, but he decided it was time to change directions. "What's your relationship to Garrett Watson?"

"Garrett?" Haley's eyes darted between Chase and Ashley. "You can't suspect him? I mean, no way is he the Rocky Mountain Killer."

He supposed it made sense she'd jump straight to the RMK considering the topic of their earlier conversation. But the way she protested on Garrett's behalf was odd. "Just answer the question," Chase insisted.

"He worked on my car," she said. "Is that a crime?"

There was a hint of belligerence in her tone. "You seemed pretty shaken when you saw him in the conference room today."

"Did I?" Haley shook her head. "I didn't even realize he was in the room. I saw Zoe and her baby."

Chase wasn't buying it. He remembered how at the hospital, Haley had asked Zoe if she'd informed Garrett of the bombing. Was that how Garrett had learned of the explosion that had destroyed his ex-wife's home? Playing a hunch, Chase said, "Garrett had a bit more to say about your relationship."

Panic entered Haley's eyes. Then she blinked several times, seeming to settle herself. "Whatever. So we had a fling when I first moved to town. I didn't know then that he was married to Zoe. I broke it off as soon as I found out. If he says anything different, he's lying."

Though she confirmed what Chase suspected, it didn't make hearing of the affair any easier. His heart ached for Zoe. "We may have more questions for you down the road. But for now, don't leave Elk Valley."

"I'm free to go?" Surprise laced her tone.

"You are," Chase said as he moved to the door. "Ashley will see you home."

Chase didn't relish telling Zoe that her ex-husband had had an affair with her colleague at the hospital. But he knew he couldn't keep this from her. Eventually, it would come to light, and she would only be hurt and angry at him if she learned he'd kept the information from her. He hoped he could comfort her without it affecting him. Against his better judgment, he was already finding himself caring deeply for the mother and child.

Zoe pushed the stroller for the umpteenth time in a lap around the conference table. At least she was getting in some steps. Kylie finally conked out and slept. A glance at the clock confirmed Chase had been gone for over an hour interviewing

Haley in an interrogation room. What were they discussing? What was Haley and Garrett's connection?

She tried to think back over the past to see if she remembered Garrett or Haley ever meeting. But nothing came to mind. Garrett had never mentioned Haley, and other than recently at the hospital when Haley asked if Garrett had been informed about the explosion, Haley had never mentioned Garrett. Yet they both had reacted peculiarly when they'd seen each other.

Zoe paused mid-lap to grab the water bottle Liam had brought her and took a long swig.

The door to the conference room opened and Chase stepped inside.

Glad to see him and anxious for answers, Zoe pushed the stroller with a sleeping Kylie to meet him at the head of the table.

"What can you tell me?" she asked softly, knowing he wouldn't divulge anything regarding the Rocky Mountain Killer investigation.

But he would divulge information regarding the explosion at her home, wouldn't he?

Chase gestured to a chair. "Please, have a seat."

Trepidation spread through Zoe as she maneuvered the stroller around so that she could sit and keep an eye on Kylie at the same time.

Once they were seated, their chairs facing each other and their knees nearly touching, Chase said quietly, "What I have to tell you is going to be hard to hear."

Her stomach dropped. That suspicion she'd had earlier raised to the forefront of her mind. "Are Haley and Garrett involved?"

He grimaced. Clearly uncomfortable. "Apparently, Haley didn't realize Garrett was married when she first arrived back in town," Chase said carefully. "Once she realized he was your husband she broke off the relationship."

Zoe couldn't assess how she felt about this revelation. Her husband had had an affair. She calculated back to when Haley had first come on board as a nurse at the Elk Valley Community Hospital. Three years ago. Around the time Garrett had taken over Watson Motors from his father, who'd retired and moved to Arizona.

Garrett had poured himself and their savings into the business. Bringing the auto-body shop into the twenty-first century, he'd claimed. At the time, Zoe had tried to be supportive even if she'd been lonely because Garrett spent so little time at home. Now she understood why.

Zoe should be shocked. But all she felt was numb. Her husband had had an affair. Long before he abandoned her and their child. She couldn't even claim his desertion on another woman.

Chase gathered her hands in his. His were warm and comforting against the flood of ice in her veins. She curled her fingers over his. Wanting, no needing, his strength and steady presence, even though relying on him wasn't a smart move. "I'd been so gullible. I mean, I suspected at times that he might be..." She swallowed back the recriminations that laid shame and blame on her doorstep. She would not own his bad behavior. His betrayal. "He told me I was being paranoid."

"Are you okay?"

Chase's soft voice grabbed her focus. The concern and compassion on his face made her want to fling herself into his arms. She squeezed his fingers. "I will be. It's a lot to process."

She needed time on her own to sort through the quagmire of her emotions. She couldn't do that with Chase so close and the temptation to lean on him for comfort and support so strong. She tugged her hands from his and stood. She had to get out of there. She needed to go someplace where she could think and pray and rage.

Chase rose to his full height, eating up the distance between them.

There was nowhere for her to go. Literally and figuratively. Her home had been blown up. Her parents lived far away. She was trapped by her isolation. And by the chair behind her, the stroller on one side and the table on the other.

And Chase stood in front of her. A handsome warrior, yet a gentle man.

Her heart battered against her rib cage. A yearning swelled within her. She met his gaze and saw the same yearning in his eyes.

His hand came up to cup her cheek, and she didn't flinch or shy away, despite her earlier need to escape. Her feet felt glued to the floor and her heart calmed. His touch was tender and light against her skin, melting the ice in her veins.

"You deserve so much better," he said, in a near whisper.

Was he talking about Garrett? Or himself?

Either way, she would decide what she deserved. Never again would she let someone else dictate her life.

And at this moment, she wanted, needed, the affirmation that she would be okay. That she was a beautiful woman who could attract a man like Chase.

She swayed toward him, the distance between them reduced to a millimeter. Questions and curiosity shone brightly in his eyes for a moment before he dipped his head and captured her lips.

The kiss was soft, probing and so welcome.

She entwined her arms around his neck, going up on tip-toe to better match him. All the hurt crowding her chest was pushed aside by a flood of warmth and affection for this man.

The soft snick of the door opening and the clearing of a throat jerked them apart.

Zoe stumbled, nearly falling back into the chair but managing to push it out of the way with the back of her knees. She skirted around the edge of the stroller and gripped the handle before she lifted her gaze to the person standing at the conference room entrance.

A woman she'd never seen before smiled hesitantly. A blonde

with bright blue eyes. She wore a jacket with the MCK9 logo on the front.

Desperate to escape as embarrassment flushed through her system, Zoe asked Chase, "Your father? Where is he?"

"The break room," Chase said, his voice husky. "Down the hall to your right. You can't miss it."

Without looking at him, she gave a quick nod then pushed the stroller past the woman standing in the doorway and headed in the direction Chase had mentioned. Her cheeks flamed. What was she doing? How could she let that kiss happen?

Oh no, her conscience chided. *You made this happen.*

And as much as she should regret kissing Chase, and probably would tomorrow, right now, she didn't regret it. At all.

Chase stood frozen in place. His whole body felt on fire. He slowly turned to see who had interrupted the moment of insanity.

CSI Ophelia Clarke.

The embarrassment crowding his chest reflected in her pretty face. Man, was he losing it to kiss Zoe in the police station. Had the parallels to his wife's death made him more invested in this case than he should have been? And now that he'd come to know and care for Zoe, he was getting in too deep. Allowing such unprofessional behavior wasn't like him. He needed to do better at keeping his emotions in check.

"Sorry," Ophelia said. "I didn't realize until I'd already—"

He held up a hand. "Not your fault. Just keep this between us, shall we?"

"Mum's the word," Ophelia said, coming all the way into the room. "I thought you'd want to know right away that the remnants of the bomb used to blow up Zoe Jenkins's home was homemade. Rudimentary."

He blew out an aggravated breath. "So basically, anyone with the understanding of engineering…?"

Ophelia made a face. "Anyone with access to the internet

can watch videos of how to build an explosive device like the one used," she said.

Acid bore a hole through his gut. "We're back to square one. We still don't know who could have planted the bomb."

Ophelia raised a piece of paper he hadn't noticed she held. "I made a list of the ingredients and supplies needed. They can be purchased at any hardware-type store."

"Give that to Ian and Meadow," he said. "They can check with the local stores. Can you and Kyle make a wider search?"

"Of course, we can."

"Thank you," Chase said. "I need to call the team together and let them know what I've learned from Haley Newton."

Ophelia stuck a hand in the pocket of her jacket and pulled out her cell phone. "I can text everyone if you'd like."

Running a hand down his face in an attempt to steady his breathing, Chase said, "I'd appreciate it. Also, can you check on the BOLO on Dr. Webb's stolen car? If they find it, I want you to process it for any evidence."

"Glad to do it," she said.

Meeting her gaze, Chase swallowed at the understanding and speculation in her eyes. Keeping his expression carefully neutral, he strode out of the conference room confident Ophelia would assemble the team while he went in search of Zoe and Kylie. His chest warmed at the thought of Zoe. *Stop.* He was protecting a vulnerable woman and child. Nothing more.

Then why did you kiss her?

He had no explanation and didn't want to examine his actions too closely.

The break room where he'd expected to find his father, Kylie, Dash and Zoe was empty.

He hustled out the exit in time to see Zoe flanked by his dad, who held Dash's leash, and Officer Steve, quickly making their way down the sidewalk. Confident that the men and his dog would keep Zoe and Kylie safe, Chase went to the men's room and splashed water on his face. "Brilliant move, Raw-lston," he said to his reflection.

He'd have to do damage control with Zoe when he got home tonight. He didn't want her to be hurt or to be thinking there was something more to their relationship than there was. More than he could allow.

But right now, he had a plan to set in motion.

Chapter Nine

Within the hour, the team had gathered in the conference room. Rocco stood near the window overlooking the parking lot, his chocolate lab, Cocoa, beside him. Seated around the long oval table were Meadow, Ian, Ashley and Bennett. Their respective dogs either sat beside their handler's chair or lay down at their feet beneath the table.

Chase had requested a whiteboard be brought in and placed where all could see it.

Along the top, he made two columns with the headings RMK and Unsub, referring to the unidentified subject targeting Zoe.

The large monitor screen facing the conference table was split with Trevor and Hannah videoing in from the safe house in Utah. On the other side of the screen was Selena and her private investigator fiancé, Finn Donovan.

The most recent text Chase had received from the RMK had put searches in other Rocky Mountain states on hold. Presumably, the RMK lurked somewhere in Elk Valley now. A horrible problem they needed to deal with.

"Let's go over what we know so far." Chase wrote on the

whiteboard in red marker. "If the text is to be believed, our serial killer is in town for the reunion."

"Do you still think the RMK plans on trying to kill Trevor at the reunion?" Ashley asked.

"He can't," Hannah said. "We aren't coming."

"Well, that's the thing," Chase said. "We need the RMK to believe Trevor is going to be at the reunion."

"You hope he shows up?" Trevor said. "As I said before, I can't remember if I RSVP'd, but I could post on the reunion social media pages saying I'm heading back to town."

"Good idea." Chase wrote that down on the blackboard. "I will also ask Zoe to spread the news that you're coming."

Hannah scowled. "When do you want us there?"

"I don't," Chase said.

"You just want RMK to think I'm coming," Trevor said. "To what end?"

There was a murmur of agreement to the question that rippled through the room.

"I have a plan, which I will tell you about in a moment." He wrote on the whiteboard. *Kidnapped Cowgirl but released puppies.* "We at least know he's got a heart when it comes to animals."

"Small comfort to those he's killed," Bennett said.

"Agreed. We have two suspects." He wrote the names *Evan Carr* and *Ryan York* on the board. He filled the task force in on what Haley had said about Naomi Carr and Shelly York.

"The victims—and Trevor—were all part of the same group of friends," Chase said. "With the exception of Peter and Trevor, they played cruel pranks on those they didn't like. And the RMK targeted them. Peter was killed for being a part of the pack. The RMK went after Trevor but wasn't successful."

Trevor scrubbed a hand over his jaw. "I just want this over."

"We all do," Chase said. Then he told them about Zoe's ex-husband. "For half a second I thought maybe Garrett Watson might be added to the list of RMK suspects, but he doesn't have a knife tattoo on his right forearm."

Chase moved to the column he'd drawn under the bomber of Zoe's house. He wrote *RMK* with a question mark beside it. "I haven't ruled out that the Rocky Mountain Killer isn't after Zoe, though there haven't been any attacks on the other family members of the victims. It seems less likely." He shrugged. "The ex-husband? Garrett Watson showed little regard for Zoe's welfare, but he did come to town to make sure his daughter, whom he claims not to want, was safe."

"There's still the question of the people who are against having the reunion and what lengths they might go to stop it," Ashley said.

"We worked our way through all of the names on the list Zoe gave us and those who made the negative comments on social media," Meadow said. "Other than Garrett Watson, no one else stands out as a possible suspect."

"I concur, boss," Rocco said. "There were many names that were from an older generation who are either infirm or have limited mobility. All the others have alibis for the days leading up to the explosion. Nothing came from the canvass of Zoe's neighborhood either. Whoever planted the bomb did so under the cover of night and was careful not to be seen by any exterior cameras."

"Which might suggest the person responsible has to be someone who is familiar with the neighborhood." Unease slithered down Chase's spine. Could one of Zoe's neighbors have a reason to target her? "What do we know about those living in close proximity to Zoe?"

"Most weren't home at the time of the explosion," Meadow said. "But we can do background checks on them all. Did Zoe mention if there was any sort of conflict with her neighbors?"

Chase shook his head. "I'll ask her about that when I get home."

He didn't miss the exchange of speculative glances among

the team. He should disabuse them of the idea there was anything untoward going on between him and Zoe, but for some reason he held his tongue. Ophelia had seen them kiss and had promised to keep it to herself. Were his growing feelings for Zoe beginning to show? He needed to do a better job of keeping his emotions under wraps.

The door to the conference room opened and Kyle and his K-9 partner, Rocky, a male coonhound with long floppy ears, stepped inside, drawing not only the humans' attention but also that of the dogs in the room.

"Hey, wanted to let you know that Dr. Webb's car was found in the parking lot of the hospital," Kyle said. "Ophelia's processing it as we speak." He and Rocky moved farther inside so he could shut the door. "And I just had a very interesting conversation with the clerk who likely sold our suspected bomber the supplies."

Chase's pulse jumped. "Please, tell me you have a description or better yet, a photo."

Kyle shook his head. "Sorry. The clerk said the person paid with cash and only gave grunted responses. The clerk couldn't say whether the suspect was a man or a woman. The store's security video feed, which I finally managed to get from the owner of the shop, shows a slim figure wearing dark clothes, a hoodie pulled up over a baseball cap, and oversized dark glasses covering most of their face. The purchase was made two weeks before the bombing."

Not a spur of the moment decision. "The suspect is a planner." The thought sent dread coursing through his veins. What was the person targeting Zoe planning next?

"Thank you, Kyle, for your hard work," Chase said. "And please have Ophelia contact me the moment she's done."

Teeming with frustration, Chase shoved a hand through his hair. They were still no closer to knowing who destroyed Zoe's home, but he hoped the car would reveal something about the person who'd tried to run them down. Were the bomber and the car thief the same person?

He put down the whiteboard marker, ready to lay out his plan. "Here's my idea. Feel free to poke holes in it. I want to get this right. Trevor is the only surviving target from that old friend group. Starting tomorrow, we are going to spread the rumor that Trevor is coming to town for the reunion. I'm going to rent a house on the outskirts of town in Trevor's name. On the night of the reunion, a small team will lie in wait for the RMK to make his move."

"What if he tries to make his move at the reunion?" Trevor asked, his voice tinny over the video feed. "You need me there."

"I have a workaround for that," Chase said. "At the reunion, we'll tell people you're in town staying at a rental but not feeling well. But before the reunion, I'll drive around town pretending to be you. We're roughly the same height and build. I'll need one of your signature silver Stetsons and access to a truck with your company logo on it."

"Thus, forcing the RMK to go to the house in order to attack Trevor," Rocco said.

"Exactly." Chase could see that the team was on board with the plan.

"Or the RMK could try to off you as Trevor as you're driving around," Bennett pointed out.

"True," Chase said. "Which is why one of you will follow at a discreet distance. And we can communicate via earwigs," he explained, referring to the communication devices that allowed them to hear each other through a small earplug.

"I can do that," Bennett said.

"Great. One other issue... I need someone to provide protection for Zoe at the reunion in case we haven't found the person targeting her by then." Chase didn't want to have to pick someone but rather hoped for a volunteer.

There was definitely an uncomfortable silence echoing through the room as the ramifications of what Chase was asking became clear. If they didn't discover who was targeting Zoe and Kylie soon, one of the task force members would be on protection detail and not in on the serial killer's potential arrest.

"I'll do it," Meadow and Ashley said at the same time.

Gratitude for the two team members and their willingness filled Chase. "Thank you both. Meadow, you stay with Zoe. Be her shadow at the reunion." At her nod, he said, "I appreciate it. Ashley, would Cade be willing to go with you to the reunion?"

"We were already planning on going," Ashley said. "My sister-in-law Melissa and her bestie, Jessie, are both planning on attending, as well."

"Good. If you all could keep your eyes and ears open, and spread the word that Trevor's in town but not feeling well, that would be optimal." Chase turned his focus to Rocco. "The same for you. You're alumni and your presence there won't be questioned, plus Sadie's on the reunion committee so it makes sense for you to be there."

"But you're also alumni," Bennett pointed out.

"True," Chase said. "I'll make an appearance early on and then duck out."

"While you're doing that," Ian said, "I'll be waiting in the house."

"Good. I'll show up driving Trevor's truck, in case the RMK is watching."

"I can stay and help with the takedown," Kyle said. He looked to Ian. "I'll join you at the house."

Ian nodded. "Sounds good."

"I'd appreciate that," Chase said. "We'll also have Deputy US Marshal Sully Briggs on standby. He'll take the RMK into custody and get him far from town as quickly as possible."

"That's a good idea," Rocco said. "There's a long line of people who would like a chance to rip into the Rocky Mountain Killer."

"Exactly," Chase said. "We want the RMK to stand trial and answer for his crimes. Not be killed in some vigilante assassination."

"I can take care of renting the house," Bennett said.

"I can make the trip to Utah and drive one of Trevor's company trucks back here," Ian said.

Pride and pleasure swelled within Chase's chest. He couldn't have asked for a better task force than the men and women sitting around the table and on the screen. Each member of the team had a specialty K-9 dog, and the combination made them a fierce force to be reckoned with.

"You guys are the best," Chase said. "I'll have Isla make the posts on Trevor's behalf routing the ISP through his company."

Chase released the team to go about their assignments. They had three days to prepare for the takedown of the Rocky Mountain Killer.

Failure wasn't an option. Not again. This time the task force would succeed. Chase sent up a silent prayer asking God for help. And doing so eased some of the anxiousness bouncing around his chest.

After putting Kylie in the playpen that now took up space in the living room, Zoe set the table while Chase cooked in the kitchen. He'd shooed her out moments ago, telling her he had everything under his control. It wasn't often somebody, offered to cook for Zoe, outside of when she went to a restaurant. Usually, once people knew that she was a chef and a dietitian, they asked her to do the cooking.

But Chase and his father, Liam, both seemed to enjoy the culinary arts. She would appreciate whatever they put in front of her.

Dash scrambled from his place near the front door as Liam appeared in the dining room doorway. He was dressed up in chino slacks and a gray blazer over a blue button-down shirt.

His hair was combed and styled. And he'd recently shaved. "You don't have to set a place for me."

Chase came out behind him and Zoe's breath caught. The man was too handsome for his own good. He still had on his work uniform but now a white apron covered the front of him, and the words *Kiss the Cook* stenciled in blue seemed to shout at Zoe, reminding her of the kiss in the conference room. Heat infused her cheeks, and she hoped the men didn't notice. She and Chase needed to talk about the kiss. About what the kiss meant. Or didn't mean.

She usually didn't shy away from hard conversations but for some reason, this one had her pulse skittering every time she thought about broaching the subject.

Chase folded his arms over his chest. "Dad, where're you going?"

"Out," Liam said, obvious excitement evident on his face.

"Okay," Chase said slowly. "Where? And what time will you be home?"

A scowl darkened Liam's face. "I don't think that's any of your business."

"I think it's lovely that you're going out. Hopefully to do something fun?" Zoe ventured, slanting a glance at Chase to gauge his reaction.

He turned his thunderous gaze to her. She lifted her chin.

"Zoe, if you don't mind—"

"I appreciate your support, Zoe," Liam broke in before Chase could finish his words.

Chase grimaced, running a hand down his face. "I just want to make sure everyone stays safe. With the RMK in town, we have no idea who will be his next target. The police department has extra patrols canvassing all areas of town and the FBI and US Marshals are here as backup and also stationed around town, keeping an eye out."

Zoe's heart melted a little, and she reached out a hand to place it on Chase's forearm. "We all appreciate your protectiveness. I'm sure your father will be careful. And it sounds like you and your team have covered all the bases. There's only so much you can control."

Liam's expression softened. "Yes, we all do appreciate your efforts. I'm going to the Rusty Spoke. It's trivia night. I'll be fine, surrounded by lots of people."

Chase's jaw set in a hard line. Zoe waited to see if he would demand an escort go with his father. But instead, he heaved a sigh. "I hope you have a good time."

Remembering the flirtatious vibe she'd witnessed between Liam and Martha Baldwin, she asked, "Will Martha Baldwin be there?"

Liam grinned. "She will. Don't wait up."

After Liam left, Chase turned to stare at Zoe. "You must think I am…" He spread his hands wide. "I'm not even sure what to say. He's my dad and I can't stand the thought of something happening to him."

"And I'm sure he has the same thoughts every time you walk out the door," Zoe said gently.

Chase seemed to think that over then gave a nod. "You're right, of course. I'm on edge. No closer to catching your bomber. I see threats everywhere."

"It's understandable," she said. "But you can't let fear rule you."

"Sometimes it's hard not to," he said, his voice breaking.

She understood. After what happened to his wife and son, Chase had become hypervigilant, wanting to keep those he loved safe. In some small measure, she and Kylie were both in that circle now. Though she couldn't say he loved her, he did care. She couldn't deny that, just as she couldn't deny she cared for him. More than cared, if she were being honest, but her developing feelings would only lead to disappointment. Heartache. The attraction between her and Chase was born out of a stressful and dangerous situation. It couldn't last, could it?

"When I'm afraid, I will trust in the Lord," she said. "That's my mantra most days. It's been hard and daunting to think about raising Kylie alone. But I know that God has me in His hands. I know He has you and Liam and the task force and this town in His hands. Circumstances may not turn out the way we want. In fact, they rarely do. That doesn't negate God's goodness."

Chase covered her hand on his arm with his own and threaded their fingers together. He brought her hand to his lips and kissed her knuckles. "You are a brave and wise woman. Zoe, I—"

The sound of the buzzer cut off his words. "The lasagna is done." He let go of her hand and returned to the kitchen, leaving Zoe to wonder what he had been about to say. Was he going to bring up their kiss?

Her pulse sped up as she transferred Kylie from the playpen to the high chair set up at the dining table. She had to work to calm her breathing as Chase brought out the pan of lasagna and a bowl of fresh green salad. He also placed a plastic bowl filled with small chunks of fruit in front of Kylie. Tenderness flooded Zoe at his thoughtfulness toward her daughter.

Chase dished up the lasagna and Zoe scooped salad onto their plates. They ate and chatted about life, books and art in a companionable way that put her at ease. Chase asked about her business and seemed genuinely interested in hearing her ideas for how to expand once her house was restored.

A pang hit her square in the chest.

How often had she longed for someone to share meals with? Someone to share her hopes and dreams with? Garrett had hardly ever been home for dinner and hadn't really been easy to confide in. The man was adept at turning the conversation to him whenever she'd tried to open up.

"I have a favor to ask of you," Chase said as he pushed his empty plate away.

Grateful to help him in whatever way, she said, "Okay."

He laughed. "You haven't even heard what it is."

She shrugged. "I owe you my life and Kylie's life. What-ever you need."

He tilted his head. "You don't owe me anything. I was doing my job."

Gesturing to the table and the house, she said, "And all of this, is just you doing your job?"

His lips curved in a half smile that was both endearing and amusing. "Maybe."

Her heart did a little jig. "What are we doing?"

His eyes widened. "What do you mean?"

"Don't play coy," she said. "We both feel the attraction."

"Attraction, yes," Chase said. "How could I not? You're a beautiful, funny, smart and caring person. But I'm not in a po-sition to offer you anything."

Just a kiss. Her heart hurt. But what did she expect? "I un-derstand," she said. "You're still grieving the loss of your wife and child. And, frankly, I don't know if I could ever truly trust my heart to a man again."

"Don't say that." Chase reached out to take her hand. "Don't paint every man with the same brush as your ex-husband. There are good men out there. You'll find the right one someday."

"Right." But it was clear he didn't consider himself the right one. She should be relieved, but instead a bruise lashed across her heart. She extracted her hand. "What was that favor?"

He hesitated then said, "I need you to help me spread the word that Trevor Gage is returning for the reunion."

"Does this have something to do with the Rocky Mountain Killer?"

He pressed his lips together. Obviously, he couldn't say.

"Never mind," she said and stood. "We can start now. Let me change Kylie into a warm outfit and we can head down-town for ice cream."

"Ice cream in October?"

"Yep. Pumpkin spice ice cream," she said, though she re-ally didn't have much of an appetite now. "Plus, if we mention

Trevor coming home to Simon Kimmer, the owner of the shop, he'll spread the word."

"Thank you," Chase said.

Zoe released Kylie from her high chair and headed for the bedroom. She could feel Chase's gaze, so she kept her head high and her shoulders back. No way would she let him know how his words had affected her. And reinforced her need to not rely on anyone else.

Chase watched Zoe walk into the spare bedroom and shut the door. The air in the house seemed to cool, or maybe it was just his blood. He'd hurt her. Unintentionally but still…his shoulders dropped with the weight of regret.

"Son?"

Chase whirled around to find his father standing in the shadows of the entryway. "How long have you been there?"

"Long enough," Liam stepped to the entryway cabinet, opened a drawer, and removed his wallet. "I forgot this and came back for it. I didn't mean to overhear."

Chase ran his hand through his hair. "What do I do? How do I make this right with Zoe?"

"You care for her," Liam said.

"Yes. But it can't go anywhere. My heart is too broken."

"Hearts mend when you let them. You are not responsible for Elsie's or Tommy's deaths."

This was an old argument between them. Chase remained silent, not seeing the point of debating his guilt when nothing could assuage it.

"I miss Elsie and Tommy," Liam continued. "I miss your mother something fierce." He moved to stand in front of his son. "But it's time to let go of the past. Forgive yourself. Elsie wouldn't want you to be alone. And I know your mother wouldn't have wanted me to be alone. I've been alone too long."

Chase wasn't sure how to respond or even how to sort

through the emotions swirling through him. Forgive himself? How? "But in moving on, won't I forget them?"

"Never. They will always have a place in our hearts. But it's time to put the past behind us. And look to the future."

"It's hard for me to think beyond the next few days," Chase replied out of self-preservation. His focus had to be on putting an end to the RMK's reign of terror. And he still had to find the person targeting Zoe. Until then he had to control his emotions and stay professional.

"You'll know when the time is right," Liam told him as he opened the door to leave. "The time is right for me. I'm going to ask Martha Baldwin out on a date."

For a long moment after his father left, Chase stared at the closed door. He was happy for his dad; he was brave to put his heart out there again. And he was right, his mom wouldn't have wanted or expected his dad to be alone forever. Just as Elsie wouldn't have wanted or expected Chase to be alone. But could Chase be as brave as his father when he still had so much guilt and sorrow pressing down on him?

Chapter Ten

Zoe forced a smile as she pushed Kylie in the stroller down the sidewalk of Main Street. The evening breeze swept over her face, cooling her cheeks. Chase, with Dash on a leash, walked beside her while behind them, Officer Steve strolled along keeping a discreet distance but close enough to be of use if anything should happen.

Trying not to view every person they passed with suspicion, she waved at several of the townsfolk who she was acquainted with. When they reached the ice cream parlor, she heard the faint ding of the bell over the door as Mayor Singh and his wife and two young children filed out.

"Zoe Jenkins," the mayor boomed. "So good to see you." He shifted his gaze to Chase. "Agent Rawlston. I hope you're taking good care of Zoe and will put whoever destroyed her home behind bars soon."

"That is the plan, Mayor," Chase answered.

"Again, I'm so sorry about the meals—" Zoe started to say but was cut off when the mayor held up a hand. He'd been so gracious when she'd called to tell him the meals she'd prepared for him had been destroyed.

"Nonsense," the mayor said. "Not your fault."

"We'll get him on that paleo diet eventually," his wife said with a smile. "It's more important that you stay safe."

"Thank you both," Zoe said.

The mayor and his family waved and headed down the street.

Chase opened the door to the ice cream parlor and looked in. "It's pretty crowded in here. Should we leave the stroller outside?"

Always thoughtful, this one. "Yes." She quickly unbuckled the straps and picked Kylie up, placing her on her hip. "What about Dash?"

"He can fit," Chase said and gestured for her to enter.

Zoe carried Kylie into the ice cream parlor. The smells of sugar and waffle cones brought back memories of summers as a kid riding her bike to the ice cream parlor with her friends. The red-and-white décor harkened back to days long gone, but the nostalgia for simpler times remained.

Zoe and Chase, with Dash close at his side, stepped into line and waited their turn at the counter behind several people ordering.

"Good evening," the young adult woman with a name tag that read Cindy said as they moved to the front of the line. The ice cream case was filled with a plethora of flavors from the standard strawberry, vanilla and chocolate to seasonal flavors and creative blends.

Cindy eyed Dash, then asked, "What can I get for you tonight?"

The owner of the ice cream shop came out from the back.

"Zoe!" Mr. Kimmer, a man in his late sixties with salted dark hair and a slow gait, moved to stand beside his employee. "I've got this."

Cindy shrugged and moved away to take someone else's order.

"Are you doing okay?" Mr. Kimmer asked. "It's just awful what happened to your house. It's just awful what keeps happening in our town."

"Yes, sir, we're fine," Zoe told him, choosing to not address the last part of his statement. She didn't want to give anyone more reason to oppose the reunion. "But we have a hankering for some pumpkin spice ice cream."

Mr. Kimmer's face lit up. "I have a special pumpkin spice sundae with caramel and pecans. Would you like to try it?"

Her mouth watered at the mention of pecans. "Of course." She turned to Chase. "What about you?"

"How can I pass up a pumpkin spice sundae?" His smile was amused and tender and intimate.

Her heart thumped against her ribs. She turned away, not wanting to fall any deeper into this man's orbit. He may be attracted to her. And he cared, she didn't doubt that. But he was doing his job. She didn't know if she could be friends with him without wanting more. She hoped so because she really liked him. Though she feared there would be a cost to her heart.

"Two pumpkin spice sundaes coming up," Mr. Kimmer said. "And a pup cup for the dog?"

"Sure," Chase said. "Dash would like that."

Remembering their purpose for the outing beyond the sweet treat, Zoe said, "I hope we'll see you at the reunion."

"I'll be there," Mr. Kimmer said without enthusiasm. "I'm just not sure how wise this endeavor is at this particular time."

"Not you, too?" Zoe said. All the divisiveness the event was causing dampened her spirits a bit. Her hopes that it would bring some comfort were slipping away. "I was hoping people would see this as a good thing for the town. People from out of state who moved away long ago are coming back. Trevor Gage, in fact, is on his way here."

"Seriously?" Mr. Kimmer said. "I never thought we'd see him back in town. You know, after all that nastiness with the Rocky Mountain Killer and the Young Rancher's Club. Trevor was a part of that group of friends, wasn't he?"

"It's true Trevor had been friends with the victims," Chase

said in a stern tone. "I don't think it's a good idea—or safe—for him to attend the reunion, but apparently he'll be there."

Zoe glanced around aware that the volume of conversation in the ice cream parlor had subsided to a few whispers as everyone seemed to be listening to the conversation. She and Chase couldn't have asked for a better way to get the news out that Trevor was coming back to town.

Was one of the people sitting at the counter or in one of the booths the Rocky Mountain Killer? A shudder of dread and apprehension worked its way through her system. Or was one of these people the person who was trying to kill her? Were they one and the same?

She was confident that whoever was targeting her wouldn't try something with Chase and Dash standing guard and Officer Steve right outside the ice cream parlor door.

"There's an open booth in the corner," Mr. Kimmer said with a wave. "I'll bring the sundaes to you."

Zoe put Kylie in a high chair, situated next to the edge of the table, then she and Chase settled in the large booth with Dash sitting at their feet underneath.

The bell over the door dinged. Zoe smiled to see her friend Sadie and her three-year-son, Myles. Myles had diabetes and had a therapy dog, an Irish setter, with him. Sadie's fiancé Rocco and his K-9, a black Lab, also stepped inside. Chase saw them as well and waved them over.

"Join us. We have room," Chase said as he stood.

Zoe wondered if he'd invited them to their table because he didn't want to be alone with her. A sadness stung her, but she shrugged it off.

Sadie scooted into the booth, settling Myles on her lap. The dogs settled under the table at their feet. Zoe marveled that the dogs all got along and were so well behaved. Nothing like the dog her parents had when she was a kid. Snickers, a Pomeranian, had been a terror, always stealing Zoe's socks and hiding them.

"I'll go place our order," Rocco said and he hustled to stand in line. His K-9 readjusted himself beneath the table so he could keep an eye on his handler.

"Isn't that Dr. Webb and his family?" Sadie gestured to the newcomers to the packed ice cream parlor. "He's been so good with Myles."

Zoe exchanged a glance with Chase. Chase had said someone had stolen the doctor's car and used the vehicle to try to run them over. By the glare on Chase's face, she surmised he wasn't happy to see the doctor. "Yes, that is Dr. Webb and his wife and son."

As if the doctor had sensed Zoe mentioning his name, he turned and waved at them. He left his family and came over to the table. "Hello, Zoe. Agent Rawlston. Sadie."

"Hi, Dr. Webb," Zoe greeted him.

Chase didn't respond, only kept his eyes trained on the doctor.

"How's Kylie?" Dr. Webb asked, his gaze on her daughter.

"She's good, no worse for the trauma," Zoe replied, aware that Chase's stare was less than welcoming. Did he still suspect Dr. Webb was behind the attacks on her and Kylie?

"Good, good. Glad to hear that," Dr. Webb said, backing up, clearly uncomfortable, before he turned and walked back to join his family.

The bell over the door jingled as more and more people entered.

Zoe settled into a conversation with Sadie about the decorations for the reunion. Though she kept an eye on Chase, who kept an eye on everyone else in the parlor.

Finally, Rocco rejoined them. "Mr. Kimmer said he'd bring our sundaes over when he brings yours." He slipped into the booth next to Sadie.

"Who knew ice cream was such a popular dessert on a late October night," Sadie said. "Maybe I need to add some ice cream to Sadie's Subs."

"It certainly couldn't hurt," Rocco said. "Everybody loves ice cream."

Zoe saw Chase nudge Rocco, then gesture with his chin toward a new group of thirtysomethings who entered the ice cream shop. "Tall, blond man."

Rocco nodded and slipped out of the booth. Chase followed him.

"We'll be right back," Chase said, his gaze on Zoe. "Don't go anywhere."

She arched an eyebrow. "Where am I going to go?"

He gave a sheepish grin and nodded.

The two men wound their way through the group, cornering the blond man.

"He's very protective of you," Sadie said with a smile lacing her words.

"It's his job. Nothing more, as he's made very clear to me."

"Yeah, Rocco tried something similar. *I don't have time for romantic entanglements.*" Sadie lowered her voice to mimic the man she loved.

Zoe laughed, even as her heart gave a little bump of hope. But she quickly slammed the hope down. Not going to happen. Chase wasn't ready to move on from his late wife. And she shouldn't be ready to trust Chase with her heart, however much her traitorous heart disagreed.

Her gaze snagged on another woman who'd entered the shop and was working her way to the counter.

Haley Newton.

Bitter resentment rose within Zoe and she clenched her teeth against the tide. Turning away, she resumed the conversation about the reunion with Sadie. "We should incorporate pages from the yearbooks throughout the decades. We could frame them and set up displays around the room."

"That's a brilliant idea," Sadie said. "I was also thinking we could ask several of the high school teachers who are coming to say a few words about each of the classes they taught."

"I love that idea."

The air around Zoe shifted and a presence loomed at her side. She glanced up and met Haley Newton's blue eyes.

"Can I help you?" Zoe was unable to keep irritation from her voice.

"I just wanted to apologize to you," Haley said. She set two sundaes down on the table then gestured toward Chase, who still stood talking to the blond man. "I'm sure he told you."

Forcing herself to answer, Zoe said, "He did."

"Here we go," Mr. Kimmer said, setting two more pumpkin spice sundaes on the table and a small scoop of ice cream in a cup for Kylie and a cup of fresh fruit for Myles. "Thank you, young lady, for your help."

Haley smiled at him. "Not at all. You had your hands full."

"Thank you, Mr. Kimmer," Zoe said. "You are a good man."

He shrugged off her compliment. "Enjoy."

When Haley continued to stand there, Zoe gave a sigh. She was going to have to hear the woman out to get her to leave them alone. "Say your piece."

"Thank you," Haley said and took a seat across from Zoe in the booth.

"Should Myles and I leave?" Sadie asked.

"No, I'd rather you stayed," Zoe said.

"Yes, that would be great," Haley said at the same time.

"Here, Myles, eat a few bites of melon," Sadie encouraged her son before digging into her sundae.

Annoyance flashed in Haley's eyes.

Not in the least bit willing to accommodate the woman, Zoe prompted. "Well?"

"I'm really sorry for any pain I caused you," Haley said in an even tone. "I met Garrett when I took my car in to be fixed after I first arrived back in town. He hadn't been wearing a wedding ring. He flirted with me and asked me out. Now that I think about it, his insistence that we had to go to the next town

over makes sense. At the time, I thought he was being chivalrous and wanting to take me to a fancy restaurant."

"Oh, that's him, chivalrous." The sarcasm was lost around a
mouthful of pumpkin spice, caramel and nuts. Zoe really just
wanted to enjoy her confection.

"Anyway," Haley said. "When I got the job at the hospital,
and I met you and we became friends… I realized what an idiot
I'd been. I broke things off with Garrett right away. I told him
never to contact me again."

Zoe carefully put down her spoon and met Haley's gaze. "I
accept your apology. This is on Garrett. He was a lousy husband and even more of an immoral man. We are both better
off without him."

The clearing of a throat brought all their gazes to Chase and
Rocco standing next to the table.

"I've overstayed my welcome," Haley said. "Thank you,
Zoe, for being such a generous person with your forgiveness."

Zoe didn't recall saying she'd forgiven the woman, but technically she forgave her. What she said was true, she blamed
Garrett not Haley. But it would take time for the sour feelings
to dissipate. She doubted she and Haley would ever be true
friends again.

Haley slid from the booth and went to the counter where
she grabbed a to-go bag presumably filled with ice cream. Zoe
watched her leave as Chase and Rocco slid back into the booth.

"That was impressive," Chase said to her.

"Yes," Sadie joined in. "You were the epitome of grace."

If only that were true. Zoe couldn't say she didn't still hold
some bad feelings toward Haley, but eventually, she would get
over it with God's help.

Her stomach twisted.

She ate a few more bites of her ice cream, which seemed
only to upset her stomach more.

"Oh, look, there's Isla and her grandmother, Annette," Sadie said.

Zoe turned to see a dark-haired woman wearing jeans and a parka. Beside her, a shorter, older woman with gray hair stood in a long wool coat. Annette Jimenez was one of Zoe's clients.

Chase waved them over.

After paying for a to-go container of ice cream, Isla and her grandmother made their way over to the table.

"Ladies, would you care to join us?" Chase asked.

Annette waved off the offer. "We just stopped in to pick up a couple of sundaes. We have a holiday rom-com starting soon."

Isla smiled. "It's that time of year."

Everyone laughed. Zoe swirled her spoon in the ice cream. A fuzzy sort of haze gripped her.

Chase leaned in close. "Would you be okay if I see Annette and Isla home, while you and Kylie stay here with Rocco and Sadie? You'll be safe."

Zoe blinked slowly. Though she understood his words, it took a moment to decipher them. With effort, she managed to say, "Oh. Sure. We'll be fine here."

He cocked his head. She smiled to reassure him. He nodded and told Rocco what he was doing. His voice sounded far away to Zoe, but she kept her gaze trained on the gooey mess she'd made of her ice cream. Beside her, Kylie banged her spoon on the table, the noise ricocheted through Zoe's brain.

Chase gently took the spoon from Kylie before he scooted out of the booth. "I'll be back in a jiff."

Dash rose and moved to his side.

Zoe watched Chase and Dash escort Isla and Annette through the crowded ice cream parlor and out the door.

Nausea roiled through Zoe's stomach. She turned to Rocco. "Would you mind grabbing to-go containers?"

"Grab me one, too," Sadie said. "This ice cream was very rich and too much for one sitting."

Rocco slid out of the booth.

"I feel bad for Isla," Sadie said.

Zoe stared at her friend and concentrated on forming words. "Annette told me Isla's been on the receiving end of some nastiness."

"Indeed," Sadie said. "I'm sure Chase just wants to make sure they get home safely."

Nodding, Zoe said, "He's a good man. I really like him." Did she slur her words? A pounding behind her eyes made her squint.

Sadie tilted her head. "Are you okay?"

"Upset stomach," Zoe replied with as much of a smile as she could muster. "Would you and Rocco walk me to Chase's house?"

"Of course." Sadie gathered her son and helped Zoe with Kylie.

"Ladies?" Rocco returned with the containers.

"I don't want the ice cream," Zoe said, swallowing back a bout of nausea. She hurried for the door with Kylie in her arms.

Outside, the cool air was a welcome relief. Zoe strapped Kylie into the stroller and nearly doubled over from the dizziness washing through her and the blood throbbing in her head.

"Everything okay?" Officer Steve asked as he came to her side.

Sweat beaded along Zoe's brow and down her back. Her hands began to shake. She headed for the nearest sidewalk bench where she could sit. She drew the stroller next to her, grateful to see Kylie had fallen asleep. Zoe wished she could go to sleep, then maybe the horrible sensations tearing through her would end.

Sadie sat beside her. "You don't look so good."

"I don't feel so good," Zoe said slowly. All the saliva in her mouth dried up. The world started to tilt. No, it was her. She listed sideways, slowly crumbling onto the bench. She could hear panic in Sadie's voice, but she couldn't make out the words as her vision tunneled into a black hole.

As they walked, Chase was aware that Dash kept looking back, as if he, too, hated leaving Zoe and Kylie's side. Chase was confident Rocco and Cocoa would protect the pair along with Sadie and her son, Myles. There was no reason to be concerned. He hoped Zoe didn't feel abandoned by him. He would explain to her later why he felt the need to make sure Isla and Annette made it safely home. He'd made a promise to himself to keep an eye on Isla and to help her however he could.

This past summer someone had done a hatchet job on the tech analyst's reputation, and had prevented her from adopting a little boy. Then someone had burned down Isla's home in an attempt to kill her. Isla was like family, as were all the Mountain Country K-9 Unit team members.

"That's strange," Annette said, breaking into Chase's thoughts.

"What is?" Chase asked.

They had just turned down the drive to Annette's home.

"I'm sure we left the porch light on," Isla said. "It must have burned out."

Caution tripped up Chase's spine as they gathered on the front porch. He reached up to test the light. Hot to the touch like a blub would be when it burned out. Still, he couldn't shake the wariness prickling his skin.

Chase held out his hand. He could just make out Isla and Annette in the ambient moonlight. "Let me clear the house."

Isla handed over the house key. Chase fitted the key in the lock and opened the door.

Dash growled and turned to face behind them. Alarm tightened Chase's muscles and his hand went to his sidearm.

"I have a gun trained on you so no sudden moves." The female voice came from a shadow near the bottom of the stairs.

Annette gasped.

Chase moved to shield Isla and her grandmother. "Who's there?"

"Everyone, step inside," the woman demanded.

Unsure what he was dealing with, Chase nudged Isla and Annette inside. He tightened his hold on Dash's leash, tugging the dog with him inside the house.

Could this be the person who had tried to ruin Isla's chances of adopting? The same person who had burned down Isla's house on the other side of town?

The same person responsible for blowing up Zoe's house? Did the two women have the same enemy?

The questions rattled around inside his mind like bees in a trap.

Isla flipped on the lights as they moved farther into the house.

The dark-hooded intruder followed them inside.

Isla gasped. "Lisa?"

Chase didn't recognize the woman with stringy blond hair and a sharp nose, but, apparently, Isla did.

"Didn't think you'd see me again?" Lisa's voice held a note of malice.

"What are you doing here?" Isla asked, her voice shaking as she stepped in front of her grandmother. "Why do you have a gun?"

Lisa's face twisted with pain. "Because of you, my brother is gone."

Brother? Chase had no clue about the drama unfolding around him. "Isla, tell me what's happening?"

Isla made eye contact with Chase. "Lisa, her younger brother and I were in a foster home together when I was a teen," she explained. "Her brother ran away and apparently, she blames me. But it wasn't my fault."

"Liar!" Lisa shrieked.

"Whoa, stay calm," Chase said. "We can talk this through."

Isla focused on Lisa. "I covered for *you*."

"You were supposed to be watching us." Lisa waved the gun. Her finger was on the trigger.

Chase's stomach clenched. "Ladies, please—"

Ignoring him, Lisa yelled at Isla. "You let him run away."

"I was making dinner. He took off because *you* were being mean to him," Isla's voice held a hard note that Chase had never heard from her.

"No!" Lisa screamed, her agitation ratcheting up. "You're responsible. You should have intervened. You were in charge."

"Isla." Chase caught her gaze again and shook his head, hoping she'd get the message and not let the woman get to her.

Isla visibly reined in her own upset. "I know it's hard for you to accept responsibility," Isla said gently. "You really need to get some help."

"Don't say that!" Lisa let out a shriek that shuddered through Chase.

"How did you find me?" Isla asked.

Chase eased his hold on Dash's leash, ready to drop the lead. He wouldn't give Dash the command to attack while Lisa's finger was on the trigger. He hoped to find another way to defuse the situation.

"Lisa, I understand you're upset," Chase tried reasoning with her. "But this isn't the way to solve your problem. We can help you find your brother. If we work together."

She steadied the gun's barrel on Chase. "You don't know anything. You can't even capture the RMK."

Chase wasn't surprised she knew who he was. He hated that her words were true.

Keeping the gun trained on him, Lisa said, "I saw the news reporting on the Rocky Mountain Killer." Her gaze turned to Isla. "I saw you were part of the team investigating. I've been in town for months."

Isla spread her hands. "What do you want?"

Sneering, Lisa said, "Old granny, here, likes to talk to the ladies at the beauty place. It was no secret you were trying to adopt a child." Lisa's eyes darkened. "You shouldn't raise a child. You're nothing and deserve to be alone like me."

Shock crossed Isla's face. "You're the one who tanked my reputation with the child protective services?" Anger reverberated through her voice.

"They had to know what an awful person you are," Lisa insisted.

Shaking her head, Isla asked, "Did you also set fire to my house?"

Lisa cackled, a strange sort of laugh that was strangled by a cough. "It's just too bad you didn't die in that fire."

Chase had heard enough. He couldn't allow this unhinged woman to hurt Isla or Annette. Chase dropped Dash's leash, knowing the well-trained dog would stay put until commanded otherwise.

"Lisa, if you know who I am, you know I'm FBI," Chase said as he stepped forward, aware that the business end of the handgun she held was aimed at his chest. "You need to drop your weapon and surrender."

She scoffed. "Right. You're in no position to demand anything. I'm in control here."

Dash growled and then let out a series of ear-piercing barks.

Lisa seemed confused by the ruckus, which allowed Chase to tackle her. The gun Lisa held went off, the bullet embedding itself in the wall several feet from Isla.

Chase wrested the gun from Lisa's hand and flipped her onto her stomach to handcuff her.

Dash sniffed the woman as Chase holstered his weapon. Dash didn't alert to indicate there was any trace of explosives on her person.

Isla quickly called 911.

Within a short time, several police officers converged on the house and took Lisa into custody.

Chase and Dash moved to Isla and Annette. "Are you okay?"

Isla had her arms around her grandmother. "We are now. I can't believe it. Lisa is the one who's been harassing me and set the fire at my house. She blames me for her brother running away."

"At least now we know," her grandmother said.

"Yes," Chase agreed. "Having her in custody will go a long way to repairing the damage she's done to you, Isla."

Two Elk Valley police officers led Lisa out as she screamed obscenities at Isla. Chase would question her later when she'd calmed down to determine if she was involved in any way with the explosion at Zoe's house. But he had a feeling she wasn't.

Chase's phone rang. The caller ID showed Rocco's number. He answered. "Hey."

"It's Zoe. She's been taken to the hospital."

Chapter Eleven

Chase raced out of Isla's house and back to Main Street where he found Rocco, Cocoa, Sadie and the children.

"Go," Rocco said. "We'll take care of Kylie."

Chase stared at his task force member, his mind running through the possible reasons why Zoe had been taken to the hospital.

He should have stayed with her. Guilt nearly suffocated him. But he'd been in a hard place, having to decide whether to stick with Zoe or see Isla and Annette home. Chase had been confident Zoe would be safe with Rocco and Sadie. "What happened? I don't understand."

"She just collapsed," Sadie said. She had both strollers in front of her. Kylie was sleeping.

Chase's heart thumped against his rib cage like a battering ram. "Is Kylie okay?"

Sadie's eyes widened. A silent oh formed on her lips. "I think so."

Chase quickly bent down and jostled Kylie, wanting to make sure the little nine-month-old woke up. Dash stuck his face inside the stroller to sniff Kylie. Kylie's eyes fluttered and she stretched. When her gaze focused on Chase's face, she smiled and babbled happily. Her gaze shifted to Dash and her little hands waved, trying to reach him.

Something inside of Chase gave way and a sob nearly escaped. This little girl had become so important to him. As important as her mother, Zoe. The realization had his breath catching. Now was not the time to examine the depths of his feelings for Zoe.

Not wanting to take any chances that Kylie had been harmed by whatever had happened to Zoe, Chase straightened and said, "We need to get to the hospital. All of us. I want Kylie to be looked at."

"We'll take our vehicle," Rocco said. "Kylie's stroller converts into a car seat."

"Lead the way," Chase said, anxious to get on the move, to get to Zoe. To find out what happened. If she died on his watch, he would never, ever forgive himself. He couldn't let another person he cared about perish because of his inability to protect them.

Thankfully, Rocco had brought his official Elk Valley PD vehicle to town. They loaded the dogs in the back compartment and the children in the back passenger seat with Sadie squeezed in between the two car seats. Chase jumped into the front passenger seat even though he wanted to take control of the SUV and drive. With lights and sirens blazing, they made quick time to the hospital.

Chase unbuckled and jumped out, released the locks holding Kylie's car seat in place and hurried into the hospital emergency room reception area. He skidded to a halt at the front desk.

"Zoe Jenkins," he said, his breath coming out in a huff. "I have her daughter. Kylie Jenkins. She needs to be seen. Call Dr. Webb, her pediatrician."

The nurse held up a hand. "Whoa, slow down. Is Kylie in distress?"

Chase looked down at the baby snug inside the car seat. Her wide trusting eyes stared up at him. His gut clenched with even more guilt and anxiety. This little girl needed her mother. This little girl had needed Chase to make sure her mother was safe. And he'd failed.

"I don't know," he finally said. "She seems okay. But her mother—"

"Zoe Jenkins has been taken to a room," the nurse said. "Let's have our ER doctor take a look at Kylie and then we'll go from there."

It took all of Chase's willpower not to rush to wherever they had taken Zoe. But right now, Zoe would want him to make Kylie the priority.

"I understand we have a little patient that might need some help?" a young female doctor said as she approached with a smile. She had long red hair held back in a braid down her back. Her white doctor's coat had the name Dr. Yvette Stinson stitched on the breast pocket. A stethoscope hung around her neck.

"Something happened to her mother, and I just want to make sure that she's okay," Chase said in a rush.

Yvette nodded with a kind smile as she bent forward to coo at Kylie. When she straightened, the doctor said, "Follow me. We'll go to exam room two."

Chase stayed right on the doctor's heels. Impatience threaded through his system and worry churned in his gut. He needed Kylie to be okay. He needed Zoe to be okay. Dr. Stinson indicated for Chase to set the car seat on the exam table, and then she proceeded to listen to Kylie's heart.

Chase paced as the doctor did a thorough exam.

He heard Rocco and Sadie talking outside the exam room. He opened the door and said, "Come in."

Sadie, Rocco and Myles crowded into the room, along with Dash. Rocco put his hand on Chase's shoulder and handed him his partner's leash. Chase gazed at Dash as more guilt flooded his system. In the rush to get Kylie into the hospital, Chase had neglected to release his dog from Rocco's vehicle. It was so unlike him. He'd make it up to Dash later with an extra chew bone. "Thank you for looking after him."

Rocco squeezed Chase's shoulder. "Of course."

"Kylie seems perfectly healthy," Dr. Stinson said. "Dad, you can take her home. She's fine."

The moniker of dad slashed over his heart. Rather than clarify his relationship to Kylie, he simply said, "Thank you, Doctor."

Sadie was at his side. "We'll stay with Kylie," she said. "If we need you, we'll have them page you. Go. Find out about Zoe. I need to know my friend is okay."

Having the reminder that Sadie and Zoe were friends helped Chase relinquish Kylie into Sadie's capable hands.

Dash nudged Chase as if to prod him into movement. Chase gave Rocco a grateful nod and hustled back to the nurses' station with Dash trotting alongside him. "Zoe Jenkins' room?"

"She's on floor three, room three-ten. I'll have the doctor meet you there," the nurse said.

With a sharp nod, Chase and Dash headed for the staircase, not wanting to wait for the elevator. They took the stairs two at a time to the third floor. They found room three-ten quickly. Taking a deep breath to calm his racing heart and to school his features into what he hoped was a neutral expression, Chase pushed open the door. He steeled himself against what he might find on the other side.

An awful beeping sound every few seconds disrupted Zoe from a deep, dreamless sleep. For some reason, she didn't want to come up from a state of unconsciousness. There seemed to be a war raging in her mind. She wanted to go back to that deep, dark abyss and yet, the incessant beeping drew her forward, until her senses gave way to awareness.

The scratchy feel of sheets on her skin made her restless. Her head tilted at an odd angle on a flat pillow. Uncomfortable from head to toe, slowly she rolled her neck and winced as the muscles protested. She swallowed, grimacing at the tender pain in her throat. Her mouth was dry. Her lips cracked. Light penetrated her eyelids. Instinctively knowing the brightness would sting her retinas, she scrunched up her eyes, wanting to hold off the inevitable.

Kylie!

The thought slammed into her as if someone had taken a fist to her jaw.

Her eyes jerked open, ignoring the painful way the sunlight streaming through the window to her right caused her eyes to water. She attempted to sit up. Her body refused to cooperate.

"Zoe, it's okay," the soft masculine voice soothed her.

Her gaze sought the source of that voice. She knew who it would be before he came into view. Chase. His expression was carefully blank, but she could see the worry in his dark eyes. He was trying so hard to be stoic. Didn't the man realize he could trust her with his heart?

She nearly laughed out loud at the stray thought, considering she had been resistant to trusting him with her heart. "Kylie?"

"Safe and healthy," Chase told her. "I had the ER doc check her over. Just in case. But she has a clean bill of health. She's with Sadie, Rocco and Myles. They will take good care of her."

Relief swept through her, bringing a wave of dizziness. She closed her eyes again, riding out the ebb until her stomach settled and the spinning in her head dissipated. "What happened?"

"We're still trying to figure that out," Chase said. "What do you remember?"

"I got up from the booth at the ice cream parlor and suddenly didn't feel well. By the time I made it outside, I felt woozy and nauseous. I was struggling to breathe."

Chase's jaw hardened. She could tell he was debating with himself how much to reveal.

She frowned. "Tell me the truth. Don't sugarcoat it. I can't stand that."

For a moment his eyes closed. When he opened them, there

was no mistaking his anger. "Someone tried to kill you. The doctors found fentanyl in your system."

Her breath stalled. "That's not possible. Is it? How?"

"We don't know. The team is working to figure it out. I don't want to jump to any conclusions until we have some answers. The paramedics gave you Narcan. If they hadn't—" His voice broke and he turned away.

Her heart stuttered at his display of emotion and the meaning behind his words. She would have died without the lifesaving drug used to reverse opioid overdoses.

Seeming to gain control of his emotions, he faced her and cleared his throat. "I'm thankful you weren't alone. Sadie called for help quickly."

Her gaze jumped to the BP monitor that had started beating faster the moment she woke up. "I need to get out of here."

"Let me find the doctor and see what we can do," Chase said.

Sudden panic had Zoe reaching for him. He grasped her hand. "Don't leave me. You can use the call button."

He nodded and reached for the button hanging over the side railing of the hospital bed.

It took another hour for the doctor to release her into Chase's care. In the emergency room waiting area she was reunited with Kylie, as Chase pushed the wheelchair.

Kylie squealed with delight as Sadie picked her up and deposited her into Zoe's arms.

Liam Rawlston walked in with a big smile on his face. "Young lady, you gave us quite the scare."

"Certainly not my intention," Zoe said back to him with a small smile.

"Your chariot awaits," Liam said. He met Chase's gaze. "Are you coming home with us?"

"I am," Chase said. "I'll meet with the team in the morning."

Zoe craned her neck to the side and looked up at Chase. "I'll be fine with your dad and Officer Steve."

"You will," he agreed. "Tomorrow."

His voice was adamant, and she decided not to argue. She didn't in fact want him to leave her. He made her feel safe and cared for. She should rebel against letting a man take care of her, but for now she was going to let the Rawlston men continue to protect her and Kylie. Because obviously the person trying to kill her was not giving up.

"Here you go, boss." Ian handed Chase a set of keys after entering the conference room serving as the Mountain Country K-9 Unit hub in the Elk Valley police station.

It was the morning after Zoe had been hospitalized, and Chase was having a hard time concentrating on what he needed to be doing. From the moment the doctor had told him that Zoe had fentanyl in her system, self-recriminations had been hounding him like dogs on the scent of fresh meat.

He took the keys and stuffed them into his pocket. "Any trouble?"

"None at all." Ian had just returned from Utah where he'd procured Trevor Gage's work truck so that Chase could impersonate Trevor. Ian moved around the conference room table and took a seat next to Meadow. "Trevor had left one of his company vehicles in the parking lot of his business. The keys were under the driver's seat like he said."

From the monitor on the wall, Trevor spoke. "I do have loyal employees."

"And the Stetson?" Chase asked.

"On the front seat waiting for you," Ian said.

The plan to convince the RMK that Trevor was back in town was coming together.

Bennett had rented a house in Trevor's name on the outskirts of town. And had mentioned to the management company that Trevor Gage was returning for the reunion. The hope was through the town's very active chatter among the residents, somehow the news would land in the serial killer's ear.

Rocco, sitting at the conference room table, filled the team in about the intruder at Isla's grandmother's home the night before. "Apparently, Isla was in foster care with Lisa and Bobby King. Both were younger than Isla. One night when the foster parents went out, leaving Isla in charge, the boy, Bobby, ran away. He was never seen again. Lisa blames Isla and was trying to ruin Isla's life."

"Any chance this Lisa King is working with the RMK?" Kyle asked from his seat across the table from Rocco.

Next to him, Ophelia shook her head. "I don't think so. She isn't from Elk Valley. I've gone through her financials, and with Isla's help we have dug into Lisa's past. There is nothing to indicate she's working with the Rocky Mountain Killer."

"Could she have anything to do with the explosion at Zoe's house?" Meadow asked, swinging her gaze from Chase to Ophelia.

"Not that we can surmise," Ophelia said. "Also Dr. Webb's car was clean. Too clean. Whoever stole it wiped every inch down. I also searched the ice cream parlor for any traces of fentanyl and came up empty. No evidence to follow there."

"A fentanyl overdose didn't just happen out of the blue," Chase said. "Someone had to have managed to slip the drug into her system." Dr. Webb would have access to the drug. He came over to talk to Zoe. As did Haley Newton. His gut twisted with frustration and anger. "I need you all to help me figure this out."

Someone out there wanted to kill Zoe. Chase was going to do everything in his power to prevent them from succeeding.

The meeting broke up and Chase returned to his office. The stress from the past few days weighed heavy on his shoulders. He was doing what he could to capture the Rocky Mountain Killer by pretending to be Trevor. He really hoped this ruse worked.

Finding the person after Zoe was going to be more difficult. The perpetrator was smart and seemed to be a step ahead of them, which suggested it had to be someone close. Someone keeping tabs on Zoe and Kylie. But who?

Elk Valley wasn't a big city nor was it a tiny town. The residents all knew each other. Was it someone who didn't want the reunion to happen? Why? Was that someone helping the RMK? Or did they fear the RMK would show up, and this was their way of thwarting the event? Only a few people outside the task force and the police chief knew that Chase had received a text from the killer stating he was in town and planning to off Trevor at the reunion. His father. And Zoe.

But the information could have been leaked. He trusted his team. He trusted his father. And no way would Zoe have said anything. None of them would deliberately reveal the information, but a slip of the tongue was always a possibility. Or a local police officer could have overheard a conversation not meant for their ears.

Rubbing the back of his neck to relieve some tension, he decided there was something he could do to make Isla's life better.

He had a few important phone calls to make. At least this was one case wrapped up. Now he had to solve the others once and for all.

Going stir-crazy, Zoe was more than ready to leave the Rawlston home and meet with the reunion committee to go over seating arrangements and the agenda. The crisp fall air seeped under the collar of her coat. She tucked a fuzzy white blanket snugger around Kylie in the stroller. Her baby waved a stuffed giraffe in her chubby hand. Love swelled within Zoe's chest.

Kylie was her everything.

Blowing out a breath, Zoe pushed the stroller down the street to the heart of Elk Valley with the town hall as their final destination. Beside her, Liam ambled along in a navy peacoat and jaunty hat covering his gray hair. Officer Steve and Meadow followed close behind, providing protection, and Zoe tried to relax.

For the past three days, the Elk Valley High School reunion committee had met via video conferencing, text and email. It wasn't ideal but it seemed to work. After today's meeting at the town hall ballroom where they were holding the reunion, Zoe and Sadie would convene at Sadie's catering kitchen so that they could work together on the menu.

The honk of a horn drew her attention to a big black truck with the logo of Gage Ranch Consulting on the side panel door. The man driving wore a silver Stetson, pulled low as to shield his face, presumably from the late October sunlight cutting through the trees lining the street. He gave a short wave as he drove past. To the pedestrians on the street, it would look as if Trevor Gage was back in town.

Zoe smiled softly and lifted a hand in greeting...to Chase, who she knew was behind the wheel of the truck. He wasn't happy that she had insisted on this in-person meeting at the town hall, but the reunion was in two days, and they needed to finalize preparations. She'd already sent ahead the projects she'd worked on while holed up at the Rawlston's. She'd decorated framed photos of various high school events throughout the years, and she made centerpieces for the tables using candles and foliage picked from Liam and Chase's backyard.

Arriving at the town hall made Zoe breathe a little easier. They made it in one piece. She hadn't realized how stressed she was on the trek over. But lately, stress seemed to be a constant companion. Except when Chase was around. His calm demeanor and steady presence anchored her in ways she'd never experienced with anyone else. She admired him so much. His dedication to his team, to the town, and to her and Kylie. He was a man of integrity and worthy of her respect.

Affection spread through her, and she knew if she weren't careful she could fall for him. She was already becoming too dependent on him, letting her heart get involved would only make her vulnerable to heartache, a state of being she didn't relish or want to experience again.

The decorating team had already started transforming the large room into a glitzy walk down memory lane. Sadie rushed forward when she saw Zoe.

As she absorbed Sadie's hug, Zoe realized how isolated she had become during her marriage. Garrett had demanded all of her attention and time. In the months after her divorce, she'd felt shamed by her failure and had kept to herself outside of the hospital and her clients.

Though she and Sadie had always been friendly, she would've categorized their relationship as more of acquaintances. But now she was thankful to say that she counted Sadie as a good friend.

"Here, let me take Kylie while you go do your thing," Liam said.

She released her hold on the stroller and gave the man a quick hug. His aftershave smelled nice, comforting. She was grateful to have him in her life. "You're the best," she told him.

With a chuckle, Liam pushed the stroller away to where a group of children ranging in age from five to preteen, who belonged to other committee members, were playing duck, duck, goose.

For a moment, Zoe watched the group with an ache in her heart. One day Kylie would be that age. Time was flying by so fast. She could only pray she'd live long enough to see her daughter grow up. But after three attempts on her life, she wouldn't feel safe until Chase caught the person targeting her.

Why did someone want her dead? The unfathomable reason proved elusive and added to her stress.

Linking her arm through Zoe's, Sadie said, "Let's make this happen."

Taking a breath to clear her nerve-racking thoughts, Zoe focused on the ballroom and making the reunion the best social event of the town's history.

* * *

After parking Trevor's truck at the Elk Valley Park and walking down the street and into the police station, Chase entered his office and removed the Stetson hat from his head. He also traded out a jean jacket for his FBI jacket, then headed to the training center where he'd left Dash this morning with the task force dog trainer, Liana Lightfoot.

Liana had worked for the county before Chase had recruited her to work with the task force. She was excellent at training in all disciplines of the working K-9, as well as therapy service dogs.

When he entered the training ring, he found Dash surrounded by Cowgirl's four puppies. He was confounded by the fact that the serial killer they were after had been decent enough to turn over the labradoodle puppies because he couldn't take care of them. Chase really hoped Cowgirl was faring well.

Chase allowed himself a few moments to just enjoy Dash being a regular dog. But soon Dash lifted his nose, turned his head and spotted him. Jumping over a couple of puppies, Dash raced to the edge of the ring. The puppies followed the big golden retriever, their happy yips echoing off the training room walls. Liana joined him outside the gate.

"Aren't they so cute?" she asked. She was a tall and fit woman with a warm disposition and was devoted to the dogs. Her long dark hair hung down her back and her dark eyes followed the puppies.

"Very," Chase agreed. His heart squeezed with tenderness. He loved dogs. Most K-9 officers did, or they wouldn't become K-9 handlers.

Dash went up onto his hind legs and put his front paws on the gate. He was nearly as tall as Chase when stretched out. Dash stuck his nose toward Chase in greeting. Chase rubbed Dash behind the ears. The dog's tongue lolled to the side in a happy response. "I hope you're being nice to those little ones," he said to the dog.

Dash's plumed tail wagged vigorously in answer.

"He's a good boy," she said. "The young ones learn from the older ones as well as from formal training."

She handed Chase Dash's leash. "Any word on Cowgirl?"

Hating to disappoint her, Chase shook his head. "We can't lose hope."

"I keep praying she'll turn up," Liana said. "But with every passing day, it's harder to stay hopeful."

"I'll let you know the minute we hear anything," Chase promised.

After leashing up Dash, Chase said goodbye to Liana, and they left the police station. They walked down Main Street, Dash sniffing the cool air.

"Hey, boss," Rocco and his dog, Cocoa, fell into step beside him. "Are you headed to town hall?"

"I am," Chase said. "You?"

"Yep. Sadie's there with the committee decorating," he said. "Any more texts from the RMK?"

Heaving a sigh, Chase said, "No. But 'Trevor' has made several passes through town and stopped at the gas station where he gassed up."

Dash was at the end of the lead, his nose twitching. An unsettled sensation dropped to the pit of Chase's gut. What scent was the dog picking up?

"Kyle and Ian are camped out in the rented house," Rocco said.

"The trap has been set," Chase said. "Now, we just have to hope he takes the bait."

Chase's cell phone buzzed inside his jacket pocket. Still walking, he took the device out. He didn't recognize the number. He pressed the answer button. "Rawlston."

The sound of maniacal laughter filled his ears. Unease slithered down Chase's spine. Hadn't Zoe said she'd heard a weird sort of laughter before the bomb that destroyed her home exploded?

He halted and held the phone away from him, putting it on speaker so that Rocco could also hear.

"Who is this?" Chase demanded.

Suddenly, Dash started pulling, straining at the end of the lead, scrabbling on the sidewalk. He nearly pulled Chase off his feet. Sharing a concerned glance with Rocco, Chase unhooked Dash and the dog took off like a rocket. Chase ran after him with Rocco and his K-9 close on his heels. Keeping Dash in sight, Chase's stomach dropped when he realized Dash was headed straight for the town hall building.

The dog veered off to the right side of the building housing the event space and came to a skidding halt. He sat by the wall and barked.

"He's alerting!" Chase told Rocco. "Evacuate the premises."

Rocco and his dog peeled away and rushed inside the town hall entrance.

Chase rushed to Dash's side and quickly attached his leash to his harness. Following the dog's gaze, Chase searched the ground on the side of the building. His gaze snagged on a patch of earth that had been disturbed near the outer wall beneath a window.

Going to his knees, the soft dirt squishing under his weight, he dug with his hands until he uncovered an explosive device.

His throat closed tight. Zoe and Kylie were in the building. So was his father. Sadie and others. They were all in danger. He couldn't let anything happen to them.

Chapter Twelve

Heart hammering in his chest, Chase sat back on his heels in the soft dirt outside the town hall building. He grabbed his cell phone, and quickly called Ophelia, the task force's crime scene expert. "I need your help with an explosive device. Bring me the portable TVC."

Chase described the cylindrical canister with a cell phone strapped to the middle by duct tape. "It's buried just outside the south wall of the town hall ballroom. The device can be remotely detonated. And could have a long range."

"Are there people in the building? You need to evacuate. I'm on my way." Ophelia sounded like she was running.

"Rocco's on it." Chase glanced toward the front of the building where a steady stream of people coming out of town hall flooded the sidewalk. He wanted to find Zoe, Kylie and his dad, but containing the device had to be his priority. The best way to protect everyone was to defuse the device before it detonated.

"I can disarm this thing," he said into the phone. "Stay with me."

"If you disturb the device, it might go off." There was no mistaking the concern lacing her words.

He considered the wisdom of her words. Better to be safe

than sorry. He tugged on Dash's leash and backed away. He'd hoped the TVC—total containment vessel—he'd helped procure for the Elk Valley PD would never be required. But after the bombing that had devastated his life, having one available gave him peace of mind. Not that it would have helped in the situation with Elsie and Tommy. He hadn't been there to help them. No one had. They'd died alone. Leaving him grieving and broken.

But he was helping Zoe and the others now. He wouldn't let anyone else die. Not on his watch.

Chase's cell phone rang again. The number was unfamiliar. Just like the last call. Scanning the area for anything or anyone out of place, his gaze stalled. There by a tree in Elk Valley Park at the end of Main Street, he saw a hooded figure.

Afraid to answer the call on his phone in case it might trigger the bomb as Ophelia suspected, Chase kept his gaze trained on the suspicious person in the park.

Ophelia joined him on the sidewalk with the TVC in tow. The spherical core chamber sat on top of a wheeled cart.

He pointed to the figure who now raised a hand in the air. Was it the phone? "I think that's the bomber."

Ophelia followed his gaze. "If that's true, we don't have time to contain the bomb. We need to get these people as far away as possible."

"You do that. I'm going after the suspect." Chase ran toward the hooded figure with Dash at his side.

Behind him, the world exploded.

He and Dash were flung forward. He landed on the ground with a thud that reverberated through him. Dash let out a bark as he crashed to the ground, but the dog quickly regained his footing.

Getting to his hands and knees, Chase watched the hooded figure run in the opposite direction through the park, getting farther away.

"Boss! You okay?" Rocco and his dog rushed up.

Getting to his feet and shaking the residual effects of the explosion from his head, Chase sucked in a breath. "Casualties?"

"No. We cleared the building before the explosion," Rocco said. "Only structural damage."

Sending up a quick, thankful prayer, Chase said, "Come on. We can't let him get away."

They raced after the bomber, running through the park straight to the parking lot. The fall leaves crunched beneath their feet and they slid on the slick, dewy ground.

With frustration, Chase watched the bomber jump into a silver truck, back up and speed away.

Unfortunately, Chase had left the keys to Trevor's truck, also parked in the Elk Valley Park parking lot, in the jean jacket in his office inside the Elk Valley police station. He'd never make it inside to grab the keys and back in time to follow the truck.

"That was Garrett Watson's company truck," Rocco said, his voice seething with anger.

Dismay and anger had Chase's hands fisting at his side. Garrett Watson had a lot to answer for.

"Was that the suspect?" Bennett and Spike, his beagle, raced to where Rocco and Chase stood in the parking lot of Elk Valley Park.

Containing his rage at Zoe's ex-husband, Chase said, "Rocco, Bennett, secure the scene. I'm going after Garrett."

"Not alone, you aren't," Bennett said, his voice hard. Beside him, his dog sat waiting to go to work. Unfortunately, having a narcotics detection dog in this instance wasn't going to help them find Garrett. "Meadow and Ophelia are on scene. I'm going with you."

Chase could see the indecision on Rocco's face. "Rocco, go make sure Sadie and Zoe and the kiddos are okay." He trusted the man would protect the women and children with his life. "Get them to safety. And my dad, too."

Without hesitation, Rocco nodded. He and Cocoa hustled away, heading back to the scene where smoke rose in dark spirals of doom to the sky. Half of the town hall ballroom was gone. Chase's stomach twisted. Zoe would be so upset. He wanted to go to her, to comfort her, but his first priority had to be bringing in Garrett Watson. The man would pay for terrorizing and attempting to kill his ex-wife.

Chase, Dash, Bennett and Spike hustled to the police station where they piled into an official Mountain Country K-9 Unit vehicle. After securing their dogs in the back compartment, with Bennett at the wheel, they drove to the other side of town where Watson Motors was located.

The vehicle barely came to a halt before Chase jumped out and released Dash. Putting the dog on a long lead, Chase stomped toward the entrance. Bypassing the reception entrance, he entered the garage where several mechanics were working on various cars and trucks.

"Garrett Watson. Where is he?" He held up his FBI badge.

An older gentleman wearing blue coveralls smeared with grease walked over. "I haven't seen Garrett all day. I'm Fred Comet, I manage the shop for the Watsons. Can I help you with something?"

"If Garrett's not here, where would he be?" Chase asked.

"I couldn't rightly say," Fred said. "But you could check out his parents' place. They live off Tiburon Road. The last I heard, old man Watson and his wife were traveling."

Chase clenched his jaw and spun on his heel. He wasn't going to take the man's word at face value. "Search," he told Dash.

The dog went into working mode, his nose twitched and lifted in the air. He started a slow procession through the garage, sniffing the workers without alerting on them. Dash moved on quickly, clearing the garage, supply closets and reception area without alerting.

Okay, maybe Garrett wasn't building his bombs here at the garage but maybe he was at his parents' home. Meeting back up with Bennett outside, Chase said, "Nothing."

"Ditto," Bennett said. "I talked to everyone. Nobody has seen Garrett today."

"We need to put out a BOLO on his truck," Chase said. He loaded Dash back into the Mountain Country K-9 Unit vehicle.

Bennett nodded and loaded his dog in the back as well.

After climbing into the driver's seat, Bennett started the engine, while Chase grabbed the dashboard radio to call in about Garrett's silver four-by-four truck with the Watson Motors logo on the sides.

The dispatch operator said, "Hold on one second." There was a moment of silence before she came back on. "Garrett Watson reported that truck stolen this morning." The dispatcher rattled off the address for his parents' Elk Valley home.

"Convenient," Chase said, not for one second believing that Garrett's vehicle had been stolen but rather that Garrett had reported it as such to cover his tracks.

Bennett stepped on the gas, and they headed to the Watson property. When they arrived at the ranch-style house, Garrett Watson stepped out the front door. Paint peeled off the banister and dead flowers in window boxes drooped.

"Did you find my truck?" Garrett asked. "I assume that's why you've made the trek out here."

"I'll ask the questions," Chase said. "You're coming with us."

"Excuse me?" Garrett frowned and crossed his arms over his chest. "You're taking me in? On what grounds?"

"On the grounds that you're suspected of blowing up the town hall building." Bennett stepped forward to grasp Garrett by the biceps. His dog stood beside him, his ears back.

"Whoa, now," Garrett said. "I don't know anything about any kind of explosions. I woke up this morning to find my truck was gone. My parents are off on a cruise now that Dad's retired. I had no way to get to town except walk, and well, that isn't happening. I'm not much for exercise."

"You can tell us all about it at the station," Chase said. "First, do I have your permission to search your property?"

"Search?" Garrett jerked away from Bennett. "What exactly are you looking for?"

"What you used to make a bomb," Chase told him.

Garrett laughed. He made a sweeping gesture with his arms. "Knock yourself out. I have nothing to hide."

Dislike for the man set Chase's nerves on edge. "We'll see."

Once again, Chase gave the command for Dash to search. They started with the outside perimeter of the house and the garage. With mounting frustration, Chase followed behind Dash while the dog continued on without alerting. They moved into the house. The odors of coffee and grilled onions turned Chase's stomach. But still Dash didn't alert.

Just because Garrett didn't build his devices at his workplace or his parents' home didn't mean he wasn't behind the attacks on Zoe. But Chase had to admit he had no cause to detain Garrett.

"Don't leave town," Chase told him.

Garrett scoffed with a careless shrug. "Until you find my truck, I have no wheels. I couldn't leave town even if I wanted to. I've already called the insurance company. It will be days before I can get a rental here."

Far from satisfied, Chase had to walk away even though everything inside of him wanted to punch the smirk off the man's face. Chase would find out how Garrett had arranged for the explosion. There was no doubt in his mind Garrett was guilty of something. He just didn't know what yet.

"I should have canceled the reunion the minute we knew the Rocky Mountain Killer was back in town." Zoe couldn't keep the self-recriminations from tainting her voice and betraying the guilt flooding her system. Her gaze went to Kylie in the playpen. She waved a toy in the air and then crawled to the edge of the pen and pulled herself to her feet.

They were safe now back in the Rawlston's home. Their

sanctuary. Was it wrong of Zoe to never want to step outside again?

"This is not on you," Chase said.

He'd returned to the house several minutes ago and explained that her ex-husband's truck had been seen fleeing the site of the explosion. But he'd also explained they had no cause to arrest Garrett yet. It just was so awful.

"Sure, it's on me," she countered, tearing her gaze from Kylie to meet his. "There was so much opposition to begin with. Somebody doesn't want this reunion to happen. I should've heeded the signs."

"We don't know that this is the work of someone in town. Or the RMK. I still suspect it's Garrett," Chase told her.

"But you didn't find any evidence to suggest he was behind this," Zoe reminded him. "Innocent until proven guilty, correct?"

She could tell from the irritated expression marching across Chase's face that in his book Garrett was guilty and proving him innocent was going to be difficult in Chase's eyes.

She hated to think that Garrett hated her so much that he would try to kill her and other innocent people. What he was supposedly doing didn't make sense.

"True. But let's just take it one problem at a time," Chase said. "Right now, keeping you and Kylie safe is my priority."

His words seeped through her, making her want to weep. Being someone's priority was a dream. Having someone to lean on and to spend her life with had led her into a disastrous marriage. But Chase was nothing like Garrett.

Chase was honorable and trustworthy.

And had a job to do. His priority should be stopping the Rocky Mountain Killer.

"I need to take Kylie and leave. That would be best for everyone," Zoe said. The idea took shape in her mind. "I should've done this to begin with. We can go visit my parents in Florida. The reunion will have to wait until—" She heaved a sigh. "Never. It was a selfish dream of mine to bring the town together."

A shudder ran through her as the memory of the explosion destroying town hall ricocheted through her mind, bringing back echoes of the explosion that had damaged her house. The fear of being evacuated, the terror of how close they all came to being caught in the blast crimped her chest.

"It was not selfish," Chase assured her. "You were trying to do a good thing. And running isn't the answer." He moved to put an arm around her waist, the warmth of his presence chasing away the icy cold seeping through her veins.

She turned to face him, her hands going to his chest. His heart beat in a steady rhythm beneath her palms. Comforting and secure. "I wish I had half the self-confidence you do."

"Believe me, I'm as flawed and insecure as anybody," Chase said to her. "I'm just better at hiding my foibles. Zoe, listen to me." He tightened his hold on her. "You're not to blame for the actions of someone else. If this is truly about stopping the reunion, the person could have gone about it in a completely different way. But they chose destruction. And whoever did this will pay."

"I'm just so grateful to God that no one was hurt today." Emotions clogged her throat. The panic when Rocco came into the event hall, his voice reverberating off the walls, telling them to evacuate, still had her heart racing.

She'd been too far from Kylie to grab her. Thankfully, Liam had had her in his arms, and he'd reacted swiftly, carrying Kylie to safety.

Yet, the fear persisted. A shiver raced over her arms and down her spine. There could have been numerous fatalities, including children. The bomber had no conscience.

Chase rubbed her biceps. "You're cold."

"It's the letdown of the adrenaline from earlier," she told him but the fear that was never far away was also chilling her bones.

He nodded and drew her against him. She clung to him, to

his strength. The lingering scent of the explosion filled her nostrils, along with the spicy masculine scent of his aftershave. It was a reminder that once again he'd saved her and everyone else's life. He was a true hero. She leaned back in his arms and looked up into his face. Words escaped her as she met his gaze. The dark depths were brimming with emotions that had her heart pounding against her rib cage, sending flutters of anticipation through her system.

Without stopping to question the sudden yearning compelling her to go on her tiptoes and slide her hands around his neck, she pulled him toward her mouth. Their lips met. He stiffened as if surprised, or was he resistant?

Mortification engulfed her. She'd overstepped. Misread the situation. Taken advantage of his kindness.

On the verge of breaking off the kiss, he softened, his arms tightening as he deepened the kiss, filling her senses with his masculinity. He tasted of safety and care. Her heart expanded and the knowledge that this man had become so important to her clamored through her mind and settled with a soft landing. She couldn't find any remorse for letting him into her heart.

Kylie's happy babbling brought Zoe back to reality. What was she doing? Becoming involved with Chase romantically would only leave her devastated in the end. She couldn't let him into her heart. She couldn't take another blow, especially when she had the very distinct feeling Chase could decimate her in ways that she'd never experienced.

Slowly, she eased away from Chase. "I'm sorry," she said. "I know you're not interested in me, and I don't know why I did that. It just…"

He brushed her hair back from her face, his touch gentle. He lifted her chin with his finger. "You don't have to apologize. The last few days have been traumatic in so many ways. I don't want to hurt you."

Too late.

Her heart ached with longing to belong to him and for them to be a family.

But she wouldn't tell him that. She hurt knowing that she and Kylie could never compete with the memory of his lost wife and child. And she was still reeling from having learned about Garrett's betrayals, more of which were coming to light even after their divorce. Was she latching onto Chase as a safe harbor when really what she needed to do was focus on herself and Kylie right now? Despite her efforts to avoid letting down her guard, somehow Chase had infused her heart with hope that maybe there was a chance for them. A pipe dream. She couldn't risk her heart again. Could she?

She placed her hand over his heart. "You're a good man. Now, it's time for Kylie and me to rest. I don't know how much more of this I can take."

He released his hold on her. She picked Kylie up and headed for the guestroom, shutting the door in time to keep Chase from seeing the floodgates open and the tears streaming down her face.

"Tell me you found something in the truck," Chase said to Ophelia the next morning.

News had come overnight that Garrett's silver truck had been found abandoned along the highway twenty miles outside of town. Ophelia had processed the vehicle before releasing it back to Garrett.

Chase had called a team meeting. Now they all crowded in the conference room again. He hated that it seemed they were spinning their wheels instead of gaining traction.

"Unfortunately, the truck had been wiped down. Exactly like Dr. Webb's car," Ophelia informed him and the rest of the task force. "Not even a stray hair."

"Whoever's behind this is very thorough and calculated," Ian said. He and Kyle had left the rental house they were using to pose as Trevor's in the care of officers from the Elk Valley PD to attend the meeting.

With the reunion now kaput, their plan to trap the Rocky Mountain Killer was on shaky ground. They couldn't let him leave town before they caught him. Chase had driven through town once again this morning, posing as Trevor Gage. But his efforts seemed futile. There hadn't been any more communication from the serial killer.

"Are we any closer to finding Evan Carr or Ryan York?" Chase tried to keep the vibration of frustration and irritation from showing, but he was doing a poor job of containing his emotions.

After the unexpected kiss last night that he had shared with Zoe, he'd had little rest. His mind played over his father's words telling him it was time to move on. To let his heart mend. Yet, he felt like he was taking advantage of Zoe in her moment of weakness. She was scared and flailing emotionally. Raising a child alone, then having someone destroying her house, try to run her over, poison her with a narcotic and then blowing up the town hall ballroom while she and Kylie were inside was enough to make anyone vulnerable enough to seek solace. Even solace in his arms. He couldn't let her make a mistake that she'd regret later. He needed to be stronger for both of them.

"We aren't any closer to discovering the whereabouts of Evan or Ryan than we were three days ago," Ashley informed him.

"They can't just have fallen off the face of the earth," Chase said. Turning his gaze to Isla, he said, "Have you tapped into all of the databases we have access to?"

She cocked her head and gave him a censoring look. "Of course, I have."

He held up a hand in apology. "I know, I know. Sorry." He ran a hand through his hair. "I don't mean to take my frustrations out on any of you."

"What do we make of Garrett Watson?" This from Trevor on the video monitor. He and Hannah sat side by side, their faces filling one half the screen. "I know you said he didn't have a knife tattoo on his forearm. But what if the knife tattoo had been a fake?"

"Unfortunately, Garrett has an alibi for the time that the Rocky Mountain Killer was seen in Idaho and in Utah," Selena said, from the other half of the monitor.

"I still think he's involved in the attempts on Zoe's life," Chase said. He didn't care if he was stubbornly clinging to that theory. He didn't like the man. And maybe that was coloring Chase's perspective. Garrett had shirked his responsibilities to Zoe and Kylie. The man wasn't trustworthy.

The door to the conference room opened. Police Chief Nora Quan stepped inside. Dressed impeccably in a tailored pantsuit in a deep plum color, the woman exuded authority and confidence. "I have some good news."

Chase perked up, hoping she would say they had a lead on Evan Carr or Ryan York, or some evidence to incriminate Garrett Watson. Something that would break their cases.

"Pastor Jerome has offered up the church's community room for the reunion," she said. "I've already informed Zoe and the reunion committee."

Chase's stomach sank. Not the news he was hoping for. "Another opportunity for the person trying to hurt Zoe to strike."

Nora leveled a finger at him, her gaze behind her glasses sharp. "I propose we go through with the reunion. The reunion itself will be heavily guarded. We continue to spread the word that Trevor will attend but then at the last moment, he decides not to for some reason. You, with your team, wait at the rental house for the Rocky Mountain Killer."

"But what about Zoe?" The question was out before Chase could filter the thought. His priorities had shifted to the woman who he was falling for. And he wasn't going to apologize.

"We will keep her under guard at your house," Nora said.

Chase couldn't argue with the plan. However, Zoe would balk. But knowing how guilty she felt for the town hall explosion, he hoped she would agree to let the reunion commence without her. It was the best way for him to do his job.

And the best way to protect her. If she were there, he didn't know if he could concentrate on the RMK when all he'd want to do was be by Zoe's side.

Chapter Thirteen

"What do you mean you want me to stay home?" Zoe stared at Chase. She couldn't have been more stunned than if he'd grown antlers and a shiny red nose.

She tucked her feet beneath her, the leather of the couch in the Rawlston's living room creaked with the movement. Chase sat opposite her in an arm chair with his hands on his knees and his intense gaze pinning her in place.

The fact that he was echoing the thought she'd had when the police chief had called with the news about using the church community room for the reunion didn't make hearing the words coming from Chase's mouth any easier to absorb.

Chase winced. "I know it's not ideal. But after what happened at the town hall, I think it would be best if you didn't attend the reunion."

"You think it would be best," she repeated with a dull ache pounding beneath her breastbone. It was one thing for her to decide not to go and a completely different issue for him to say she shouldn't go.

Because he thought it would be best.

How many times had Garrett made a decree, claiming he knew better than her? Too many to count. She hadn't recognized his chauvinism until long after they'd married. She'd mistaken his need to be in control and to make the decisions as his way of caring for her. Was she making that same mistake with Chase?

"I'm just saying…" Chase held his hands up in a gesture of surrender. "If you were the target of the bombing, and we have to assume you were, then maybe it would be better if you didn't go. Safer for everyone. Especially you and Kylie. You are my only concern."

Irritation and guilt swamped her. He was nothing like Garrett. He'd proven that over and over. He was a man of honor and integrity. A protector and a gentleman. Her shoulders slumped. "You're right, of course. I'm being silly. I shouldn't attend."

"Not silly," he countered. "The reunion is your project. I hate that you'll have to miss it. If I could be in two places at once, I'd go with you and keep you safe."

And he would. She didn't doubt it for a moment. But it was more important for him to stop the serial killer terrorizing the town than for her be at the reunion. "I can coordinate with Sadie as much as possible so that she's not left with all the responsibility."

"That's perfect." Chase's voice was filled with relief. "I'm sure she would appreciate your thoughtfulness."

"At least somebody does," Zoe groused and immediately regretted her words.

She knew it wasn't fair to be taking her upset out on Chase. He was only trying to protect her. That's what he did. Protected people. Her heart rate ticked up at the thought of what his job might cost him. When she'd come out of the town hall building, she'd seen Chase running through the park and had sent up prayers that he would be safe, more than a little concerned for him.

It was hardly fair for her to begrudge him the same concern.

She needed to trust that God had all of them in his hands.

But that wouldn't stop her from worrying about Chase.

She sent up a silent prayer for God to suppress her growing affection for the man. But that was becoming harder with every passing moment. Especially since she knew he was going to continue with his plan to impersonate Trevor Gage and hopefully lure the Rocky Mountain Killer into a trap. It was dangerous.

Chase was putting his life on the line for them all.

"I'm sorry. You don't deserve my snark," she said, contrition making her wince. "I'm just frustrated."

"As long as you're safe, I'll take any snark you want to throw my way. I can handle it," he replied in a husky voice that sent a ribbon of affection and admiration through her.

He wasn't the type of man to take offense or be too sensitive of criticism. She really liked that about him.

Her staying home, safe with Meadow and Officer Steve standing guard, would help Chase stay focused on what he needed to do.

She sent up a silent prayer that Chase would come through this unscathed and the Rocky Mountain Killer would be caught.

Chase left his house wearing his Mountain Country K-9 Unit uniform of light gray jacket and slacks, secure in the knowledge that between Meadow, her K-9 partner Grace, and Officer Steve, Zoe and Kylie would be well protected. His dad was also staying home, too, since he had not graduated from Elk Valley High School, having moved to Elk Valley in his mid-twenties for a job with the fire department.

Chase carried a duffel bag containing Trevor's silver Stetson and one of his company logo jackets to his Mountain Country K-9 Unit vehicle. He opened the back compartment for Dash to jump in.

Earlier in the day, he'd parked Trevor's truck at the church and walked away wearing his Trevor disguise. So now when he reached the church parking lot, he brought the vehicle to a halt next to Trevor's truck.

Leaving Dash comfortable and safe in his compartment, Chase entered through the main entrance. He stopped by the welcome table to grab his and Trevor's name tags. Peeling off the back of the stickered name tag, he placed his own name on the breast pocket of his uniform while tucking Trevor's name tag into his pocket.

Moving farther into the church's community room, located below the sanctuary, he scanned the space. Tables had been set up all around with donated and borrowed tableware. There wasn't much in the way of decorations since everything Zoe and her committee had used to decorate the town hall ballroom had been destroyed. He noted the gathering was rather small, consisting mostly of first responders, who were local to Elk Valley and a few old-timers like Mr. Kimmer from the ice cream parlor and his wife.

Rocco approached. He'd left his K-9 partner at home as well.

"Not a big turnout," Chase commented.

"Honestly, I think most people are skittish about attending, seeing as the last venue was blown up and all," Rocco said, with a wry twist of his lips.

Sadie joined them, linking her arm through Rocco's. "This will be a dry run. We'll do another reunion, maybe next year."

"Zoe will be happy to hear that," Chase said.

"It was her idea."

Chase wasn't surprised. The woman was always thinking ahead. One of the many reasons he admired and respected her. She was a strong and capable woman who was also thoughtful and kind. He didn't like being here without her.

Stay on task, he silently reminded himself.

"I hear that Trevor has made an appearance," Sadie said loudly. "Someone said he wasn't feeling well and is in the bathroom."

Chase appreciated Sadie's help. He scanned the room again. Ashley and her husband, Cade McNeal, along with Cade's younger sister, Melissa, stood talking with Jessie Baldwin from the Rusty Spoke.

"I'll go check on Trevor," Chase said and strode away.

He stopped to say hello to Ashley and her family. Raising his voice to ensure he was overheard by the other attendees, he said, "I was going to check on Trevor in the restroom. Sounds like he might have a little bit of food poisoning."

"Oh, that's horrible," Ashley said. "Let us know if we can help."

After making a show of checking the bathroom, Chase returned to say loudly, "Trevor went out the side door and is headed back to his rental. He's pretty sick."

Ashley and Cade helped spread the word around the reunion space. With a nod of appreciation to Ashley, Chase walked out of the church into the parking lot.

Careful to stay out of the overhead lights, he stepped between Trevor's truck and his vehicle. After opening the truck's passenger door, he used the remote for his K-9 unit vehicle to release Dash. The dog quickly made the transition from the K-9 unit to the truck.

"Floor," Chase murmured to Dash. The dog settled on the floorboard, his head resting on the bench seat.

Placing Trevor's Stetson on his head, Chase closed the door and walked around the back end of the truck.

The sensation of being watched had the fine hairs on the back of his neck quivering.

He sent up a quick prayer that Dash hadn't been seen.

Marveling at how easy praying was once again becoming, Chase started Trevor's truck and backed out of the parking spot. He pulled down the visor, hoping to help shield his face from view. Driving down Main Street slowly so anyone watching would think Trevor was at the wheel, Chase kept an eye on his rearview mirror for a tail while also scanning the alleys of the business he passed, searching for any signs of a threat.

His cell phone dinged.

He waited until he was out of town before fishing the cell phone out of his front jeans pocket. Checking for signs of another vehicle and seeing none, he pulled to the edge of the road to read the text. The number was blocked. Adrenaline spiked through his veins.

Poor Trevor! Food poisoning will be the least of his worries when I'm done with him. Sorry, you won't reach him in time even if you leave the reunion now.

With a growl, Chase tossed the phone onto the bench seat. Aloud he said, "Bring it on."

Dash made a noise in his throat as if in agreement.

Pulling the truck back onto the road, Chase sped to the rental house. The two-lane road was quiet and dark. No headlights behind him but that didn't mean a vehicle wasn't back there, staying in the shadows. Foreboding gripped his gut. The houses on this side of town were spaced out with long driveways. He turned down the one for the rental house.

The ranch-style house with its low-pitched roof and large windows stood dark at the end of the lane. Even though Chase knew two of his task force members were inside, there were no signs of life. He hit the garage remote and waited while the door opened. He pulled the truck into the empty garage and hit the remote again to close the door.

Grabbing his phone, he climbed from the vehicle and released Dash.

Dash hopped out and sniffed around but didn't alert.

Chase opened the door leading from the garage to the kitchen and said to Dash, "Quiet. Search."

Dash slipped inside without a sound and disappeared into the body of the house to do his job of searching for any sort of explosives.

Chase entered the house, awareness sliding over his skin.

"Hey, boss," Bennett's voice came at Chase through the darkness.

"Everything good here?" Chase asked, closing the garage door behind him, and letting his eyes adjust to the darkened interior.

Bennett sat at the kitchen counter, a darker shape against the inkiness of the unlit house. "We're good."

Off to the left, sitting at the table deep in the shadows of the dining room were Kyle and Ian.

"Any problems?" Kyle asked in a low tone.

"Maybe. I can't say I was followed but you know that feeling when you're sure someone is...?"

"Oh, yes," Ian said. "Know it well."

"I received another text from the RMK," he told them. "Another threat against Trevor. He knows Trevor left the reunion not feeling well."

"We'll be ready when he comes," Bennett said in a hard tone.

Dash returned and sat at Chase's feet. Though it was a good sign the house wasn't rigged with explosives, the grip of dread didn't let up. Chase motioned for Dash to lay down near the back door. Since Trevor didn't have a dog, he couldn't let Dash be seen.

"I'm going to step out front and grab the newspaper I saw lying on the porch," Chase said. "If I was followed, I want the person to see Trevor and think he's unaware."

Bennett slipped off the stool and moved to stand next to Chase. "We have your back."

Without turning on the porch light, Chase stepped out of the house. The eerie sensation of being watched triggered another quiver of alarm. But he didn't pause to scan the area. Better to let whoever was out there think he was oblivious. He bent to retrieve the copy of the *Elk Valley Daily Gazette* and then stepped back inside the dark house, shutting the door behind him with a soft snick. He reached for the wall switch and turned on the living room overhead light.

"There are NVGs on the recliner," Kyle told him, referring to night vision goggles, which would come in handy if the power went out.

Chase moved deeper into the room and switched on a table lamp next to the recliner facing the television. The curtains were all drawn. He pushed aside one of the living room curtains and then, keeping the Stetson and jacket on to make himself more of a target, Chase turned off the overhead light and sat in the recliner with his back to the window.

He tucked the NVGs against his side and grabbed the remote for the TV. Whoever was out there would hopefully think Trevor was relaxing and watching television, completely oblivious to the threat against him.

The local news shifted to an older sitcom that didn't hold any appeal.

Chase removed his phone from his pocket and sent a text to Zoe, asking if everything was okay.

Within seconds, the ding of an incoming text showed her picture popping up.

He read her message with relief.

All good here. About to put Kylie down for the night. How's it going there?

He was about to answer when his phone rang. The sound was startling in the quiet of the house. The caller ID said it was Isla.

He hit the answer button and put the phone to his ear. "What can I do for you?"

"I just wanted to let you know that, through some clever maneuvering, if I say so myself, I managed to discover the person who hacked Garrett Watson's computer."

Chase sat straight up. His heart bumped with anticipation. "Who?"

"Haley Newton."

Haley Newton? Chase didn't quite know what to do with

that information. Why would Haley hack Garrett's computer and send vicious posts to the reunion website? What was in it for her? Did she dislike the thought of the reunion so badly but was too afraid to own her opinion that she had to use Garrett to express her opposition? Why go to all that trouble?

"Chase, someone's outside," Ian's voice drew Chase's attention.

Finally.

"Good work," he said softly to Isla and hung up.

He would deal with Haley Newton later. Right now, he had the Rocky Mountain Killer to contend with.

Zoe held the phone, staring at the screen in anticipation of Chase's response. Her fingers tightened around the device when no answering text came through. Was he in trouble? Just not willing to answer the question? Had she overstepped? Worry chomped a hot trail through her, making the muscles of shoulders bunch with dread.

She tossed the phone onto the dresser and picked up Kylie from where she was playing on a learning mat laid out on the floor of the spare bedroom.

"Time for bed, sweetie pie," she cooed. She carried Kylie to the changing table. "How about bunnies tonight?" She picked up a fuzzy one-piece pajama set and shook it in front of Kylie.

Feeling a nudge at her thigh, Zoe glanced down to find Meadow's dog, Grace, had followed them into the guestroom and taken a seat next to her. She held up the jammies to the sleek-looking vizsla. "What do you think? Cute, right?"

Grace's tongue lulled out the side of her mouth and her thin tail thumped against the floor.

Zoe chuckled. "I'm not sure you understand me, Grace, but I am thankful you're here along with Meadow and Officer Steve."

Just as she got Kylie changed out of her outfit and into the fuzzy bunny pajamas, a scraping noise on the outside wall of the house grabbed her attention. Grace stood and stared at the window. Her tail stood straight out from her body and her front right paw was up. Her whole body looked like she was pointing at the window.

Zoe's heart jumped into her throat. She took a calming breath and hugged Kylie to her chest.

Given all that had happened in the past few days, she wasn't taking any chances. "Come on, Grace," she coaxed. "Out."

Grace ran ahead of her and straight to Meadow's side.

Zoe carried Kylie into the living room where Liam and Meadow were playing a card game. The lights were low, the curtains closed. On television a classic movie played. Officer Steve wasn't in the room. The kitchen was dark as well.

Meadow glanced up and immediately put down her cards and stood. "What's wrong?"

Grimacing but not willing to let it go, Zoe said, "I heard a noise outside. I'm being paranoid, I'm sure."

"Probably Officer Steve doing his rounds," Meadow said. "But to be on the safe side, I'll check in with him. Liam, take Zoe and Kylie into the bedroom and lock the door behind you."

Taking the vizsla with her, Meadow stepped out the front door.

"Okay, let's get into the guestroom." Liam hustled Zoe and Kylie out of the living room, careful to keep them away from the windows. They filed down the hall and into the guestroom. Zoe sat on the bed with Kylie snug in her arms. Liam paced a short path from the door to the crib.

After several moments of silence, Zoe said, "Shouldn't they be back in the house by now?"

The concern on Liam's face ratcheted up Zoe's anxiety. Though he didn't say anything, she could tell he was worried.

What if something happened to Officer Steve or Meadow or Grace?

Please, Lord, keep them safe.

Sudden barking from outside sent shudders of fear sliding

across Zoe's skin. Something was wrong. She jumped from the bed and crossed the room to the dresser where she'd left her phone. "I'm going to text Chase."

The door to the room burst open. Zoe spun around .

Standing in the doorway with a gun in her hand was Haley Newton.

Chapter Fourteen

His heart rate jumping, Chase remained seated in the recliner with his back to the window of the rental house. Someone was outside. The RMK? "Where is the person?"

"Back of the house," Kyle answered. "Going to comms."

Chase sensed rather than saw Bennett, Ian and Kyle taking defensive positions while staying in the shadows.

Slipping the earbud communication device out of the pocket of his flak vest and jamming it into his ear, he said in a whisper, "Test."

"Yes," Ian's voice sounded in Chase's ear along with a click.

"Yep," came Kyle's soft reply followed by another click.

"Good to go," Bennett said and added a click.

The clicks would be used when voices could reveal their positions.

His phone vibrated in his shirt pocket. No time to check it. The RMK was on the premises. At least, Chase hoped it was the serial killer.

Rising slowly from the chair, Chase turned off the TV and the table lamp, throwing the house into darkness.

"Dash," he called softly.

His partner moved silently to his side. For a big dog, Dash could do stealth well.

Putting on the night vision goggles, Chase moved down the hall toward the back bedroom with Dash at his heels. He froze as he heard a faint noise. Dash turned to face the closed door to their right. The would-be intruder had gained entry through the window of the second bedroom.

Patting his side quietly, Chase indicated for Dash to move with him past the room. They entered the master suite where Chase took off the night vision goggles and turned the light on, shutting the door to the room. Dash stared at him, waiting for instructions.

Chase wanted the intruder to think Trevor was heading to bed.

Humming loud enough to be heard outside of the closed bedroom, Chase moved around the room as if oblivious to the fact that somebody had just entered the house uninvited.

In the attached bathroom, Chase turned on the shower. He moved back into the bedroom, closing the bathroom door behind him. He turned out the bedroom light, slipped on the NVGs, and waited. Dash's body quivered with energy next to him.

The click of the door handle being turned had Chase's senses jumping into alert mode.

The bedroom door swung open. A masked man stepped through the doorway. He was tall and broad-shouldered. There was something familiar about the set of his shoulders.

And there was no mistaking the weapon in the man's hand.

Chase allowed him to step all the way into the room and head toward the bathroom where supposedly Trevor was now vulnerable in the shower.

Three quick separate clicks in the earpiece alerted Chase that Bennett, Ian and Kyle were coming through the bedroom door behind the suspect.

Removing his NVG, Chase said, "Lights."

The moment the word left his mouth, he launched himself at the Rocky Mountain Killer.

The overhead flicked on.

Chase wrapped his arms around the man's waist and drove his shoulder into his kidneys. They both tumbled to the ground. Dash clamped his powerful jaw around the intruder's ankle, eliciting a scream of pain.

The gun went off. The sound echoed in the room. The bullet embedded in the wall.

Then the other men piled on. Ian wrestled the gun away from the intruder's hand.

Bennett whipped out zip ties and secured the man's arms behind his back.

"Out," Chase gave the signal for Dash to release his hold on the intruder. Dash complied and backed up but stood ready to attack again if need be.

Kyle quickly zip-tied the man's ankles together.

They flipped the intruder onto his back. He wore a black balaclava mask with only his blue eyes visible. Blond hair peeked out from the edges.

Fully expecting it to be Ryan York, Chase gripped the edge of the mask and ripped it off the man's face to reveal blue eyes wild with rage, a patrician nose and square jaw.

Evan Carr.

"Evan!"

Bennett's shocked tone drew Evan's gaze to his brother-in-law.

"You! Why are you here?" Evan sputtered.

Grabbing Evan's sleeve, Bennett pushed up the material to reveal the knife tattoo on Evan's right forearm. Bennett sat back on his heels. "Naomi is going to be devastated."

Chase didn't envy Bennett having to tell his wife, Naomi, that her brother was the Rocky Mountain Killer. That Evan, in his sick and twisted way, was avenging what had happened to his sister at the Young Rancher's Club dance ten years ago.

"I did it for her! They deserved to die," Evan screamed and bucked against the restraints. "Get Trevor out here. I want to look him in the eye and tell him he deserves to die."

"Trevor's not here," Chase said. "Ian, can you alert Sully? He's close by waiting for our call."

Ian nodded and walked out of the room, dialing his phone. He would bring the deputy marshal to the rental house to take Evan into custody.

"Where is Cowgirl?" Kyle asked.

"I want a deal," Evan demanded.

Of course, he did. Didn't all suspects say that when caught? "I'll talk to the state's attorney, but tell us where Cowgirl is now," Chase countered.

Evan clamped his lips together.

"Come on, Evan," Chase coaxed. "You set the puppies free. Don't leave Cowgirl to fend for herself. I know you love animals."

"They're better than people," Evan sneered.

Thinking of Garrett Watson, Chase was tempted to agree. "Where's Cowgirl?" Chase repeated. "Who's going to feed her? Take care of her?"

After a moment, Evan grumbled, "She's in the caves on the south side of Laramie Mountain."

"Got it," Kyle said, already heading out the door.

Chase remembered what Haley had said about an incident in the caves, so he pressed Evan, "What happened in the caves? Why did you kill Seth Jenkins, Brad Kingsley and Aaron Anderson ten years ago?" He knew, but he wanted to hear it from the killer.

Evan's face shuttered for a moment, becoming a mask. Was he going to deny it? But then, his gaze flared with pure venom. "Those rotten pigs humiliated my sister," Evan said. "Where's Trevor? He was one of them."

"Why kill Peter Windham? He was Naomi's friend," Bennett asked.

Evan turned his wild-eyed gaze to Bennett. "He knew what they were doing. He didn't warn her."

"You are so wrong," Bennett said. "Trevor did like Naomi, and Peter knew that he did."

"No, that's not true!" Spittle flew from Evan's mouth. Now that the man was talking, it was clear he wasn't going to stop. "Peter should have told Naomi and not let those pigs make fun of her."

"Okay, sure," Bennett conceded through clenched teeth. "He should have warned her but that didn't mean he deserved what you did to him."

"What about Henry Mulder and Luke Randall?" Chase asked of the two victims killed just months ago.

Evan practically growled as he struggled against them. "Pigs. They liked their pranks. I should have known they weren't my friends. They lured me to the cave and left me stranded, lost and alone all night. With rats!" A shudder of revulsion wracked Evan's body. "I was a kid!"

So, his history with these boys went back further than they'd previously thought. The group hadn't only mistreated Naomi but Evan himself.

Sully, along with two other deputies Chase didn't recognize, entered the room. "So, this is the infamous Rocky Mountain Killer?"

"He's confessed," Chase said and gestured to the Glock 19 lying on the floor. "I'm confident the bullets from that gun will match the ones taken from the victims."

"I like when it all comes together," Sully said. "Less headache that way."

The two deputies pulled Evan to his feet.

"Wait!" Chase remembered the devastation to Zoe's house and the town hall. The way Zoe had seemed so close to death in the hospital. He had to find out if they were connected. "Evan, why go after Zoe Jenkins?"

Evan wrinkled his nose. "Seth's sister?"

"Yes." A knot formed in Chase's gut. He wanted to reach out and wrap his hands around Evan's throat. "Why have you been trying to kill her? Why blow up her house? And the town hall? Where did you get the fentanyl?"

Evan shook his head. "I don't know what you're talking about. I don't mess with explosives. Too dangerous. Or drugs. And I wouldn't hurt a woman. Even if she is that pig's little sister."

The dread that had been dogging Chase intensified. If Evan wasn't the one targeting Zoe...then who? Haley Newton came to the forefront of his mind. She'd messed with the reunion's social media pages. But why? By her own admission, she was the one to break off the affair with Garrett when she realized he was married. Had she just been so against the reunion she thought to tank it with her nasty posts but hadn't wanted anyone to think it was her? Was she the one targeting Zoe? He couldn't come up with a motive.

"If you have more questions for the suspect, you'll have to ask them at the justice center in Laramie," Sully said.

Chase's phone vibrated in his pocket, reminding him he had incoming texts. Maybe Isla had found more information on why Haley Newton would hijack Garrett Watson's computer.

First, he thumbed open the text from Zoe.

911 hurry help

The words leapt out at Chase like a slap across the face.

"Something's happening at my house." He ran through the rental with Dash hot on his heels. In the garage, he hit the remote to open the door and he and Dash jumped into the cab of Trevor's truck.

Bennett climbed into the passenger seat. "Let's go."

Gratitude tightened a band around Chase's chest. He'd picked wisely when he'd brought his team together. He put the truck into reverse, backed out of the garage and maneuvered around the marshal's vehicles, then took off down the highway toward town.

Horrible scenarios marched through his mind. What was happening to Zoe? To Kylie? They had to be so scared. Guilt clogged his throat. If he'd looked at her text when it first came in, he could be there already making sure they were safe. But he'd put capturing the RMK ahead of the woman he loved. Taking down Evan Carr hadn't been as satisfying as Chase had imagined.

He pressed harder on the gas pedal. The truck strained beneath his grip. He had so much to make up for. He had to get to Zoe. His family. He had to tell Zoe he loved her.

Please, Lord, let me get there in time.

"Zoe?" Meadow called from the front of the house.

Haley put her finger to her lips and waved the gun at Zoe and Liam. She whispered, "Not a sound."

Zoe shifted, turning slightly so that she could lay Kylie in the crib, and dropped her phone onto the mattress. She quickly tucked the blanket around it. Chase would come once he saw her text. She clung to that knowledge with all the hope she could muster. She lifted a silent prayer, asking God to please make Chase hurry.

"I said don't move," Haley's hissing voice was sharp and tinged with something that made a shiver of fear race through Zoe.

The woman was not in her right mind.

For the life of her, Zoe couldn't begin to guess why Haley was trying to kill her. They'd been friendly before Zoe learned of Haley and Garrett's affair. Haley had apologized. She'd seemed truly contrite. This didn't make sense.

Zoe lifted her hands and turned so that her body blocked Kylie from view. The baby snuggled into her blanket and cooed softly. The sound seared Zoe's heart.

Haley shut the door to the guest bedroom and locked it. A

moment later, Meadow was banging on the door, and they could hear Grace barking.

"Zoe, it's Meadow. Are you okay? Where's Liam?"

Haley walked farther into the room, setting the duffel bag she carried at the foot of the crib. In a low whisper, she said to Zoe, "Tell her you're fine or I'll shoot her through the door."

"We're fine," Zoe called out, her voice shaky. "Liam's with me. We're putting Kylie down to bed. We'll be out shortly."

"Why is the door locked?" Meadow rattled the handle. "I can't find Officer Steve. I'm calling for backup."

Haley whipped around, aiming the gun at the door. She fired off two rounds. The wood of the door shattered around the bullets, but no sound came from the other side.

Zoe yelped. Liam rushed toward Haley, but she swung the weapon and aimed at his chest, forcing him to a halt. He held up his hands and backed up.

"Oh no, you don't, pops," Haley said. "Zoe, open the duffel bag. There are zip ties in there. You secure old pops here."

Fearing that Meadow and her dog were hurt or worse, Zoe slowly bent down and unzipped the duffel bag. And found a silver galvanized pipe with lots of wires sticking out of it. A pipe bomb. Not that she'd ever seen one in real life but she couldn't turn on the news lately without some reference to these horrid devices. She fell back on her behind. "There's a bomb here."

"Get the zip ties and put them on. Hands and feet," Haley insisted. She alternated aiming the gun at Zoe, Kylie and Liam. "You'll do as I've said or one of you three is going to die with a bullet in the head."

Swallowing back the panic and fear, Zoe reached into the bag, careful not to jostle the scary-looking canister with wires protruding from it, and pulled out a handful of zip ties.

She moved to Liam, looping one around his wrists. Tears clouded her vision. She pulled the ties tight but not too tight for fear of hurting him. She did the same for his feet.

"It's okay," Liam murmured. "We'll get through this."

As much as she wanted to believe him, doubt crowded her mind.

Please, Lord, please, Lord, the prayer played on a loop in her brain.

"Now zip tie your own hands and feet together," Haley demanded.

Zoe frowned and threaded the ends of a zip tie together, then put her wrists through the zip tie.

"Use your teeth to tighten it," Haley said.

Bitter anger prompted Zoe to say, "You're the one who blew up my house. And the town hall."

"It's amazing the information on how to build a rudimentary bomb can be found on the internet. They get the job done though." With the gun, Haley emphasized her words, "Do it now."

Zoe used her teeth to tighten the zip tie, but she left it loose enough so that it wouldn't bite into her skin and would hopefully give her room to slip out if there was an opportunity to escape.

"You'll never get away with this," Liam said. "My son will stop you."

Haley swung the gun toward him. "Shut up!" She rushed forward and grabbed a roll of duct tape from the duffel. She tore off a piece and slapped it over Liam's mouth.

Risking that she'd silence her as well, Zoe pressed, "But the fentanyl? How? Why?"

Dropping the duct tape on the floor, Haley laughed. "Easy peasy. I bought it off the street. You'd be surprised what's available out there. When I saw you going into the ice cream parlor, I knew that was my chance. I offered to help old man Kimmer. He had his hands full. It was quite brilliant of me. I sprinkled the liquid drug on your sundae. By the time I set it in front of you it had seeped in. You never even tasted it."

Of course. Haley brought over the sundaes, arranging them

on the table and Zoe had eaten it, none the wiser. "You stole Dr. Webb's car? And Garrett's truck? Again why?"

"It's easy to duplicate a key with the right tools." She scoffed. "I'm not dumb enough to use my own vehicle. Too bad your boyfriend has such quick reflexes. I would have taken you both out with the doc's car." She waved the gun again at Zoe. "Take a seat, both of you," Haley said.

Liam and Zoe sat on the edge of the bed. Zoe didn't point out she'd neglected to zip-tie her feet together.

Haley grabbed the duffel bag and pulled out a cell phone. The kind one buys at convenience stores.

"You should say your prayers," Haley said with a sneer.

Anxiety quaked through Zoe. "Haley, please don't do this," she pleaded. "At least, tell me *why* you're trying to kill me?"

The incredulous look on Haley's face would have been comical if the situation wasn't so terrifying. "Why do you think?"

The only reason that made any sense had Zoe's stomach clenching. "I assume this has something to do with Garrett." Her heart tore in two. "Did he pay you to do this?"

"Pay me? Of course not. He can't pay me anything. He can't marry me because of you," Haley practically screamed.

What? Confusion and anger raised Zoe's blood pressure even more. "Of course, he can marry you. We're legally divorced."

"You're bleeding him dry. You and the brat." Haley gestured with the gun toward the crib where Kylie had fallen asleep. "He's barely staying above water with all the money he shells out each month."

Zoe's breath stuttered. She hated seeing that weapon pointed at her daughter. Hated more to think this was all so cliché. "This is about the alimony and child support money?"

"He can't marry me while you're taking all his hard-earned income. That's what he said. I know if I get rid of you then he can marry me." She sounded like a petulant teenager.

Zoe's mouth dropped open, but she couldn't form words. All of this destruction so she could be with Garrett.

Finding her voice, Zoe said, "Haley, I will tell the judge I don't need the money from Garrett anymore. Please, don't do this. We can figure this out. You can have Garrett with my blessing."

"Too late now. You should've refused the money to begin with. You let that good man go. Now he's going to be mine."

Refraining from rolling her eyes, Zoe pointed out, "He cheated on me. And not just with you."

"Maybe. But that was before he met me. Not after," Haley insisted. "We love each other. Now we can be together." Her eyes glazed over as if a memory surfaced. Her voice softened. "I was robbed of a future with my first love, Brad."

Zoe didn't want to feel empathy for this woman over the fact Brad had been murdered by the RMK.

Clarity returned to Haley's gaze. "But I will get to be with Garrett." Haley reached into the duffel and lifted the bomb carefully out of the bag. To Zoe's horror, Haley set it inside the crib with Kylie. "If you try to lift Kylie out of this crib, the bomb will go off."

Liam yelled a protest behind the duct tape covering his mouth.

"No!" Zoe jumped to her feet. "What if she moves?"

Haley shrugged, a malicious smile crossing her face. "Hopefully, she's not a restless sleeper. Either way the bomb is going off." She reached into her pocket and pulled out a phone. "I can remotely detonate the bomb, as well." She waved the gun again at Zoe. "Sit down. No more talking."

She moved to the door. "I'm coming out of the room now. Deputy Ames, if you're still out there, know that I will kill all of us with one press of a button."

There was no answer from outside the bedroom door. Zoe's heart plummeted. Grace didn't even bark. Tears streamed down Zoe's face.

Cautiously, Haley opened the door. She peeked out, then flung the door wide. The hallway was empty. Zoe breathed a sigh of relief. Hopefully, Meadow had gone for backup. But they had to get to Haley before she pressed that button on her phone.

Haley backed out of the room then turned and ran.

Chase's phone buzzed again. The engine of the truck whined with the way he was pushing the vehicle to go faster.

A glance at his phone revealed it was Meadow calling. He tossed the cell to Bennett who hit the answer button and put it on speaker so they both could hear.

The tires of the truck hugged the pavement as he drove. They'd passed the destroyed town hall. "Tell me!"

"There's an intruder in the house," Meadow said. "I took gunfire. I can't find Officer Steve. Zoe, your dad and the baby are locked in the spare bedroom. The gunfire came from that room. I'm outside waiting for backup."

Fear pelted Chase like giant balls of hail. "Five minutes out." Terror at losing the people he loved most in the world a second time stole his breath. He struggled to suck in oxygen and fought the dizziness of grief and pain.

"I put an alert out to the team at the Elk Valley PD. Whoever's inside the room won't get away," Meadow said.

But they could kill his family. He blinked rapidly to keep his focus on the road.

"Let Ian know," Bennett said. "He's still at the rental house."

Remembering Isla's phone call, Chase said, "Do you think it's Haley Newton?"

"I don't know," Meadow replied. "I didn't see the person. They slipped inside while I was checking on Officer Steve. Zoe heard a noise outside."

The thought crossed Chase's mind that maybe Officer Steve was in on it, but he had been with them when the person had tried to run Zoe down in Dr. Webb's stolen car.

The sound of gunfire erupted on Meadow's end of the call.

"Meadow!" Chase and Bennett both yelled.

Breathing heavy, she said, "Taking more gunfire. It's coming from the front window."

"Don't fire back, you might hit Zoe, Kylie or my dad." Chase took a curve too fast. The truck slid but he managed to right the vehicle and proceed.

"Rocco and Ashley are here now," Meadow said.

"Stay back!" a female voice screamed. She said more but Chase couldn't make out the words.

"Meadow, what's happening?" Chase demanded to know.

"A woman is at the front window," Meadow said. "She's demanding we stay back or she's going to blow up the house."

Chapter Fifteen

The echoing sounds of gunfire rang in Zoe's head. With each shot, she flinched. Her gaze jumped to Kylie. The baby still slept. Zoe sent up a grateful prayer that her daughter was apparently impervious to the noise.

Liam made a sound behind the duct tape. Maneuvering herself so she could reach his mouth with her bound hands, Zoe carefully peeled the tape off his face.

"I appreciate that you didn't tighten these zip ties super tight, but I can't get out of them," Liam groused as he struggled to pull his wrists from the restraints. His skin was turning red and raw from his efforts.

Zoe jumped up from where she sat on the bed and took a quick peek out the doorway where Haley had disappeared down the hall. She could see Haley at the front window, gun in one hand and the phone in the other. She'd slid the window open and fired at someone outside.

Where was Meadow? Was that who Haley was shooting at?

Zoe had to get Liam and Kylie out of the house. Fast. And in one piece. Though how, she didn't know. What had Chase said? One problem at a time.

First, she needed to barricade the door to prevent Haley from returning and then they had to ditch the restraints. Zoe moved cautiously to the door and shut it, praying Haley wouldn't hear the click. "Can you hop quietly over to the dresser?" she asked Liam.

With his feet bound, he moved slowly to the dresser. Together, they pushed the large piece of furniture in front of the door. Liam wobbled, nearly losing his balance. Zoe gripped his arm, holding him steady, and helped him back to the edge of the bed.

Zoe grabbed the diaper bag where she'd stashed a nail filing kit. Though she couldn't separate her hands, she could still use them enough to open the bag. She rooted around inside until she found the zipped case. She breathed a sigh of gratefulness to see the small set of manicure scissors inside. She pulled them from the case and hurried to Liam.

"These will have to do," she said.

She worked on the restraints holding his wrists together. Bit by bit the little blades of the scissors chopped through the plastic until finally it gave way. Liam grabbed the scissors from her hands and went to work on the tie around his own wrists. She kept the tension taut on the plastic until it finally broke apart.

Liam then went to work on the restraints around his ankles. Zoe ran to the crib. But she was afraid to pick up Kylie.

Had Haley been telling the truth that if Kylie moved the bomb would go off?

Kylie twitched in her sleep, sending Zoe's heart pounding so hard she thought she might crack a rib. She put a hand on her baby's back, just barely touching her so as not to add more weight to the mattress. Kylie stilled beneath her touch.

There had to be something they could do. Liam joined her at the end of the crib.

"I can try to disarm this," Liam said.

"Are you trained?" Zoe asked with hope.

Liam made a face. "No. Chase is, though."

Zoe's phone was laying inside the crib underneath Kylie's

blanket. Did she dare reach in and remove it? Would doing so blow them all to bits?

"I can't get my phone without risking our lives."

A face appeared at the bedroom window that looked out over the backyard. Zoe swallowed a scream the second recognition took hold.

Chase.

Zoe's knees nearly buckled but she managed to stay upright without grabbing the edge of the crib.

Liam hustled around the crib to slide open the window. He and Chase worked to pop the screen out. Then Dash jumped through the window and landed on the floor.

"Silence," Chase commanded the dog.

Dash folded himself into a laying position, but his attention stayed riveted on the bomb in the crib. He didn't make a sound. Even his tail remained still and upright. But Zoe could feel the tension in the dog. It matched her own.

Liam quickly explained the situation with the bomb and Haley. "The woman is clearly unstable."

"I'll worry about her after I get you three to safety. Dad, help Zoe out," Chase said reaching his arms up for her.

Zoe shook her head. No way was she leaving Kylie with a bomb in her crib. "I can't leave without my daughter. I won't."

Liam grasped her biceps. "You have to trust Chase. I know this is hard. But he is our only hope of getting Kylie out of this alive."

Zoe's gaze bounced from Liam to Chase to Kylie. She would do anything for her daughter. Even relinquish her baby's well-being to the man she'd come to love. Her breath caught but there was no time to process the ramifications of loving Chase.

She pushed against Liam, saying, "You first."

She would never forgive herself if Chase's father perished.

Liam shook his head. "You know I won't go until you do."

She could tell from the stubborn jut of his chin, so like his son's, that he would not budge unless she agreed. She nodded. Liam released his hold on her and hustled her to the window.

With a longing glance at her child, Zoe sent up a desperate plea to God above to protect them all. *Please protect Kylie.*

She climbed over the window ledge and practically fell into Chase's waiting arms. She clung to him for moment. Then relinquished her hold so he could help his father out. The backyard was dark behind them, the light from the room illuminating a small stretch of grass under their feet.

Gripping Chase's hand, Zoe said, "Please, save my baby."

He squeezed her hand and without another word heaved himself up and over the window ledge into the room.

Zoe went on tiptoe, grasping the edge of the window so that she could see over the ledge.

With her heart in her throat, she watched as Chase approached the crib.

Careful not to jostle the crib, Chase studied the bomb laying on the mattress just a mere two inches away from Kylie's little body. The baby slept soundly. Chase sent up a grateful praise to God for the huge favor.

It looked like the bomb had a small bubble level attached to wires on either side of the level's frame.

Taking a deep breath, he reminded himself he'd trained for situations like this. But he'd never had to operate under such dire circumstances. His inclination would be to wait for the bomb squad. The techs who handled this on a daily basis would have no trouble. But there was no time to wait for them to arrive from Laramie.

Meadow and the others were keeping Haley distracted, but she might return to the guest bedroom at any moment and discover it barricaded. Chase had no doubt she would press the send button on the cell phone she carried.

Even if he managed to detach the scale from the bomb, there was still the chance she could detonate before he could remove Kylie. He rushed back to the window. "How much does Kylie weigh?"

"At her last pediatrician appointment, she weighed eighteen pounds, four ounces," Zoe said. "Why? What are you thinking?"

It was crazy and risky what he was thinking. Something only done in movies. But if he could find something that weighed roughly the same as Kylie—no, he would need another set of hands. And there was no way he was bringing Zoe or his dad back into the room.

His best option was to disconnect the scale from the bomb, get Kylie out then take down Haley.

Shaking out his hands to rid himself of the tremors created by the fear sliding along his flesh, he squatted down to get a better look at the bomb. He traced the lines of wire to the cylindrical pipe they were attached to. Underneath the bomb was the receiving cell phone that would detonate the explosive if triggered. This bomb looked similar to the one that had taken out the town hall building.

He drew back in surprise. The two wires coming out of the scale seemed to be the same wire. A trick? A way to get Zoe and his father to cooperate?

What she that devious? Or rather, that clever.

Carefully, with his fingers hovering over the wires, Chase traced them all the way around the device till his fingertips touched. Yes, it was the same wire attached to both ends of the level.

"Okay, Lord, I know I've been mad at you and taken my anger and frustration out on you, but somewhere deep inside I have at least a mustard seed of faith that tells me you will protect Kylie. I don't know why you didn't protect Elsie and Tommy," his voice hitched as he was slammed with emotion.

"I don't believe there's a reason for everything." That platitude people had given him after the death of his wife and child made him so angry. "But I do believe bad things happen to good people. That's what happened to Elsie and Tommy. They were good and a bad thing happened to them. Please don't let a bad thing happen here."

Chase grasped either end of the wire. "Amen. Please Lord."

Holding his breath, he yanked both wires out of the level.

Nothing happened.

He bowed his head in relief, but only for a second.

They weren't out of the woods. Quickly, he gathered Kylie to his chest. Disturbed, she let out a cry. He stuck his pinky into her mouth, and she began to suck.

Swiftly, he lunged for the window and handed Kylie out to Zoe's waiting arms.

"Get as far away as you can," he said.

"What about you and Dash?" Zoe said, her gaze piercing him.

"I have to take down Haley," he said.

"Please, be careful," Zoe pleaded.

"I will." Chase straightened away from the window and started to turn.

"Wait, Chase!" Zoe whispered.

He quickly stuck his head back to the window, afraid something else was wrong. "Zoe?"

"I love you," she said.

Stunned, he could only stare.

His father urged her away from the house. She turned and ran toward safety with Kylie held close. They ran through the backyard to the back gate. The same gate Chase had come through moments before.

Shaking his head to dislodge the bombshell Zoe had just dropped on him, he refocused on what he needed to do.

He scrubbed Dash behind the ears, and said, "Time to work."

Dash seemed confused for a moment. His gaze went to the bomb and then to him. Chase moved to the door of the spare room and pushed the dresser out of the way. When he stepped out of the room, he heard Dash jump off the bed. The dog brushed up against his side. Thankfully, the rest of the house was in shadows as he and Dash crept forward.

When they reached the opening to the living room, he spotted Haley standing in front of the open side of the sliding window taking pot shots at the officers outside through the screen. She paused and crouched to reload her weapon with bullets she pulled from her jacket pocket. She appeared none the wiser that he'd freed her hostages.

Chase squatted down, waiting for her to stand up again. When she did and resumed her position with her back to him, he whispered into Dash's ear, "Bite."

Dash didn't hesitate. The dog sprang forward, running silently down the hall, aimed at Haley's back. Chase followed steps behind his partner. Dash launched himself at Haley, his large front paws hitting her upper back and throwing her face forward against the glass of the sliding window. Chase lunged for the hand holding the phone. He bent her wrist back, forcing her to drop the device.

She screamed and twisted, trying to get the gun in her other hand aimed at Chase. He shoved her harder and sent her crashing through the open side of the window, taking the screen with her. Chase barely managed to keep from following her out.

She landed on the rosebushes, stunned and screaming with pain from the bare bushes' thorns tearing into her skin. The gun fell from her hand. Then the task force team members and all of Elk Valley PD descended on her.

Chase was confident they would take her into custody without incident. He doubted she would be able to move after that landing.

He and Dash went out the front door and handed off the phone to Ophelia.

"The bomb's in the crib in the guest bedroom. The only room with the light on." He told her.

Once again, she'd brought the TCV and, with help from Kyle, rolled the total containment vessel into the house.

"Chase!"

Zoe's yell drew his attention. Zoe, Kylie and his father hustled down the sidewalk. Along with them was Officer Steve.

He and Dash ran to meet them.

"We found him behind some bushes in the house down the street," Liam said. "He has a nasty contusion on the back of his head. He needs to see a paramedic."

Liam led a groggy Officer Steve away.

Chase swept Zoe and Kylie into his arms. "Haley's been taken into custody. You don't have to fear her anymore."

Zoe buried her face into his chest. "She wanted to marry Garrett but apparently, he said he couldn't afford to marry her because he had to pay me alimony and child support. I don't think Garrett was aware of what she was doing." She shuddered in his arms. "Thank you. Thank you again for saving our lives."

He pulled back so he could look into her beautiful and sweet face so full of heartache and hope. "I would do anything for the women I love. I love you, Zoe. And I love Kylie. I hope one day we can be a family."

He held his breath. What would she say?

Tears streamed down Zoe's face. She lifted up on tiptoe to press her lips against his. The world slowed and all he wanted was this moment to last forever.

Kylie squirmed between them, babbling, "Dodododod."

They laughed, breaking the kiss, but held onto each other.

Then Dash was there, squeezing his way between them as if he, too, wanted to get in on a hug.

"Is that a yes?" Chase whispered. "Will you marry me?"

"Yes! A thousand times yes," Zoe said.

"Sorry, I didn't mean to overhear, but I did and I'm so excited," Liam said wrapping them all in his arms. "This is going to be fun."

Epilogue

"Welcome, everyone," Zoe said from the front of the large event tent erected in the middle of Elk Valley Park. Twinkle lights strung from the overhead support poles provided a soft glow for the late afternoon Thanksgiving feast about to commence. Propane-fueled heaters had been brought in to keep the November chill at bay.

The long tables were decorated with brocade fabric runners in bright harvest colors. Battery-powered tea lights surrounded by fall foliage made of silk, and small gourds in various shades of orange, brown, yellow and red made for a festive autumn-themed gathering. Seated at several of the tables were the task force members and their families, plus their K-9 partners lying at the feet of their handlers.

Deputy US Marshal Sully Briggs and Chase's boss, Cara Haines, who had flown in from Washington, DC, for this evening of celebration, had taken their seats among the task force members, but notably at a distance from each other. Chase had noticed some tension between them but refrained from probing into their business. He knew they had some sort of history but did not know the details.

More tables were occupied by the Elk Valley Police Department and other honored guests, such as Mayor Singh and his family, and Pastor Jerome. This was a private event for those close to the investigation, but plans were in the works for a large town function in the spring to celebrate and heal from all that the RMK had put the community through.

But Chase only had eyes for the woman he would soon call his wife. His heart expanded, brimming with love for Zoe and Kylie. Every passing day since they'd brought both the RMK and Haley Newton to justice, he'd counted himself the most blessed man alive. Actually, long before then, but he'd only admitted his love for Zoe to himself and to her on that late October night. His happiness had grown exponentially since.

"Okay, you all, settle down," Sadie said from her place next to Zoe.

Chase bounced Kylie on his knees, waiting for the two women to say their piece before it was his turn.

"We thank you all for coming to our inaugural Thanksgiving dinner," Zoe said.

"Tonight, we will offer both traditional Thanksgiving fare and several healthier options," Sadie said with a smile.

Cheers went up all around the space.

Zoe added, "But first, Chase has a few words to say." Zoe's smile was tender and filled with love.

For a moment, Chase was lost in that smile and the depth of love in her eyes.

Then his father was taking Kylie from his arms. Beside Liam, Martha Baldwin bumped his shoulder. "It's my turn, you know."

Liam laughed and handed Kylie over to the older woman. They'd become quite the item, his dad and Martha.

Chase moved to stand next to Zoe. She squeezed his arm, her touch lingering for a moment, and it took all his willpower not to pull in for a kiss. Then she and Sadie took their seats.

"We have a lot to be thankful for," Chase began. He could hardly believe how his life had changed in the past nine months. Though he still missed Elsie and Tommy, the hollow space in his heart had healed and he had allowed love to fill him again with hope.

"The Mountain Country K-9 Unit accomplished what we set out to do." He couldn't keep the pride out of his voice. "We brought the Rocky Mountain Killer to justice. The US Marshals have him in protective custody, awaiting trial. We all know it could be a while before he faces his sentencing. But he is no longer anonymous. He is no longer the mystery bogeyman haunting this town."

The applause was deafening inside the enclosed space.

His chest swelled with pride. After nine long months, his team had put their killer behind bars. It was still hard to believe Evan Carr had been behind the terror the whole time. So much destruction in the name of revenge.

Chase's gaze met Naomi's across the tent. Holding her son in her lap, with Bennett's arm around her, she smiled. But there was a sadness in her eyes. It would be a long road for her, seeing the fallout of her brother's actions. But the MCK9 unit would be there for her.

When the applause died down, Chase continued, "We recovered Cowgirl safe and sound. Our expert dog trainer, Liana, has been working hard to retrain her." Chase nodded to the task force dog trainer. "Liana, would you like to say a few words?"

From her place at the table, Liana stood. "Despite the demons that drove Evan Carr to commit his horrendous acts, he was kind to Cowgirl and her puppies. Our veterinarian has given them all a clean bill of health. Cowgirl's behind in training, but she's eager to please and ready to learn. She's going to make a great therapy dog. And the puppies are showing promise as well."

Another round of applause erupted. Another thing to be grateful for—all the dogs were safe and back in the task force's care. And they'd finally located Ryan York. The marshal's service had found him hiding out in the back waters of Florida.

He'd said he was afraid that the Rocky Mountain Killer would come after him. He'd made a life for himself in Florida and would remain there.

Chase's gaze sought the team's technical analyst. "Isla, I believe you have something you'd like to share?"

Isla jumped up, excitement oozing off her. Her grandmother sat beside her beaming.

"Thanks to someone—" Isla sent Chase a meaningful glance. "Who called child protective services and the adoption agency and convinced them to reopen my case, my dream of being a mother is about to come true."

More applause erupted.

Chase shook his head and waved away their complimentary praise. "I only did what was right. Plus, once we captured Lisa and it became clear she had been the one sabotaging Isla, there was no reason for CPS or the adoption agency to not approve of Isla." He paused and turned his attention back to Isla. "Go ahead. Tell them."

He would not take her thunder way.

Looking happier than he'd seen her in the whole time they'd worked together when he'd brought her on as the team's technical analyst, Isla said, "I've been cleared by CPS. And the adoption agency called to inform me that the little toddler, Enzo, who I had hoped to foster and adopt before Lisa's sabotage, had been placed with another family but things didn't work out and they asked if I was still available to foster him with the intention of adopting him." She bounced on her heels. "Of course, I said yes! I should have him within the next few weeks."

This time the celebration wasn't contained to applause as several people jumped up to hug Isla.

Chase waited, letting the merriment die down naturally.

Once everyone had settled again, he said, "I have one more huge announcement to make before we can eat."

"My stomach is rumbling," Bennett called out.

People laughed.

Chase held up his hand. "You're going to want to hear this." He turned his attention to Cara. She nodded. He raised an eyebrow, silently asking if she wanted to make the announcement. She shook her head and with a flick of her hand gestured for him to proceed.

It gave him pleasure to say, "Because our team was so successful, the FBI has asked us to remain active."

A cheer went up.

"But what about those of us who live in other states?" Hannah yelled out. Trevor grinned next to her.

Once again, Chase held up his hand, waiting for silence. "Our headquarters will be based here in Elk Valley, but those of you who live elsewhere can remain where you are and be mobile."

Grateful smiles and nods met his announcement. And Chase took in each one of them. Ashley standing in the corner with Cade. Bennett still holding Naomi. Selena beaming at her fiancé, Finn. Kyle taking Ophelia's hand in his. Meadow and Ian exchanging jokes with Rocco. Trevor leaning over to kiss Hannah's cheek.

Chase turned his attention to Zoe and Sadie. "Ladies, I think it's time to roll out the Thanksgiving feast."

Zoe and Sadie disappeared through one of the tent flaps to the mobile truck waiting on the other side. Chase made his way to the table where he sat next to the empty seat Zoe would take. Liam and Martha joined him, putting Kylie in the high chair between Chase's and Zoe's seats.

The tent flaps parted and a team of volunteers from town proceeded to lay out the feast on an empty table in the center of the tent space.

Pastor Jerome stood to say a quick blessing, asking God's protection over the task force, all the people of Elk Valley and all the people of the country who the task force would one day help. "And God bless this food as we give thanks for Your blessings. Amen."

Chase met Zoe's gaze over Kylie's head, counting their love among their blessings.

* * * * *

Don't miss the stories in this mini series!

MOUNTAIN COUNTRY K-9 UNIT

Search And Detect
TERRI REED
Month 2024

Perilous Christmas Pursuit
LENORA WORTH
November 2024

Lethal Holiday Hideout
KATY LEE
November 2024

MILLS & BOON

Sniffing Out Justice
Carol J. Post

MILLS & BOON

Carol J. Post writes fun and fast-paced inspirational romantic suspense stories and lives in the beautiful mountains of North Carolina. She plays the piano and also enjoys sailing, hiking and camping—almost anything outdoors. Her daughters and grandkids live too far away for her liking, so she now pours all that nurturing into taking care of two highly spoiled black cats.

Books by Carol J. Post

Love Inspired Suspense

Midnight Shadows
Motive for Murder
Out for Justice
Shattered Haven
Hidden Identity
Mistletoe Justice
Buried Memories
Reunited by Danger
Fatal Recall
Lethal Legacy
Bodyguard for Christmas
Dangerous Relations
Trailing a Killer

Canine Defense

Searching for Evidence
Sniffing Out Justice

Visit the Author Profile page at LoveInspired.com for more titles.

Fear thou not; for I am with thee: be not dismayed;
for I am thy God: I will strengthen thee;
yea, I will help thee; yea, I will uphold thee
with the right hand of my righteousness.
—*Isaiah* 41:10

Thanks to my sister, Kimberly Coker, for helping me plot my books and being the navigator on all my research trips. You're the best sis ever!

Thank you to my editor, Katie Gowrie, and my critique partners, Karen Fleming and Sabrina Jarema, for making my stories the best they can be.

And thank you to my husband, Chris, for your unending love, encouragement and support. Thanks for all the things you do, too, like making sure I have clean clothes and something to eat when I'm on deadline and buying me chocolate. After forty-three years, I'd still do it all over again.

Chapter One

The sun shone from low in the eastern sky, casting long shadows over the group gathered at the edge of the parking lot. Beyond the Blackwater River State Park campground lay hundreds of acres of pine forests, swamps and scrubby ridges. Somewhere in that vastness of nature, a twenty-six-year-old woman had disappeared.

Kristina Ashbaugh-Richards swiped a hand across her forehead, slick with beads of sweat. At barely nine in the morning, it was already hot and humid. Of course, Florida was always hot and humid in early August, even in the Panhandle. Her T-shirt was damp where her pack rested against her back, and she was looking forward to shedding the hiking boots she'd put on an hour and a half earlier.

She took a swig from her water bottle. One end of a leash circled her wrist, the other end attached to her golden retriever's collar. Bella wasn't the only dog there. Almost forty Escambia County search and rescue volunteers had gathered, about half of them with a canine partner.

Three people stood in the center of the semicircle of volunteers, one holding a stack of papers. She'd introduced herself as Teresa. "The info on our lady is all here, including a picture."

She handed the stack to the gentleman next to her. "Eddie's going to give one to each of you. You're looking for Julia Morris—dark hair, shoulder length. She's slender, in good shape, enjoys the outdoors. A week ago yesterday, she left her home in Fort Walton Beach to do some wilderness camping in the Blackwater Forest, a nature photography trip. She was to report back to work Monday morning. When she didn't, her coworkers got concerned and called the authorities. She apparently never made it home from that camping trip."

Kris reached down to scratch the top of Bella's head. The dog was standing at attention in her black-and-orange vest, Search & Rescue printed across both sides. Her muscles were stiff with anticipation. This was their first search and rescue mission in more than a year and a half. Though it had been a while, Bella obviously hadn't forgotten. Nothing brought working dogs more satisfaction than participating and succeeding in what they were trained to do.

After assigning grids to the volunteers and giving them items of the missing camper's clothing, those in charge released them to begin. Bella strained at the leash, eager to start the search, and Kris's pulse picked up speed. She'd stayed away far too long.

After she'd taken a few steps, someone spoke a short distance behind her. "Glad I caught you. Sorry I'm late."

The male voice brushed her mind with a vague sense of familiarity. She cast a glance over her shoulder but couldn't see past the others in the party.

"Glad you made it. I'll team you up with Kristina Richards and her dog, Bella."

At Teresa's words, Kris gave a tug on the leash. "Hold on, Bella."

She waited for the others to disperse. When the newcomer turned to face her, her stomach did a free fall, then tightened into a solid knot.

His jaw went slack, but he recovered instantly. A slow, easy smile spread across his face. He'd always had an infectious smile. She wasn't susceptible anymore.

Kris squared her shoulders as Teresa led him in her direction.

"Tony, this is Kristina Richards and her dog, Bella. Tony Sanderson."

Tony nodded. "We've met. We were friends through high school, then lost touch."

Friends. Was that what he called it?

"Great. I'll let you get on your way."

Kris set out again, letting Tony fall in next to her. She wouldn't wait on him, although she likely wouldn't have to. He looked like he could keep up with her just fine, even on her morning runs. He'd filled out nicely since high school, but other than that and how the lines of his face had grown more mature, he hadn't changed a lot. His sandy blond hair was as thick as ever, and those deep brown eyes still seemed to hold a hint of humor.

"How have you been?" His question cut across her thoughts.

"Okay." She focused her gaze straight ahead. She wouldn't make small talk. "How much do you know about what we're doing today?"

"I know we're looking for a young woman who never returned from a wilderness camping trip. What else can you tell me?"

She removed the paper she'd folded and stuffed into her pocket. "Here's her information. She was reported missing after she didn't show up for work yesterday."

He read what she handed him and passed it back. "Where are we headed?"

"We take the catwalk, then head northeast into the woods. Since she was off-grid, no one knows where she set up camp. She left her phone in her car, probably figuring she wouldn't have service anyway."

Several minutes passed in silence before he spoke again. "So, you're Richards now. You're married?"

"No." He'd probably assume she was divorced and hadn't taken back her maiden name. She wouldn't bother to correct him. She wouldn't ask if he was married, either, because she really didn't care.

She'd work with him, though, and not let their past interfere with the job they had to do. A young woman was counting on them. Even if they were paired up on future searches, she'd deal with it professionally.

As they moved along the catwalk, they were silent except for the clomp of their shoes against the wooden planks. Bella trotted as far ahead as the leash would allow, tail wagging. Sounds of the swamp surrounded them—the calls of birds, the buzz of insects and the occasional croak of an alligator.

When the catwalk ended, Kris consulted her GPS and headed into the woods. A rustle sounded some distance to their right, likely one or two of the other volunteers. Her own search area was still some distance away.

Finally, she checked her GPS again and gave Tony a nod. "We're getting close."

She knelt next to Bella and held the T-shirt she'd been given in front of the golden retriever's face. After the dog gave it several sniffs, Kris straightened. "Bella, search."

The dog's demeanor shot from carefree to focused. She moved forward, nose sniffing the air, head swinging side to side as she tried to pick up the scent. Kris led her in a broad zigzag pattern, covering the area thoroughly. Watching her dog wrapped up in the joy of the search, she could almost pretend they were alone.

Until Tony broke the silence. "I love watching these canines do their thing. How long have you had Bella?"

At the mention of her dog, some of the prickliness subsided. "Five years."

"Have you been doing this all that time?"

"No. Bella finished her training three years ago."

"I just joined the group last year, after I moved from Fort Walton Beach to Pensacola."

Great. They were living in the same town again. "I figured you'd want to be closer to Sanderson Charters." She managed to suppress the disdainful nose crinkle that usually accompanied her saying the name. When their dads had parted ways, Tony's had opened a competing business an hour away and took a lot of Ashbaugh customers with him.

"I'm not working in the charter business. I went into police work instead. Dad was a little disappointed, but Nick's doing the business with him, so it all worked out."

She nodded. She'd known Nick, too. He'd been a year ahead of them in school. Apparently, Tony's big brother didn't have the same moral standards Tony did.

She dipped her gaze to the ground. All the while he was badmouthing Jerry Sanderson, her father had had no right to talk. He was now doing prison time for drug running while Kris and her twin, Kassie, were managing his charter business.

Morning slid into afternoon with no success, and Kris slipped the backpack straps from her shoulders. "I'm starved. How about we take a break?"

"You won't get any argument from me."

While she took a bowl from her pack and filled it with water, Tony sat on a downed tree trunk and removed a sandwich from his own pack. He was dressed in khaki shorts, making her wish she'd opted for something cooler than jeans. At his right hip, the bulge of a holster was barely apparent under his T-shirt. Although she felt comfortable in the woods, having an armed escort couldn't be a bad thing.

Kris refilled Bella's empty bowl with kibble and removed her own sandwich from its plastic bag. By then, Tony was halfway through his.

He patted the log. "Have a seat."

After sinking onto the rough bark, she bit into her sandwich. Peanut butter and honey had never tasted so good.

Tony took a long swig of water. "From what I've seen, the dogs get discouraged when they search all day and don't find anything."

"They do. Sometimes we'll hide something and have them find it, so they can feel like they did a good job."

He held out a hand, palm up. "Is it okay if I pet her?"

"Sure."

Bella approached, and he scratched her cheek. After downing the last bite of his sandwich, he gave her a two-handed rubdown. "I always enjoy seeing the K-9 officers with their dogs."

"What agency do you work for?"

"Pensacola P.D."

"Do you know Jared Miles?"

"We've met. He's in patrol, isn't he?"

"Yeah."

"I'm in criminal investigations. I take it you know him."

"He's my sister's fiancé."

"Kassie or Alyssa?"

"Kassie. Alyssa took off after she turned eighteen and hasn't been back since. We don't hear much from her." Unless she needed money.

Oh, yeah. She wasn't going to converse with him beyond what was necessary to complete their assigned task. Unfortunately, it was too easy to slip back into the camaraderie they'd shared as teenagers, before he'd humiliated her in front of the entire student body.

Kris finished her sandwich and returned the baggie and other items to her pack. They'd just started out again when the radio she carried crackled to life. One of the dogs had picked up a trail.

Tony looked at her. "We keep searching, right?"

"Yes. We should know something soon."

Soon ended up being less than twenty minutes later. The dog lost the trail at the Blackwater River. Moving a good distance in either direction produced nothing. Neither did crossing the river and searching the other side. Their camper either swam downriver or left in a boat.

They continued their search, moving deeper into the woods. The air hung heavy and damp with Florida's relentless summertime humidity. A breeze moved past them, then disappeared again.

Kris wrinkled her nose. "Ugh. Smell that?"

"There's a dead animal nearby."

Over the next several minutes, the odor grew stronger.

Tony waved a hand in front of his face. "That's bigger than a squirrel or armadillo."

Kris stepped around a tree and looked to her left. Her chest clenched. Her mouth worked, but nothing came out because her throat had closed up.

She grasped Tony's upper arm. He looked at her, then beyond her. His eyes widened, and his jaw went slack for the second time that day.

Whispered words escaped his mouth, barely audible— "Not again."

He moved closer to the body, and she did, too, because she couldn't seem to extricate her fingers from his biceps. A breeze rustled the trees around them, sweeping away some of the stench of death, and thunder rumbled far in the distance.

She swallowed the bile rising in her throat. Someone had taken a hammer—or something—to the side of their camper's head. Dried blood matted the dark brown hair, and pieces of bone and tissue protruded from the crater.

She squeezed her eyes shut and pressed a shaking hand to her mouth. Tony wrapped an arm around her and led her a few yards away. When he stopped, he still didn't release her. As soon as her legs no longer felt as if they'd buckle, she would step away.

She shook her head. "Why didn't Bella pick up the scent?"

"She's not a cadaver dog, is she?"

"You mean the woman was killed somewhere else and dumped here?"

"I don't know. That's not our camper, though."

"She fits the description."

"This body has been here for at least ten days. But we need to call this in."

She stepped to the side, and he let his arm fall. While he radioed what they'd found, she knelt on the ground, arms wrapped around Bella's body, face buried in the golden fur.

Soon, he approached. "They're calling the authorities. I'll need to bring them back here. I'll walk with you until we meet up with them."

As they approached the catwalk, voices reached them from up ahead. Soon, four Santa Rosa County personnel came into view. Kris bid Tony farewell with a boulder-size knot in her stomach. Whether from being forced to spend the day with him or capping it off with the grisly find in the forest, she wasn't sure. Probably both. As a detective, maybe Tony was used to dealing with dead bodies. She wasn't.

Thunder rumbled again, closer than before.

"Come on, Bella." She picked up her pace to a jog, determined to reach her car before the rain moved in.

She didn't make it. Five minutes later, the sky opened up. Shortly after that, she loaded a sopping wet dog and her own dripping self into her red CR-V. She pulled her phone from her pack and called her best friend, hoping to cancel dinner plans. "I'm finished. Have you started cooking yet?"

"The casserole's in the oven, waiting for you to arrive."

She'd been afraid of that. "I need to borrow some dry clothes."

"Sure thing. We're getting the same storm. Maybe it'll pass before you leave here."

Kris ended the call and heaved a sigh. Forty minutes to Fort Walton Beach and an hour home, when she longed to head straight to Pensacola, pick up Gavin from the babysitter and spend the evening locked in her house, loving on her little boy and her dog.

But she couldn't let down her best-ever friend. Shannon and her boyfriend had broken up last night, and tonight she needed company. During the darkest period of Kris's life, Shannon had been there for her. Kassie had tried, but Kris had always felt closer to her best friend than either of her sisters.

When she pulled into Shannon's driveway, the rain was still coming down in sheets. She grabbed her umbrella and, after letting Bella out, made a dash for Shannon's front porch. Once there, Bella shook the water from her fur, showering Kris.

"Really?"

Moments after she rang the bell, the door swung open, and music spilled from the house. The smile Shannon wore held a lot of sympathy. "Come in. Here are some dry clothes." She handed Kris a T-shirt and yoga pants.

"I'll put Bella in the garage. Otherwise, your place will smell like wet dog."

"Go get changed. I've got Bella." Her voice was raised to compete with what poured from the sound system. She loved her music. Any time a popular band performed within a hundred-mile radius of Fort Walton Beach, she was likely in the audience.

As Kris headed down the hall, Shannon's voice followed her. "Come on, sweetie."

The smile she'd worn upon greeting her was a good sign. So was the lack of red, puffy eyes. She was handling the breakup well. Of course, Shannon always handled breakups well. She'd had enough practice. She threw off boyfriends like Kris cast off hand-me-down clothes.

When Kris walked into the kitchen, Shannon was throwing away an empty dog food can.

"You fed her. Thanks." Her friend didn't have a dog, but Kris kept a stash of food there.

"I even toweled her off." She removed a casserole dish from

the oven and placed it on a potholder in the center of the table. "Cheesy ground beef, the cheater's version of lasagna. Have at it."

Kris spooned a good-size serving onto her plate. "It smells fantastic."

Shannon sat opposite her. "Did you find your camper lady?"

"No. About forty of us were looking, a bunch of dogs, too, but there was no sign of her."

"That doesn't sound good."

"It gets worse. Tony and I discovered a body."

Shannon's eyes rounded. "Like a dead person?"

"Yep."

"Not the camper."

"No. He said the body had been there longer than that."

Shannon took a swig of iced tea. "Who is this Tony person? Someone good-looking and eligible, I hope."

"Definitely good-looking." As much as she hated to acknowledge it.

"And eligible?"

"I don't know." He hadn't been wearing a ring. Not that she'd specifically looked for one. He'd held his sandwich in his left hand, and she hadn't been able to help but notice.

Shannon laid down her fork with a sigh. "What do you mean, you don't know? Girl, you need to ask these kinds of questions."

"Why, when I couldn't care less about the answers?"

Shannon shook her head in that *what-am-I-going-to-do-with-you?* way.

"I did get his full name."

"That's a start."

"Tony Sanderson."

Shannon's mouth fell open and snapped shut again. "Oh, *that* Tony."

"Yeah. Another reason to add to my usual one for why I don't care whether he's available or not."

Shannon shook her head. "I'm so sorry. I should never have

conned you into writing that note. I thought if he knew how you felt about him, he'd see y'all were meant to be more than just friends. I had no idea he'd use the note as a weapon."

She shrugged. "It's not like it permanently scarred me. You know, the whole sticks-and-stones thing." Except that whoever said words couldn't hurt apparently lived under a rock.

Kris scooped another bite of the noodle-beef-cheese mixture onto her fork. "Enough about Tony. How are *you* doing?"

"I'm all right. It was time." Shannon's gaze dipped to her plate, and she played with her food for several seconds, spearing and twirling it on her fork. Finally, she met Kris's gaze. "Carl was starting to scare me. He has anger issues."

Kris frowned. "Any chance he'll come back and try to hurt you?"

"I don't know." She squared her shoulders and lifted her chin. "But I say we banish both Tony and Carl from the rest of our conversation tonight. Let's plan another trip on the water."

"Already?" She and Shannon, along with Bella and Gavin, had spent the past weekend on Shannon's small cabin cruiser.

"It'll do us both good." Shannon spooned a bite into her mouth. "I wonder who the cute guy was that we passed on the water."

"We passed several cute guys on the water."

"The one we came up on early Sunday morning, with the cutoff jean shorts and no shirt."

Oh, yeah, him. They'd heard a splash ahead of them. As they'd approached, their engine on low, he'd been standing with his back to them, working over the side of the boat. Then he'd whirled, an anchor line or maybe cast net in his hand. "He didn't look thrilled to see us."

"We were scaring away his fish."

"Or maybe it was because you were shining your flashlight in his face."

"It wasn't in his face the whole time. Most of the time I had it aimed at his chest and abs. Very muscular ones, I might add."

Kris shook her head. Granted, the guy looked like he lived at the gym, but she wasn't nearly as swayed by good looks as her friend was.

"I should have asked if he was single, except I wasn't until last night." Shannon released a wistful sigh. "Maybe if I hang out at the public boat ramps, I'll run into him again."

"Shannon!"

"What?"

"You just got out of one relationship, and you're already trying to jump into another one."

"That's the best way to recover. If the horse throws you, get back in the saddle." Her tone grew serious. "It's like I've been telling you. No one will ever *replace* Mark, but isn't it time to get back out there? I mean, how long has it been since the accident, sixteen months?"

"Eighteen." Plus one week and two days.

"A year and a half. If Mark could talk to you right now, he'd say he doesn't want you pining away for him. He'd want you to be happy."

"I *am* happy." Relatively speaking.

She stood to take their plates and silverware to the dishwasher. Shannon followed with the casserole dish. By the time she'd put away the leftovers and cleaned the dish, Kris had finished wiping the counters.

She hung the dishcloth on the oven door handle. "Would you be disappointed if I ate and split?"

"Maybe a little, but I understand. After the day you've had, you're probably wiped."

She gave her a tired smile. "Wiped doesn't begin to describe it."

Kris walked from the kitchen. "I need to use your restroom before I leave." Then she'd get Bella and be on her way.

She stepped into the small room and hit the double switch, turning on the light and the exhaust fan. A minute later, the ring of the doorbell barely penetrated the rumble of the fan motor.

Her stomach tightened. *Carl.* Who else would it be at eight thirty at night, in weather like this? Hopefully the breakup hadn't ticked him off too badly.

"Don't answer it."

Shannon probably wouldn't hear her shouted words over the music, but she should have the sense to keep a locked door between herself and a possibly irate ex-boyfriend.

Kris stood and flushed the toilet. Washed and dried her hands. Opened the door. Shut off the light and exhaust fan.

The hair on her arms stood on end. Something wasn't right. If Shannon had opened the door, there would be arguing. If she'd kept it closed and locked, there'd be pounding and demands that she open it. But all was quiet except the music.

She tiptoed down the hall to the driving beat of Crossfade's "Cold" and stepped into the living room. Nothing was amiss. The wall to her left blocked the view of the kitchen. She moved forward, and the wall ended, opening the living room to the kitchen/dining area.

Blood *whooshed* through her ears, and her knees started to buckle.

A man stood between the table and the cabinetry, his back to her, a knife gripped in one latex-covered hand, his other stuffed into the pocket of his jeans. Shannon lay at his feet in an expanding pool of blood, hands clutching her stomach and chest, one leg slowly bending and straightening.

Kris pressed a hand to her mouth to stop the scream rising in her throat. But the gasp had already escaped. The intruder turned. It wasn't Carl. It was the boater she and Shannon had met early Sunday morning.

As he leaped toward her, his foot slid backward on the tile, slick with Shannon's blood, and he landed hard on that knee. Kris bolted across the living room. By the time she threw the deadbolt and opened the door, heavy footsteps pounded behind her.

She flew down the porch stairs. Cold rain poured down on her, drenching her for the second time.

She looked frantically around. There was no one to help her, no traffic in either direction. She ran for the side of the house. The intruder shot outside the same moment she rounded the corner. Had he seen her? If so, he'd be on her in moments. Her best option was to hide.

She climbed over the viburnum hedge that lined the side of Shannon's house and lay flat against the stucco wall. The hedge was thick, the branches of each shrub intertwining with the limbs of the next. If he wasn't looking, he'd never see her.

Heavy footsteps moved closer. As she peered between two of the shrubs, sneakers passed within feet of her face. She held her breath, heart pounding so hard it hurt. *Keep going.* Once he left the yard, she could make a run for a neighbor's house and have them call the police.

A rustle sounded nearby, then another and another, each closer than the last. Her heart almost stopped. He was searching the hedge for her.

She low-crawled away from him, keeping her side pressed against the house. When she reached the front corner, she sprang to her feet and sprinted toward the road. A vehicle approached from her left. Her heart leaped into her throat. If she ran into the street in front of him, maybe he'd stop and help her.

The killer's footsteps pounded closer. By the time she reached the edge of the road, she could hear his labored breaths. A hand brushed her back.

She ran into the street. The headlights shining through the downpour were closer than she'd expected. The driver hadn't seen her. He'd never get stopped in time.

She made a desperate lunge, steeling herself for the sickening thud of metal against flesh. And the searing pain that would follow.

If she survived at all.

* * *

Tony jammed on his brakes, sending the Tundra into a skid. A sickening thud reverberated through the cab. A body rolled across his hood, slammed into his windshield and fell to the pavement.

Two figures had appeared out of nowhere. In the dark and pouring rain, he hadn't seen them until they'd been right in front of him. The larger one was lying in the road next to him. He wasn't sure about the smaller one. If he'd missed her, it hadn't been by much. He unfastened his seat belt and turned on his flashers. Before he could open the door, the man beside him rose and took off at a limping run.

Tony stepped from the truck. The man was headed down the property line between two houses. The smaller figure was running down the street toward his parents' place. That was where he was supposed to be.

He charged after the larger one. Someone didn't run after being struck by a car without good reason. Maybe they'd both committed a crime. Or maybe the man had been chasing the smaller person, who'd been trying to escape.

By the time he reached the backyards, he'd already lost sight of the man. For the next ten minutes, he darted from yard to yard, periodically stopping to listen for signs of movement. Finally, he had to admit defeat. In daylight, the injured man would never have escaped him. In the dark and pouring rain, visibility was too limited.

He jogged back toward his Tundra. The rain was slackening. As he neared the street, music flowed into the rainy night from one of the homes. It had barely registered when he'd stepped from his truck.

He continued forward. The yellow glow of his emergency flashers pulsed through the rain. The two people had apparently run out of the house that lay beyond. The front door was open, and light shone from beyond that first room.

He knew the woman who lived there. A friend had dated

her briefly in high school. That had been before his family had moved from Pensacola to Fort Walton Beach at the end of his senior year. Her parents had done the same two years later, buying a house on the same street. Was she the smaller figure he'd almost hit? He couldn't say. Everything had happened too fast.

He approached his truck, which waited just outside the glow of a nearby streetlight. Two feet away, he skidded to a stop. A soft, shifting light came from inside the cab. Someone was in his truck, possibly with a cell phone. Maybe his. He'd left it sitting in the cup holder after letting his mom know he was on his way.

He approached slowly and drew his weapon. If the man had doubled back and was waiting for him inside the truck, he wouldn't be caught off-guard. He stepped closer. Definitely the glow of a cell phone. Someone sat on his passenger floorboard, head lowered, legs curled beneath them. The figure didn't belong to a man.

He holstered his weapon. She posed no threat. She held the phone in one hand and touched the screen with the other. She was shaking so badly, whatever she keyed in likely didn't resemble her brain's commands.

He hesitated. If she was the person he'd almost hit, and she'd been fleeing for her life, he didn't want to terrify her further.

He tapped on the window. She dropped the phone and scrambled onto the passenger seat, fumbling for the door handle. When he swung open the driver door, light flooded the interior of the cab. "It's okay. I'm a police officer. I can help you."

Her head swiveled toward him, and her eyes widened. His did, too.

Kris? She should have been back home in Pensacola. What was she doing hiding in his truck, a dripping, quivering mess?

He hurried around to the passenger side. When he opened the door, she looked up at him, her face streaked with tears, her short, dark hair plastered to her head. He reached into the truck to put a comforting hand on her shoulder. "Tell me what happened."

"Boater...knife...blood...everywhere." She was hyperventilating, gasping after every word. She ended the jumbled sentence with a sob.

He glanced behind him. "Where is Shannon?" She still lived there. The last he'd heard, her parents had let her assume the mortgage while they'd moved on. Taking cover inside would be safer than sitting outside with the man he'd hit on the loose.

"He stabbed her."

"Who stabbed her?"

"The boater." Another sob shook her shoulders.

"Did you call 911?"

"I tried."

That was what she'd been trying to do when he'd first seen her. He retrieved his phone from the passenger floorboard and made the call. When finished, he bent over to bring himself eye-to-eye with her. "They're sending police and ambulance. Is Shannon inside?"

Kris nodded.

"I'm going to check on her. Okay?" Maybe she was still alive. An ambulance would arrive within five or six minutes, but in situations like this, seconds counted.

She grasped his free hand. "Don't leave me."

"I won't, but you need to come up to the house with me."

"No, no, no." She shook her head so violently she sprayed him with rainwater.

"You don't have to come inside. Just wait on the porch."

She drew in a stabilizing breath. "Okay."

He helped her from the truck. She and Shannon Jacobs had been friends all through school, a friendship they'd obviously maintained. Though he didn't have the details, something horrific had happened here tonight.

She ascended the three steps and stopped at the open door, eyes averted so she couldn't see inside. "Please let Bella out."

"Where is she?"

"The garage."

"Give me a minute to check on Shannon."

"Okay. My purse is in there, too."

He nodded. That was why she didn't have her own cell phone or the means to drive away to safety.

When he stepped into the living room, his position offered him an angled view of the dining area. Two legs were visible around the living room wall, from the calves down. One foot was clad in a sandal, the other bare, its covering likely lost in the scuffle. The driving beat of a song he didn't know rammed into him, pounding in his chest. Ignoring it, he moved toward the kitchen.

Shannon lay faceup next to the kitchen table, blood pooling around her torso. One arm was bent, that hand resting on her abdomen. The other was extended at an angle from her body, palm up, fingers curled. Drying blood coated the underside of her hand and forearm.

His heart twisted. He dealt with violence on a regular basis. None of the cases were easy, but they were especially difficult when he knew the victims.

Careful to not disturb the scene, he squatted to press two fingers to her carotid artery. Nothing.

He rose and looked around the room. A purse hung over one of the chairs. If there'd been a struggle, nothing in the kitchen revealed it. The counters were spotless, bare except for a canister set and toaster oven. The only items occupying the table were a centerpiece, a napkin holder, and salt and pepper shakers.

He opened the door off the side of the kitchen. Bella wandered into the room and sniffed him.

"Hey, Bella. Let's go see your mommy." If the purse belonged to Kris, he'd let the crime scene people bring it out when they arrived.

As he walked back to the living room with the golden retriever in tow, sirens sounded in the distance. Kris was standing on the porch gripping the side railing.

Her gaze snapped up to meet his. "Shannon, is she..."

He nodded. "I'm so sorry."

The dog rushed to her, and she squatted to bury her face in the blond fur. Her shoulders shook with silent sobs. Tony wished he could be the one providing her comfort. At one time, he would have been. Then something had happened, something she was still holding against him, based on her coolness toward him this morning.

The first hour, the tension between them had been thick before she'd finally relaxed into her job. She'd had a crush on him throughout their junior and senior years, and the entire school had known about it before he had.

Their fathers had parted ways on unpleasant terms, too, at least on the Ashbaugh side. Not Jerry Sanderson. The man lived out his faith everywhere he went. It was an example Tony still tried to follow.

He cleared his throat, and she looked up at him, her face streaked with tears. His chest tightened. "Do you think Bella would be able to pick up the killer's scent?"

"Possibly." She swiped her hands across both cheeks. "It's worth a try."

The first police car arrived a minute later, followed by an ambulance. Two officers stepped from the cruiser, and Tony approached the driver. He knew him from his years with Fort Walton Beach. "Parker, good to see you again." He nodded at the partner.

After returning the greeting, Bradley Parker looked toward the house, where Kris waited on the porch. "When we were dispatched, they weren't sure what kind of call it was."

"When I called it in, I wasn't sure myself. Turns out it's a homicide. The lady that lives here sustained multiple stab wounds."

Parker looked at his partner. "We need the CSI people out

here." He brought his attention back to Tony. "And we'll put out an APB for the suspect."

"He left on foot." Tony glanced at Kris. "The lady on the porch was here when it happened or got here right afterward. The guy went after her, and she ran. She can probably give a good description." He moved toward the porch, and Parker followed.

"I can tell you what he looked like." Kris had obviously been listening. "He was five ten or five eleven, well-built, with blond hair. It was long for a guy, touched his shoulders."

Parker made notes in the pad he'd taken from his pocket. "Facial hair?"

"Goatee and mustache, closely cut."

"Tattoos?"

"None that I saw."

After Parker radioed in the description, Tony motioned toward Bella. "Her dog is trained in search and rescue. I'd like to see if they can track him, in case he's still in the area."

"That's good. I'll go with you." He turned to his partner. "Stay here. Meet with the detectives and crime scene folks if they arrive before we get back."

Tony pointed out the path he'd seen the suspect take. Bella moved forward sniffing the air, and Tony followed Kris and her dog.

Parker fell in next to him. "Isn't the rain going to affect her ability to pick up the trail?"

Kris cast him a glance over her shoulder. "Golden retrievers are air scent dogs, so bad weather doesn't limit their ability."

"That's good." Parker lowered his voice. "How are you involved?"

"She ran out in front of me." He also kept his volume low to avoid distracting the woman and dog working in front of them. "I missed her but hit the guy pursuing her."

"Where is he?"

"He took off, and I lost him. It was dark and pouring rain."

He shifted his attention to Bella. She was working off-leash, Kris following at a slow jog. The dog's demeanor was different from when they'd performed their search in the woods. Her movements held excitement, as if she'd picked up on what her human wanted and was sure the prize was just ahead.

Bella led them between two other adjoining yards before turning to trot along the edge of the road. Suddenly, she stopped and retraced several steps. After walking in a couple of circles, sniffing the air, she sat.

Kris sighed. "She lost the scent. The killer probably got into a vehicle here."

As they headed back toward Shannon's house, Parker introduced himself to Kris and engaged her in conversation that centered around Bella. He loved dogs and seemed fascinated with Bella's abilities. Or maybe he was trying to put Kris at ease. If so, he was succeeding.

When they got back to Shannon's, the CSI people hadn't arrived yet. Kris leaned against her car, and Parker approached. "Do you mind answering a few questions?"

"Not at all."

He pulled a notepad from his pocket. "What happened here tonight?"

"I had dinner with my friend Shannon. I went to use the bathroom before leaving, and when I came out, she was on the floor bleeding. A man was standing over her with a knife."

"Did you hear anything before you came out?"

"Between the bathroom's exhaust fan and the music playing, I barely heard the doorbell. The guy took off after me but slipped in Shannon's blood and fell. That gave me a chance to get out."

"Do you know who he was?"

"Shannon and I met him while we were boating this past weekend."

"Do you have a name?"

"Just a first. Joe. It was early Sunday morning, shortly before daylight. We were in Choctawhatchee Bay, had lines out behind us and were trolling. We heard a big splash, figured someone had dropped anchor. Shannon shined her flashlight in that direction, and a boat was there."

"Do you know what kind?"

"An older Sea-Pro, white with blue trim, twenty-one foot, a one-hundred-fifty-horse Yamaha on the back."

Parker lifted his brows. "Those are some impressive details."

"My dad owns—owned a charter business. I know boats."

"I don't suppose you noticed the registration numbers."

She gave him a half smile. "I'm good but not that good."

"That's where this Joe was?"

"Yeah. He was standing with his back to us, leaning over the side holding a rope or something. He turned around, still holding it in one hand, and lifted the other to shield his eyes from Shannon's flashlight."

"What happened then?"

"I jumped on him for sitting there without at least a stern light. We could have hit him. He said the bulb had burned out."

"Any other conversation?"

"After Shannon asked and he told us his name, she swung the flashlight around to introduce the two of us. Shannon's always been super friendly."

Parker frowned. "First names or last names, too?"

"First names."

"Anything else?"

"I think that's it. We motored away."

After several more questions, Parker took down Kris's contact information. "The detectives will want you to do a composite and will probably ask you to try to point out where you saw the boater. That splash you heard probably wasn't an anchor. They'll want your friend's phone, too. Do you know where it is?"

"On the kitchen counter. She was cooking when I called her with my ETA. I noticed it when I got there."

Tony shook his head. "It wasn't there when I went inside."

"It had to be. It's beside—" Her eyes widened. "He took it."

"What do you mean?" Parker asked.

"The killer. I told you he was standing over Shannon holding a knife. His other hand was in his pocket. I'm guessing he'd just swiped Shannon's phone."

Lead filled Tony's gut. "That's not good."

"Why?"

As soon as she'd asked the question, her jaw went slack. "He took Shannon's phone, hoping it would help him locate Shannon's friends."

Tony nodded, that lead weight expanding into a boulder.

"One friend in particular."

Chapter Two

Kris sat in a well-lit room at the Fort Walton Beach Police Department, the only sounds the soft strokes of a charcoal pencil against sketch paper.

The woman sitting across from her had introduced herself as Monica. She had a soothing voice, gentle smile and relaxed manner that put people at ease. Once assured that Kris was comfortable, she asked basic questions first—shape of the face, hair texture and length, absence or presence of facial hair and other broad characteristics.

Now, after rounding out the face slightly, making the eyes deeper set and squaring up the jaw, she was completing the finishing touches.

Finally, she laid the pencil down and turned the sketch pad around. "How is that?"

"Perfect." A shudder shook her shoulders. Maybe a little too perfect.

She could have come up with a decent composite just with what she'd seen in the glow of Shannon's flashlight. But the image of him standing over her friend's body, and the coldness in his eyes when they met hers, would remain with her the rest of her life. Last night, that image had haunted her dreams.

With time, it would fade. It would have to, or she'd die from sheer exhaustion.

Monica thanked her, and Kris rose. "Thank *you*. It's pretty amazing how you can take something from someone's mind and transfer it to paper."

Monica rose, too, and shook her hand. "You made it easy."

Kris walked from the building and made her way toward her car. It had been a long day, one that had started with a trip on the water. She'd led the detectives to the location, or what she believed was the location, the best she could. She was confident she'd gotten close. Her sense of direction was good, but she knew the waters around Pensacola much better than those around Fort Walton Beach.

She pressed the key fob, and the locks clicked. At least she had nowhere else to go but home, once she picked up Gavin from the babysitter. Tomorrow, she needed to get back to the charter office. This morning, she'd managed to return some phone calls from yesterday that had been forwarded to her cell phone and had gotten a couple of charters scheduled. But after spending Tuesday on the search and rescue mission and being tied up in Fort Walton Beach all day today, her work was probably piling up. They'd hired a part-time accounting person, and Kris and Kassie traded off with helping Buck, their captain, with charters, but Kris tried to make it into the office three or four half days each week.

She settled into the driver's seat and pulled her phone from her purse. She'd promised to text Kassie when she was on her way back to Pensacola.

Kris had called her after getting home last night, even though it had been late. The sleepiness in her sister's voice had fled instantly when Kris told her what had happened. She'd even offered to cancel the appointments she had at her salon today and accompany her to Fort Walton Beach. Kris had told her it wasn't necessary, but the offer had meant a lot.

There had been so much competition between them as children, which had continued as friction well into adulthood. In recent weeks, the friction had lessened, and the arguments had grown less frequent.

She wasn't holding her breath, though, thinking everything would be perfect from this point forward. She was too pragmatic. Unrealistic expectations only led to disappointment.

Before putting her phone away, she shot off a second text, this one to Tony. She'd rather not have any more contact with him. But last night, he'd insisted that she save his name and number and call him if she needed anything. He'd then amended those instructions to include keeping him posted on everything related to Shannon's death and any threats to herself. He'd made it clear that he expected a text before she left Fort Walton Beach. She'd reluctantly agreed.

He hadn't even wanted her to return to her home. She'd argued that she lived an hour away, and the killer had no idea where to find her, that it had taken him almost two days to find Shannon. He'd argued that her car had been sitting in Shannon's driveway the night she was killed. She'd responded that people couldn't look up owner information with a tag number, that it wasn't public information, and he'd insisted that didn't rule out the possibility. She'd reminded him that the killer had rung the bell, and Shannon had let him in, and she wouldn't do anything that careless.

The argument hadn't ended until she'd agreed to look at her options, which would take time. Until then, she'd be as safe locked inside her house with the alarm and her dog as she'd be anywhere else.

Maybe she was putting more confidence in Bella's abilities than she should. After all, she was trained in search and rescue rather than taking down bad guys, like her future brother-in-law's dog, Justice. But she was super protective of both her people and would likely tear up anyone who tried to harm them.

After pressing the send icon, she dropped her phone into her purse and pulled out from the parking lot. Soon she was on Beal Parkway headed toward US 98, which would take her all the way to Pensacola. Ahead of her, a car sat on one of the side streets, waiting to pull onto Beal.

She glanced in her rearview mirror. Right now, Fort Walton Beach was the most dangerous place she could be, and she wouldn't risk picking up a tail and leading someone to her home.

In the second she'd checked her mirror, the car she'd noticed earlier had started to shoot out in front of her. With a gasp, she jammed the brake. Her purse flew forward, making a somersault before landing on its side on the floorboard, contents strewn around it. She pressed the horn long and hard instead of calling the rude driver names.

After turning onto 98, she left Fort Walton Beach and drove through Mary Esther. On the long stretch that followed, traffic was moderate. Vehicles traveled in small clumps with large gaps between.

When she came upon a pickup pulling a landscape trailer, she moved into the left-hand lane. The burgundy SUV some distance behind her did, too. So did an older white pickup truck behind it.

As soon as she swung back into the right lane, the SUV sped past her, a middle-aged woman at the wheel. The pickup remained in the left lane, not traveling much faster than the landscaper. Maybe that was his normal traveling speed, considering the age of his truck. Or maybe he was staying at a distance so she couldn't identify him.

As the gap between them increased, some of the tension leached from her shoulders. She increased her speed some more. The truck didn't.

She released a sigh, the last of the tension fleeing. In less than thirty minutes, she'd be loading Gavin into his car seat and heading for home. At just after four, it wouldn't be time for dinner, but she'd start preparing it. They'd eat at five, watch a movie of Gavin's choice, likely involving a princess or super-hero, and then go to bed early.

When she looked at the rearview mirror again, her heart leaped into her throat. The truck had sped up and was rapidly bearing down on her.

She glanced around her, her mistake immediately obvious. No other vehicles traveled with her. She was in one of those gaps she'd thought about earlier, alone with her pursuer. Trees lined both sides of the road, a grass median in the center.

She floored the accelerator and watched the speedometer climb. Seventy...seventy-five...eighty. Still the truck advanced. The speed limit here was fifty-five. At twenty-five miles an hour over, she should attract the attention of a cop. If there were any cops around. There weren't.

The pickup truck roared up next to her, engine wide open. She glanced at the driver. Although he'd hidden his long hair under a bandana, she had no doubt. She was looking at the boater.

She slammed on her brakes the same moment he swerved to the right. His rear bumper almost clipped the front of her car. He slid off the right shoulder, taking out a section of guardrail, and bounced back on, brakes depressed.

She mashed the accelerator and whipped around him in the left lane, making frequent glances in her rearview mirror. For several seconds, he weaved, trying to regain control of his truck. Soon he was speeding toward her again.

She squeezed the wheel until her hands ached. Other vehicles traveled some distance ahead, a semitruck in their midst. She just had to reach them before the pickup caught up with her.

As he closed the gap between them, she moved over to strad-dle the broken line separating the two lanes. For the next min-ute or two, she held that position, moving right when he tried to squeeze around her on the shoulder and left when he tried to squeeze around her on that side, all the while hoping he didn't have a gun. She needed to call for help, but her phone was somewhere on the floorboard, along with the rest of the contents of her purse.

Ahead of her, two vehicles moved into the left lane to pass the tractor trailer. She backed off the accelerator slightly. If she timed it correctly, as soon as she reached the other vehicles, she could pull up next to the semi and match its speed until she figured out what to do.

As she got closer, a blue Pontiac approached the semitruck in the right lane. It was the only vehicle that hadn't yet passed. She backed off the accelerator some more, eyes on the Pontiac. *Stay where you are.* A few more seconds and she'd swing all the way into the left lane, ready to travel next to the trailer.

The car's left signal came on. "No!" She hit the brakes, and the pickup truck moved to the right. The driver started to change lanes, then jerked back fully into his own.

Kris breathed a sigh of relief and was traveling next to the trailer seconds later. The pickup was right behind her, about three car lengths back. There was nothing he could do to her now, with her somewhat protected by the truck. If he had a gun, he'd have already shot her.

The speed limit reduced as she passed into Wynnehaven Beach. If the traffic cooperated, she'd keep her position next to the semi. Retrieving her phone from the floorboard while stopped at a red light wasn't going to happen—there weren't any traffic signals along this stretch of highway.

Soon she left the small town behind. The speed limit increased to fifty-five, and trees again lined both sides of the road. Each mile was taking her closer to Pensacola, leading a killer straight to her home. She needed a plan.

Another small town lay just ahead—Navarre. As she drew closer, her pulse picked up speed. Her idea just might work.

She drew up even with the cab of the semi. In the distance, 87 veered off to the right, with a long, gentle exit lane. If she timed it right, she could whip off 98 and onto 87. By the time the driver of the truck knew what she'd done, he'd be well past the exit.

She eased past the semi, staying in the left lane. The pickup crept forward, too. Ahead, a double white sign showed 98 West continuing straight ahead, 87 North to the right.

She waited to make her move, gripping the wheel, jaw tight, back straight. The exit lane began, but she couldn't act yet. She had to wait until the road started to split.

Now! She floored the accelerator and turned the wheel to the right, crossing in front of the semi and onto 87, missing the truck's front bumper by less than twenty feet.

A horn sounded behind her, long and loud and angry. She cringed and waved. "Sorry." The driver would understand if he knew her situation.

There was no way the pickup could have followed, but she checked her rearview mirror anyway. Another vehicle was making its way off 98, a little silver car.

She continued around the long, gentle curve. The ordeal wasn't over yet. The Chevy pickup driver would take the next road and double back to look for her. She had to find somewhere to hide. Then she could retrieve her phone and call 911.

She needed to get away from 87. It was the first place the killer would look for her. But she had no idea where to go. As many times as she'd been through Navarre going to and from Shannon's, she'd never strayed off 98.

She slowed to take the next right, Harrington Drive. A block ahead, a sign announced Santa Rosa County Library. She turned into the parking lot and slid into a space next to a cargo van.

Once she'd shifted into Park and killed the engine, she ran around to the passenger's side to move her purse and retrieve her phone from the pens, receipts and other items littering her floor. Then she stood at the front of her car and made the call she'd been dying to make for the past thirty minutes. Her red CR-V wasn't visible from Harrington. But she wasn't taking any chances. She'd remain poised and ready to run into the library at the first sign of a white pickup truck.

There would be no relaxing evening at home tonight. She needed to come up with a plan. Even without the ability to get into DMV records, it would just be a matter of time until the killer found her. He'd probably start with Navarre and the surrounding communities and expand outward from there. Eventually his search would lead him to Pensacola.

Right to her and Bella and Gavin's doorstep.

Tony had been right. She needed to find another place to live.

And she needed to do it fast.

Tony stepped from the police station into the heat and humidity of an August afternoon. Judging from the few puffy white clouds in the sky, they weren't going to get a repeat of last night's storms.

He'd started the day attending a briefing. One of the discussion items had been Shannon's murder. Though it had happened in Okaloosa County and was in the jurisdiction of the Fort Walton Beach PD, the details of the case were being disseminated to all the surrounding agencies.

Last night's search had produced nothing—no prints, no evidence, no witnesses. Today, authorities had requested location information from Shannon's cell phone provider. Kris had also tried to point out the location where she and Shannon had come upon the boater and then helped the artist create a composite of the killer. If her memory for faces was as good as it was for boats, she'd make the ideal witness.

Tony climbed into the driver's seat of the black Chevy Tahoe, his department-assigned SUV. Since Kris had just texted him to say she was leaving Fort Walton Beach, he now had her number, too, had even saved it in his contacts.

He hoped she wouldn't mind him using it, because that was exactly what he intended to do. Granted, it wasn't his case, but he had a personal stake in it. He knew the victim, his parents lived a few doors down and now someone he cared about was in the killer's crosshairs.

He cranked the vehicle, and before he could back out, the ringtone on his phone sounded. He wouldn't have to call Kris. She'd beaten him to it.

He swiped to accept the call. "Hey, you."

"Hey."

It was just a single word, but it held a lot of tightness. Between their time together in the woods and their interaction last night, he'd thought they'd come to a truce.

Or maybe that was fear he heard. "Is everything all right?"

"Shannon's killer came after me."

"Where are you?" Wherever she was, he'd go to her. She could explain everything then.

"Navarre. I'm at the Santa Rosa County library. The police will be here any minute."

Good. She'd dialed 911 before calling him. "I'm on my way. Stay put until I get there."

Whatever had happened, he wouldn't let her drive home and walk into her house alone. Once they arrived, he'd thoroughly check everything. Then he'd make another attempt at trying to talk her into staying somewhere else.

He ended the call and headed in that direction. Navarre was only thirty-five minutes away. Slightly less if he hurried.

As soon as he turned off of Harrington, he scanned the library's parking lot. A Santa Rosa County sheriff cruiser sat in one of the parking spaces, but Kris's red CR-V wasn't there. Had she decided not to wait for him?

He continued his approach, drawing closer to a white cargo van that was almost too long for its space. Beyond it, a red bumper came into view. The van had enabled her to effectively hide from anyone who ventured past.

After pulling into a parking space, he got out and approached her car. She stood next to it, talking to a sheriff deputy. Another was inside the cruiser on his radio.

The first deputy nodded at him and turned his attention back to Kris. "Anything else you can tell me?"

"That's pretty much it. I figured this would be a good place to hide out while I called you guys."

Tony watched the deputy walk toward his vehicle. When he approached Kris, she gave him a weak smile. "I'm sorry to run you all the way out here, but I'm glad you came."

"What happened? I know you just relayed the whole thing to the deputy, but maybe you can give me the CliffsNotes version."

"When I was on one of those deserted, wooded stretches of 98, a pickup truck pulled up next to me and tried to run me off the road. It was the same guy who killed Shannon. I jammed on my brakes, and while he was trying to regain control of his truck, I sped past him then drove like a maniac until I was able to get next to a semi."

"How were you able to lose him?" In broad daylight, with good weather and rural surroundings, that had to have been quite a feat.

"Let's just say there's a pretty ticked-off truck driver on 98 right now. At least, there was as of about thirty minutes ago. I cut across in front of him to make an emergency exit onto 87. The killer couldn't get around the truck in time to follow me."

And then she'd hidden out at the library, concealed by a cargo van. She obviously thought quickly under pressure. Of course, she'd always been smart. If it hadn't been for their joint study sessions, he'd have probably failed high school chemistry.

"What kind of pickup was the guy driving?" The deputy would have asked that question, too. But he wanted to know for himself.

"A Chevy. I noticed the bow tie on the grill when he was behind me."

"Do you know what kind of Chevy?"

"A white one." She gave him a half smile. "I'm afraid I don't know trucks like I know boats. I do know it was older, though, maybe not an antique, but probably pretty close."

"During the brief time he was in front of you, you didn't happen to notice any part of the tag number, did you?"

"Uh-uh. I was too focused on trying to stay alive."

He put a hand on her shoulder and squeezed it. "You did good." He dropped his hand. "Are you going home now?"

"Yes, after I pick up Gavin from the babysitter."

So she had a kid. Likely an ex-husband, too. Though they were the same age, his life was a lot less complicated. He'd fallen in love a couple of times but had come out of the experience without any attachments. They'd both been fine Christian women. One of the relationships, he'd ended. The other, the woman had. Both times, the decision had been somewhat mutual. Those women were now happily married, and there were no hard feelings on either side.

She opened the Honda's door and slid into the driver's seat.

He stepped closer. "I know I said this last night, but you need to get somewhere safe. You've been in danger since the moment you and Shannon heard this guy dumping whatever it was that he dumped. He has no idea what you might have seen. He already killed Shannon, and now he's coming after you. Except he'll be more determined. Not only is he afraid you witnessed whatever went down on the water, you can also identify him as Shannon's killer."

"I know. I've been thinking about it."

"Do you have a friend you can stay with, or maybe Kassie?"

"Someone I'd feel comfortable piling in on with a kid and a fairly large dog? That friend is dead."

Her tone held hardness. Bitterness seemed to have replaced the brokenness he'd seen last night. He hoped over time she'd see her way past it.

She heaved a sigh. "I don't want to put anyone else in danger—my friends or my sister."

"What about the space above Ashbaugh Charters? Is it still vacant?" It wasn't an ideal solution, especially if the killer discovered her maiden name, but it might be a safer option than home, depending on how secure her house was.

"No one is staying there, if that's what you mean. I wouldn't classify it as vacant. It's been used as extra storage space for years, so it's filled with dusty old boxes. Some critters have probably taken up residence there, too."

"How about if we go by on our way to your house? We can check it out together."

"Sounds good. But don't say I didn't warn you."

"I'll be prepared for the worst."

He walked to his vehicle and followed her from the parking lot. Twenty minutes later, they pulled into two of the parallel parking spaces lining Government Street. Located at the edge of the Seville Quarter, the New Orleans–style building housed the charter office and another space, each with a second story. Back when their fathers had been partners, her family had owned the entire building.

He stepped from his vehicle and met her on the sidewalk in front of a fifteen-paned French door. Above it, gold script on a one-by-three-foot sign spelled out Ashbaugh Charters. The other half of the building was vacant, as evidenced by the for-rent sign in the front window.

Tony nodded in that direction. "If the space above the charter office is uninhabitable, what about up there?"

"Kassie and I have it listed for rent. We'd have to change our ad. 'Space comes with a squatter already installed upstairs.'"

He gave her a playful poke in the side. "You can't be a squatter on your own property."

"I guess not. But I think I'd be much safer with an alarm. That space has been empty so long, it's not protected by a security system. The charter office has one."

"Monitored?"

"Yep. It's even got a motion sensor, which we'll have to disable if I'm going to stay there."

She unlocked the front door and swung it open. The squeal

of the alarm began instantly. After punching in the code and locking them in, she walked to a wooden door in the back right corner of the lobby area.

"Follow me."

She swung open the door, revealing a narrow wooden staircase, and flipped the light switch next to it. "I haven't been up here in ages, so I have no idea what we'll find."

"We'll make the discovery together."

He followed her up the stairs. Dozens of dusty boxes filled the space, along with some old chairs, folding tables, a broken-down vacuum and what looked like boat parts. The most recent additions had been thrown in haphazardly, boxes not stacked, items left in the middle of the floor.

He surveyed the mess. "It's actually not as bad as I thought. Most of this stuff could be stacked against the wall."

"There's not even a bed up here."

"We can clean everything up and move one in."

She crossed her arms and leaned against a stack of boxes. "I keep hoping I'll wake up and realize this is all a bad dream, that Shannon will be calling any minute to make plans for our next get-together or tell me about her latest crush." Her gaze dipped to the floor. "I called her parents last night. I wanted them to hear it from me instead of the police. Her mom fell apart. She put Shannon's dad on. He handled it a little better than she did, but neither of them will ever get over this."

She looked up at him, her eyebrows drawn together. "You have to catch this guy."

"We're doing everything we can."

She looked around the room and heaved a sigh. "There's no way I can face this tonight, or even next week. Even with help."

"Don't worry about it now. We'll pick up your son. Then I'll follow you home. Once there, we'll figure out the safest place for you to be, and I'll make that happen."

She looked at him with raised brows. "When did you get so bossy?"

Without further argument, she bounded down the stairs in front of him. She was the same size she'd been in high school—slender, petite, obviously active. She'd been a runner then. If she still ran, recent events were going to curtail that activity for a while.

He reached the lobby and followed her to the door, where she pressed a button on the alarm panel to arm the system. A sense of protectiveness surged through him. Based on what he'd seen in his headlight beams last night, the man chasing her was at least a head taller than she was and probably double her weight. Left to face him alone, she wouldn't stand a chance.

He'd see to it that didn't happen. If he couldn't be with her himself, he'd make sure someone else was.

For the past ten years, he'd felt bad about how they'd parted at the end of high school. Throughout junior and senior high, he'd considered her one of his closest friends. Somehow, he'd hurt her without intending to. He'd always tried to follow the advice in Romans to live at peace with everyone, as much as he was able, but with their fathers parting ways, summer break rapidly approaching and his family moving to Fort Walton Beach, whatever had gone wrong between them had seemed to put a permanent wedge in their relationship. It was a loss he'd felt for a long time, one that was still there, ten years later.

Then yesterday, God had put her in his path, not once, but twice. Maybe this time he wouldn't blow it.

God, please give me a chance to make right what I messed up in the past.

Chapter Three

Kris pulled into her driveway, Tony's department-assigned vehicle behind her. He'd followed her to the babysitter's house, where he'd waited in his vehicle.

While she helped Gavin from his car seat, he approached. As much as she'd rather deal with everything after a good night's sleep in her own bed, something told her the discussion about her living arrangements was nowhere near over.

She removed the straps from Gavin's shoulders and took his hand. When he'd climbed from the car, she picked him up. Tony was standing several feet away, watching her.

"This is my son, Gavin."

"Hello, Gavin. How are you?" Although he greeted him, even offered him a small smile, he didn't step any closer. His back was rigid, his jaw tight.

Was he judging her—a single woman with a kid? The Sanderson family had always been über religious. Based on the things her father had told her, it had all been for show.

But Tony knew she was married, or had been. The day of the search for the missing camper, Teresa had introduced her as Kris Richards. He'd even asked about the name change. Apparently, he just didn't like kids.

She looked at her son. "This is Mr. Tony. He's a policeman like Uncle Jared. Can you say hi?"

Gavin raised his hand in a little wave, and Kris headed up the curved concrete walkway toward the front door. Blooming annuals lined the path on either side of her. Perennials formed a backdrop in varying shades of green, their spring blooms having shriveled and fallen off some time ago.

"You're still in the home where you grew up."

She looked at Tony over one shoulder. "Yeah, I moved back when…a year and a half ago. It was a good arrangement. Gavin and I didn't have to be alone, and Dad got good home-cooked meals. The only downside for him was that he couldn't drink around Gavin and me or even come home smelling of alcohol."

Her father's alcoholism wasn't any secret. Neither was her mother's desertion, taking off to the Bahamas with her boyfriend. Or the conflict between her and her sisters. Since their fathers were in business together and they'd developed a friendship of their own, Tony had had a front-row seat to the rotten Ashbaugh family dynamics.

The contrast between them and the picture-perfect Sandersons had been huge. The messed-up Ashbaughs had probably been a topic of conversation around the Sanderson dinner table more than once.

She stepped onto the front porch and unlocked the door. After disarming the alarm, she invited him inside.

"You and your son live here alone now?"

So he knew the situation with her father. Another thing for the Sandersons to gloat over. Of course, if Tony had access to the internet, TV or a newspaper, he would have known. The entire story had been quite public—her father's disappearance and the charges when he'd shown back up.

She and her father had shared a special bond, and all her life, she'd made excuses for him. A few months ago, she'd finally taken off the blinders.

"Yes, it's just us and Bella."

As soon as she said the name, the golden retriever padded into the entry to greet them. As Kris closed and locked the door behind them, Tony knelt to pet the dog. He was far better with animals than kids.

He straightened and frowned at her. "You're definitely not safe here."

"I have an alarm." But it no longer brought the comfort it had before.

"This place is huge. There are too many ways in."

He was right about the size. The Victorian-style home right on Bayou Texar *was* huge. It had been in her family since her great-grandparents had had it built at the turn of the last century.

"If someone kicked in the door and triggered the alarm, how long do you think it would take the police to get here?"

"I don't know." A lot longer than it would take an intruder to run upstairs and kick in her bedroom door. Dread trickled through her, and she tightened her hold on her son.

He followed her to the kitchen, where she laid her purse on the counter and lowered Gavin to the floor. He looked up at Tony and then back at her before trotting off to the family room.

His little-boy voice drifted back to them. "I'm gonna pway wif my twuck."

Tony crossed his arms. "If you stay at the charter office, you'll be right downtown. The police would be there in a minute or two. Someone would have to be pretty desperate to break in the front door six feet from a well-lit, well-traveled road."

"The back door opens into a parking lot. It's much more deserted back there."

"Not as deserted as behind the house."

He was right again. The family room, dining room and downstairs bedroom all had double French doors overlooking the backyard and offering a view of the bayou beyond. Someone could break out a pane of glass in any of them and reach through to unlock the door. Or they could just kick the door in. Unfortunately, neither location felt safe.

She pressed her lips together. "No serious discussions on an empty stomach. I'm going to get some supper ready. Would you like to stay?" Maybe he'd say no. She was too tired to try to make polite conversation. But after everything he'd done for her in the past twenty-four hours, the least she could do was feed him.

"That sounds great."

"We'll be having leftovers." One more opportunity for him to back out. When she'd fixed her and Gavin's dinner Monday night, she'd made extra, as she often did, planning to reheat it two nights later. If Tony wanted to stay, she could stretch it, especially if she added a salad and some bread.

"Hey, I'm a single guy. You'd be appalled at some of the things we eat and call dinner. Leftovers are fine. Do you need any help?"

"I've got dinner covered if you wouldn't mind taking Bella out." A neighbor had come over to walk her at lunchtime. "Her leash is hanging in the foyer by the front door."

Tony walked from the room, and she pulled two casserole dishes from the fridge, one holding chicken divan and the other cooked rice. After taking the chill off with the microwave, she put them into the oven on low and set to work making the salad.

She was almost done when Tony reappeared, Bella trotting after him. "Potty break complete. What else can I do?"

"You can make yourself at home."

Once she'd finished the salad, she sliced and buttered some Italian bread and sprinkled it with garlic. Soon a childish voice drifted to her from the front of the house.

"See my twuck?"

Uh-oh. Gavin was apparently trying to engage Tony in conversation. She'd better go rescue him—Tony, not her son.

When she walked into the living room, Tony was standing

in front of the fireplace, holding a picture frame to his chest and looking down at Gavin.

"That's a nice dump truck. Did Mommy get it for you?"

"No. Aunt Kassie."

Kris stepped into the doorway and leaned against the jamb. "She got it for his second birthday a few months ago."

He placed the frame back on the mantle. It held a picture of Mark, one of her favorites. He was wearing his blue dress uniform, standing between two poles, one holding an American flag, the other the Air Force flag. The picture was taken right after he'd received the Air Force Achievement Medal.

Tony nodded toward the photo. "I take it that's Mr. Richards?"

"Yes, Mark."

His gaze went to the flag sitting in the center of the mantle, folded inside its triangular wood-and-glass display case. "I'm sorry for your loss."

"Thank you."

Several moments of awkward silence passed before she pushed herself away from the door jamb. "I'm going to go toast the garlic bread, and then dinner will be ready."

"How about if I set the table?"

"Sure."

She headed back to the kitchen with Tony and Gavin in tow.

Once the garlic bread was toasted, Tony helped her place everything on the table. "For leftovers, this looks great. It smells wonderful, too."

"Thanks. This is one of my favorite meals. Super easy to make, too."

When they'd all sat, Gavin folded his hands and looked at Tony. Mealtimes with Kassie and Jared always began with prayer. In Gavin's mind, company at the dinner table meant someone would be saying grace.

Instead of dishing up the food, Tony looked at her, waiting.

She dipped her chin. "Go ahead."

He offered a simple prayer for protection and ended with thanks for the food. Gavin echoed his "amen" with a hearty one of his own. Tony was probably impressed.

She should set the same example for Gavin that had been set for her. By her mother, anyway. Until she decided to take off.

She picked up her fork and stabbed a piece of cubed chicken. "I don't suppose you heard anything today about the missing camper."

"Not a thing."

"Or the woman we found in the woods?"

"Not yet. It'll take time to identify her."

"When we discovered her, you said 'not again.'" She'd found the comment odd but had been too addled at the time to question it. "What did you mean?"

His gaze shifted to the side, and several seconds passed in silence. Finally, he spoke. "Three months ago, I worked a case where a woman disappeared from Milligan. Her car was abandoned at the edge of a wooded area along Route 90. She was found near Pensacola two days later." He cast a glance at Gavin before continuing. "Same shape as the woman we found."

Head smashed in with a blunt object, maybe a hammer. At two years old, Gavin likely wasn't tuning in to any of their conversation, but it was sweet of Tony to consider it. "The case you worked, the lady was dark-haired and slender, like our Julia Morris?"

He nodded, his expression grim. "That victim and now the woman we discovered. If we find that Julia Morris met the same end..."

She finished the thought for him. "You have a serial killer on your hands."

His gaze locked with hers. "Don't talk to anybody until the police are ready to make it public."

"I won't."

He opened his mouth as if to say something else, then

stopped. But she didn't need him to voice the thought aloud. She could see it in his eyes.

"Dark hair, slender, physically fit. I match the profile. But so do countless other women." Maybe she was at risk, but the possibility was slim. The threat from the boater was much more real.

Throughout the rest of the meal, Tony stayed true to his promise to not force her to discuss her living arrangements. Once they'd each taken their last bite, though, that restraint ended.

"Are we in agreement that the charter office would be safer for you guys than here?"

"Probably."

"Do you have a better suggestion?"

"Mark's parents would be ideal. His father is a retired military man with a decent collection of guns. And he knows how to use them."

"Great. How about calling them now?"

"Not so fast. There are two problems. First, they live in Ohio, so I'd be leaving Kassie to handle the charter business alone, on top of her responsibilities with her salon. I'm afraid it would be too much for her."

"It would be temporary." Tony frowned. "If this guy has his way, you won't be around to help her with the business...ever. And someone else will be raising your son."

She suppressed a shudder. If Tony hadn't been headed to his parents' house at the moment she'd run into the street last night, and if there'd been no semitruck to aid in her escape from 98, she wouldn't be standing in her kitchen right now arguing about living arrangements.

"What's the other problem with staying with your in-laws?"

"They just left for a Mediterranean cruise and won't be back for two weeks."

He gave her a sharp nod. "So, if you do decide to stay with them, what are your intentions for the next two weeks?"

She pulled her lower lip between her teeth. The thought of staying in the huge old house alone terrified her. She'd thought she could do it. That had been before the second attempt on her life. "I'll move into the space over the charter office."

He expelled a breath, both his shoulders and his facial features relaxing. "Tonight?"

"Tomorrow. I'm too tired to even think of tackling it tonight."

"All right. I'll help you with the move. Meanwhile, I'm sleeping downstairs, either on one of your couches or in your guest room. I'll look around and decide which."

She cocked one eyebrow at him. "You really *have* gotten bossy."

Whatever argument she would have come up with a few hours ago didn't make it to her lips. In fact, it didn't even form in her thoughts.

She didn't want Tony with her. He taken that stupid note she'd written and mocked her with it. It had happened more than a decade ago, but she still wasn't ready to let it go.

Right now, though, none of that mattered. Because tonight, Tony was exactly what she needed—someone who would offer the comfort of his presence with no pressure for anything more.

Maybe eventually she would be able to once again think of him as a friend. But that would be all. Her heart still belonged to Mark. If she ever reached a point where she was ready to move on, it would have to be with a man who liked kids. That requirement was non-negotiable, because she and Gavin were a package deal.

Tony pulled out from the parking lot of Captain Joey Patti's Seafood Restaurant, a plastic bag in the seat beside him. It held two grilled mahi fish tacos and was currently filling the confines of his truck with mouthwatering aromas.

Once he got to his apartment, he'd call Kris and see what her schedule looked like. He hadn't talked to her since he'd dropped her off at the charter office that morning. She'd warned him then that she had a full day, with two back-to-back charters, as well as some paperwork to handle at the office.

Even though it was now five o'clock in the afternoon, her work wasn't over. His wasn't either. They both had a long evening ahead of them.

He was actually looking forward to it. Spending time with Kris was every bit as enjoyable now as it had been when they were in high school, maybe even more so. He could just about see something serious developing between them. She was smart, witty and ambitious. And she was beautiful. Falling for her would be so easy.

But he wouldn't do it. She had a kid, and he'd made a vow fourteen months ago. Never again would he be responsible for someone else's child.

He backtracked a short distance down Garden Street to make his right turn onto Coyle. Palmilla Apartments was ahead and to the left. The recently built complex was large and upscale. His own apartment was tiny—just an efficiency—but it was nice. And it was plenty for a petless, childless single guy.

Once inside, he laid his bag on the small kitchen table, sank into a chair and dialed Kris's number. While waiting for the call to connect, he offered a brief prayer of thanks for the food. Her "hello" came right on the tail of his silent "amen."

He put her on speaker and pulled the Styrofoam container from the bag. "How is everything going?"

"Good. My charters went well. Kassie came in the last part of the day, and we tackled some of the mess upstairs."

"Wow, you guys are ambitious." She sounded a lot more energetic than last night.

"Don't get your hopes up too much. We hardly made a dent in it."

"No problem. We'll get as far as we can. I've got the day

off tomorrow, so whatever we don't get done tonight, we can finish in the morning."

"That'll work for me, too. I don't have anything till the afternoon."

He picked up the first taco. "Are you still at the charter office?"

"No, I rode home with Kassie. We're having dinner in a few minutes. What about you?"

"I got takeout from Captain Joey Patti's."

"Mmm, the best. Not to say that my sister isn't feeding me well."

"When you're done, how about if I take you to get whatever you guys will need over the next few days? Then we can go by the charter office."

They'd agreed last night that she shouldn't drive her car until this was over or she was able to leave town altogether. The killer knew what she drove, was confident enough in that fact to chase her down 98. No, that candy-apple-red CR-V needed to stay in her garage.

His phone vibrated, and an incoming call flashed across the top of the screen.

"I gotta go. My captain's calling."

He touched the screen with one pinkie to accept the call. "Hey, Keith. What's up?"

"I know you're done for today and are supposed to be off tomorrow, but we've had a new development."

"What kind of development?"

"Pictures. Quite a few of them."

"Of?"

"Slender women with dark hair."

Tony laid down his taco and sat up straighter.

His captain continued. "When you guessed we might have a serial killer on our hands, it looks like you might have hit the nail on the head."

"I want to see them. I'll be there in about ten minutes."

He ended the call and inhaled his last taco, leaving the pita chips and salsa for tomorrow. On the way down to his vehicle, he called Kris back. "I'll be a little later. I've got to go back to the station. I'll call you when I'm done."

Six minutes after leaving his apartment complex, he was there. Palmilla's location was another one of the reasons he'd chosen it.

He hurried into the station and met Keith in his office. "So, what's the story?"

"Santa Rosa County got a call. A maid in a cheap hotel in Holley. She was cleaning the room of one of the guests. He'd only been there for three days, but she claimed that, the way he looked at her, he gave her the willies right from the get-go."

"That's where the pictures came from?"

"Yep. He had them in a dresser drawer and didn't have it closed tight. She got curious, pulled it open farther and recognized several pictures of Julia Morris lying on top."

"The missing camper."

"Yep. She'd seen the news story that aired last night, with the plea that anyone with any information come forward. She called 911 from her cell phone and hurried out of the room as the guy was pulling up. He took one look at her and shot out of there as if the whole county was in hot pursuit."

"Did the hotel clerk have any information? Name, address, vehicle description, tag number?"

"They got it all. It just wasn't any good. He gave a false ID, and the tag was stolen. The only thing they had was that he was driving a white Chevy pickup, older model."

Tony stiffened. Just the kind of truck Shannon's killer was in when he went after Kris. But that didn't mean much. White was the most popular color for pickup trucks. His Tundra was even white.

Keith continued. "The guy wrote '95 on the paperwork, but that detail may not be any more accurate than the others. Based on the description your lady friend gave yesterday, it was pretty close. If it's the same truck."

His captain handed him a stack of photos—the copies that Santa Rosa County had distributed to the other agencies. "We're going to keep an eye out and see if he returns to claim his possessions, but it's not likely. He didn't leave anything of value. Nothing that offered a clue to his identity, either."

Tony looked at what he held. The top photo resembled what they'd been given the day of the search. Definitely the missing camper. She was walking, almost in profile, a camera hanging from a strap around her neck, trees in the background. Leaves encroached on the edges of the photo and in the foreground, as if the one doing the photographing had taken advantage of the foliage to conceal himself.

He slid the photo to the back of the stack. The next several featured Morris also, all taken around the same time. The odds of finding her alive had gone down each day she'd been missing. With the find of the photos, they'd dropped to near zero. How long did the creep stalk his prey before moving in for the kill? Where had he disposed of her body?

A few photos later, the subject changed—the same dark hair, the same slight build, but different features. Tony's jaw tightened. "Amanda Driscoll."

This was probably the reason Keith had called him. Driscoll was the Milligan woman who'd been killed and had her body dumped near the outskirts of Pensacola. Like with Morris, there were a half dozen photos, obviously candid shots.

Tony didn't recognize the next subject. "Who is this?"

"Dawn Baucom."

"The name doesn't ring a bell."

"That's the woman you and your friend found in the woods on Monday. They just ID'd the body this afternoon."

Tony nodded. Three young women—two dead, one missing. Appearance a common thread between them. Now definitively connected.

He slid the next three photos under the stack, like he had the others.

A smiling face stared up at him, glowing with a natural beauty. Skin tanned to a healthy glow. Hair cut in a pixie, the short strands lying in soft layers. Dark eyes tugged at him, even from a photograph.

His chest tightened around a cold knot of dread. One more young woman connected to the others. One more target of a serial killer.

"That's the only woman we haven't yet identified." Keith's words sliced through his scattered thoughts. "You know her?"

He nodded. They hadn't identified her yet because she hadn't been reported missing or found dead.

But she'd been targeted. She'd landed in the killer's sights, and it would just be a matter of time.

Yes, he knew her.

He forced the response through a constricted throat.

"Her name is Kristina Ashbaugh-Richards."

Chapter Four

Kris pushed herself away from Kassie's dining room table.

"Dinner was delicious. Thanks for the invite."

Kassie always claimed that Kris was the gourmet cook of the family, but Kassie didn't do so badly herself.

Kris wiped remnants of baked chicken and scalloped potatoes from her little boy's face and hands. He didn't eat the green peas with nearly as much gusto as he had the rest of his dinner.

She pulled him from his high chair. "Go play while Mommy helps Aunt Kassie clean up the kitchen."

He ran from the room and disappeared down the hall, Bella following. A half minute later, the clatter of plastic and metal told her he'd dumped the toy bin in the spare bedroom.

Kris winced. "I should have told him to take out one toy at a time. Tony will be here any minute."

"Let him play. I'll pick up the toys after you guys leave."

Kris stacked their plates and laid the silverware across the top before heading to the sink. "When Tony showed up to help with the search efforts, I wasn't thrilled, even less so to be stuck working with him as my partner. But I have to admit, as much as I hated seeing him, I'm really lucky to have him hanging around right now."

Kassie frowned. "Luck has nothing to do with it."

Kris rolled her eyes. "I know, it's all about God."

She tried to tamp down the annoyance surging through her but wasn't quite successful. She'd liked her sister better before she'd gotten back into church and started thinking that God was the answer to everything.

Kassie rinsed the last of the plates Kris had brought over and put it in the dishwasher. "God is guiding your life, even if you don't see it now."

Kris swiped the sponge back and forth across the counter with more force than necessary. "He's guiding my life the same way He guided the pickup truck driver to cross the center line and hit Mark head on? The same way He guided Mom to take off and leave us behind? Thanks, but no thanks. I'll do without His guidance."

Kassie didn't respond. When Kris looked over at her, her eyes held sadness.

The annoyance instantly morphed to guilt. She shouldn't have snapped. Her sister's mini sermons were only because she cared.

Kris heaved a sigh. "I'm sorry. Things are tough right now, but I don't mean to take it out on you."

"It's all right." Kassie gave her a small smile. "You've been through a lot, and the recent events aren't helping any." Her smile faded. "Are you okay with seeing so much of Tony?"

She shrugged. "Not really. It's silly since it was so far in the past, but it still hurts. I plan to, at some point, let him know how much of a jerk he was."

Kassie smiled more fully. "That will probably do you both good."

Kassie closed the dishwasher door and pressed the start button. She'd heard about Tony's cruel prank at the time. It wasn't because Kris had told her. They hadn't had the type of relationship where they'd shared secret crushes, or much of anything else, for that matter.

No, Kassie had known because everyone else had. Tony had shared the note Shannon had conned her into writing with all of his friends, who'd shared it with their friends. At least she'd only had to endure the taunts and jeers for a couple of weeks. School had been almost over, and Tony's family had moved to Fort Walton Beach right after that.

Kassie hung the dishcloth over the handle of the oven door. "You're leaving your car parked in the garage till this is over, right?"

"Yeah." It would be a pain having to rely on Kassie and Tony for transportation, but since the killer knew what she drove, tooling around town in it would be reckless, if not downright stupid. Going anywhere alone wasn't too smart, either.

The ring of the doorbell cut across her thoughts, and she walked from the kitchen. "That's Tony."

"Check the peephole before you open the door." The admonition followed her into the living room.

It wasn't necessary. She was naturally cautious. Even more so now.

When she swung open the door, Tony stood on Kassie's porch in jeans and a burnt-orange polo shirt, his sandy blond hair mussed by the moderate breeze. The same attraction she'd felt in high school surged through her, and she tamped it down.

She gave him a relaxed smile. "I hope you're not going to regret this." If he expected to have the space over the charter office livable in time to sleep there tonight, it was going to be a long evening.

She didn't get a return smile. His mouth was set in a straight line and creases of worry marked his face. She dipped her gaze to a small stack of papers clutched in his right hand.

Kassie appeared beside her holding Gavin's hand. "Hi, Tony. Long time no see."

Instead of returning her greeting, he gave her a quick nod. "You ladies need to see something. May I come in?"

Kris's pulse kicked into high gear. Whatever he held, it wasn't good.

Kassie motioned toward the couch. "Have a seat."

Kris sat on one side of him, her sister on the other. "Come here, sweetie." Kris patted her lap, and Gavin climbed into it.

When she looked down at what Tony held, her own face stared back at her. The image looked as if it had been blown up, making it somewhat grainy. What little background was visible was too blurred for her to identify where she'd been at the time the picture was taken.

"Where did you get that?"

"It was turned over to the police."

"By who?"

"A maid in a hotel in Holley."

She shook her head, more confused with every answer. "How did she get it?"

"She was cleaning a room, found a drawer full of photos. She recognized the missing camper from the news story and called the police. There were pictures of two other women, the homicide case I told you about and the woman we found in the woods."

"But why—" She swallowed the rest of the question. Her picture was there because she fit the profile. A wave of dread washed through her, chilling her all the way to her core.

She didn't have just the boater to fear. She'd somehow come to the attention of a serial killer. He knew where she was and had gotten close enough to take her picture.

Tony's grip tightened around what he held. "I'm ready to get you moved to the space over the charter office, and I fully intend to stay there with you. But I'd rather see you safely away from here."

"I don't know where to go other than Mark's parents' place." She squeezed Gavin against her chest. Anything that put her in danger threatened her little boy, too.

Tony looked at Gavin. "You might want to think about having him stay with someone else."

"As long as I've got your protection, I think he'll be safest with me." Dropping him off somewhere else was a poor option. He hadn't slept in his own room since Mark was killed. In fact, he wouldn't go to sleep without her lying down next to him. Leaving him in someone else's care would add trauma on top of trauma.

She again lowered her eyes to what he held. "You have other pictures?" His stack looked like it contained at least three or four.

"There are three more." He slid the top one to the back.

In the next photo, she stood at a grill smiling over one shoulder, a long-handled spatula in her right hand.

"Wait. I recognize that picture. I was at Shannon's. This was a couple of months ago. We were grilling out after spending the day on her boat."

"You ladies were apparently being watched."

"No, Shannon took the picture. I was so windblown, I didn't want her to. I threatened to beat her with the spatula. Then to add insult to injury, she posted it on Facebook." She shook her head. "I never knew what she was going to do."

Pain stabbed through her. Shannon was one of a kind. That unpredictability made her fun. She was a cheerleader, a shoulder to cry on, a confidant—the best kind of friend.

Tony showed her the other two pictures, both ones she recognized as having been taken by Shannon.

She looked up at him. "I don't know about the first photo, but he got the others from Shannon's Facebook page. Her profile isn't public. The man who attacked her took her phone, so he had access to those pictures." It wouldn't have been difficult. Shannon had never set up a password to lock her phone.

Her heart was pounding in earnest now. "You know what this means? The boater is your serial killer."

"I think you're right. Everything you witnessed just might help solve this case."

She nodded. If her eyewitness account led to his capture, how many lives would be saved? Some serial killers' sprees went on for years. But would his capture be worth Shannon's death? Her parents wouldn't think so.

She shifted on the couch to face Tony more fully. "The killer didn't take those pictures. He hasn't found me." The cold dread that had seized her earlier released some of its grip.

Tony's jaw tightened. "He will. It's just a matter of time. He followed you as far as Navarre. I'm sure he's searching for you. How long do you think it'll be before he reaches Pensacola?"

Kris swallowed hard. Tony was right. The fact that the killer didn't know where she lived didn't mean she was safe.

Tony continued. "Now he has three reasons to kill you. He believes you saw him dump whatever he threw off of his boat. Chances are good it was a body. You're also a direct witness to Shannon's murder. If those aren't good enough reasons to come after you, he realizes you fit the profile of the girls he takes. He has targeted you to be one of his victims." He held up the stack of photos. "This is proof."

She pressed her lips together, the delicious meal Kassie had fed her congealing into a lump.

Kassie shifted at the other end of the couch. "You need to get somewhere safe, and the charter office isn't it."

"Anywhere I go, I'll be putting someone else in danger. Except for Mark's parents." The odds of the killer following her to Ohio were slim. The odds of him being able to get past her father-in-law and his arsenal of weapons were even slimmer.

She drew in a deep breath. "I'll message them on Facebook. They're already posting pictures galore, so they should see it soon. In the meantime, we need to move ahead with our original plan." She looked at Tony. "If you're still okay with sleeping on the couch in the office, I'll feel safe upstairs."

She'd stay holed up inside with Gavin and her dog. Kassie

could pick up groceries or anything else she needed and also walk Bella. So could Tony.

Tony. She hadn't wanted to see him again. Now they were not only having daily contact, he was going to be sleeping right downstairs. Instead of consternation, the thought brought relief.

Regardless of everything that had happened in the past, his presence in her life now was a godsend. She would soon be at the charter office with Tony securing her safety. It was exactly where she needed to be, at least until Mark's parents returned and she could hightail it for Ohio.

Two weeks. With Tony's help, she could hang on that long. She would stay busy with the charter office duties and her son and her dog.

And she would try to not make herself crazy by focusing on the danger she was in.

Kris moved about the small kitchen in the back of the charter office. Gavin sat in his high chair a few feet away, playing with a couple of matchbox cars. Bella had already eaten and lay against the wall, almost out of her way, but not quite.

One small and one medium-size pan sat atop the two-burner stove, steam seeping out around their lids. The kitchen wasn't large enough or well-equipped enough for any gourmet cooking, but the pasta and spaghetti sauce that were almost ready would be more than sufficient.

Two nights ago, she and Tony had gotten Gavin's crib and a full-size bed from one of her spare bedrooms moved and assembled upstairs. They'd also packed up enough personal belongings to last the next two weeks.

Last night, they'd done some more cleaning upstairs and compacted everything even more so Gavin and Bella would have room to play. Between the kitchen and bathroom downstairs and the makeshift bedroom upstairs, she couldn't say it was comfortable, but it was livable. She'd made it through two days. Twelve to go. Eventually, she'd be counting off the hours.

Not only was she scared half out of her mind, staying cooped up inside was about to push her over the edge. From the time she was little, she'd always been an outdoor girl. Running with Gavin hooked into his stroller, going out on Shannon's or one of her dad's boats, working in her yard—it was where she recharged and found her peace.

The metallic click of the lock up front, followed by the alarm tone and four beeps told her Tony had arrived. Kassie had left fifteen minutes ago, knowing Tony was on his way.

Kris walked from the kitchen in time to see Tony step into the hall. He was carrying a TV, the handles of a plastic bag looped over one arm.

"You brought a TV?"

"And a DVD player, along with a collection of some of the older Disney movies."

Warmth swelled in her chest. He'd obviously made his movie choices with Gavin in mind.

Over the past two days, she'd come to the conclusion that he didn't dislike kids, he was just uncomfortable around them. Apparently, he didn't have friends or family members with little ones. Maybe he needed more exposure to find out they didn't break or bite.

Not that it would make a difference for her. In less than two weeks, she'd be on her way to Ohio and wouldn't return until the killer was behind bars. Between the composite the police had and her description of the truck, the case shouldn't drag on for long. Once they caught the killer and she returned, except for the occasional search and rescue operation, there would be no reason for her and Tony to continue to have contact.

The thought didn't bring the relief she would have expected it to. The more time they spent together, the more they were falling back into the camaraderie they used to share, and she was once again looking at him as a friend, one she still found attractive. But she was long past high school crushes.

Tony drew in a deep breath. "Dinner smells good."

"Spaghetti. The pasta has another two minutes."

Instead of continuing to the kitchen, he stepped into the office on the left, formerly her dad's, now shared by Kassie and her. "I had another reason for bringing the TV. Or if you don't have cable here, we'll use one of the computers. At the station today, they were talking about the storm headed this way."

"Storm?" She hadn't heard. Of course, she hadn't watched the news in the past two or three days, either.

He set the TV on one corner of the desk, opposite the computer monitor. "Yep, a tropical storm. It's probably been upgraded to a hurricane in the past couple of hours."

"Are we in the cone?"

"Not at the moment, but you know how these things can shift."

She nodded. Having lived in Florida all her life, she was no stranger to hurricanes. The devastation Michael caused when it hit their area in 2018 was still fresh in her mind.

Tony pulled a stack of movies and the DVD player from the bag and placed them beside the TV. "What do you say we eat, watch a Disney princess fall in love, then see what we can find on the storm. If we can't find anything, we'll check the NOAA website."

"Sounds good."

She led him into the kitchen where Gavin was pushing his cars back and forth across the tray, making motor and crashing noises.

Tony gave him a couple of stiff pats on the shoulder. "Hi, Gavin." At least he was trying.

After draining the pasta, she dished up one large plate and one small one, then handed the tongs and serving spoon to Tony. A new sense of dread was now piled on top of the one that had been a constant companion for the past several days.

The storm was a good five or six days out. Maybe it would track even farther away and miss them entirely. Not that she wished it on someone else. She just had enough to worry about without dealing with hurricane prep, likely damage to her home and power outages that could go on for weeks.

After cutting up Gavin's spaghetti, she took the little metal cars and put his spoon and plate in front of him. When she'd sunk into her own chair, Tony sat opposite her, took Gavin's hand and reached across the table to take hers. She completed the circle by holding her son's hand.

She'd never shared a meal with any of the Sandersons without someone blessing the food. For the past two nights, that "someone" had been Tony. And it had felt good.

That comforting sense of family had struck her every time the three of them had joined hands, and she'd had to tamp down a longing she hadn't even known she'd had. Whatever she was longing for, it wasn't anything within her reach—not with Tony, maybe not with anyone. Her first responsibility would always be to her son.

Tony had just finished his prayer when his ringtone sounded from inside his pants pocket. Before swiping and putting it to his ear, he glanced at the screen. "It's my dad."

While Tony talked, Gavin made some unsuccessful attempts to spoon spaghetti into his mouth before foregoing the utensil and using his fingers. Oh, well, she'd clean him up when they finished.

Tony ended the call and laid his phone on the table. "Dad has a large charter Monday afternoon, and his first mate has the flu. He's not likely to be over it by then. Since I've got tomorrow and Monday off, he asked if I could help him."

She nodded, pushing aside the vague sense of disappointment settling over her. He'd talked about hanging out with her at least part of both days. It would have helped pass the time.

He picked up his fork and took a bite. "Mmm. I'm guessing this didn't come out of a jar."

"It did, but I doctored it up."

"I can tell." He took a couple more bites. "You can cook for me anytime."

He gave her a smile of approval, and her stomach responded with a flutter. She promptly squashed it. "Thanks for the compliment."

He took a long swig of iced tea. "If we weren't trying to keep you hidden, I'd bring you with us on Monday's charter."

She looked at him with raised brows. "I'm afraid I'd turn you down on that one."

"Why? You love boating. It would be fun."

Was Tony really that clueless or was he goading her? "I love boating with Buck, our charter captain. I loved boating with Shannon. I have no interest in being on the same boat or even in the same town as your father."

Maybe that was harsh, but thinking about Jerry Sanderson's betrayal always brought out the worst in her.

Tony frowned. "My dad has nothing against you or your family. The animosity has always been one-sided."

She laid down her fork. "It was your father who broke up the partnership, not mine. Then he opened a competing business forty-five minutes away, doing everything he could to take all of my father's business with him. Then he spread all kinds of lies about my family."

Throughout her rant, Tony's eyes had grown wider, his jaw more slack. "What kind of lies?"

She opened her mouth to respond and snapped it shut again. The words to back up what she'd just said weren't there. Her father had made all kinds of accusations, but now that Tony had pinned her down, she couldn't remember him giving a single example.

She shrugged. "Just lies. I don't remember the details." *Wow, that was pathetic.* Time for a change in topic. "Any progress on Shannon's case?"

"Her cell phone provider got back to us. They pinged her phone and got nothing. The killer apparently took what he wanted and destroyed the phone."

She hadn't expected any different. Killers were usually smart enough to not walk around with their victims' phones.

When they'd finished eating, Tony insisted on washing their dishes since she had cooked. By the time he finished, she had Gavin cleaned up and dressed in his pajamas.

Tony met her in the hall. "Does Bella need to go out?"

"Not till bedtime. Kassie took her out before she left." She led him into the office and sat on the couch with her son. Bella lay at her feet.

Tony handed her the stack of movies. "Are there any of these Gavin hasn't seen?"

She looked through them—titles like *The Little Mermaid*, *Sleeping Beauty*, *Aladdin*, *Snow White* and *Beauty and the Beast*. When he'd finished plugging everything in and hooking the DVD player to the TV, she smiled up at him. "He's seen them all, but that's okay. He watches them over and over and never gets tired of them."

She handed him *Aladdin*, and he put it into the DVD player.

"I got all these from a guy I work with. I think his kids are older than we are. He originally had VHSs and sometime back traded them out for DVDs for his grandkids."

Over the next hour and a half, Gavin slid from her lap to nestle between Tony and her. By the time the movie ended, he was leaning heavily against her arm.

"I think he's asleep." She'd let him sleep until she was ready to go upstairs herself. She'd feel more secure if that upstairs room didn't have French doors leading onto a balcony. The doors were protected by the alarm, but still.

There was also the potential visibility from the street. The doors had curtains over them, but they were thin—only slightly more substantial than sheers. It was better than nothing, though. Anyone looking up from outside would only see vague shadows.

She twisted and shifted her son until he lay across her lap. In this position, she could face Tony more fully.

"I really appreciate all you're doing, seeing to our safety."

"I don't mind a bit." He gave her an apologetic smile. "I'm hoping this makes up, at least a little, for my being so clueless in high school."

"It does. But it wasn't the clueless part that bothered me. It was the cruel part."

"What do you mean, *cruel*?"

"I'd had a crush on you our entire junior and senior years. Knowing you were leaving for Fort Walton Beach, Shannon insisted I should let you know and conned me into writing that note. Stupid, I know. But you could have just told me you weren't interested instead of trying to humiliate me with it."

He stood, shaking his head, confusion written all over his face. "What are you talking about?"

"Shannon said she gave you the note and you put it in your backpack."

His eyebrows drew together, forming vertical creases between them. "Shannon didn't give it to me. I never saw it until someone showed it to me. I snatched it and kept it, hoping nothing would come of it. I didn't want anyone giving you grief over it."

She hesitated, doubt seeping into what she'd believed for so long. "Why would Shannon lie about it?"

"I don't know. But she didn't give it to me." He paced to the other side of the room and back again. It didn't take long. "All the time we spent studying together, did you ever know me to have a mean streak?"

"No." He'd been nice to everybody, had even stuck up for the underdog. But why would Shannon say she'd given him the note when she hadn't?

She inhaled sharply. Shannon hadn't come right out and said she'd given it to him. She'd said it was tucked securely into his backpack. Kris had assumed the rest. Did Shannon back out of giving it to him personally and instead slip it into his pack without his knowledge? If so, someone obviously noticed, took the note and shared it with the student body.

He looked down at her, his eyes pleading. "If I never had a mean streak, why would I intentionally destroy a friendship, one that I valued the way I valued ours?"

He spoke with such conviction, her chest squeezed. She'd thought he valued her friendship. She had certainly valued his. That was why the situation had hurt so badly. Was it possible she'd been angry with him all this time for something he hadn't done?

His confusion was so real, he had to be telling the truth. If she'd been wrong about him for so long, was it possible she'd been wrong about his father, too?

She swallowed hard. "I believe you."

His breath released in a rush. "Thank you."

The way they'd parted had obviously bothered him. It had bothered her, too. They could now renew their friendship without that ugliness hanging over them.

But that was all. Regardless of Shannon's prodding, considering anything more seemed like being unfaithful to Mark. Yeah, it was irrational, but that was how she felt.

Tony circled behind the desk and eased into the chair. "Since there isn't a cable hookup anywhere, how about if I bring up the NOAA website on the computer? I can angle this so you don't have to disturb your little one until you're ready to head upstairs."

After several clicks, he turned the monitor around. "Here we go."

She leaned forward to see what he'd pulled up. The eastern edge of the five-day cone barely touched Florida. Mississippi and Louisiana weren't likely to fare as well.

"I know this sounds really selfish, but I can't help but hope that cone moves even farther west or peters out altogether." Of course, the latter wouldn't happen. Over water, especially warm water, storms only gained strength.

He circled the desk again to sit on the couch, then squeezed her shoulder. "Whatever happens, we'll get through it."

We? That was what he'd said. And she didn't doubt it. He'd already proved he was willing to be there for her. She couldn't start depending on him, but for right now, she'd take whatever support he wanted to offer. For the past eighteen months, she'd faced every problem alone, and she was getting tired.

"What's on your agenda for tomorrow?" He'd already told her he wasn't working.

"Church in the morning. The services are live streamed, so we could watch it right here."

Another *we*. She'd pass on this one. "That's okay. You go ahead. I don't want to keep you away from your church." She'd rather do a Disney marathon than have to sit through Tony's church service. She got her fill of sermons with Kassie.

"I don't mind missing the service if I get to watch it here with you."

"That's all right. I'll read or do something with Gavin."

He lifted his eyebrows. "We used to go as kids and enjoyed it."

Yeah, they had. They'd even gone to the same church. His whole family had attended. Though Kris's dad had never gone, her mom had regularly taken her and her sisters. Then she'd stopped.

That had been her dad's fault. He'd always been jealous, convinced he'd lose her to someone else. Kris had thought he was imagining things, until her mother took off. Watching her walk away from her faith had shaken Kris's own. God taking her husband had dealt it the final death blow.

She scooped Gavin up in her arms and scooted forward on the couch. "I'm turning in. I need to get this guy in bed."

"I'll take Bella out for her final time tonight. Then I'll be ready to hit the sack, too." He cast the couch a sideways glance. "Such as it is."

She followed his gaze. It was a good ten or twelve inches too

short to accommodate his six-foot frame, but he hadn't com-
plained once. Instead, he'd lain on his back, one knee bent, the
other foot resting on the floor. By the time the two weeks were
over, he was going to be glad to see her safely out of town, just
to get back in a real bed.

She waited in the office while Tony slipped out the back
door with Bella. The lock clicked over. The dog's potty breaks
didn't take long. The parking lot occupied the space directly
behind the building. Although the patch of grass bordering the
sidewalk was a short distance away, it was still close enough
for Tony to keep the back door in sight.

When he returned, she followed him down the hall with
Gavin and waited while he peered out the plate glass window
in the darkened lobby. They'd followed the same routine the
past two nights, with Tony checking to make sure no one was
within sight of the building. The kitchen window had vertical
blinds, and the bathroom was windowless. But the large window in front was uncovered, as was the door. Since her stay
was temporary and she was avoiding the lobby, they hadn't
gone to the trouble of installing blinds.

"The coast is clear."

At Tony's words, she shifted Gavin to her hip to free one
hand and slipped around the corner to the closed door. As soon
as she swung it open, Bella shot around her and up the stairs.

When Kris gripped the handrail, ready to follow, Tony spoke
behind her. "Are you okay carrying him?"

"I'll make it. I do this at home regularly."

"Your stairs at home would probably pass Florida building
codes. These wouldn't."

He was right. They were far too steep. At the turn of the last
century, laws were different from today.

By the time she reached the top, Bella was already stretched
out in the middle of the bed. Kris bid Tony good-night with
a wave and a tired smile, and he closed the door downstairs.

She approached the crib with her sleeping son. The forty-watt bulb in the simple ceiling fixture left a lot of the room in shadow, but that was okay. The dimmer the lighting, the lower her chances of being noticed from the street.

When she laid Gavin in his crib, he barely stirred. He'd likely sleep soundly all night. He'd started sleeping the night through at nine weeks old, and now at two, he rarely awoke before seven o'clock.

If only she could be so blessed. The past two nights, she'd woken almost every hour. She would blame it on being in a strange bed, but she hadn't slept any better at home. As soon as she hovered near sleep, the image of Shannon lying on the floor in a pool of blood would slam into her mind. If it wasn't that image, it was others—the decomposing body in the woods, skull smashed in; the pickup truck next to her, a killer at the wheel with murder in his eyes; the missing camper, vibrant and healthy one short week ago, likely now dead. When she slept, those same images invaded her dreams.

She moved back to the stairway to close and latch the safety gate. Having the door at the bottom of the stairs made sense when the upstairs space was used for storage. But a steep open stairway with an active little boy in residence was a recipe for disaster.

The safety gate had been Tony's doing. When they'd finished moving some things in and setting up the beds that first night, Tony had made a two-in-the-morning run to Walmart. Before three, he'd had the gate installed.

She flipped the light switch at the top of the stairs, and the room fell into virtual darkness. Once her eyes adjusted, enough light from the street filtered through the thin curtains to enable her to safely move around the room without the aid of the light fixture.

As heavily shadowed as everything was, the room didn't look half bad. She and Tony had gotten all the boxes stacked neatly against the back wall. Yesterday, Tony had shown up with a couple of huge plastic totes for all the miscellaneous pieces and stacked them next to the boxes. The only things too large to go into the totes were the vacuum, some fishing poles and a couple of wooden oars. He'd stood them up in the back corner.

At her insistence, they'd put Gavin's crib against the boxes. She wanted him as far away from the French doors as possible. It was probably irrational. If someone came through those doors, Gavin wouldn't be any safer at the far end of the room than in the middle, but positioning herself between the doors and her son couldn't be a bad thing.

Kris slipped into the T-shirt and yoga shorts she'd brought to sleep in. "Come on, Bella. Move over." She gave the dog a push. She didn't budge.

An adult golden retriever sprawled in the center of her king-size bed at home was okay. It wasn't going to work in a full-size bed, not if she expected to get any sleep.

"Okay, bed hog." She slid both hands under the dog and rolled her onto her back. "You're not taking your half out of the middle."

Once she had the dog situated, she picked up her Kindle from the box she'd repurposed as a nightstand. Maybe she'd eventually fall into a dreamless sleep.

The reading should help. The book she'd started earlier in the week was a romantic comedy. She was a quarter of the way through. What she'd read so far had offered a little bit of romance and a whole lot of comedy. Exactly what she needed.

She settled back with the book. Soon, soft snoring created a backdrop for her thoughts. It wasn't coming from the man downstairs. She had no idea whether Tony was asleep or whether he was a snorer.

Bella left her no doubt. *Great.*

She looked at her dog in the soft glow emitting from her reader. She lay stretched out on her side, facing the crib, her back to Kris. Gavin was still in the same position he'd been in when she'd laid him in the bed. That made two of them getting a good night's sleep.

She returned her attention to the story. She would read till her eyelids grew heavy. Just a little longer. If she didn't stop until she could no longer stay awake, maybe she'd actually sleep. Soon the words began to blur. Every time she blinked, her eyes stayed closed a little longer.

A soft rattle came from somewhere nearby. Her eyes shot open, and she lay frozen, body rigid, Kindle clutched facedown against her chest. What had she just heard?

She rolled her head toward the balcony. Beyond the filmy curtains, a shadow shifted. The next moment, both doors exploded inward with a crash, jerking a scream from her throat.

A man stood silhouetted against the light pouring in unobstructed from the street below, a knife clutched in one hand. The shrill squeal of the alarm filled the room.

Bella sailed off the bed amid a flurry of sharp barks. Kris rolled across the space just vacated by her dog and sprang to her feet next to Gavin's crib.

On the other side of her bed, dog and man stood facing off, about five feet apart. Bella stopped barking long enough to release some angry growls, then resumed.

The man advanced a step and swung the knife.

Kris's heart leaped into her throat. "Bella!"

The dog jumped back, her barking even more ferocious. She moved side to side in front of the intruder, blocking his way to her people. She would protect them or die trying.

The man advanced, swinging the knife, and Bella retreated. Kris leaned over Gavin's crib to snatch one of the wooden oars that stood in the corner and held it like she would a baseball bat. Bella backed around the foot of the bed and toward the crib. Kris released another long scream as her dog moved closer. Now Gavin's screams joined her own.

Less than a minute had passed since the intruder had broken through the doors, but already her time was running out.

Backed against the wall between the bed and crib, there was no means of escape.

The knife slashed through the air again, and she swung the oar. He threw up his left arm to block the blow. The oar connected with a solid *thwack*.

The door at the bottom of the stairs creaked open. Relief surged through her. It was premature. The man made one more angry slash, this time at her rather than her dog. She jerked backward as the sharp tip of the blade grazed her throat. The sting barely penetrated her fear.

"Kris!" Tony's scream accompanied his pounding footsteps. But the intruder had already sailed over the bed and was running for the damaged doors.

Kris's knees buckled, and she dropped the oar. As Gavin's screams echoed through the room, she collapsed to the floor in a crumpled heap.

Chapter Five

Tony charged up the stairs, taking them two at a time, weapon drawn. He'd been dead to the world. Kris's scream had jarred him instantly awake. Her son's distressed cries and the squeal of the alarm had chased away any grogginess that might have remained.

Kris had screamed several times. She was now quiet, but sharp, frenzied barks came from beyond the latched security gate.

God, please let her be all right.

Instead of fiddling with the latch, he leaped over the barrier and into the room. Her son's screams quieted to soft sobs. Kris was sitting on the floor between her bed and his, one hand curled around the side of her neck. The balcony doors were wide open, and Bella was outside looking through the railing, her barks piercing the squeal of the alarm.

Ignoring the longing to comfort Kris, he ran onto the balcony. A large pocketknife was lying on the floor, the blade exposed. After stepping around it with little more than a glance, he peered over the edge of the railing, searching the street below. A figure disappeared around the corner of the building.

He pulled his phone from the pocket of his gym shorts. He'd

put it there when he'd grabbed his weapon. The security company would have already notified the police, but he had something to add—a vehicle description.

When he stepped back into the room, Kris was on her feet, hand still pressed against her neck. She was wearing a T-shirt and a pair of those stretchy pants women often wore while exercising. Her hair was mashed down on one side and sticking up in spiky disarray on the other. The fear emanating from her twisted his heart.

He laid his weapon on top of one of the stacks of boxes and then dialed 911 as he approached her. "It was him, wasn't it?"

She nodded, eyes wide. Bella padded in from the balcony and circled the bed to press herself against Kris's leg. One of the wooden oars lay on the floor next to her. She'd apparently tried to use it as a weapon.

When the dispatcher came on, Tony explained what had happened and gave a description of the truck. They would put out an APB and have units search the area. Meanwhile, police would arrive any minute. If not for the alarm, they would probably already hear the squeal of approaching sirens.

"How about if we go downstairs, shut the alarm off and meet the police?"

She nodded, her eyes still wide. "He found me. He knows where I am. He tried to cut Bella." She lowered her hand and looked at it. "He cut me."

Panic stabbed through him, and he rushed toward her.

She held up her hand. "I'm okay. It's not much more than a nick."

His breath expelled in a rush. A blood smear marked her palm, a matching one on her throat. She was right. It wasn't bad, certainly not life-threatening. But that didn't dull the sense of protectiveness shooting through him, or tame the urge to wrap her in his arms and hold her until all threats were gone. Before he could act on the impulse, she turned to lift Gavin from the bed. Then she knelt to wrap one arm around her son and the other around her dog.

Yes, the killer had found her. The thought put a cold lump of dread in his chest. It probably hadn't even been that difficult. If he'd checked out Shannon's friends before destroying her phone, he'd have found Kris's profile and seen her name. *Richards* may not have led him anywhere, but an internet search of *Ashbaugh* would pull up the charter company. Finding her there would have been a long shot, but it was one that had paid off.

After retrieving his weapon, he led her toward the stairs, her son's hand tucked into hers. "We've got to get you somewhere safe."

"I know." Her voice was soft.

"Somewhere away from here."

She followed him down the stairs, matching her son's pace, one slow step at a time. At the bottom, she turned toward the hall, still holding Gavin's hand. "I'll be right back."

Tony continued across the room and punched the code she'd given him into the alarm panel by the front door. Now a more distant sound reached him, the scream of approaching sirens.

Kris reappeared a minute later and sank into the chair behind the desk. The blood smear on her throat was gone, an inch-long red line in its place, barely visible in the soft glow of the streetlights drifting through the window.

She dragged Gavin onto her lap. "I have a friend from high school who moved to Texas. I haven't talked to her in ages, but we are Facebook friends. I could message her and see if she could put me up for the next week and a half."

"That sounds like a good plan." Anywhere except Florida. Georgia and Alabama, too, because they were both too close to Pensacola.

Tony moved to the front door to watch for the responding officers. Judging from the volume of the sirens, they were close.

Soon flashing blue lit up the street and reflected off the buildings. A Pensacola Police cruiser pulled into one of the parallel parking spaces in front, K-9 Unit displayed on the side. A German shepherd dog sat in the back. The driver door swung open, and a familiar figure climbed from the driver's seat.

Tony cast a glance at Kris. "The police are here, more specifically, your future brother-in-law."

"Jared?" Kris rose, letting Gavin slide from her lap, and approached the door.

As Jared moved closer, Tony hit the light switch. Relief flooded the other man's features. Kris swung open the door. After wrapping her in a hug, Jared held her away from him, looking her over. "You're all right?"

"Thanks to Bella and Tony."

"When the call was dispatched and they gave this address, I about had a heart attack."

As Tony watched the exchange, warmth filled him. Kris was obviously close to her future brother-in-law. From the little bit he'd seen, she was finally enjoying some closeness with her sisters, too, at least one of them. The constant friction he'd seen between the twins as teenagers seemed to have disappeared.

"Tell me what happened."

"The killer climbed onto the balcony, kicked in the doors. Bella charged at him, barking and growling, but he had a knife." She put a hand to her neck. "He got me, but just barely. I'm all right."

Tony's jaw tightened. "He apparently dropped the knife on the balcony in his haste to escape."

Kris looked at him sharply. "He did? Maybe you can get prints."

"Maybe." It wasn't likely. If he'd worn gloves to kill Shannon, he'd have taken the same precautions coming after Kris.

Jared's thoughts had apparently followed the same track. "Could you see if he was wearing gloves?"

"Not really. The light was behind him. He was swinging the knife, and Bella was backing up, trying to stay out of his reach. There are a couple of paddles up there, like from a canoe or rowboat. I grabbed one and tried to club him with it, but he blocked it."

Tony smiled. "You were going to fight off a killer with an oar."

She returned his smile. "Only until you got up there with your gun. In the meantime, I was determined he wasn't going to get close enough to me or my son to use that knife."

Jared continued. "What happened then?"

"Tony headed up the stairs, and he took off." Her gaze met his. "I think he expected me to be alone. He wasn't counting on you or my dog."

As she talked, Jared made notes. "An APB has been issued, so units are searching for the truck. Can you tell me what he was wearing?"

"Blue jeans and a dark-colored shirt, black or navy blue, maybe even dark green."

"I take it you're positive it was the same guy you saw at your friend's house the night she was killed, and the one who came after you earlier this week?"

"I'm positive. Like on the road, he was wearing a bandana, his hair hidden underneath."

"Anything else you can tell us?"

"That's all I can think of."

"We'll take the knife into evidence, hopefully lift some prints, if not from tonight, maybe previously." He paused. "You're not going to stay here, are you?"

That last question came from Jared as a friend rather than an officer. Good, someone else to convince her to leave. Now it would be two against one. Except she'd already agreed to leave the state.

"I was thinking about getting in touch with a former friend who now lives in Texas."

Uh-oh. Tony frowned. "Was?"

"I'm having second thoughts."

"Why?" His exasperation came through in his tone. He

should have known her agreeing to leave had come too easily. Kris had always been independent, someone who would balk at being put in a position to have to ask for favors.

She heaved a sigh. "If I leave, I'll escape for now, but eventually I'll have to come back. My life is here."

"If this guy gets a hold of you, you won't have a life to worry about." *Come on, Jared, help me out here.*

Kris continued. "He's killed four times in, what, the last three months?"

Tony pressed his lips together. Four times that they knew of. It could be more. "Let's not make it five."

"My leaving isn't going to prevent that fifth killing. Likely, just the opposite. You don't have a single lead other than an old pickup truck with a bogus tag. And you wouldn't even have that if he hadn't come after me. With no leads and no idea when or where he'll strike next, how many women will have to die before you catch him?"

Jared put a hand on her shoulder. "You don't need to play the hero. If you can get somewhere safe, that's what you need to do."

Thanks, buddy. "Jared's right. You see to the safety of yourself and your son, and law enforcement will handle things here."

"I can't do that and live with my decision." Her gaze dipped to the floor. "I keep thinking about the woman we found in the woods and the woman you mentioned from Milligan who was killed the same way. I'm still haunted with thoughts of the camper we searched for on Monday, knowing she's probably lying in a shallow grave or in the woods somewhere."

Or at the bottom of the Gulf.

She looked up at him, her expression earnest. "Think about it. You're desperate to catch this guy. That's almost impossible without knowing when or where he's going to strike next. We still don't know the *when*, but we can anticipate the *where* because we know the *who*."

Tony shook his head. "Absolutely not. We're not going to use you as bait. You need to think about your son."

She bristled. "I *am* thinking about my son."

He winced. He hadn't intended to disparage her parenting skills, but he was desperate to make her listen to reason.

She heaved a sigh. "As long as this guy is out there, I won't be safe anywhere. It took him two days to find me. How long before he connects me with Mark's family? After tonight, I'm no longer sure he won't somehow track me down in Ohio. Here, I don't just have the police looking out for me, I have police who also happen to be personal friends of mine."

She put one hand on his shoulder, the other on Jared's. "I trust you guys to keep us safe."

Jared frowned. "We can't be with you twenty-four seven."

"Someone can. Maybe not with me, but watching." She dropped her hands. "I've thought about asking Kassie to let Gavin stay with her. But she would have to leave him with his babysitter while she works. I'm afraid it would be too easy for the killer to use him to get to me."

Tony pressed his lips into a thin line. She was right, on all counts.

"If I leave and more young women lose their lives at this guy's hand before he's caught, do you really think I could come back and pick up as if nothing happened? That's assuming I even make it back home. At this point, I can't guarantee that I would."

She'd made her point well. He didn't even have a valid argument. But that didn't mean he had to like it.

He gave her a sharp nod. "We'll talk to the folks in charge and come up with a game plan."

Whatever they decided, he'd make sure she had ample protection.

He'd thought God had brought her back into his life so he could make right what he'd messed up in the past. But that wasn't the only reason. He'd also been put here at this specific time to protect her, maybe even to help guide her back to the faith she'd once had but rejected.

Was there another reason that he hadn't considered? The attraction was definitely there. So was the deep friendship they'd always shared, which made a good foundation for any romantic relationship.

No, no matter how much his heart was urging him otherwise, he wouldn't even consider it. She had a kid. After his niece had died while in his care, no way would he put himself in a position where he would be responsible for little Gavin.

Anything beyond their simple friendship was off the table.

He'd keep reminding himself of that fact. Daily.

Hourly, if he had to.

Jerry Sanderson turned the boat into the waves and hit the throttle. The bow rose, cutting a path through the choppy surface.

Kris closed her eyes and tilted her head back, relishing the sun on her face and the wind in her hair. In another hour, they'd be back at the marina in Fort Walton Beach where Sanderson kept his three boats.

Though she'd had no desire to spend the day on the water with Tony's father, here she was. She'd come along because she'd felt that she had to.

It wasn't that she owed Tony's father anything, because she didn't. But she owed Tony, big time. Even though two unmarked units would be watching the Ashbaugh Charters office, after Saturday night's incident, he'd been ready to renege on his offer to help with the charter, refusing to leave her alone. With everything he was doing for her, no way was she going to force him to choose between her and his father.

As much as she hadn't wanted to come, it hadn't been bad. Jerry Sanderson had been too occupied with his customers and captaining the boat to interact with her much beyond welcoming her aboard and flashing her the occasional friendly smile.

Tony was staying pretty busy with his first-mate responsibilities, too.

That was all right. Just being on the water was entertainment enough. After being holed up in the charter office for the past four days, she'd have almost agreed to get on a boat with Jack the Ripper for an opportunity to soak up some sunshine. Even Gavin had seemed to be getting cabin fever. Her usually easygoing, compliant child had been especially disagreeable since yesterday.

She opened her eyes to look at her son, who was sitting in the lap of one of the customers, eyelids at half-mast, fingering the beads on her bracelet. Nineteen-year-old Emily had no interest in fishing and had signed up for the charter only because her boyfriend had. As someone who loved kids, it hadn't taken her long to decide that she'd rather play with Gavin than hold a fishing pole.

The rest of the group consisted of two women and four men. All seven were Florida State University students enjoying the last week of their summer break before the start of the new school year.

Tony moved from his position next to the helm to sit beside her. "Have you enjoyed yourself?"

"Totally. I'm glad I came." Not that she'd felt she had a choice. But Tony would be glad to know the afternoon hadn't been drudgery.

Being a nonpaying passenger, she hadn't felt right using the Sanderson bait and equipment, but at Tony's insistence, she'd done a little fishing herself. She'd had some nibbles that had resulted in nothing but lost bait. So she'd finally put up the pole and kicked back to relax. It was what she'd been doing ever since.

She looked out over the water, with its moderate chop, then up where puffy, white clouds were scattered across a blue sky. The sun was about two-thirds of the way through its descent, leaving them plenty of daylight left to make it in. She and Tony would even be back in Pensacola before dark.

Some distance off their starboard bow, another boat paralleled their path. Jared had agreed to remain a short distance away in his own boat, keeping watch and making sure no one got too close. He was no doubt armed and ready to use whatever he was carrying.

Tony smiled at Gavin, whose eyes were now closed. "I think we wore out your little one."

"We did." A hint of pink stained her little boy's cheeks and upturned nose. Florida sun could be brutal, especially in August. But Gavin wasn't sunburned; she had him too well slathered. The same windburn likely marked her own cheeks.

When they got back to the marina, Emily stood and passed her sleeping bundle off to Kris. Gavin stirred then rested his head on her shoulder and was out again.

Each of the charter customers said their thanks and goodbyes and filed off the boat.

Jerry Sanderson put a hand on Kris's shoulder. Kindness filled his eyes, and the smile he wore crinkled the skin at their corners. "I enjoyed having you and your little boy spend the afternoon with us. Thanks for coming."

"Thanks for having us." She turned to step off the boat. She didn't want to like this man, but it was hard not to. The warmth and acceptance she sensed from him cast doubt on all the negative things her father had said about him.

His voice halted her escape. "I was really sorry to read about your father's arrest and drug charges."

She turned to look at him. The sincerity in his words was reflected on his face. Suddenly the image she'd created of the Sandersons sitting around the dinner table disparaging the Ashbaughs and gloating over Bobby Ashbaugh's downfall no longer seemed plausible.

She shifted Gavin onto her hip. "Did you know before what he was involved in?"

"I had my suspicions. That's why I split with him and went off on my own."

She frowned. "And took a lot of Ashbaugh business with you."

"I didn't take a single name, phone number or email address. When I walked away, I completely started over. I did a lot of advertising to get the word out, and God blessed my efforts."

She narrowed her eyes. "You're telling me you didn't trash my father's reputation in the community?"

"I told my wife. I felt she deserved to know why I was breaking off an eight-year partnership."

Kris looked at Tony. "Did you know that's why they split?"

"Not until just now."

She looked from Tony's father to Tony and back to his father. Sanderson didn't even tell his sons? Everything he was saying was in complete opposition to what her father had told her for years.

More lies piled on top of all the others. Over the past few months, her father had shattered every ounce of trust she'd ever had in him.

She met Mr. Sanderson's gaze. "I'm finding out I've spent a lot of years believing lies."

He gave her a sad smile. "I'm sorry. We've been praying for you and your sisters. And since finding out what you've been through this week, we're really doubling down on those prayers."

She turned an accusing glare on Tony and then softened it immediately. He wasn't sharing personal information about her for no reason. He'd have had to tell his dad something about why he was dragging her along on today's charter. Coming from Tony, whatever excuse he gave would be nothing but the truth.

"Thank you." She meant it. Not that she believed in prayer, but it was the thought that counted.

After saying their farewells, they walked to where Tony

had parked his Tundra. Kris buckled Gavin into his car seat and climbed into the front. Tony slid into the driver's seat and cranked the engine. "How about we stop somewhere and pick up dinner when we get back to Pensacola so you don't have to cook."

"I'm all for that." She loved to cook, but not after a day on the water, especially with the added stress of having to spend it with Tony's father. Of course, that was stress that had turned out to be unnecessary.

Less than an hour later, Tony drove slowly down Government Street, approaching the charter office. "Did you notice the dark SUV we just passed?"

She looked in the side mirror. "Parallel parked on this side of the street?"

"Yep. That's one of ours."

She nodded. It sat facing Ashbaugh Charters, on the opposite side of the road, a short block away. With the fading sunlight and the tint of the windows, she couldn't see the occupants. "They're keeping an eye on the building?"

"Yep. I'm sure there's an unmarked unit in back, too, like this one—not close enough to be obvious but where they can still see the back door."

He'd told her yesterday that they were there. Seeing one of them for herself brought a lot of relief.

Thanks to Tony and his brother, Nick, the building had been secure by midafternoon yesterday. On his way to church, Nick had stopped by Lowe's and then dropped off wood and other materials to replace the damaged door jamb. After lunch, Tony had gotten everything fixed and working properly again. Fortunately, the doors themselves had been salvageable.

Between the materials delivery and actually performing the work, Tony had brought up his church service on the TV in the office. When he'd asked her to join him, she'd made up some excuse about needing to bathe Gavin. Then she'd felt guilty and ended up coming in to sit with him near the end of the service.

Mark had tried to get her to attend, too. He'd become a Christian shortly before the accident. Maybe he'd have had an impact on her eventually. Unfortunately, God took him before that could even start to happen.

As they drew closer to the building that housed the charter office, Kris's chest tightened. A burgundy Sorento sat parked in one of the parallel spaces in front of the building. "Kassie's still here."

"At almost seven thirty?"

Her stomach drew into a knot. Kassie had been at the charter office when she'd left late that morning with Tony. Why would she still be there, especially with everything that had been going on?

Granted, it wasn't dark yet. It was just nearing dusk. And police were watching the place. But why tempt fate?

Tony eased into a spot across the street. The charter office lights weren't on. The lights next door were.

Kris released a relieved breath. Kassie was apparently showing the retail space and apartment above to a potential renter.

"I'm going to check on her. Can you come along?"

"If you hadn't asked, I would have insisted."

They crossed the street, and when Kris stepped inside, the door at the bottom of the stairs was open a full ninety degrees. Two voices came from above, Kassie's and a male voice.

The layout of this space was the same as in the charter office—narrow stairway leading to the upper story. On this side, though, the apartment above had been refurbished years ago to include a kitchenette and a small bathroom.

Tony pulled the door shut behind him, and Kassie's voice grew closer. "So, what do you think?"

"It's perfect. I'll have the music store I've been wanting to open for ages and be able to live above it."

Good. It looked like they were going to finally have the place rented. The monthly payments would help cover some of the expenses, and in her situation, having a close neighbor held a lot of appeal.

"That sounds great." Kassie started down the stairs. With the angle of the door and where she was standing, Kris couldn't see her, but her sister's footfalls on the stairs told her where she was.

Then heavier footsteps joined the lighter ones, and their future renter continued. "The lease on my apartment in LaGrange isn't up for another four weeks. If I pay you this month's rent, will you hold it for me?"

"How about we say half and call it even? I'm glad to have you back."

Back? So it was someone they knew. Even better.

Kassie stepped around the door, and the smile she was wearing broadened. "Oh, hey, I didn't know you guys were back."

"We just got back. I saw your car parked out front and the lights on in here and figured—"

She swallowed the rest of her words when their new renter followed Kassie into the lobby.

Kassie squared her shoulders. "Kris, I'm sure you remember Spencer Cavanaugh."

Her voice was a couple of pitches higher than normal, and her pose said she was preparing for a battle.

"Yes, I remember." Where Kassie's tone was higher and tension-filled, her own was low and cold. "Hello, Spence."

Of course she remembered him. Druggie, wannabe rock star and their younger sister Alyssa's no-good former boyfriend. And Kassie was agreeing to rent to him? Had she lost her mind? His music store would probably be a front for a drug operation or prostitution ring or something equally seedy. If that was who her close neighbor was going to be, she could live without one.

Kassie introduced the two men, who hadn't previously met. Besides Spencer being two years behind them in school, their circles of friends hadn't intersected. Tony had run with the good kids. Spence…hadn't.

Kris looked at Tony and Spence. "Can you excuse us for a few minutes?"

She grabbed Kassie's wrist and led her out the front door. The SUV was still there, parked a short distance away. They'd be safe standing out front long enough for her to talk some sense into her sister, who had somehow lost hers.

"You're not seriously thinking of renting to him, are you?"

"He's not the same man we knew seven or eight years ago."

"And you can somehow guarantee that he's not going to be dealing drugs out of our building?"

"He won't."

"How do you know?"

"He's changed. He's not even a drug *user* at this point. He's spent six years serving our country."

Kris frowned. So he'd been in the military. That didn't mean that once he got away from the discipline and back in his hometown he wouldn't return to his former lifestyle. After all, how many times had she and Kassie gotten their hopes up that Alyssa was finally going to get her act together, only to be disappointed?

"He's even playing guitar with his church's worship team now."

Great. No wonder Kassie was all gung ho about renting to him. She probably figured he was one more person she could get to try to influence her wayward sister.

Maybe Kassie was right, though. If he really had changed, it wasn't right to hold the things he did as a teenager against him. But now that she was thinking about it, what irritated her the most was the fact that Kassie had made the decision without her input.

She crossed her arms. "You should have talked to me. Decisions related to the charter business, we make together."

"I'm sorry. It's just that Spence and I have been talking for the past hour. That's why I'm here so late. I knew that once you got reacquainted with him, you'd agree with me."

She still wasn't ready to let it go. "Just remember, when he destroys the place or we've got cops making drug busts right next door to us, it's all going to be on you."

She spun and stalked to the door. When Kassie followed her inside, Spence lifted his brows. "Should I be warming up my pen, or is our verbal agreement off?"

Kassie tilted her head to the side. "Before you sign the lease, my sister might need some convincing."

Spence nodded. "I can understand that." He locked gazes with Kris. "I provided your sister with some references—my employer, my current landlord. I've only had one since my discharge from the army. I'm happy to answer any questions you might have for me, too."

Kris asked about his military background, his work, his friends, his activities, even his involvement with his church. Within thirty minutes, she was as convinced as Kassie apparently was. He really had changed.

Maybe dumping Alyssa was the smartest thing the man had ever done.

Chapter Six

Tony got a Coke from the vending machine, popped the top and took a long swig. Several counties were working together trying to solve the string of murders and had almost nothing.

The crime scene investigators had been able to lift prints from the handle of the knife, but there'd been no match in IAFIS. Either their killer had never been arrested or he'd worn gloves and someone else had handled the knife before he had. Kris had been right. Their greatest chance of catching him was watching for him to come after her again.

He walked toward his captain's office. He'd check in before calling it an afternoon.

When he rapped lightly on the open door, Keith looked up from the papers on his desk. "Come in. We just got word from Fort Walton Beach."

Tony eased into one of the chairs opposite the desk, his heart beating faster. "Yeah?"

"Some fisherman snagged a body. Young woman, slender, dark hair, head smashed in with a blunt object. She had a concrete block tied around her waist. They're waiting for positive identification, but she fits the description of your missing camper."

Tony nodded. "It would make sense. The dogs lost her trail at the Blackwater River and were never able to pick it up again. The Blackwater River flows all the way to the Gulf. Did they say where they found her?"

"Not too far from the inlet between Destin and Okaloosa Island, where Choctawhatchee Bay connects to the Gulf. The location was about a half mile from the location your lady friend pointed out. Either she'd missed it by a little bit or the body had drifted."

Even though he hadn't expected any different, the news was still like a kick in the gut. He knew her name—Julia Morris. He'd studied her picture and searched for her with the others, hoping the day would somehow have a positive outcome.

He pressed his lips together. "That makes three, same profile, all killed the same way."

"Four, counting the woman he stabbed to death last week."

And he was determined to make Kris number five.

"We're watching her." Keith had just read his mind. He knew about their longtime friendship, but if he suspected that there was anything more than that, he was wrong.

Keith leaned back in his chair. "We're watching her too closely for him to get anywhere near her, but hopefully not closely enough to tip him off." He paused. "I'll keep you in the loop, in addition to the regular briefings."

"I appreciate it."

As he walked through the parking lot toward his vehicle, he put a call through to Kris. She answered after the first ring.

"I'm heading your direction now. Anything you want me to pick up?"

"Milk. Other than that, we're good. I've been holed up in the office answering calls this afternoon. It's about time to close up, so Kassie's going home, and I'm getting ready to start dinner."

"What are we having?"

"Chicken Alfredo."

"I'll be there in twenty minutes."

She was feeding him another one of his favorites. This protection detail he was on had some great benefits. He'd had more home-cooked meals in the past week than he'd had in the past twelve months. He was going to be disappointed to see it come to an end and not just because she was feeding him well. He was really enjoying her company. Once they caught the man and the danger to her was over, he'd do everything he could to maintain the friendship they'd reignited. He'd somehow just have to keep a rein on his emotions.

That hadn't been a problem before. She'd always been nothing but a friend—one of the best. He'd dated other girls, but pursuing a romantic relationship with Kris had never crossed his mind.

That had changed. She was a woman now, and an attractive one at that. After ten years apart and all the time they were spending together, it was getting harder and harder to continue thinking of her as simply a friend.

He disconnected the call and slid into the driver's seat. He hadn't wanted to leave her at all. But he couldn't very well park himself at the charter office twenty-four seven. He had to leave her safety in the hands of the officers keeping watch. And the Lord. He was doing plenty of that, too—he'd been sending up pleas for her protection for the past week.

When he arrived at the charter office, Kassie was just leaving. He greeted her at the door.

"Good day, I assume?"

"Yep, uneventful."

"Those are the kind to have."

As soon as he stepped inside, mouthwatering aromas wafted to him. His stomach growled. That sandwich and chips he'd eaten at lunchtime were long gone.

He locked the door behind him and set the alarm. When he reached the kitchen, Kris stood at the stove stirring something in a pot, her back to him. The contents of another pot were boiling, judging from the steam pouring out. Probably pasta, or maybe the chicken if she hadn't cooked it in advance.

He squeezed past her to put the milk he'd bought in the small fridge. "Dinner smells wonderful."

She cast him a sideways glance without halting her stirring of whatever was in that pot. "Thanks. It'll be ready in about forty-five minutes. It would be sooner if I wasn't limited to two burners."

He scanned the small kitchen. Bella lay under the table against the wall. A carton of heavy whipping cream and an open one-pound box of butter sat on the counter next to a grater that had small bits of what looked like parmesan cheese clinging to it. There wasn't a store-bought jar in sight.

"You're making it from scratch. I thought you were going to do things the easy way while here."

"You can't get much easier than Alfredo."

"Can I help you with anything?"

"I appreciate the offer, but more than one person moving about this kitchen is a crowd. You can just have a seat and keep me company. I'd say you could entertain Gavin, but he's pretty good at entertaining himself."

"How about Bella? Can I feed her?"

"I already did before I started cooking, and Kassie took her out before she left."

He squeezed past her again to take a seat next to her son. The little boy sat in his high chair, a coloring book open on the tray in front of him and a fat red crayon clutched in one hand. Seven other crayons were scattered about the tray, the empty box lying in the corner.

"What are you coloring there, buddy?"

"A house and a twee." He put the red crayon to the paper and began coloring in the leaves of the tree. Maybe it was fall in his picture. In North Carolina.

He picked up a yellow crayon and pointed to the object in the forefront of the picture. "Doggie."

"Is that Bella?" He had the color right.

"No, 'nother doggie."

Instead of coloring the dog, he moved the yellow crayon back and forth across the roof of the house.

Kris cast him another glance. "How was work?"

"Not bad. I handled a couple of new cases—a house robbery and a sexual assault."

"I thought homicide detectives just handled murders."

"That's how it is in large cities, but in smaller towns, detectives handle all kinds of investigations."

Kris moved to the fridge and pulled a plastic package from the freezer. "Do you like spinach?"

"Not by itself, but in Alfredo I do."

"Good. Otherwise, I could substitute broccoli."

"Either one is fine." In fact, he'd eat whatever she wanted to cook.

"They found the missing camper."

She spun to face him, hope in her eyes.

"Some fisherman snagged her body this morning."

Her shoulders drooped, and she seemed to deflate. "I hate that. I really didn't expect anything different, but I was still holding out a sliver of hope that she'd somehow turn back up alive and well. At least now her family will have some closure. Not that that's any real consolation." She paused. "Where did they find her?"

"About a half mile from the place you pointed out to them."

She nodded. "I was close."

"You did good."

When she had dinner ready, she took the coloring book and crayons away from her son. He didn't protest. Of course, the same delicious aromas that had been tormenting Tony had probably been teasing Gavin for the past forty-five minutes.

Kris put a small spoonful of pasta on a plate and, after spooning the chunky sauce over the top, placed the plate in front of her son. When Tony carried his own food to the table,

Gavin hadn't touched what was in front of him. Instead, he was sitting with his hands folded, obviously waiting for someone to say grace. That someone would be him, as it had been for the past week.

Gavin really was a good kid. Kris was doing an amazing job of raising him by herself. Someday God would bring a man into her life, someone who would be worthy of the love of both her and her sweet little boy. He prayed that would be a godly man who would restore her faith in God and people.

After Tony had blessed the food, Kris picked up her fork. "Have you heard any more about the storm?"

"I haven't seen it for myself, but they say the track has been moved farther east."

She leaned back in her chair, face creased with concern. "That puts us in the cone."

"It's also been upgraded from a Cat. 2 to a Cat. 3." Not to compound her worries, but she needed to be prepared.

The creases deepened. "I'm worried about my house. It's right on the water and has those French doors across most of the back, not to mention all the windows."

"Do you have storm shutters?"

"I do. They're in the garage, but it's a huge job getting them installed. Mark and I helped Dad do it for Michael."

"I think we're still looking at landfall late Thursday night." He pulled his phone from his pocket.

"Who are you calling?"

"Dad and then Nick."

A few minutes later, he disconnected the second call and laid the phone facedown on the table. "It's settled. Dad and Nick will meet us there at two o'clock tomorrow afternoon. They're bringing Mom and Joanne, too."

"Joanne?"

"Nick's wife."

For several moments, Kris didn't say anything. Her eyes

grew moist, and she blinked several times. Finally, she spoke. "Doesn't everybody have their own preparations to make?"

"I don't have anything to do except stocking us up on supplies. That's one advantage of apartment living."

"But your dad and mom don't live in an apartment, and I'm guessing Nick and Joanne don't, either."

"They don't, but they assured me they'll be able to get it all done."

"Tell them thank you, and I'll feed everybody."

"That sounds like a fair trade."

When they'd finished eating and cleaned up the mess, Bella and Gavin followed them to the office, which was also doing duty as a combination living room and guest bedroom. Tony sat at the desk to navigate to the NOAA website.

"After we see what this storm is doing, what do you say we watch another Disney movie? Gavin can pick this time."

"That sounds good."

As soon as she sat on the couch, Gavin climbed onto her lap and Bella lay at her feet. An image filled the monitor, much scarier than the last time he'd checked.

"The track is quite a bit farther east." He turned the monitor around. "We're right in the middle of the cone. Unless it totally hooks to the right in the next thirty-six hours, I'm afraid we're going to get slammed." There was probably plenty of news footage of the areas that had already been hit, but seeing it wouldn't do Kris any good. He walked around the desk. "Let's watch that movie now." After handing the stack to Kris, he smiled down at her little boy. "What movie do you want to watch?"

Kris thumbed through them, and Gavin snatched one from the stack. "Boody and Beast."

Tony took the case from him. "*Beauty and the Beast* it is."

After turning the monitor back around and moving the TV to the center of the desk, he slipped the DVD into the player. When he'd taken his place on the couch, Gavin slid from Kris's lap.

"Where are you going, sweetie? Let's sit in Mommy's lap and watch the movie."

Tony watched the little boy as he looked from him to his mother and back to him again. Maybe he didn't want to watch the movie. In that case, Kris would have to find something else to entertain him.

After one more glance at his mother, the little boy pointed at him. "Tony."

The next moment, he was climbing into Tony's lap.

Tony stiffened, one hand gripping the arm of the couch, the other curled into a fist. His heart pounded as if he'd just taken a flight of stairs at a full run.

More than fourteen months had passed since he'd last held a little one. He'd always loved kids and had jumped at the chance to babysit his niece. Then the unthinkable had happened.

Nick and Joanne didn't blame him. They'd insisted it wasn't his fault, that SIDS was a silent killer that struck with no warning. It didn't matter what they said because he'd never been able to stop blaming himself.

"Tony?"

He released the breath he'd been holding and looked at Kris. Her eyebrows were raised, and silent question filled her dark eyes.

"He won't bite. He won't break, either."

Wouldn't he? How could she be so sure? Little Zoe did.

"He's potty-trained, too. You don't even have to worry about being wet on." She gave him a smile, but he couldn't bring himself to return it.

Her smile faded, and she stood to lift her son from his lap.

"Tony." The little boy's voice held a note of protest. He tightened his fingers around Tony's shirt, instantly losing his grip when Kris straightened with him.

"What's the deal with you and kids?"

He shrugged, the motion feeling awkward. "I'm just not comfortable around them."

"It's more than that. You act like you're scared of them."

He winced. She was too perceptive. But he wasn't about to tell her his deepest, darkest secret. He hadn't told anyone outside his family.

"Something happened, didn't it?" The words were soft, barely above a whisper.

He didn't respond.

"Tony?"

"Let it go." He spoke through clenched teeth.

"If you want to talk about it, I'm a good listener."

He shot to his feet. "No, I don't want to talk about it." His voice was raised, the words sharp, but he couldn't seem to soften them. He had no desire to open old wounds, and she shouldn't be pushing him. It wasn't any of her business anyway.

He brushed past her and into the hallway. As he stalked into the lobby, a knock on the front door sent his heart into his throat and instantly dissolved his irritation.

He skidded to a stop. If whoever was there posed a threat, the officers standing guard outside would have been on him before he could reach the front door.

He peered through the panes of glass in the French-style door as he approached. Relief whooshed through him. Now he recognized the visitor. He was the owner of one of the neighboring businesses. Tony had seen him coming and going a couple of times. Tonight he was holding a large box.

Tony shut off the alarm and opened the door. "Yes?"

"I have something for Kris. It was delivered to me by mistake, left at my front door. I've had it since midafternoon, but I got busy and couldn't make it over here. When I was leaving, it looked like there was a light on in the back over here, so I figured I'd give it a shot."

Tony looked down at what the man held. It didn't have a UPS or FedEx label. Instead *Kristina Ashbaugh-Richards* had been written across the top with a black Sharpie, the charter office address below. There was no return name or address. His chest tightened around a growing lump of dread.

The man held up the box. "Do you mind giving it to her?"

"Sure. Thanks." If there was a bomb inside, the man would likely be in pieces, scattered all over Government Street, instead of standing on the charter office doorstep.

Tony swallowed hard and took the box. It weighed so little it almost felt empty. Whatever was inside was soft, judging from the muffled sounds it made when he tipped the box. Maybe he should see what was inside before giving the box to Kris. Would she perceive that as an invasion of her privacy? If so, he'd apologize later.

He'd just add that apology to the other one he owed her. Now that he'd calmed down, he had to admit that he shouldn't have snapped at her. She was only offering a listening ear, something that, if he knew Kris, would have come with ample amounts of moral support.

First, he needed to see what was in the box.

When he turned around, Kris was standing at the end of the hall, Gavin in her arms. "What did Don bring over?"

"I don't know yet. There's no shipping label and no return address, which I find a bit suspicious. Would you like me to open it?"

"Please."

He set the box on the lobby desk and pulled the scissors out of the desk caddy. While he sliced through the tape sealing it, Kris remained standing at the end of the hall rather than venturing into the lobby.

He lifted the flaps and sucked in a sharp breath.

"What is it?" Kris's voice held a slight quiver.

"A stuffed animal."

She lowered Gavin to the floor and moved closer. When her eyes met Tony's, she hesitated.

The item in the box wasn't a gift. It was a threat, one with a whole lot of rage behind it.

Kris had thwarted his attack not once, but three times. First, she ran from him at Shannon's, leading to him being struck. She evaded him traveling on US 98. Then he couldn't get to her at the charter office because she had Tony's and Bella's protection. She was a witness. She fit the profile, and he wanted her badly. Now, he was furious.

Yes, the box held a stuffed animal, a dog. At least that was what it had been, before someone had gone crazy with a knife. Soft white stuffing was mixed with chunks and strips of blond fur. If the legs and tail were somewhere in the mess, he couldn't see them.

The head, though, had been left intact, leaving no doubt as to the breed. It was a golden retriever.

"Tony?" Kris's tone held hesitation mixed with a solid dose of dread.

Gavin grasped the hem of her shirt and molded himself against her leg, obviously picking up on his mother's fear. As she moved closer, Tony fought the urge to close the flaps on the box, to tell her it was nothing. Anything to keep from upsetting her.

She would never let him get away with it.

When she reached his side, she grasped his arm, likely for support, then dipped her gaze to the contents of the box. A tortured wail poured from her and ended in a sob. Gavin burst into tears next to her.

After taking two steps back, she picked up her son and squeezed him to her chest, silent tears streaming down her face. Tony wrapped his arms around both of them, and Gavin's wails quieted to sobs.

He pressed his face to the top of Kris's head and whispered into her hair. "It's okay. I'm right here. I won't let him hurt either of you or your dog."

But was it a promise he would be able to keep? As diligent as he'd been, the killer had still come into her room while he'd been asleep downstairs. He would have to figure out a better way to protect her. Later.

Right now, Kris needed his comfort as much as his protection. So did her sweet little boy.

For the next several minutes, he held them, comforting and consoling them, offering reassurances.

And trying hard to not think about the longing that rose up inside him or how good it felt to hold them both in his arms.

Tony stood at the grill, his father and brother on either side of him. A couple of Pensacola PD officers were nearby keeping watch, hidden by shrubbery and other natural barriers. Someone was out front, too, watching from their vehicle. He hadn't seen the two in back in quite some time, but when he'd made a quick run to Publix for some salad fixings an hour ago, the vehicle in front had still been sitting at the edge of the road one door down.

It had been a good day. The six of them had worked in pairs getting all the shutters installed on the lower floor. Then Tony and Nick had worked from ladders to take care of the upper story while their dad had stayed on the ground to hand the panels up to them. None of them had wanted the women clinging to ladder rungs fourteen feet off the ground.

Now shutters protected every window and door except the front entry door, and Kris's generator was loaded into the back of his Tundra. Since she wouldn't be staying at her house, she was letting Kassie use it. If they lost power and it wasn't restored soon, he'd clean out her refrigerator and bring her food to Kassie's.

Currently, she was inside the house, hard at work on the rest of that dinner she'd promised, with the assistance of his mom and Joanne.

Gavin and Bella were inside, too, along with Gavin's babysitter. Kris had contacted her before they'd left the charter office, and the older woman had entertained both Bella and Gavin while the rest of them had worked.

Tony still hadn't told Kris that he was sorry for snapping at her last night. An apology would require an explanation. It was a conversation he'd been starting to prepare himself for while standing in the charter office lobby.

Then he'd looked in the box.

They'd eventually watched the movie, at Kris's suggestion. It had provided a good distraction for Gavin. He wasn't sure about Kris, but it hadn't done a thing for him. Not that he wouldn't have found it entertaining under different circumstances.

Nick elbowed him in the side. "You think you ought to flip that last steak before it's completely charcoaled on the one side?"

He slid the spatula under the ribeye and made a quick flip of his wrist.

"Sorry, a little distracted." Maybe he should let Nick man the grill.

Nick gave his shoulders a brotherly squeeze. "You've got reason to be, especially after last night's threat. Joanne and I are praying for you guys."

"Thanks."

"We're not praying only for protection."

"What do you mean?"

"Have you considered the possibility that God might have brought you back into her life for more than protection?"

"I don't know if she's even a Christian. Best-case scenario, she has strayed far from whatever faith she may have had as a child." Had his brother forgotten the command to not be "unequally yoked"?

"Maybe you're supposed to be salt and light for her."

He could go along with that. She'd given him a flat-out no when he'd asked her to watch his church service with him, but then she'd conceded. Granted, she'd missed most of the service, but it was a start. He wouldn't give up working on her, either.

"Your brother is right."

Great. Now his dad was chiming in, making it two against one.

His dad continued. "Kris has been through a lot. Besides losing her husband, she's been failed by some of the Christians in her life. Her mother walking out on her had to have had an impact on her."

Tony frowned. "It didn't help, either, that her father told her all kinds of lies about you, likely one of the most prominent Christian men in her life."

Nick nodded. "It's up to us to show her what true Christian love looks like. Then who knows where things might lead?"

Tony gave his brother a stern sideways glance. He didn't need to be a mind reader to know the direction his brother's thoughts had taken. "They're certainly not going to lead where you're thinking."

"Why not? She's a pretty girl. You guys have always had a good friendship."

He narrowed his eyes. "She has a kid."

"What does that have to do with anything? You love kids."

"You know the answer to that."

Nick planted both fists on his hips. "I know *your* answer, but it's really messed up."

"Hand me that platter." He would put an end to this topic of conversation. "It's time to get these off the grill."

Nick handed him the empty platter with a sigh. It wasn't the first time they'd had this conversation, and it wouldn't be the last.

Tony slid each of the seven steaks from the spatula to the platter and ended with a small hamburger on top for Gavin. Nick walked across the deck ahead of him and swung open one of the French doors leading into the dining room.

The table was already set with seven place settings, complete with china, full silver service and cloth napkins. Two foil-covered casserole dishes sat nestled into metal racks. In the center of the table, three candles rose from a base of fresh greenery.

Although a picnic on paper plates would have sufficed for his family, with Kris, he didn't expect anything less than the spread before him.

Kris walked into the room carrying a bowl of tossed salad, and his mom and Joanne followed with a variety of salad dressings. Gavin's babysitter slid him into the high chair and sat next to him, and everyone else took their places at the table. Before seating herself, Kris removed the foil from the Pyrex dishes, revealing scalloped potatoes and broccoli casserole.

His father scanned the offerings. "Kris, you outdid yourself."

"With all the work you guys did this afternoon, I owe you a few more dinners like this."

His father gave her a warm smile. "Sweetheart, you don't owe us anything. You didn't even owe us this, although we're going to enjoy it immensely. What we did this afternoon is what friends do for each other."

"Thank you."

There was a catch in her voice. When Tony cast her a sideways glance, she was blinking away moisture. Outside, Nick had mentioned showing her what true Christian love looked like. His dad was an expert.

Being the elder of the group, his father offered a prayer of thanks for the food. Dishes were passed, and everyone settled into easy conversation.

Kris looked around her son to address the babysitter. "Mildred, where are you waiting out the storm?"

"I'm going to my daughter and son-in-law's place. It's farther inland."

Tony's father nodded. "We're doing the same thing. Betty and I are too close to the water, so we're going to wait it out with Nick and Joanne. What about you two?"

"Tony and I are going to my sister's place. Her fiancé works nights for Pensacola PD in patrol and will be on duty, although

I'm sure they'll be holed up at the station during the worst of it. Meanwhile, we'll be hunkered down with Kassie and her fiancé's grandmother."

"I'm sure they'll be happy to have you there."

After everyone had had their fill, Kris and Joanne cleared away the plates and almost empty casserole dishes and returned with a stack of small plates, peach cobbler and what looked like homemade whipped cream. Last came a pewter cream and sugar set and two carafes containing coffee, one decaf and one regular, according to Kris.

Oh, man. He should have saved room for dessert.

He was halfway through the tasty treat when a little voice came from the other side of Kris.

"May I be escoosed?"

Kris looked at his plate, which was empty, just like his dinner plate had been. "Sure, sweetie."

Before she could stand, Mildred picked up her napkin and started to wipe his hands. "I'll get him."

When she'd set him on the floor, he looked up at her with a big smile. "Tank you."

Then he showered Tony with that same smile before running from the room. Something stirred inside. Nick was right. He did like kids. And Gavin was a hard one to not fall in love with.

Some of his good behavior was probably innate—he was just a compliant, easy child. But Tony couldn't discount the excellent parenting he was receiving. If somewhere in the distant future he was ever ready to raise a kid, he hoped it would be one like Gavin.

One by one, each of those gathered finished their dessert and sipped their coffee. As conversation continued, relaxed and natural, a sense of nostalgia settled over him. How many times had he and Nick, along with Mom and Dad, sat around this very table, sharing a meal with the Ashbaughs? Their fathers hadn't just been business partners, they'd been friends.

Sarah Ashbaugh was gone, and Bobby Ashbaugh was in

prison, but would the Sandersons and the other Ashbaughs eventually be able to find their way back into friendship? It looked like it tonight. Even Kris was talkative and relaxed.

Tony leaned back in his chair, full to the point of being almost uncomfortable. If he had Kris cooking for him on a regular basis, he'd have to step up his gym workouts or take up running. In fact, if he had Kris cooking for him, it would be the latter, with her at his side, Gavin in a jogging stroller in front of her. The image he created had a lot of appeal.

The little boy padded back into the room holding a stuffed white rabbit and squeezed between his chair and his mother's. Tony slid back and over, giving him more room.

Instead of climbing into his mother's lap, he turned toward Tony and held out both hands.

Tony swallowed hard, his throat working. He didn't look around the table, but judging from how conversation had come to a sudden stop, every eye was on him, even Mildred's. If he ignored those pleading eyes and outstretched hands, his family would know why. Mildred wouldn't. Neither would Kris.

He slid his hands under Gavin's arms and lifted him onto his lap. The little boy clutched the rabbit against him and snuggled against Tony's chest.

Was the boy trying to make him uncomfortable? Or win him over?

Winning him over wasn't necessary. He'd done that almost right from the start.

Gavin looked up at him and held the rabbit up for inspection. "Bunny."

Tony smiled. "That's a nice bunny. What's his name?"

"'Noball."

"Snowball. That's a good name for a white bunny."

"Uh-huh."

Gavin again held the rabbit against his chest and nestled closer to Tony. As conversation around the table resumed, Tony remained ultra-aware of the warm bundle in his lap. Warmth gradually pushed away his nervousness. When he looked at Kris, she was watching him with a soft smile.

Yes, Gavin had won him over, but he wasn't the only one. So had his pretty mother. Could there possibly be a chance for them? If Kris returned to the faith of her childhood and was eventually able to move past the death of her handsome Air Force husband, could they have something much deeper than friendship?

No. How could he even think about getting a ready-made family after Nick and Joanne lost their child while she was in his care? After three miscarriages and losing the one child they'd been able to have, watching him hold Gavin was probably sending a red-hot poker through their hearts.

He shifted his gaze to the opposite side of the table, where Nick sat with his wife. Instead of pain on his brother's face, Tony saw joy. The man was even smiling. So was Joanne.

They'd told him over and over that they didn't blame him. They'd insisted it could have happened with anyone, them included. Maybe they'd really meant it. Maybe someday he'd believe it for himself.

That day hadn't come yet.

Next to him, Kris pushed her chair back. "I'd better work on getting this mess cleaned up so we can all get out of here before dark."

With six of them handling cleanup and Mildred keeping both Bella and Gavin out from underfoot, everything was done in record time.

They moved into the large foyer, with its curved stairway rising to the second floor. At the front door, his dad thanked Kris for the meal and wrapped her in a warm hug. She stiffened for a brief moment before relaxing and returning the hug.

Tony stepped onto the porch first, Nick and Joanne behind him. His parents and Kris followed. Finally, Mildred walked out holding Gavin's hand in hers. The sun had sunk below the horizon, and the final remnants of daylight were barely hanging on.

Tony started down the porch steps toward the curved walk that led to the driveway. His truck sat some twenty feet away, behind Mildred's Camry, Kris's generator in the bed. His parents and Nick and Joanne had ridden together in his dad's F-250, parked on the opposite side of his Tundra.

An explosion rent the silence of the evening, the force knocking him against the porch railing. Behind him, someone screamed. Or maybe it was several someones.

He turned around. Mildred had scooped up Gavin and fled back inside. Kris was following. His father had stepped in front of his mother, as if to shield her with his own body, and Nick had Joanne wrapped in a protective hug.

When he spun back toward the driveway, the front half of his truck was in flames.

"Kris, get me a fire extinguisher."

When he'd arrived, his gas gauge had registered three-quarters. If the tank ignited, it would take out his dad's truck, Mildred's car and possibly Kris's detached garage.

Kris appeared on the porch with a fire extinguisher a half minute later. He didn't need to tell her to call 911. The officers watching the house were driving in their direction and would have already radioed dispatch. More units would be on their way, as would a fire truck.

If the explosion had happened a minute later, an ambulance would have been needed also. Actually, several ambulances.

Thank you, God.

When he got within ten feet of his truck, he pulled the pin on the extinguisher, took aim and squeezed the lever. The stream of dry powder shot from the end of the nozzle. Twenty seconds later, that stream was gone. Fortunately, all that remained of the fire was some smoke.

The unmarked unit drew to a stop at the edge of the road,

and the driver exited. "We've already called it in. Are you guys all right?"

"Except for being a little shaken up, we're fine. I just don't understand how someone got close enough to plant a bomb with you guys sitting fifty or sixty feet away."

"It wasn't planted here. You did leave for a short time this afternoon."

The man was right. He'd made his Publix run without giving it a second thought. Big mistake. Police were watching everywhere Kris went. They weren't watching him. Although he hadn't been in the store more than fifteen minutes, it had been enough time for someone to attach a bomb to his truck.

Kris moved up next to him. She'd apparently left Gavin inside with Mildred. "As soon as Mark's parents get back, I'm heading for Ohio."

She'd already let him know they'd responded to her message. She was welcome and could stay as long as she liked.

"That's a good idea." It was what he'd wanted her to do all along.

"You could have been killed. So could your parents and brother and sister-in-law." She shifted her gaze to the officer who had joined them. "As much as I want to make it easier for you to catch this guy, my presence is putting people I care about in danger. I can't stay."

Tony nodded. He was thinking about her while she was thinking about others. The reasons for her leaving didn't matter.

As long as they could keep her location a secret from the killer, she'd be safe.

That fact just about made it worth losing his truck.

Chapter Seven

The wind howled and rain beat against the roof and the plywood covering the windows. Around the room, several candles flickered from places well out of the reach of Bella's tail or nose. They'd lost power an hour ago. Already, the house was getting stuffy.

Although it was nearing midnight, Kris was too wound up to feel sleepy. The threat to her dog, the bomb planted under Tony's truck and now the storm hammering them—it was almost enough to make her want to beg for help from the God she hadn't spoken to since learning of Mark's death.

According to Tony, a security camera near the charter office had captured a boy of about ten or twelve setting the box containing the shredded stuffed animal in front of the neighboring store, but none of the cameras had picked up whoever had passed it off to him to begin with. This morning, Tony had gotten a rental and was still waiting to hear whether his truck would be declared a total loss. The preliminary investigation had determined that a homemade bomb had been taped to the Tundra's engine splash guard and remote detonated as they walked out the door.

What wasn't determined was whether the killer was just issu-

ing a warning or whether he'd planned to blow up the car with
Tony, Gavin and her inside. If the latter, maybe he'd changed
his mind when he'd seen that two other couples would likely
be collateral damage.

Kassie rose and walked to the double window, now covered
with plywood. She didn't look any more relaxed than Kris felt.
Neither did Tony. Even Ms. MaryAnn, Jared's grandmother,
was wide awake.

Only Gavin was oblivious to the storm raging outside.
Around ten, Kassie had made him a bed of blankets in the
corner. He'd snuggled with Snowball and gone promptly to
sleep. Kris envied him. She wasn't likely to sleep soundly again
until she got to her in-laws' house late Saturday night. Leaving
somehow felt like letting the killer win, but last night's attack
was the final straw.

Kassie cupped her hands on either side of her face and peered
through a small cutout in the plywood.

"See anything?" Kris asked.

"Nothing except a river flowing over the Plexiglas."

Tony shook his head. "I can't believe you have windows in
your plywood."

"That wasn't my doing. The prior owners had an overly curious twelve-year-old that kept wanting to peek out the front door
during Michael. So the dad cut an eight-by-ten opening in a
couple of the larger sheets and screwed Plexiglas against them."

She walked back to the chair she'd been sitting in. "It would
probably be a great idea if it wasn't pitch black out there and
the wind wasn't throwing solid sheets of rain against the front
of the house."

A muffled crash sounded from the back, and Kassie jumped.
"I hope that was just a limb and not the whole tree."

Kris winced. A huge oak tree stood in the backyard about
twenty feet from the bedrooms. If one of the larger limbs hit
the house, the roof would likely have extensive damage. If

the whole tree came down, it could take out the back half of the house.

Kassie picked up the flashlight she'd put on the coffee table before the power had gone out.

Tony rose, too. "I'll follow you."

Kris gave Ms. MaryAnn an uneasy smile. "I think it's going to be a long night."

"It is. But this isn't my first rodeo." She returned Kris's tight smile with one much more relaxed. The woman had a sense of peace about her that was at odds with the storm raging outside. "Jared put plywood on the windows, and we secured everything the best we could. The rest is up to the Lord. Of course, Jared and I prayed for protection over the house before he headed to the station and I came over here."

"If you want to extend some of those prayers to include this place and my house on Bayou Texar, we won't complain."

"We're already praying for protection here, but I'll be happy to include your place, too."

Kris waited for the mini sermon, but it didn't come. According to Kassie, Ms. MaryAnn was instrumental in getting her back into church, which led to her renewing the commitment she'd made as a child. But maybe preaching at her wasn't Ms. MaryAnn's style.

"Thank you for the prayers." Though she appreciated them, she didn't have near the confidence in them that Ms. MaryAnn seemed to have. Her own peace of mind came from good, solid storm shutters. And insurance.

The wind intensified, the howl becoming a roar. Gavin hugged his stuffed rabbit more tightly and released a sigh without waking up. The eye wall of the storm was supposed to pass about forty miles west of them. The fact they weren't getting the eye directly wasn't much consolation. The winds on the right side of the storm were always the strongest.

She frowned at Jared's grandmother. "Jared isn't out in this, is he?"

Ms. MaryAnn shook her head. "They're waiting it out at the station. As soon as it's safe to venture out, they'll be ready to respond to emergencies." She paused. "I don't know when his shift will actually end. I think it'll be all hands on deck for a while. Besides other emergencies, with power out and businesses shut down, there's always the concern about looting. But he'll make it home eventually."

Kris nodded. "Home" for Jared was currently with his grandmother. He'd moved in four months ago when she'd returned home after finishing rehab for a broken hip.

Now she was fully recovered, or close to it. In fact, she was already looking forward to getting back out on the pickleball court, which was how she'd broken her hip to begin with.

Jared was still there, without any immediate plans to leave. During his grandmother's convalescent period, he'd gotten to know Kassie and had fallen in love. Now he wasn't in any hurry to return to his home in nearby Nice. Ms. MaryAnn didn't seem to be anxious to throw him out, either.

Kris cast a glance toward the hallway. What was taking Kassie and Tony so long? Any discussion they might be having wasn't penetrating the howling of the storm outside. As much as she wanted to know how Kassie's house was faring, she didn't want to leave her son or Jared's grandmother to find out.

Finally, Kassie walked back into the room and laid the flashlight on the table.

Tony was right behind her. "There's no water coming in, not yet, anyway. No drips, no wetness on the ceiling as far as we can tell."

Kassie eased down on the couch next to Kris. "Thank the Lord, it looks like we dodged a bullet on that one."

Kris pursed her lips. "I hope mine is also faring well."

Tony eased down on her other side and gave her a casual sideways hug. "With those hurricane shutters we all installed, it should breeze through this."

Yeah, he was right. Her house was as protected as it could

possibly be, thanks to Tony and his family. They'd worked so hard, sacrificing their time for her when they'd obviously had their own homes to secure. They'd made it fun, too. The friction that had always characterized the Ashbaugh relationships had somehow bypassed the Sandersons.

It had all made for a really emotional day. The love and acceptance she'd experienced from the people she'd so long viewed as her enemies had put her on the verge of tears more than once. Even more unexpected was the longing that had risen up at odd times—the desire to be a part of this family. She wasn't naïve enough to believe the Sandersons were perfect, but compared to the Ashbaughs, they weren't far from it.

And then there was Tony. Learning what had really happened all those years ago, finding out that he had valued her friendship as much as she had valued his, had made it hard to hang on to her heart. But how could she give her heart to Tony when it still belonged to Mark? Tony deserved better than that. Gavin did, too. Tony was making headway—he was a lot more comfortable around him than he'd been at first. But her little boy deserved to have someone who was all-in.

She shook off the impractical thoughts. She and Tony would never be more than friends. The dream of becoming a part of his family was nothing but a fantasy. She had no doubt Tony cared for her. But he hadn't given her a single hint that he was interested in anything more than friendship, or that he was even attracted to her. Hugs had been for the sole purpose of providing comfort. That fierce sense of protectiveness he displayed was nothing more than he'd feel for any other woman, both as a cop and as a man.

She would never belong to the Sanderson family, but maybe she could eventually be a part of one just like it.

Tony took his arm from around her shoulders and leaned against her to pull his phone from his pants pocket. She watched his fingers slide across the screen.

How you guys faring?

The contact name across the top was Nick Sanderson. Yep, Tony backed up what she'd just been thinking. Instead of viewing everything in life as a competition, Tony and Nick cheered each other on, celebrating each other's accomplishments.

She and Kassie were slowly getting there. It had only taken them twenty-seven years. But when it came to Alyssa, they were still nowhere close.

She wouldn't be getting a text or phone call from Alyssa tonight. She was likely too wrapped up in her own problems to think about checking on her older sisters who were in the middle of a Cat. 4 hurricane.

Tony's phone buzzed with a reply.

Good so far. You?

Something hit house but seems OK.

Prayers.

Same here.

Yeah that was a conversation she and Alyssa would have... like never.

Kris's phone started to ring from its place on the end table, and she lifted her eyebrows. Maybe she'd been thinking bad thoughts about her younger sister unjustly. She rose and snatched up the phone. Alyssa's name wasn't displayed. Instead, the screen showed Blocked.

That didn't mean anything. It could still be Alyssa. Maybe she'd had to have her number changed and was having to lie low. Kris wouldn't be surprised. Whenever Alyssa found her way out of trouble, it didn't take her long to find her way back in.

Kris crossed the room and swiped to accept the call. The gravely voice on the other end of the line definitely wasn't Alyssa's.

"I was going to make it fast, but you've ticked me off. Now you'll go like the others."

Her breath hitched, and she stood frozen for several moments. Finally, she found her voice. "Who is this?"

Silence. She was speaking to dead air.

"Kris?" Tony rose and crossed the room. All other eyes were on her, too.

She slowly lowered the phone. "It was the killer. He said he'd planned to kill me fast, but now he's going to make me go like the others."

She shuddered at the image that flashed into her mind and stuck there in glaring detail—dark brown hair matted with dried blood, skull smashed in, bits of bone and tissue protruding. She shook her head to try to clear the image. It didn't help. Tony stepped closer and drew her into his arms. She slid her own around his waist, surrendering to the comfort and protection he offered.

When they'd found the body in the woods, he'd put one arm around her and pressed her against his side. The night of Shannon's murder, he'd reached into the truck to squeeze her shoulder, as he had on several occasions since.

This was different. Now he stood with both arms wrapped around her, squeezing her against him, the side of her face pressed against his chest. It had been eighteen long months since a man had held her like that, and tears rose up from some unknown place to sting her eyes. She would let him be her rock, however temporary that might be.

She spoke into his shirt. "My number was in Shannon's phone. He's been hanging on to it all this time."

Tony rested his chin on the top of her head, making her feel even more cocooned. She drew in a deep breath and released it slowly, allowing the tension to drain from her body.

"In a little over twenty-four hours, you'll be on your way to Ohio. In the meantime, I'm not going to let you out of my sight."

She closed her eyes. Soon she'd be gone, far away from Pensacola and all its threats.

Far away from her family. Far away from Tony.

Safety was requiring too much sacrifice.

How long would it be before she'd get her life back? Sometimes serial killers escaped justice for years. Some were never caught.

Would it ever be safe for her to return home?

And what about her relationship with Tony? After dinner last night, Gavin had climbed into his lap, and he didn't look ready to bolt from the room. He'd seemed to relax, had even wrapped an arm around her little boy.

How long would it take for Gavin to weave his way into Tony's heart so thoroughly that that "package deal" would be exactly what he wanted? And how long would it take for her to let go of everything she had with Mark and love again?

If she could stay, would there be a chance for Tony and her?

Maybe she would never know.

Yes, safety was requiring far too much sacrifice.

Kris stepped over a downed tree limb and made her way through the thick carpet of twigs and leaves that covered Kassie's yard. Tony walked next to her, Kassie a short distance ahead. A large limb lay on the roof, the source of the crash they'd heard last night. Other smaller ones were scattered about the asphalt shingles.

The power was still out. It likely wouldn't be restored for several days, much longer in outlying areas.

Kassie peered up with a frown. "That probably did some damage, but I'm guessing it's just surface. If it had put a hole in the roof decking, I'd have some major water stains in my spare bedroom."

Tony nodded. "I'll try to get up there today to clean off the roof and see what we have."

"If we need to tarp it, I've got a couple in the garage."

That would be a common sight for the next few months—neighborhoods a patchwork of blue tarps.

Tony continued. "Let's check the rest of the house. Then we'll see how Ms. MaryAnn's place fared."

They'd left her inside with Gavin. She'd agreed that she didn't need to be traipsing through an obstacle course so soon after recovering from a broken hip. She'd already announced her plans for a long nap as soon as she could safely return home.

When they'd all finally gone to bed at three in the morning, the outer bands had still been battering them. Kris had carried Gavin with her to the spare bedroom, Tony had stretched out on the couch and Ms. MaryAnn had insisted she'd be quite comfortable in the recliner.

Those nap plans Ms. MaryAnn had mentioned had a lot of appeal. Maybe Kris would be able to squeeze one in herself this afternoon. Making a drive from Florida to Ohio in her sleep-deprived state didn't seem much safer than staying where there was a killer after her.

When they'd finished circling the house, Kassie crossed her arms. "I know how I'll be spending my day. It'll take hours to haul the limbs to the road and rake the yard. Then I'll see how much cleanup I can do next door by the time Jared gets home."

That would be another common sight—huge piles of yard debris stacked along the road until the authorities could haul it all away.

Kassie continued. "But first, the plywood has to go so I can open the windows. We'll want to get the generator hooked up, too."

Since it had been in the bed of his truck and the explosion had just impacted the front, the generator had survived. It wasn't powerful enough to run the air conditioner, but they could keep their phones charged and have lights. The refrigerator and freezer would work, too.

Tony looked at Kassie. "I'll do what I can, until I get called in, anyway." He shifted his gaze to Kris. "Once we get the plywood down and the generator going, we'll check your place."

An ache formed in her stomach at the thought. Homes right on the water almost always fared worse in hurricanes.

At least her protection detail was back on this morning. She'd been relieved to see the SUV when she'd peered out the front door upon getting up.

Tony held out a hand. "Let's check your neighbor's place. I'm sure she's anxiously awaiting word."

Jared's grandmother's yard looked much the same as Kassie's—buried beneath a blanket of limbs, twigs and leaves. The house itself was fine. Even the shed out back was untouched. Maybe the prayers the older lady had sent up had done some good. Hopefully, they'd worked for the Ashbaugh family home, too.

Kassie fell into step beside Kris. "What do you say we have Tony hook up the generator, and while he's taking down plywood, we can whip up some scrambled eggs and sausage for this hungry bunch?"

"That sounds good."

"We'll need to check the charter office building, too."

Kris followed her into the house while Tony headed to the garage to get them some temporary power. If the office building sustained damage, Kassie would be dealing with it alone, on top of handling the operations of the charter business and keeping Kassie's Kuts running smoothly.

Kris pulled the door shut behind them. This was the worst possible time for her to bail. If she had another option, she'd take it.

Ms. MaryAnn looked up from the book she'd been reading to Gavin. He sat in her lap, Snowball clutched against his chest.

"How bad is it?"

"Not bad at all," Kassie said. "Everything's a mess, but it doesn't look like there are repairs to make beyond some possible missing or damaged shingles. Tony's hooking up the generator so we've got lights and refrigeration, and we're going to make some breakfast on the camp stove."

"Good. Your little one here has been saying he's hungry. I told him his mommy and auntie would be back inside in a few minutes."

She returned to her reading. It was a story about Noah's ark. Kassie had several Bible stories mixed in with the popular fairytales, and when given a choice, those were what she usually read to him.

Kris didn't mind. Despite her own lack of faith, she had no problem with her sister teaching him about God. Even though she'd turned her back on God, she couldn't get away from the feeling that she'd be shortchanging her little boy if she didn't at least expose him to Christianity so when he got older, he could make an informed choice.

But she had time. Bringing him to church wasn't that important at his age. Or maybe it was.

She and Kassie had just started breakfast preparations when most of the lights in the front of the house came on.

"Woo-hoo!" Kassie gave her a big grin. "We've got power. Since the AC isn't kicking on, I'm guessing we've got Tony to thank rather than Florida Power."

While waiting for the sausage patties to brown, Kris glanced into the living room. Tony was right outside the front window, judging from the whine of the screw gun. The plywood shifted, and glove-covered fingers wrapped around the top and bottom.

When he'd set the large sheet aside, he smiled at her through the glass. She gave him a friendly wave, and her heart made a little flip. Fortunately, he couldn't see the latter. She needed to get a grip. Finding out she'd had a crush on him in high school had probably been uncomfortable enough for him. If he had an inkling of the feelings she was struggling with now, awkward wouldn't begin to describe the experience.

Maybe she was being too hard on herself. With everything she'd been through the past year and a half, it was no wonder her emotions were all over the place. Once she was out of danger and got settled back into her old life, she'd regain the control she craved.

She and Kris had just finished the eggs and sausage when the front door creaked open.

Tony stepped into the kitchen. "That's it. The windows are all uncovered, and the pieces of plywood are stored back in your garage."

Kassie carried a stack of paper plates and plastic cups to the table. "Perfect timing. Breakfast is ready. I don't entertain like my sister does." She plunked two cartons on the table—one of milk and one of orange juice—next to a carafe of coffee. "Especially right after a hurricane."

"Hey, as long as there's plenty and it tastes good, I'm happy. Based on what I'm looking at and how it smells, you succeeded on both counts."

The food had just been blessed and passed when Kris's phone buzzed with a text. She'd left it charging on the kitchen counter. It was probably someone checking to see how they'd weathered the storm. They could wait until she'd eaten.

She refused to entertain the other possibility, that the killer was making another threat, this one by text.

Tony's buzzed a few seconds later, and he pulled it from his pocket. "Uh-oh."

"What?"

"A mobile home park got hit hard. Apparently the storm spawned a tornado. A lot of the homes are flattened. Not everyone evacuated."

"We're doing a search and rescue operation?"

He narrowed his eyes at her. "There's no *we* to it."

Her heart kicked into high gear. She always felt a bit of an adrenaline rush when she got those notifications. Even more so now.

"Your guys can watch me there just as well as here or at the charter office. Even more so. The place will be crawling with law enforcement and rescue workers."

"Don't even think about it."

"This is likely your last shot at trying to catch this guy when you have an inclination of when and where he might strike."

And if they were successful in apprehending him today, she wouldn't have to flee her home.

Tony was quiet. Whether he was considering her words or thinking of ways to strengthen his argument, she wasn't sure.

"Look, if I leave, there's no guarantee that he won't somehow find me. The only way I'll truly be safe is for you guys to get him off the street."

She looked at her sister. "Kassie, tell him I'm right. I can't leave you to handle everything on your own. I need to make this one last-ditch effort to ensure my safety and preserve your sanity."

Kassie held up both hands. "Don't involve me in this. I totally get where you're coming from, but I can see Tony's point, too."

Kris shifted her gaze to Ms. MaryAnn. She'd take an ally wherever she could get one.

The older woman shook her head. "I'm not touching this one."

Tony heaved a sigh. "I'm not saying yes, but I'm not saying no, either. I'll talk to those in charge and see how they want this to go down.

"Good."

All she could do was wait and see. Without the blessing of the police, she wouldn't even attempt it, no matter how many rescue workers were around.

Not even with Tony at her side.

Chapter Eight

Tony eased the Nissan Rogue to a stop at a darkened traffic light, Kris in the passenger seat beside him and Bella in the back. Gavin had stayed behind with Ms. MaryAnn. Tony hadn't received word yet on the fate of his Tundra. In the meantime, the rental wasn't a bad ride.

After waiting for a vehicle to pass in front of him, he looked both ways before creeping through himself. With no working traffic lights in town, every intersection was being treated as a four-way stop.

He glanced in his rearview mirror. The vehicle that had been parked in front of Kassie's this morning was framed there. It would stay with them throughout the day. Kassie was behind it, waiting to get through the same intersection they'd both just cleared.

The dark traffic lights weren't the only sign of the storm that had ravaged the area last night. Signs in front of businesses had been blown out, leaving only the frames. The wind had lifted several carport roofs, curling them back over houses or tearing them completely off and depositing them some distance away.

They'd only gone a few blocks but had already passed two houses split almost in half by huge uprooted oak trees. Road crews had come through and cleared the main streets, but debris covered the parking lots, driveways and yards.

He glanced over at Kris. Her eyebrows were drawn together, forming vertical creases between them. The view outside the SUV's windows wasn't doing anything to alleviate that concern.

He still hadn't apologized to her for snapping at her a couple of nights ago. He should have done it right away, but there'd been the situation with the box. The next day, they'd been busy with hurricane prep. Yesterday, he'd worked his shift, and they'd gone straight to Kassie's.

He drew in a stabilizing breath. He needed to tell her he was sorry, and putting it off wasn't going to make it any easier.

"I owe you an apology."

She didn't respond. When he cast her a sideways glance, she was staring out the front windshield, waiting for him to continue.

"You were right that something happened. You asked me what it was, and I didn't want to talk about it." He still didn't.

She crossed her arms. "I would say I shouldn't have pushed, but I didn't push. I just offered a listening ear."

"I know you did, and I was wrong. I shouldn't have snapped at you."

He turned onto Yates. It hadn't been cleared like the main roads. Small limbs and twigs crunched beneath his tires as he proceeded toward Kris's street. He weaved around a large tree limb that someone had pulled toward the edge of the road.

Kris sat in silence. He did, too. But he wasn't finished, not by a long shot. He just couldn't seem to find the words.

She uncrossed her arms and let her hands rest in her lap. "You know all about my dysfunctional family. You were there when my mom took off. That was ten years ago. In all that time, none of us have gotten so much as a postcard. She embraced her new life and made a clean break with the old, even though that old life included three devastated daughters. And you know that messed-up younger sister I have? She's twenty-five and still hasn't gotten her life straightened out. And then there's my dad. He wasn't just an alcoholic. He was also a drug runner."

She heaved a sigh and let her head rest against the seat. "I know we're just friends, and that's all we'll ever be, but even friends share with one another."

"I know." He didn't acknowledge her statement that they'd never be more than friends, or the unexpected stab of pain that shot through him with the thought. He couldn't tell her how he felt, that he was dangerously close to falling in love with her. The confession would serve no purpose. He wasn't the father her little boy needed, but someone out there was. Both Kris and Gavin deserved that chance for happiness.

He crept down the road, glad for the distraction of driving. If he didn't have to look at Kris while he told his story, he wouldn't have to see the judgment in her eyes.

"June, a year ago, Nick and Joanne took a weekend trip for their anniversary. They left me to take care of their ten-month-old daughter. I put her to bed and went in to check on her a short time later. She was sleeping peacefully. I turned on the TV, watched a movie. When it was over, I wanted to check on her once more before heading to bed myself."

He tightened his fingers around the steering wheel as unwanted images crashed into his mind. After drawing in a stabilizing breath, he continued.

"I opened her door and tiptoed into her room. I could barely see her in the light coming in from the hallway. She was lying on her back, the way I had left her, her face turned toward me. But something didn't look right."

"Oh, no." She whispered the words. She'd already figured out where the story was heading.

"Her stomach wasn't rising and falling, and even in the poor lighting, her coloring looked wrong." Or maybe that part had been his imagination, fear taking over. "I turned on the bedside lamp, and her lips had a bluish tint. Her ears did, too. I checked, and she definitely wasn't breathing."

The events that followed played through his mind, almost immobilizing him. A warm hand settled over his, still gripping the wheel. The touch gave him the strength to continue.

"I tried to revive her. I dialed 911, put the dispatcher on speaker phone and continued to work on Zoe through the whole conversation. Nothing I did worked."

Not even prayer. Granted, his prayers weren't eloquent. They were nothing but *God, please* over and over. He didn't know whether Nick and Joanne had ever asked why, but *he* certainly had.

He stopped in Kris's driveway. The unmarked vehicle following them parked at the edge of the road, and Kassie pulled in behind the Nissan. Except for the debris scattered around it, the house looked much the same as it had when he'd left it two days ago. If there was damage, it was most likely in the back.

He killed the Rogue's engine and let his hands fall to his lap. "If only I would have checked on her sooner. I waited the entire length of the movie."

He turned his head until his gaze met hers, steeling himself for the blame he expected to see. There wasn't any. Instead, sympathy and understanding filled her eyes.

She shook her head. "You had already checked on her, and she was fine. This could have happened at any time. She could have stopped breathing when you were sound asleep."

"But she didn't. This happened on my watch. If I would have checked on her sooner, I might have been able to save her. Or if I had decided to read instead of watch TV, I might have heard something. This is all on me. That's why I've vowed to never again be responsible for someone else's child." Maybe he shouldn't even be responsible for his own.

Her face fell. Was it from the realization that they could never be together? Or was what happened a non-issue because she wasn't interested in anything more than friendship anyway?

She spoke softly. "Do Nick and Joanne blame you?"

"They never have. They've insisted that the outcome probably wouldn't have been any different if they'd been there."

No, his brother and sister-in-law didn't blame him, but he'd never been able to stop blaming himself. How would he ever move past the trauma of holding his dead niece in his arms?

"They're right, you know. Sudden infant death syndrome has taken countless babies' lives. This wasn't your fault. You can't keep living under a burden of guilt that isn't yours to carry."

She again rested her hand on his, this time sliding her fingers into his palm. Her reassuring squeeze conveyed her acceptance. It was like salve on the tattered pieces of his heart.

"Thank you." He returned the squeeze. He appreciated the thought, but it didn't change anything. He had let his niece die while he'd been watching TV thirty feet from where she'd been sleeping.

He forced a small smile. "Are you ready to check out your place?"

"As ready as I'll ever be."

They stepped from the SUV, and Kassie met Kris at the passenger door.

"It's still standing, so that's a good sign."

Kris opened the back door, and Bella jumped out. Not only was the house still standing, but viewed from the front, there wasn't any obvious damage. They'd know for sure once they checked the upstairs for water intrusion and walked around back.

Kris unclipped her keys from her purse and made her way toward the front door, Kassie following. Tony trailed behind. There was a sidewalk under him somewhere, hidden beneath all the leaves and twigs that had blown from the trees.

The flowering plants and other ornamentals he'd admired on prior visits were buried also. He'd make it a point to get over here as soon as possible and see what he could salvage of all her hard work.

When Kris opened the front door, Bella was the first one inside, clearly excited to be home. After a quick tour of the first floor, Kris hurried up the stairs and into her bedroom. It looked the same as it had the last time he'd walked in, minus Gavin's crib, which he'd disassembled and taken to the office.

Tony looked up at the ceiling, something he hadn't done the last time he'd been here. "It looks like you have some staining."

Kris nodded. "That was from Michael. We ended up getting the roof reshingled, courtesy of the insurance company. We just never got around to hitting the ceilings with a stain blocker."

She frowned. "After this much time, there's probably no excuse. For the past several years, Dad had been dealing with his issues and sort of let the place go. And since I moved in here a year and a half ago, any repairs beyond the urgent just haven't been high on my priority list."

She led them into the two spare bedrooms and finally the large room at the other end. Judging from the masculine furnishings and the appearance of having been untouched for months, it had likely been her father's room.

Each of the rooms along the back had the same staining, which Kris insisted hadn't changed. Apparently, the roof had held up well.

Kris led them toward the stairs. Upon a closer look, it wasn't just the ceiling that needed attention. The hardwood floor needed buffing and waxing, and the walls could do with a fresh coat of paint.

Maybe he could announce a Sanderson work day. He didn't even have to get the go-ahead from his father or brother. They'd be on board. So would his mom and Joanne.

Except Kris might not appreciate being their project. She'd accepted help with hurricane prep. She'd had no choice. Aside from the fact that someone was trying to kill her, she would never have been able to handle all those shutters by herself, especially on the second-floor windows.

But this was different. There was no nature-imposed deadline. She would insist that she could handle it, that she'd get to it eventually. He could be just as insistent.

When they exited and circled the house, the side and back looked much the same as the front.

Tony picked up a two-foot-by-three-foot piece of thin plywood, its edges weathered and rotting. One side was painted white, and an oval hole had been cut out, with a screen stapled over the opening

He held up the piece. "Looks like you lost some soffit."

Inspection of the eaves confirmed his suspicions. Judging from the voids, more than one piece had come down.

He turned around and looked toward the water, past a large cypress tree. "Oh, man, your gazebo is flattened."

Kris followed his gaze, and hardness entered hers. "Good riddance. I've always hated that thing anyway."

At his lifted brows, she continued. "My dad had it built right after my mom left, like a monument to her infidelity."

He stepped to the side to gain a clearer view of that part of the shoreline. Boards were strewn along the beach, with railings and sections of roof mixed in. The floor had even been lifted from its supports and lay much closer to the water than he remembered.

Something else was there, too, protruding from the sand. Something that didn't look like wood or any kind of construction material.

Without offering an explanation, he walked toward the water's edge. Three of the gazebo's support posts were still embedded in the ground. The other three were missing, washed somewhere down the beach or out into the bayou.

But it was what was in the center of those remaining posts that had snagged his gaze and held it.

Bones.

Were they human? He couldn't be sure, but they looked a lot like a femur and the two smaller bones in the lower leg.

A soft gasp behind him was the first indication that someone had followed him. Kassie and Kris stood side by side, eyes wide. Each had a hand covering her mouth.

Bella shot past them and started to dig. Tony sprang toward the dog, but before he could reach her, Kris's voice cut through his panic. "Bella, come."

Her tone was commanding, with a mild sternness. The dog obeyed immediately, trotted to her and sat down at her side.

He looked back at the find on the beach. Bella had unearthed some smaller bones. Without poking around, he couldn't say for sure, but if he had to guess, he'd say he was looking at part of a human hand.

He pulled his phone from his pocket. "We need to call the authorities. This will need to be preserved and properly investigated."

Kassie looked at Kris. "Do you think Dad knew someone was buried here?"

Kris shook her head. "I don't know. Maybe he didn't. Maybe it was coincidental that that's the spot he picked to build the gazebo."

Kassie gave her the same *get real* look she used to give her when they'd argued as teenagers.

But Kris wasn't that naïve. The lack of conviction in her tone said she didn't believe her words any more than he and Kassie did.

He had questions of his own, beyond *Did he know?* What he really wanted to find out was whether Ashbaugh had anything to do with disposing of the body, or even more importantly, whether the death had happened by his hand.

Maybe the biggest question of all was whose bones were they? Did those bones have anything to do with their mother's disappearance? Neither Kassie nor Kris was ready for a bombshell like that.

He'd known about their mother leaving and how it had affected each one of the girls. He'd been there to see the devastation. Their father had retreated into the bottle and never found his way out. Kassie had cried for weeks on end. Kris's pain had rapidly turned into hatred. Alyssa had simply gone off the deep end.

Identifying the bones would take time, but he was confident what they would reveal. Learning their mother didn't leave them by choice would be good for Kris, but finding out her father likely killed her and hid her body under the gazebo would shatter her. Whatever the outcome, he'd be there for her.

Kris spun away from the gazebo's remains. "We'll let the authorities handle it."

As she stalked toward the house, Bella trotted behind her, and Tony fell in next to her. Her jaw was set in determination. Whether it was a refusal to believe her father could have done the unthinkable or a determination to be strong whatever the outcome, he wasn't sure.

She'd always been close to the man, had even seemed to put him on a pedestal. Watching him fall from that position of honor in her thoughts to a lowly criminal had to have devastated her.

Kassie trailed behind them, not attempting to engage her sister in conversation. He and Kassie had both spent enough time with her to know better than to try to talk to her when she was upset. Even a comforting hug wouldn't be well received right now, no matter how badly he wanted to give it.

She rounded the corner of the house and headed for the front door, key ready. "I'm locking up. My phone's in my purse, but it's probably time to be heading out."

Tony frowned. He'd rather she not remind him. As much as he didn't like it, Kris was right. Allowing her to participate in the search and rescue operation, under the watchful eye of the Pensacola Police Department, was their last best chance to catch this guy.

Everyone else had agreed, too. Besides the unmarked unit currently waiting beside the road, several other law enforcement officers would be on site in plain clothes, spread throughout the park, keeping watch while they blended in with the rescue workers.

God, please give us a break.

He wanted to catch this guy in the worst way. He just didn't want to put Kris in jeopardy in the process.

And please protect Kris while we try to do this.

Bella picked her way up a haphazard mountain of wallboard, studs, pipes, insulation, electrical wiring and broken glass while Kris waited on the ground a few yards away.

The dog was working off leash. Based on the excitement rippling through her body, someone was buried somewhere in the hodgepodge of building materials that used to be a double-wide mobile home.

Tony stood with Kris, watching Bella move across the pile, alternating looking down and lifting her head to sniff the air.

Suddenly, the dog stopped, stood stock still, then sat.

Tony leaned toward Kris. "What's she doing?"

"She just alerted." Kris's pulse kicked into high gear, and she hollered at a rescue worker standing in front of a home catty-corner from them. "We've got someone over here."

The man hurried toward them, speaking into his radio as he walked. Within a minute, two others had joined him.

Kris turned away to head down the street. As much as she'd love to see the fruit of Bella's labor and actually witness the rescue, the two of them still had work to do.

There were two more damaged homes to check on her assigned street. The residents of both had told the manager of the park that they would evacuate, so those homes had been assigned a lower priority and left till last.

Those evacuation plans weren't always a sure thing, though. The resident of the home they'd just left had done the same thing and then apparently changed their mind. He or she was likely regretting the decision.

Kris walked down the street toward another collapsed home.

The damage to the park was clearly the work of a tornado. It had touched down at one edge and then cut a jagged path through the center, leaving some homes untouched and others completely demolished.

The place they'd just left had been Bella's second find of the day. The first one had happened just before lunchtime. The dog had worked tirelessly since they'd arrived—seven straight hours with a couple of short breaks.

With plenty of workers wandering around the park, Tony's primary job had been protecting her. So far, his protection hadn't been needed. There'd been no sign of the killer or anyone who looked at all suspicious.

It made sense. To attack her when she was surrounded by so many people, the man would have to be insane. Or incredibly bold.

She'd been hoping for the latter. After succeeding several times, killers sometimes got overconfident and took reckless chances just for the thrill of it. It was often those reckless chances that gave the authorities the breaks they needed to catch the guys.

So far, that wasn't happening. It was late afternoon, and the search was drawing to a close. The slim chance that she wasn't going to have to leave for Ohio early tomorrow morning had gotten even slimmer.

The search for survivors in the wreckage of the last two homes didn't take long. No one was there. She headed back toward the Nissan, which Tony had parked at the end of the next street over. He walked next to her, his T-shirt spotted with perspiration and the radio he'd carried all day attached to the waistband of his jeans.

He pulled the keys from his pocket but was too far away to use the fob. "Any ideas for dinner?"

"Not a clue."

"I vote for takeout."

"Sounds like a plan." The last thing she felt like doing was cooking. "I need to go back by the house so I can get packed for my trip north."

"We'll need to make it fast. I want to get you inside your sister's house well before dark."

She frowned. "I'll do my best."

Gathering their things together for the stay above the charter office had been a breeze. But how would she even begin to pack for an out-of-state trip with no idea of how long she'd be gone?

When they reached the end of the road, they rounded the corner. The Nissan sat in the distance. A boy of about twelve or thirteen barreled toward them, with one of the men who'd been watching the charter office about twenty feet behind him.

Tony sidestepped, his arms shooting out to grab the kid. As the boy veered around him, Tony extended his foot. The kid went briefly airborne before crashing to the asphalt. Tony dropped to his knees next to him and grasped his arms before he could rise and take off again.

The man who had been chasing him closed the gap between them, breathing heavily. "He put something on the windshield of the Nissan, an envelope or piece of paper. When he saw us approaching, he ran."

Tony pulled the kid to his feet, and he made a futile attempt to twist away. "Let me go."

"Not yet. First, we're going to see what you left for us."

Keeping a firm grip on the boy's wrist, Tony led them to the rental vehicle. A sheet of paper was folded in thirds and tucked under one of the wiper blades. Tony removed it, handling it much more carefully than the kid probably had.

After passing the boy off to the other man, he unfolded the sheet, touching just the corners. Kris craned her neck, but couldn't read what was there.

Tony skimmed the page, and his features darkened. "Did you write this?"

"No. I don't even know what it is." He looked from Tony to the other man. "Are you guys cops or something?"

Neither of them answered the question.

The kid tried again to jerk his arm free. "Look, I didn't do anything wrong."

"Then why did you run?"

"The guy who gave me this said to make sure no one saw me."

"What guy was that?"

"I don't know who he was."

"What did he look like?"

The kid's gaze shifted to the side. "I didn't pay any attention."

"What was he driving?"

"I didn't pay any attention to that, either."

Tony continued as if he didn't notice the obvious signs the boy was lying. "Where did you meet this guy?"

"On the road that runs in front of the mobile home park."

"So, he gave you the note. Then what?"

"He said he'd give me twenty bucks if I put it on your windshield."

"Anything you can tell us that will help us find this guy?"

"Uh-uh."

"What's your name?"

"Noah."

Tony bent at the waist, putting him almost eye level with the kid. "Let me tell you something, Noah. We *are* cops. The note you delivered threatens this lady's life. That puts you in a lot of trouble, so you'd better start talking. What did the guy look like?"

He hesitated only a moment longer. "He had blond hair, a little past his shoulders, and a beard and mustache."

Tony straightened. "How about his vehicle?"

"He got out of a car."

"Not a pickup truck?"

"No, definitely a car."

"What kind?"

"I don't know."

Tony narrowed his eyes.

"I'm telling you the truth. It was silver, or more like gray, because it wasn't shiny. It looked older. But I don't know what kind it was."

"Two-door or four-door?"

"Four-door."

Tony looked at the other man. "How about calling it in? He's probably long gone, but we know we're looking for an older gray sedan. Same suspect."

While the other man spoke into his radio, Tony shifted his attention back to the kid. "Anything else you noticed?"

Noah shook his head. "Don't tell him I told you. He looks really strong. If he found me and knew I told, I think he'd hurt me."

"It'll be our little secret."

Kris watched Noah hurry away and turned to Tony. "What does the note say?"

She steeled herself for his answer. He'd already said it contained a threat. Judging from the anger on his face when he'd read it, the threat was serious.

He moved to stand beside her and held the note where she could see it.

Large block print filled the page, written with a Sharpie.

YOUR TURN. I'M READY FOR BOTH YOUR DOG AND YOUR BOYFRIEND.

She looked up at Tony. "I'm leaving in less than twelve hours. If you can keep me safe that long and see me on my way, by this time tomorrow, I'll be arriving in Cincinnati."

"I'm not letting you out of my sight. Let's hurry and get what you need from your place." He looked at the other man. "You're following us?"

"All the way to the charter office, then others will take over."

As he walked away, Tony opened the back door of the Nissan. Bella hopped in and stretched out beside Gavin's car seat. "I know John will be sitting right out front, but I want to make this as quick as we can."

"Will do." If she forgot anything, she'd buy it in Ohio.

She climbed into the passenger seat and looked back at Bella. "You worked hard today. Good girl."

Her tail pounded the seat.

Tony cranked the engine and drove toward the park entrance. As he drew to a stop, waiting for traffic to clear, she looked in the side mirror. A dark Ford Explorer sat directly behind them, John at the wheel.

Tony pulled out, and she looked over at him. "I was really hoping you guys were going to catch this guy today. I know it was a long shot, but still."

"I had hoped so, too." He slid her a sideways glance before returning his eyes to the road. "I don't want you to leave."

She studied him, waiting for him to continue. He wasn't relaxed. She could see it in the tightness of his jaw, the tension in his shoulders, the way he was gripping the wheel. Was he developing feelings for her that went beyond friendship and wasn't sure how to tell her?

What about her own feelings? In spite of how hard she'd fought it, she was falling for him. A wave of guilt swept through her. If she was thinking of moving on this quickly, what did that say of the importance of what she'd had with Mark?

Seconds ticked by in silence, except for the hum of the Nissan's engine. If Tony was having romantic thoughts toward her, he didn't seem very anxious to admit it.

She released a sigh. "I don't *want* to leave."

Maybe she should make it easier for him and share her own feelings. But what if she was misreading him? What if he still thought of her as simply a close friend and she confessed to feeling more?

No, she'd been there, done that and was still embarrassed by it. If he wanted to pursue a romantic relationship with her, he was going to have to spell it out clearly…in neon. She wasn't about to put herself out there a second time.

She shifted her gaze to stare out the front windshield. "One good thing came out of today. Now you know you're not just looking for a pickup."

"I know. Either he ditched the pickup, or he owns more than one vehicle."

A heavy silence descended between them again, the weight of words not shared. He'd told her this morning about what had happened with his niece. Maybe he had let that be a barrier between them—the fear that something like that could happen again. They could work through that.

There was one other barrier, one that she didn't want to think about. Through her adolescence, her mother had often warned of the dangers of being "unequally yoked." Though she'd never said an unkind word about their father, Kris had been able to read between the lines: if she'd have married a man who shared her faith—not just shared it, but really tried to live it out—the relationships in their home would have been far different.

Tony would have been raised with the same strong beliefs. He'd apparently never wavered in his commitment to God. She and Kassie both had, but Kassie had come back. Kris would, too, when she was ready.

That day was getting closer. All of her excuses for walking away were crumbling. Her mother hadn't left her faith and her children. The results wouldn't be back for some time, but Kris didn't need positive identification to know that those bones hidden under the gazebo belonged to her mom. The Sanderson family hadn't failed her, either. Contrary to her father's lies, Jerry Sanderson had done nothing but show Christian love and kindness.

The only thing she still had to come to terms with was God taking Mark. Over the past eighteen months, she'd asked why dozens of times. She hadn't gotten an answer, or even any sign that God was listening. Maybe He was, and she just couldn't hear Him through the anger and mental and emotional anguish.

She let her head fall back against the seat, and soon her eyelids grew heavy. Tomorrow she'd have to be up before daylight, and she was already exhausted. The eleven-hour drive was going to require cold AC, upbeat music and multiple cups of coffee.

By the time they'd picked up Gavin from Ms. MaryAnn's it was dusk. Tony pulled into her driveway, and John parked the Explorer at the edge of the street.

When she reached for her door handle, Tony held up his hand. "Wait here while I check the house."

"Good idea." She and Gavin and Bella would be safe with John sitting twenty feet away.

She handed him her keys, and he returned a few minutes later. "All clear. Let's make this fast."

As Tony headed to the living room with Bella, she removed a flashlight from the hall closet. The final remnants of afternoon sunlight drifting through the windows left most of the house in shadow. That minimal light wouldn't last long.

She picked up Gavin and hurried up the stairs. After putting him in his crib with a variety of toys, she clicked on the flashlight and entered the large walk-in closet. One large and one medium-size suitcase should do it. She laid them open on the bed. There was no time for her usual detailed packing list. She'd do her best, but she'd probably be making an emergency shopping trip in the near future.

She pulled a few pairs of jeans and dress pants from the closet, then chose coordinating blouses. Next would be shorts and shirts. Shoes, too. All she'd brought to the charter office was her hiking boots, tennis shoes and a pair of boat shoes. She piled each item on the bed as it came to mind. What if her stay extended into late September or October, even November? She and Gavin would need warm clothes. Sweaters, jackets, mittens, knit hats. She heaved a sigh, suddenly stalled out.

The problem was she didn't want to make this trip. Under normal circumstances, she loved visiting her in-laws. She'd felt close to them almost immediately upon meeting them. But this was different. She was having to leave Tony, with no idea of when she'd see him again. Another pang of guilt stabbed her. Mark had been gone a year and a half. How long was long enough?

"Kris?" Tony's voice drifted up from the bottom of the stairs.

"Don't rush me." She snapped her mouth closed, but the snippy words had already escaped. "I'm sorry. I'm almost done."

"I was just letting you know I'm taking Bella out. I think she needs to go. She's standing at attention at the front door."

"Go ahead. We'll be down in about ten minutes."

When she'd folded and packed her clothes into the larger suitcase, she started on Gavin's. Less than ten minutes later, she was ready.

"Come on, sweetie." She lifted him from the crib.

After wheeling both suitcases down the hall, she hollered at Tony from the top of the stairs. "We're done. Can you lug the suitcases down?"

No answer.

"Tony?"

He apparently hadn't come back inside yet. Ten minutes was more than enough time for Bella to do her business. Maybe he was at the road talking with John.

"Okay, buddy. Let's go find Mr. Tony. Hold Mommy's flashlight."

"'Kay."

Leaving the suitcases there, she picked up Gavin and headed down the stairs, the beam of the flashlight bouncing along the wall at her side. The light that had shone through the windows when she arrived was gone.

When she crossed the foyer to the front door, it was locked. That made sense. Tony wouldn't leave them in an unlocked house, even when he'd be right outside. Maybe he'd left her keys inside and was currently locked out.

After putting Gavin down, she swung the door open and stepped onto the porch. "Tony?"

Still no answer. Where was he? Had he walked Bella around back?

She glanced at the Explorer still sitting beside the road. She couldn't see inside.

"Tony?"

Still no answer. The hair on the back of her neck stood on end. Something wasn't right.

She backed into the house. Before she could get the door closed, a figure shot across the yard and charged up the front steps. She slammed the door. As she reached for the lock, the door exploded against her, knocking her into the Bombay chest on the opposite wall.

She screamed loud and long. Gavin stood a few feet away, clutching the flashlight, his own wail dissolving into hysterical sobs. An icy block of dread filled her chest. The boater stood staring down at her, holding an object she didn't recognize in his right hand, illuminated by the beam of the flashlight.

She stepped in front of Gavin, shielding him with her own body. He dropped the light and wrapped both arms around one of her legs, still sobbing.

"What do you want?" It was a stupid question, but maybe if she stalled, it would give Tony or John time to come to her aid.

"You're what I want." He looked down at Gavin. "This one's just insurance, something to guarantee that you'll cooperate."

He raised his arm. "Do you know what this is?"

The flashlight was still on, its beam making a diagonal path across the hardwood floor. It no longer illuminated what he held.

"It's a Taser. Have you ever seen what one of these can do to a full-grown man, especially when set on high? Right now, your boyfriend is lying in your side yard pretty much incapacitated. So is that plainclothes cop you had watching you. They'll both recover pretty quick. I'm not sure about the dog."

The panic over Bella's fate barely registered before the man pointed the weapon toward Gavin. "Just think what this could do to a little boy."

She dropped to her knees. "Please. Do whatever you want to me, but don't hurt my little boy."

"Take his hand. We're gonna walk outside to that white Nissan, and you're gonna drive us."

"I don't have the keys."

He reached into his front pocket with his free hand. When he pulled it out, a ring of keys dangled from his index finger.

Tony's keys.

He'd been in such bad shape the killer had been able to take his keys without him putting up a fight. How could one man sneak up on two trained police officers and incapacitate them both?

As her abductor led her to the vehicle sitting in the drive, he held the Taser flat against his chest, inconspicuous to anyone who might happen to see them. But there was no one outside, no kids riding bicycles, no adults on evening strolls.

He opened the driver door and the one behind it, then reached for Gavin's hand. The little boy drew back, clinging to her leg, cries renewed.

"Tell him to get in the back."

"I'll put him in his car seat. Come here, sweetie."

She lifted him into the vehicle. After he'd climbed into his seat, she struggled to clip the straps with shaking hands.

"Don't bother fastening him in. He won't be there long."

She swiveled her head to look over her shoulder, fear almost immobilizing her. "What are you going to do to him?"

"Nothing if you follow my instructions exactly."

He grabbed her by the hair to pull her from the vehicle. After shoving her into the front seat, he climbed in behind her. "Drive."

He directed her around a couple of corners. "Pull over here."

She did as instructed and shifted the vehicle into Park. They'd hardly left her neighborhood. Two houses stood across the street, a small patch of trees to her immediate right.

"Get out."

"What about Gavin?"

"Get him out, too."

After scrambling from the vehicle, she leaned into the back to pull her son from his car seat. He had stopped crying some time ago, but his body shook with each shuddering breath. She clutched him to her chest and glanced around her. The front end of a car was barely visible between two of the trees.

The man gripped her upper arm and led her to an old Oldsmobile, its body a dingy gray in the moonlight that filtered through the trees. Likely the same car Noah had described.

After taking Tony's keys from her, he tossed them some distance away and handed her a different set. "Put your kid in the back and get in."

She did what he'd told her. There was no car seat, but that was the least of her concerns. Soon they were again on their way, eventually headed west on 98. A couple of miles from the Florida–Alabama line, he instructed her to take a left. Where was he taking them?

Shortly after she'd reached the 55-mile-an-hour speed limit, he tapped her on the shoulder. "Pull over here."

She pressed the brakes and came to a stop on the shoulder, in front of a brown Tarkiln Bayou Preserve State Park sign. There were no other vehicles, and both the entry and exit gates were closed and locked.

"Hand me the keys."

She turned off the car and passed the keys to him. When she looked back at her little boy, his thumb was in his mouth, and his eyes were round in the light of a half-moon. Her heart squeezed in a painful combination of love and fear.

God, if you're listening, please protect my boy. I don't deserve any favors, but little Gavin is so young and innocent.

"Get out of the car."

The terse command cut across her thoughts, and she scrambled onto the asphalt shoulder. The road wasn't well traveled. No one had come from either direction during the minute or so they'd been stopped.

The killer climbed from the back seat, pulling Gavin out with him. "Come on, little boy. We're going for a walk."

Kris's thoughts spun. What was he going to do to them? Did he plan to take them into the woods and kill them? The park covered more than four thousand acres. How long would it be before someone discovered their bodies? Was he going to do to them what he did to the woman she and Tony discovered? A shudder shook her shoulders and rippled down her spine.

He moved into the woods, Gavin's hand in one of his, the Taser in the other. She had no choice but to follow. After traveling about forty feet, he released her little boy's hand and turned to face her. "We're going back to the car now."

What? Did he change his mind? What was the point of their little detour?

She picked up her son, and he wrapped both arms around her neck. She'd hardly gone two steps when the man's words stopped her cold.

"Not him. You and me."

She spun and squeezed Gavin so hard he squirmed in her grasp. "We can't leave him alone out here in the dark."

"Actually, we can and we will. The question is whether we leave him conscious or unconscious. Dead or alive. Put him down."

"No, I can't..." Her throat closed up, and her brain stalled out. The killer was letting Gavin go, but he was leaving him alone in a deserted park, pine trees all around, water just past the end of a long catwalk.

Warning flared in the man's eyes, and he held up the Taser.

"Please, let me take him somewhere safe."

The warning turned to anger. He flipped a switch and the red light of a laser appeared.

"This is armed, ready to fire. As you can see, your son is the target. So let's try this again. Put him down."

She lowered Gavin to the ground, and he held up both hands, sobbing. When he called for her, her heart broke. The killer gave her arm a yank, and she bit back a shriek.

"You might want to make sure he stays here so he doesn't get run over."

"Please let me talk to him."

Although he didn't give her permission, his hold on her relaxed.

She dropped to her knees again and hugged Gavin to her chest. "Baby, you stay right here. Put your arms around this tree and don't move until a nice policeman comes for you. Can you do that?"

He nodded, his eyes round. Big tears made rivulets down both cheeks.

She guided his arms around a pine. "Hang on to this tree and don't let go." He was just obedient enough to do it, all night if that was how long it took.

The man pulled her to her feet and gave her a shove. She stumbled forward, then cast a glance over her shoulder. "Mommy loves you so much, but she has to go with this man." She choked back a sob.

He dragged her toward the car, and cries of "Mommy" followed them, shredding her heart even further. A sense of hopelessness descended on her, and the tears she'd managed to hold at bay for her son's sake flowed freely.

God, whatever happens to me, please protect my little boy.

When they reached the car, instead of directing her to the driver's side, he kept a tight grip on her arm while he opened the trunk.

"Get in."

She shook her head, trying to back away. "Please don't put me in the trunk."

He glanced toward the woods, fingering the Taser. He didn't say a thing. He didn't have to. The silent threat was just as effective as any words he might use. She scrambled into the trunk and sat, hip wedged against the spare tire.

"Good girl. I think I'll even reward you by making a little phone call." He touched three numbers and pressed the phone to his ear. "I'm calling to report a child left unattended at Tarkiln Bayou State Park. A little boy, about two or three."

Without waiting for a response, he ended the call. Kris slumped forward, face against her knees and shoulders shaking with sobs she didn't even try to hold back. But now her tears were those of relief.

"Thank you." She lifted her head and drew in a shuddering breath. "Thank you, thank you."

And thank you, God. He'd answered her prayer.

Her abductor's lips curled back in a sneer. "I did it for him, not you. He doesn't deserve to suffer. You do."

Without any warning, his fist slammed into the side of her head. Stars exploded across her vision, tiny points of light that rapidly faded and disappeared. Darkness encroached from all sides, slowly extinguishing the moon's soft glow.

The trunk's lid slammed closed.

The suffering he mentioned had begun.

Chapter Nine

Tony struggled to his hands and knees, muscles still in spasm from a sustained Taser shock. One minute, he'd been following Bella around the side of the house, waiting for her to do her business. The next he'd had 50,000 volts of electricity coursing through his body with nothing more than the one-second warning of a twig snapping behind him.

He'd just started to recover from the Taser shock when his attacker had pressed a stun gun to his neck, and the excruciating pain had begun anew.

He'd heard Kris step outside and call his name but hadn't been able to respond. His jaw had been clenched, and every muscle in his body had contracted and released in rapid, painful spasms. Then he'd lost consciousness.

He pushed himself fully upright and pulled one barb from his abdomen and the other from his hip. Bella was lying a few feet away, whimpering. When the man had attacked him, the dog had approached growling, her stance aggressive. Without letting his finger off the Taser's trigger, he'd jammed the stun gun against the dog's neck then finished him off.

"Hang on, girl." He'd have to see to the dog later. He stumbled toward the front of the house on sluggish legs, reaching for his radio with one hand, his weapon with the other.

His weapon was gone.

He radioed dispatch to request backup. His attacker could still be on the property, possibly even inside with Kris and Gavin.

He crept forward. As he rounded the front corner of the house, his gaze swept the driveway, and his stomach dropped. The Nissan was gone.

He charged up the porch steps, willing his stubborn limbs to hurry. The front door was open, a flashlight's beam shining across the foyer floor.

"Kris?" He stopped at the bottom of the stairs and hollered again, knowing all along that the darkened house was empty.

He could guess what had happened while he was out. The man who'd attacked him had gone after Kris and taken both her and Gavin away in the Nissan. A vise clamped down on his chest, and his knees went suddenly weak. *Oh, God, please keep them both safe.*

He radioed dispatch again with an update. "We have a kidnapping. We're looking for a white 2023 Nissan Rogue."

Or maybe not. The man had probably parked his own vehicle nearby and traded them out. "Also put out an APB for a white Chevy pickup, maybe around 1995. An older gray sedan, too."

He stepped back onto the porch. Where was John? How could this happen with two trained police officers protecting her?

He approached the Explorer and opened the driver door. Light flooded the interior. John was gone.

Using the flashlight on his phone, he circled the house. When he reached the back, he swept the beam of light around the yard. Jean-covered legs and shoes were barely visible at the edge of a small grouping of trees. He hurried in that direction, his heart in his throat.

When the legs drew up, Tony released a relieved breath. He might be injured, but he was at least alive.

He dropped to his knees next to his fellow law enforcement officer. Rope secured his ankles. His arms wrapped the tree trunk behind him, his wrists bound on the other side. A piece of duct tape covered his mouth. Two wires trailed away from him, the probes apparently behind him.

"This is going to hurt." Tony reached for the tape and gave it a swift yank. "What happened?"

John barely winced. "I thought I might have seen movement next to the house but wasn't sure."

While he continued his explanation, Tony untied his hands.

"I drew my weapon, went to investigate. Next thing I knew, I was getting Tased from behind. Didn't think the creep was ever going to let off the trigger. By the time I could move again, he had me bound and gagged."

When his hands were free, he rubbed one wrist and then the other before reaching down to release his ankles. "What about the lady and her boy? I heard a vehicle start up and feared the worst."

Tony pressed his lips together, the tightness in his chest returning full force. "You're right. They're gone. Do you have your weapon?"

"No. The guy took it as soon as he had me tied up." He pushed himself to his feet. "You want to pull those things out of my back? I'm not sure I can reach them."

Tony moved behind him. One probe had hit the center of his left shoulder blade and the other a couple of inches below his waist.

He removed them one at a time. "I hate to admit it, but I'm in the same boat you are—surprised, Tased and disarmed."

Sirens sounded in the distance, and John glanced in that direction. "I'm guessing you already called it in."

"Yep. I'm going to check on the dog. She got zapped with a stun gun."

John headed toward the front, while Tony continued across the back of the house to the other side. Bella had risen and was plodding away from him on unsteady legs.

"Bella."

The dog turned to look at him and released another whimper. He hurried toward her and took her face in his hands. Then he massaged her, from her neck all the way down her back. "Are you all right?"

She pressed her face against his leg and wagged her tail.

When they reached the driveway, two Pensacola Police cruisers drew to a stop at the edge of Kris's front yard, lights flashing. Lettering on one identified it as a K-9 unit.

The driver door swung open, and Jared Miles stepped out, creases of concern etched into his features. "It's Kris, isn't it?"

He nodded. "Gavin, too. The guy came out of nowhere, Tased me."

He'd promised to keep them safe. How could he have let this happen?

Jared put a hand on his shoulder. "You did what you could."

He swallowed hard. "Can you let Kassie know?"

She'd pray until Kris was found, adding strength to his own incessant, desperate prayers.

"Sure." He stepped to the side and pulled his phone from his pocket. While he made the call, the other officer approached.

"Rick Danforth. Can you fill us in on what happened?"

As Danforth jotted down a few notes, their radios crackled to life. The authorities had found the Nissan. Tony had guessed right. It wasn't much more than a block away. That meant Kris and Gavin were likely in either the white pickup or the gray sedan.

The dispatcher's voice came through their radios a second time, dispatching units to Tarkiln Bayou Preserve State Park. They'd received an anonymous call about an abandoned child.

Tony looked at John. The rental car would be out of commission until Crime Scene finished processing it. "Can you take me there? Depending on the circumstances, we might need Bella."

"Absolutely." John headed toward the Explorer, digging his keys from his pocket.

Tony whistled for the dog and fell in next to him. "It's got to be Gavin. Someone discovering a lost child would stay with him until the police arrived. The call was anonymous. This person doesn't want to be discovered, but he also didn't want harm to come to the boy."

"Why take him and leave him in the park? Why not leave him here?"

"What better way to ensure Kris's cooperation than to threaten her son?"

"Makes sense. The timing is right, too. Almost twenty minutes has passed since I heard your car start up. Tarkiln Bayou Park is about ten minutes southwest of here. That leaves enough time for him to switch vehicles, drive to the park, drop off the boy and make the call."

John climbed into the driver's seat, and Tony circled around to the passenger side to let Bella into the back. Before getting in, he hollered at the men still standing in the drive.

"Have them search the area for the Chevy pickup and gray sedan I called in earlier. Check along 98, going west." It wouldn't make sense for the killer to go to the park and then head east on 98, backtracking through Pensacola. No, they were heading west, into Alabama.

God, please let the authorities catch up with them before they leave the highway.

Tony slid in opposite John and sent up yet another prayer of protection for both Kris and Gavin. When John stopped in front of the closed entry gate ten minutes later, two marked units had just arrived. He and John stepped over the gate and into the parking lot with the four officers.

Tony took charge. "Let's spread out." He pointed to one of the men. "You, follow the catwalk and check the water's edge."

He motioned to two others. "One of you take the woods to the right of the catwalk, the other the woods to the left. The rest of us will fan out from there. We think the little boy's name is Gavin."

Bella suddenly stood at attention, staring into the woods, body rigid with tension.

"What is it, girl? Do you hear something?"

The dog barked once, and a ripple went through her body.

He looked at the men "Go. Start your search. We'll keep in touch via radio."

Without waiting for a response, he bent over to hold Bella's face in his hands. "You know where he is, don't you, girl?" He straightened and held out a hand, index finger extended. "Go find Gavin."

Bella trotted into the woods, sniffing the air the same way she'd done when they'd searched for the missing camper. After going a few yards, she came to a sudden stop, her ears lifting slightly.

The next moment, she charged ahead, leaving Tony scrambling to keep up. Soon he lost sight of her.

"Bella. Where are you, girl?"

After several moments of silence, excited barks echoed through the woods. He ran toward the sound. The dog was sitting on her haunches in the patchy moonlight, Gavin in front of her.

He sat on the ground, legs extended in front of him, arms wrapped around a tree to his right. Now that Bella had fallen silent, Tony could pick up what the dog had apparently heard—soft whimpers.

Tony spoke into his radio. "The child is found."

He dropped to his knees next to the little boy. Although the dog was pressed against him, he still sat with his arms wrapped around the tree.

"Come here, buddy. Let Uncle Tony take you home."

Gavin let go of the rough trunk and reached out his hands.

Tony picked him up and held him against his chest, whatever uneasiness he'd once had completely gone. Little arms went around his neck, and warmth filled his chest. Thanks to Bella, he'd found Kris's little boy and played a part in his rescue.

Without relaxing his embrace on Gavin, he rose and headed back toward the front gate. God had answered his prayer. Half of it, anyway. He lifted his eyes heavenward, gratitude swelling inside.

Thank you, God, for keeping Gavin safe.
Please do the same for Kris.

Pain. The full length of her body. It was everywhere—her ankles, her hip, her wrists, her shoulder, her head...

Especially her head.

Where was all the pain coming from? She struggled to open her eyes, but her eyelids seemed to be weighted down.

After a couple more attempts, they slid open a sliver. Scuffed hardwood planks extended some distance in front of her, running under a small table and disappearing at a log wall. She was on the floor of what looked like a rundown cabin. A man sat at the table nursing a can of soda or beer, a lantern burning in front of him.

Kris let her eyes fall shut again. Where was she?

When she tried to shift her position, she couldn't do it. Her hands were tied behind her back, her ankles bound. Tape covered her mouth.

Memory rushed back to her with the force of a tidal wave. The boater had abducted her. He'd somehow gotten past both Tony and John. He'd taken her son, too.

But Gavin was safe. The man had called the police. By now, her boy would be in Mildred's care, or possibly Kassie's.

She tried to lift her head, and a moan escaped through her nose. The figure in the chair shifted. The next moment, a blinding light shone in her face, and she squeezed her eyes shut again.

"After two hours, you finally decided to join the party. I guess I hit you harder than I intended. Sometimes I don't know my own strength."

She opened one eye a sliver. Nothing existed except that blinding beam of light, which cast everything else into total blackness.

Suddenly, it clicked off, and his chair scraped against the hardwood floor. She watched him rise and approach, his footsteps slow and deliberate.

He stopped in front of her and knelt down. "I'm going to pull the tape now. Don't bother to scream, because there aren't any people for miles. You'll just tick me off, which would be a huge mistake."

He picked at one corner of the tape until he had enough loose to get a good grip. Then he ripped it away in one angry motion. Fire shot through the lower part of her face. She winced but didn't cry out. Based on the condition of the victim she and Tony had found in the woods, losing a few skin cells was probably pleasant compared to what he had in store for her.

He stood and pulled an object from his pocket. It didn't look like the Taser, but with the lantern at his back, she couldn't say for sure.

For several moments, he stared down at her, his face cast in shadow. Was he trying to decide what to do with her? Or was the wait part of the torment?

He flicked his wrist and a blade extended. Panic pounded up her spine. He was going to stab her to death like he did Shannon.

Instead, he stepped over her. For a good half minute, she held her breath, waiting for the piercing pain of a knife wound or a boot to the kidney or another blow to the head.

It didn't come. One large hand wrapped hers, and the smooth edges of the knife slid between her wrists. With a couple of rapid, upward slices, she was free.

She pushed herself into a seated position, her legs extended in front of her. Soon he had sawed through the bindings securing her ankles. He lifted her to her feet and threw her into the other kitchen chair.

Over the next several minutes, he finished his beer and pulled another one from a cooler against the wall. The place likely didn't have electricity, even if the power had been restored. If he wanted cool beverages, he'd have to make it to a store sometime in the next few days. Or maybe he planned to kill her before his ice ran out.

He sat across from her again and popped the top on his beer. "Are you thirsty?"

She looked at him with raised brows. Was he showing a smidgeon of concern? She'd pass on the beer, but a bottle of cold water was really appealing. "A little."

"Good."

He took a long swig of the beer. As the minutes ticked by, he made no move to get her anything. Instead, he picked up a small block of wood and shaved slivers off of it with the knife he'd used to cut her bindings.

She looked around the cabin. It was small, the main part a single room that housed a small living area and a kitchenette. At the end of the short counter, an open door led into a darkened room, probably a bedroom.

Where were they? Were they still in Florida, or had he taken her to Georgia or Alabama? He said she'd been out for two hours. That meant they could even be in Mississippi.

Looking outside didn't offer any clue as to her whereabouts. All was dark beyond the four cracked and dirt-caked windows. Come morning, she might be able to see through them.

When she met his eyes again, he was watching her. "You're probably wondering where we are. We're deep in the woods where no one will find us. This place has sat undisturbed since before I was a teenager."

He returned to his carving, his movements rhythmic. Outside, the high-pitched buzz of cicadas formed a muffled backdrop for the scrape of his knife against the wood.

"You know, you're special. Not like the others. I've got you, but you made me work for it. Trust me, you'll pay for those times you thwarted my plans."

He spoke without looking at her, his attention on the block of wood in his hand. He cut off another thin slice, letting it fall to the growing pile of shavings already there. If what remained of the original block was supposed to be a work of art, it hadn't begun to take shape yet.

"You were actually doing me a favor, because it'll be so much more satisfying in the end. A prize worked for is more rewarding than one that comes too easily."

He laid down the wood and then folded the knife. Leaving the beer can sitting on the table, he walked to the cooler again and returned with a bottle of water. Without a word, he plunked it on the small table, sat and resumed sipping his beer.

Kris eyed the water bottle, droplets of moisture clinging to it. It was sitting between them, closer to her than it was to him. Had he intended it for her?

She could surely use it. While searching for survivors in the park, she'd tried to stay well hydrated. That was hard to do in the sun with temperatures in the midnineties. She hadn't had anything to drink since arriving at home, and she was beyond thirsty.

She looked at him for silent permission, but he had resumed his carving.

"Thank you for the water." If he didn't want her to have it, he'd stop her.

Except for the jerky movements of the knife, he was still, his eyes fixed on his project.

She slowly reached for the bottle, giving him plenty of opportunity to intervene. She clasped her hand around it, slid it closer, unscrewed the lid.

She touched the top to her lips, and cool, refreshing water

flowed into her mouth. His chair scraped across the hardwood floor. Before she could react, his open hand connected with her cheek, sending the bottle flying. It landed on its side against the wall, water pouring from its top.

She pressed a hand to her stinging cheek. He'd set her up.

"These games aren't so much fun, are they? It's a lot different being on the receiving end."

What games? Before she had a chance to voice her question aloud, he jerked her up from the chair, one meaty hand wrapped around her upper arm. Her shoulder gave a crack of protest.

"Now it's your turn to be hungry and thirsty." He dragged her toward the doorway into the darkened room, and she stumbled after him. The space had probably been a bedroom at one time, but the only sign of its former use was a dilapidated chest of drawers standing in one corner, a two-foot-by-three-foot window nearby.

He stopped in front of a closed door, likely a closet, still maintaining his viselike grip on her arm. "I hated the dark, but you didn't care."

She looked at him in the soft glow of the lantern spilling in from the main room. What was he talking about?

After swinging open the door, he threw her inside, slamming her body into the back wall. "Now you're going to pay."

The door banged shut, leaving her in pitch blackness except for the sliver of dim light that found its way under the door. "It's finally your turn to be locked in a dark closet."

Instead of leaving the room, he paced for some time outside the closet door. "Are you sorry yet?"

Sorry for what? Evading him?

As he paced the room, she felt the walls for any weak boards that might offer a means of escape. There were none.

If he left her alone and she could escape the closet, maybe she could climb through the bedroom window. She reached for the doorknob and turned it slowly. It moved about one-eighth of a turn and stopped. It was locked.

He suddenly banged on the door, and she drew back her hand with a stifled shriek.

"How does it feel, Lana?"

Footsteps retreated, and another door slammed.

"I'm not Lana." Her shouted denial probably didn't even reach him.

A sense of hopelessness bore down on her, threatening to crush her. She was trapped in a remote cabin with a madman with little chance of rescue.

She sank down the wall and sat on the floor, knees drawn up to her chest. The small space didn't allow for any other position.

She wasn't Lana, had never met her and had no idea who she was.

But she was paying for every one of her sins.

Chapter Ten

Tony walked from the police department building, shoulders slouched and worry gnawing a hole in his gut. They'd soon be coming up on twenty-four hours since Kris was taken and were nowhere near finding her. He'd put in a long shift, tracking down every lead they'd gotten. There hadn't been many. At different times throughout the day and early evening, all the local television stations had been airing the composite Kris had done a couple of weeks ago.

With tens of thousands of homes without power, it wasn't having near the impact it normally would. The only people with the ability to view what was being aired were those with backup generators or battery-operated, digital-ready TVs with exterior antennas.

Even so, the police had gotten two leads. One was from an older man, calling about a guy who had moved in next door to him a couple of weeks ago. Tony had to admit there was a resemblance, but it wasn't a strong one. After talking to the guy, his employer and his family, they'd eliminated him. The other lead had been an even bigger stretch.

Several agencies had put helicopters in the air, looking for either vehicle, as well as anything that might provide clues in the case.

Tony tried to not think about what she was experiencing—the fear, the terror, the emotional and physical suffering. The killer had intended to silence her the way he'd silenced Shannon. How long had it taken him to realize Kris fit the profile of his victims? Not long, based on the pictures found in the motel room. Sometime between her encountering him when he'd dumped the camper's body and the night of the storm, she had moved from a witness to be silenced to another victim to torment. He'd made that clear in his phone call.

Tony slid into the driver's seat of his department-assigned vehicle. If he had any idea where Kris's abductor had taken her, he'd get out there and search for her himself.

One thing was sure. The man hadn't followed Highway 98, at least not for any length of time. Several agencies had swarmed the highway for miles in both directions, searching for the white Chevy truck and the gray sedan. Either Kris's abductor had fled in yet another vehicle, or he'd traveled some distance away from 98.

Last night, he and John had dropped Gavin off with Kassie, then retrieved his department-assigned vehicle. He'd also left Bella there, with the understanding that he'd be picking her up again if there was any chance she could assist in finding Kris. Unfortunately, he had no idea where to even begin looking.

He cranked the vehicle and shifted into reverse. Processing the Nissan had turned up nothing. The prints they'd identified were his. The ones not in the system had probably belonged to Kris.

They were all out of options. Except prayer. Of course, he'd been praying almost nonstop since Kris disappeared. So had Kassie and Jared and his mom and dad. Nick and Joanne, too.

Last night, he'd almost told her how he felt. He'd said he didn't want her to leave. He'd meant it with every fiber of his being. She'd waited for him to continue. He hadn't been able to bring himself to do it. He wasn't the father her little boy should have. He'd never be able to step into the shoes of the man smiling out from the frame on her fireplace mantle. So what was the point of telling her that he was falling for her when they'd never be more than friends?

But maybe he should have, because now he was looking at the possibility of losing her, leaving all those words forever unsaid. *God, please let me see her again.*

He'd almost reached the edge of the parking lot when his cell phone rang. When he looked at the screen, his pulse kicked into high gear. His captain was calling him.

"Hey, Keith."

"You'd better get back in here."

Tony pulled into the nearest parking space, heart pounding. "What's going on?"

"There's a guy here you'll want to talk to."

After killing the engine, he jumped from the vehicle and jogged toward the building. Light poured out from inside, the backup generators having kicked in right after the power went out two nights ago. When he reached his captain's office, another detective, Robbie Sanchez, was standing there, along with a man Tony had never met.

Keith stood and made introductions, then continued. "Kenny here is pretty sure he knows our guy."

Kenny nodded. "I grew up in Perdido, Alabama, about an hour northwest of here. Moved to Pensacola about five years ago. From age thirteen on, there was another kid I used to hang with, Brent Wadsworth. Although I haven't seen him for about two years now, the composite I saw on TV looks just like him."

"How about a last known address?"

"Last time I talked to him, he was living in Cantonment, about a half hour north of here."

"Did he mention where?" Sanchez asked. "A street name or anything?"

"No."

Tony frowned. "After taking the lady from her home on Bayou Texar, we know he stopped by Tarkiln Bayou Preserve State Park. If he was headed toward Cantonment, that detour would have taken him far out of his way."

Kenny nodded. "That park is just a little way off 98, right?"

"It is."

"If he hopped back on 98 and headed west into Alabama, after ten or fifteen minutes, he could drive north for an hour and run right into Perdido, our old stomping grounds."

"Is there somewhere around there that you think he might have taken her?"

Kenny pursed his lips, brows drawn together in concentration. "It's a long shot. I don't know if I could even find it. When we were fifteen, Brent discovered an old, abandoned cabin in the woods. We used to hike to it and hang out."

Tony looked at Keith. "I'd like to pick up Bella and have Kenny try to take us out there."

"Go. Meet back here in thirty minutes. We'll have a group ready to go."

Tony hurried from the building, dialing Kassie as he walked. She answered on the second ring.

"I'm picking up Bella. We have a lead."

He didn't want to get her hopes up in case it didn't pan out. But she probably needed a spark of hope as badly as he did.

"That's awesome. I'll be praying even harder, if that's possible."

When he arrived at Kassie's a few minutes later, she was waiting out front for him, Bella in her vest, her leash attached to her collar.

She handed him the looped end. "Text me as soon as you know something."

"I will."

He opened the back door for the dog. "How is Gavin handling everything?"

"Not well. He keeps crying for his mother."

Tony's heart twisted. The poor child lost his father. *God, please don't take his mother away, too.*

When he returned to the station, plans were well underway. Besides Sanchez, Jared Miles was there with his dog, Justice.

Keith walked them all outside. "We're coordinating with a SWAT team out of Mobile. Everyone will rendezvous in the Perdido Elementary School parking lot."

Tony looked at his captain. "I'd like to have Kenny ride with me if that's okay."

Keith nodded. "Sure."

"We'll be the lead vehicle, since Kenny is the only one who knows where we're going."

"I'll do my best, anyway."

Tony hurried to his vehicle, Kenny following. When they'd both climbed into their seats, he pulled from the parking lot and made his way toward 98, struggling to keep his speed down to a justifiable level.

Kenny looked over at him. "I understand this lady isn't the only one."

"She's not."

"I've been on vacation up in Wisconsin for the past two weeks, so I didn't see the composite aired until tonight."

"That's understandable."

"These women and the one you're looking for, are they dark-haired, slender build, fairly attractive?"

Tony cast him a sideways glance. "Yeah. Why do you ask?"

"His sister was dark-haired."

Several moments passed in silence. Tony eased to a stop at a darkened traffic light. When he looked at the other man, he was frowning. "Did he not get along with his sister?"

"It was a lot worse than that." Kenny's face was creased in the soft moonlight. "Their mother left them alone a lot, usually left his older sister in charge of him. She apparently resented being responsible for her kid brother and took it out on him."

After checking for traffic both directions, Tony pressed the gas. "She hit him?"

"Yeah. Tormented him other ways, too."

"Do you know where she is, his sister?"

"No. I never met her. They were both removed from the home when he was six and she was thirteen, then adopted into different families. But he had a couple of pictures of her."

Several more seconds passed in silence. There was more to the story, something that apparently bothered Kenny all these years later.

"Tell me about these pictures."

"They looked like school pictures. He showed them to me a couple of times." He sucked in a deep breath. "Brent used to draw a lot, make pencil sketches of animals, superheroes, people he knew, you name it. He had a lot of talent. But the sketches he did of his sister were really disturbing."

"Disturbing in what way?"

"In a lot of the drawings, she was bound and gagged. In all of them, she'd been beaten or shot or stabbed. They were really graphic for being done in charcoal pencil."

"Did he say the girl in the drawings was his sister?"

"Yeah. Even though it was obvious, I asked. He used to say that someday she was going to pay for the way she treated him. I always told him to let it go, that she wasn't worth the energy he was expending on her. I even talked to the school counselor once."

"How did that go?"

"She didn't let him know that I had said anything. She just brought him in and talked to him about his home life, both with his adoptive family and with his birth mother. Brent had been through counseling before and had figured out how to give all the right answers. He was good at acting totally chill, like nothing bothered him. The counselors never saw the side of him that I saw. He could go from happy to furious and back to happy again without breaking stride." Kenny sighed. "Now

I find out I was friends with a possible future serial killer. I should have pushed harder."

"Hey, don't beat yourself up. You did a lot more than most teenagers would have done. You had no way of knowing this would happen. It wasn't your fault, so don't carry the guilt for it."

He turned right onto 98. They were now headed west, the Alabama border not too far ahead. In a little over an hour, they'd meet up with the Mobile SWAT team.

"How many has he killed so far?"

Kenny's voice held a lot of heaviness, the weight of regret. Tony hoped he'd figure out how to let it go.

"Four." If they didn't find Kris tonight, she'd likely be number five.

No, he wouldn't even go there.

The man sitting beside him was the best lead they'd had since Amanda Driscoll disappeared from Milligan almost four months earlier.

Would this lead be a dead end too?

God, please help us find them.

And please don't let it be too late.

Kris dragged her eyes open and lifted her head with a moan. She was back in the closet. Judging from the fact that there was no sliver of light under the door, it was night. She'd lost all track of time, each painful hour bleeding into the next.

The last thing she remembered was sitting, tied to the kitchen chair, while her captor delivered blows to her head, face and stomach. It wasn't the first beating she'd received that day, but it was the worst. She'd apparently lost consciousness.

She closed her eyes and let her head rest against her knees. From what she'd gathered listening to his disjointed stories, Lana was an older sister who had subjected him to a lot of abuse. How many of the stories were true and how many were the creation of a tormented imagination didn't matter. She was paying for every bit of that abuse, whether real or imagined.

The bedroom door creaked open, and the soft glow of the lantern shone under the closet door. Her breath caught in her throat. As his heavy footsteps moved closer, her heart pounded out an erratic rhythm. What punishment was he going to mete out this time?

The knob rattled, and the door swung open. She sat huddled on the floor, unable to rise. Not only did her entire body hurt, her ankles were bound and her hands were lashed together behind her back. He'd bound her hands in the early morning hours. After she'd kicked him in a futile attempt to avoid his fists, he'd bound her feet also.

He'd never reapplied the tape over her mouth. There hadn't been a need. Screaming would only make things worse. He'd warned her.

She didn't lift her head until the toe of his boot slammed into her side.

"Wake up. It's time."

Time? Time for another beating or time to die?

He gripped her upper arm and hauled her to her feet. Then he threw her roughly over his shoulder. As he walked into the multipurpose room, she lifted her head to scan the space. One chair was angled away from the table, a beer can sitting there. The lantern shone from its usual spot in the center of the table.

Next to it lay a hammer.

No, no, no. He was finally finished toying with her. It was time for her to join the others.

He crossed the room and stopped a few feet from the door. Instead of bending to put her on the floor, he flipped her over and dropped her from shoulder height. She landed on her back, face up, arms trapped beneath her. The blow forced a grunt from her mouth.

When she tried to draw in a breath, her lungs seized up. No matter how she tried, her chest and throat remained paralyzed. Her heart slammed against her ribcage, and her thoughts spun. The panic gripping her probably made it worse, but she couldn't keep it at bay.

Her captor walked to the table, gait relaxed. The invisible bonds around her chest began to release, and she struggled in a constricted breath. The breaths that followed became easier.

When he turned to face her again, he was holding the hammer. The panic began anew. She was going to die. In the span of less than two years, little Gavin would lose both his father and his mother. But Mark's parents would raise him. They were good people.

And Tony. She should have told him how she felt about him. Instead, she was getting ready to pass from this life with all those emotions unexpressed.

And what about God? She'd let the fire she'd had as a child die when she'd thought her mother had left. When Mark had been killed, she'd finished stamping out what little spark remained. Now she was going to meet a God she'd spent the last ten years ignoring.

The killer slowly circled her, tapping the head of the hammer against his other palm, his gaze predatory.

This was it. Any second now, he'd start swinging.

God, please forgive me. Prepare me to meet You. Please watch over Gavin. And please somehow let Tony know that I love him.

The man completed another circle then stopped in front of her. His jaw was tight, his eyes narrowed. "Aren't you going to say something?"

She stared at him in dumb silence. What was she supposed to say?

He gripped the head of the hammer with his other hand. "I hold all power over you. I hold the power of life and the power of death."

He was right. And it only made her situation that much more

hopeless. He needed to just do what he was going to do and get it over with.

Anger flared in his eyes. "Say something."

What? Was he actually wanting her to talk him out of it?

No. Nothing she could say would make him rethink what he was about to do. He wanted her to plead for her life.

Was that what Shannon had done? Probably. Each of the other women, too. And he'd gotten some perverted thrill from listening to their pleas, a heady sense of power, finally being the one in control.

She wouldn't give it to him.

She wouldn't beg for mercy, but she wasn't giving up, either.

"You're right. You do have all the power. You have the power to take my life, to leave my little boy an orphan. But you also have the power to make the right choice, to be better than Lana. She was cruel. No one deserved to be treated the way she treated you."

The anger left his eyes as suddenly as it had come. Instead, there was hesitation. Maybe she was getting through to him. Was it her sympathy with his plight that was reaching him, or was he able to relate, just a little bit, to Gavin? She'd continue to hit him with both.

"I'm sorry you had a cruel sister instead of a loving mother." Maybe she was going out on a limb, but a loving mother wouldn't have let anyone torment him so severely. "You're better than Lana. You can rise above all the wrong she did to you." She pushed herself to a seated position, hands still tied behind her. "You met my son. You saw what a sweet little boy he is. He might even remind you of yourself at that age."

He lowered the hammer slowly until both hands came to rest at his sides. Had she actually talked him out of killing her?

"Every little boy deserves to grow up with a loving mother. You deserved that, and I'm so sorry you didn't get it. But please don't take that away from my little boy."

She waited for a response but didn't get one. Instead, he continued to stare down at her, lips pressed together, creases of indecision between his eyebrows. If he'd just say something, anything.

"Please untie me and let me go back to my son." Since she'd been unconscious when he'd brought her in, she had no idea where to go. But if she could get out of the cabin, she'd figure it out.

His eyes widened and his lips curled back in a sneer. "No!" The single word was a bellow, so sharp and loud she flinched. "I'll never let you go. You have to pay."

He raised the hammer and swung it downward in an arc. As she twisted and rolled, the hammer's head grazed her shoulder. Pain shot all the way down her arm.

When he swung a second time, she rolled again, and the metal end missed her head by mere millimeters.

For the past twenty-four hours, she'd heeded his warning not to scream. Now she screamed. She couldn't help it. It didn't matter that it was pointless, that no one would hear her. After the first scream came another and another, rising up from somewhere inside, seemingly of their own accord. Fear, anger and hopelessness melded together, too violent to contain.

This was it. He had won. And it wouldn't end here. He'd continue to kill, again and again.

He raised the hammer again.

Resisting was only delaying the inevitable. But she wouldn't make it easy on him.

She wouldn't give up until she had no strength left to fight.

Chapter Eleven

Tony zigzagged between trees at a full jog, Bella next to him. Jared was on his other side, Justice just ahead of them. Counting Kenny, Robbie Sanchez and the four SWAT guys out of Mobile, there were currently eight men and two dogs crashing through the trees.

But there was no time for the stealth they'd all started with. The enraged bellow and the subsequent high-pitched screams had told them all that Kris's time was almost up.

God, let us get there before it's too late.

Another scream split the night. It set every nerve in his body on edge, but it also sent relief flooding him. As long as Kris was screaming, she was still alive.

They all charged into a small clearing. Just ahead, a dilapidated cabin sat washed in the unfiltered glow of a swollen half-moon. Without slowing, Tony slammed his shoulder into the door.

It burst inward with little resistance. A few feet away, Kris lay on the floor, hands tied behind her back, ankles bound. A man stood over her, face twisted in rage, a hammer raised over his head. Justice lunged, going airborne for several feet before sinking his teeth into the man's raised arm.

While others restrained the suspect and Jared called off his dog, Tony dropped to his knees in front of Kris, his heart twisting. Although she was still conscious, she looked as if she'd been through a boxing match. Her face was misshapen, and even in the poor lighting and shadows cast by those gathered, it was obvious the bruising was extensive. One eye was swollen completely shut, the other open only halfway. She released a moan and let that eye shut, too.

Tony looked back at the others. "She needs medical aid, pronto."

But Sanchez was already calling it in. Bella approached and sat in front of Kris, releasing a whimper.

She opened her eye again and tried to smile with swollen, blood-caked lips. Bella gingerly licked her cheek and whimpered again.

Kris shifted her gaze from her dog to Tony. "You came."

He swallowed around the sudden lump in his throat and took her hand in his. "You're safe now. I only wish we could have found you sooner."

He squeezed her hand, foregoing the hug he wanted to give her. Behind him, someone was reading the suspect his rights. Sanchez was still speaking with dispatch, and a conversation was going on between two of the SWAT guys.

But Tony's main focus was on Kris. She was alive, the only victim to survive abduction by this man. *Thank you, God.*

Her fingers tightened in his, ever so slightly, and her eye drifted shut again. "How did you find me?"

"A former friend came forward, knew about this place from when they were teenagers."

But even Kenny's help wouldn't have been enough without Bella. Not finding either the pickup or the sedan, they'd finally stopped along 61 and headed into the woods. A short time later, Bella had picked up the scent, leading them in a slightly different direction.

"Without Bella, we would never have found you in time."

"Good girl." Her speech was slurred, her eyes still closed.

"Help is on the way." He squeezed her hand again.

She returned the gesture, or at least tried to. Her grip was so weak, it was hardly detectable. Her fingers gradually went limp.

Tony squeezed her hand. "Kris?"

No response.

He cupped her battered face. "Stay with me, Kris."

More of Sanchez's conversation drifted to him, words and phrases like "head injury" and "medevac."

"Hang in there, sweetheart."

God, please let her be okay. After saving her from a madman, they couldn't lose her to her injuries.

He'd cared for her since adolescence. Now he loved her.

Would he ever get the chance to tell her how he felt?

Should he?

Two hours later, Tony paced the surgical waiting room of Ascension Providence in Mobile. Kassie, Jared and his family waited with him. Robbie Sanchez had ridden from Pensacola with Jared and had agreed to take Kenny and both dogs back with him in Jared's cruiser.

Mobile had been hit as hard as Pensacola, but the lights were on here. Hospitals were always the first to get power restored.

After being carried through the woods on a stretcher, Kris had been airlifted to the hospital and rushed into surgery as soon as doctors had determined she had a skull fracture with bleeding on the brain.

He'd called his dad before leaving the cabin to ask for prayers. Instead, when he'd arrived, both of his parents, as well as Nick and Joanne, had been waiting for him.

Since then, he'd alternated between worrying and praying. He'd tried sitting a couple of times, but with all the pent-up anxiety, he hadn't been able to stay still. At this point, pacing suited him better.

The door to the waiting room swung open, and the surgeon

stepped inside. Tony's heart seemed to lodge in his throat, and he suddenly couldn't breathe. It seemed like an eternity passed before the doctor spoke.

"She came through the surgery well and is resting comfortably. She'll be kept sedated for a few days, but we don't foresee there being any complications."

Tony's knees went weak, and he sank into a chair. *Thank you, God.*

The doctor continued. "She'll be in recovery for an hour or so, then moved into ICU. You can all go get some rest."

When they stepped into the hall, Nick fell in beside him.

"What are you going to do when she wakes up?"

"I'm hoping I'll be here."

"As a friend or something more?"

He slid his brother a sideways glance, one with a little bit of annoyance. They'd had this discussion several times already. Tonight, he was too exhausted to rehash it.

"You've fallen in love with her. I can see it every time you look at her."

"So now you've turned into a mind reader."

"I don't have to be a mind reader. It's all over your face."

Yeah, it probably was. It didn't matter. No matter how much he loved Kris, he couldn't bring himself to feel that he deserved fatherhood.

"Do you believe that God is in control?"

"Of course, I do."

"Do you think He'd somehow turned His back or gotten preoccupied, and Zoe died when He wasn't looking?"

"Of course not." He lowered his gaze to the floor. No, God hadn't turned His back, but Tony had.

Nick stopped walking to grab Tony's shoulders, then gave him a rough shake. "How long do you plan to keep punishing yourself for something that was completely out of your control?"

"I don't know."

Nick dropped his hands. "You need to let it go."

Let it go. Wasn't that what he had, in so many words, just told Kenny? It was easier said than done. Right now, he needed to be by himself and pray.

Nick moved ahead of him to catch up with Joanne, but Tony held back, hands curled into fists. Maybe his brother was right. Maybe he needed to take his own advice. Could he really let it go and leave the rest to God?

God, I need Your help. I can't do this on my own. Help me give this up to You.

A hint of something good stirred inside, a sort of release— a sense of freedom that was close enough to touch but too far away to grasp and claim. He'd held on to the guilt for fourteen long months, mentally beating himself up time and again.

He slowly uncurled his fingers, opening his hands. *God, take the pain, take the regret. Help me to release it all to You.*

An invisible weight seemed to lift from his shoulders, and he drew in a deep breath. Nick and Joanne didn't blame him. They hadn't right from the start. Nick had told him over and over to stop blaming himself.

He was finally ready to listen.

Determination surged through him. The next few days would seem like years, but as soon as Kris woke up, he'd tell her how he felt. Maybe she wouldn't be ready for anything more than friendship. Maybe she thought he'd make a lousy father and she'd be better off raising Gavin alone.

Whatever the outcome, he wouldn't leave her side until she knew exactly where he stood.

Kris drifted on a blanket of clouds.

She had no idea where she was but really didn't care. At least not enough to open her eyes. She was comfortable. And she was safe. For some reason, the latter seemed to really matter.

She drew in a deep breath and released it slowly. The clouds dispersed, and the surface behind her back firmed up. She wasn't floating. She was lying in bed, a pillow beneath her head.

When she opened her eyes, her surroundings were foreign. She wasn't in her bedroom. The ceiling was closer than her ten-foot ceilings at home, with fluorescent lights set in, currently off. A tall, narrow window that didn't appear capable of opening occupied part of the pale wall to her left. Where was she?

Memory rushed back to her and images flooded her mind—the rundown cabin, her captor standing over her, fists clenched, the hammer moving at lightning speed toward her head.

Her gasp sounded amplified in the silence of the room. A rustle nearby was the first sign that she wasn't alone. Her heart kicked into high gear, and her breathing turned to shallow pants.

When a familiar face moved into her circle of vision, the panic swirling through her subsided. Tony was there. But where was her son?

"Gavin?"

"He's fine. Kassie and Mildred are trading off taking care of him."

When she tried to smile at him, her cheeks seemed to resist the motion. Her lips did, too. It would take time for her face to return to normal.

"How long have I been asleep?"

He pulled out his phone and did some math in his head. "About eight hours...plus three days."

"Three days!" How was that possible?

"They had to do surgery and kept you sedated afterward to give your brain a chance to recover."

"Have you been here the whole time?"

"Just about. I was off Sunday, and I'm using vacation time the rest of the week. That padded chair against the wall actually reclines and doesn't make too bad of a bed."

The thought of his remaining by her side almost continuously sent warmth flooding her chest. Granted, he was just a friend, but she couldn't ask for a better one.

"So, how bad do I look?"

"A lot of the swelling has gone down, but you're sporting some pretty interesting colors, from yellow to blue to purple to black."

"Can you find me a mirror? On second thought, I think I'll take your word for it." Maybe by the time she had to actually look at herself, a lot of the bruising would fade.

He eased down next to her and took her hand in his. "I should probably call for a nurse now that you're awake. I'm sure the doctor will want to check you out."

The reluctance in his tone told her he wanted to be alone with her now that she was conscious. She wasn't about to object.

"I don't think I'll die from neglect in the next few minutes."

"Good." He squeezed her hand. "Sometime when you're feeling up to it, I'll fill you in on the events leading up to your rescue. Lots of people were praying, and God answered. If not for a vacation ending just in the nick of time and a dog with a super sniffer, things would have turned out differently."

"I'd love to hear about it. I have to admit, I wasn't holding out much hope. When you burst through that cabin door, I thought I was seeing things."

"The more we learned, the more concerned we were. The killer had an older sister who abused him horribly when he was a young child."

"Lana."

He lifted his eyebrows and tilted his head.

"He kept calling me Lana. He was punishing me for everything she did to him."

He pressed his lips together. "In doing some checking, the authorities learned she disappeared from her home in Mississippi eight months ago. Her body was found a week later, her head smashed in with a hammer. Her murder is still un-

solved. She was petite and dark-haired, just like all the women
he abducted."

"He was arrested, right? He's locked up?"

"Yes. He'll pay for his crimes."

"Good." She would eventually be called on to testify. Having to relive the events of this past weekend wasn't something
she relished. But Tony would be right next to her. She released
a sigh. "I'm so glad it's over. For everyone."

She searched for the bed control and pushed the button to
raise the back. A dull ache filled her skull, intensifying the
more upright she became. She stopped at about thirty degrees.
At least she wouldn't be trying to converse lying flat on her
back.

"Have they identified the bones under the gazebo yet? That
seems like forever ago."

"I just found out this morning." He hesitated, frowning.
Sympathy filled his eyes, mixed with a lot of concern.

"It's okay. I'm pretty sure I already know where this is
going."

He nodded. "The bones belonged to your mother."

Knowing what was coming didn't help. The news still ripped
the foundation from under her. It was one more blow in a series of blows.

Their mother had loved them and hadn't left them by choice.
But any sense of closure or other relief she may have felt was
crushed by the knowledge that their father had killed her.

She turned her face toward the window and blinked back
tears. Tony squeezed her hand.

"There was a suitcase buried with her."

She rolled her head back to the other side and looked at him
sharply. "So she was planning to leave." It didn't take a genius
to put the pieces together. She was packed and ready to run off
with her boyfriend, her father discovered her plans, flew into
a rage and killed her.

"She was going to leave, but she was planning to take you three girls with her."

"How do you know that?"

"She'd packed her journal. It was lying underneath her clothes, sealed up in a gallon Ziploc bag."

"You guys read it?" Her chest tightened with the sense that they'd violated her mother's privacy.

"Not me personally. I've been here with you. But, yes, the crime scene people looked at it. It's evidence."

"Will they give it back to us eventually?"

"I'm sure that won't be a problem when they're finished with the case."

She dipped her gaze to her lap. She'd been angry with her mother for so long, had even vowed that if she ever returned, she'd spit in her face. Now she wanted nothing more than to hold in her hands the book where her mother had poured out her heart.

"Your dad will likely be charged with murder."

"He'll never stand trial. They recently diagnosed him with stage-four liver cancer." It would be a sad end to a sad life. She paused. "What else was in the journal?"

"I just got a brief summary, but I know she wrote a lot about his drinking and jealousy and fits of rage, and that if he ever laid a hand on any of you three girls, she'd leave. Then she learned that he was engaged in some activities that could put you girls in danger. That was when she decided to take off with you."

He squeezed her hand again. "One thing was clear from everything she wrote. She loved you, all three of you. She wouldn't leave you by choice."

Kris remembered that day well, coming home from school to find her father in the kitchen, head in his hands, an open bottle of whiskey in front of him. She'd instinctively known something was wrong. Her mother had never allowed him to drink at home.

Kris had called out to him, and he'd looked at her with puffy, bloodshot eyes. A piece of paper had lain on the table in front of him. She'd moved close enough to read what was there—a note from her mother.

She looked at Tony. "But she left a note. I saw it. She explained that she couldn't take it anymore, that she was going to meet her boyfriend in the Bahamas and run away with him. She said to tell us girls that she was sorry."

"That totally disagrees with what she'd written in her journal. Was the note handwritten?"

"It was typed, but she signed it. I recognized her signature."

After reading the note, she'd run upstairs to find Alyssa holed up in her room with the door locked, refusing to let anyone in. Kassie had arrived home a few minutes later, shock dissolving to sobs when she'd gotten the news.

Tony frowned. "She might have left a note, but based on what she'd written in her journal, that wasn't it."

It was possible. Her father could have taken her signature from the note she wrote, typed his own and copied it with her signature at the bottom.

"Based on the journal entries, your mother was taking you three girls out of the home and leaving."

She drew her eyebrows together. "But she bought a plane ticket to the Bahamas. The information was on the credit card. Dad showed it to us. There was only one ticket purchased."

"Did anyone actually verify that she was on that flight?"

"Probably not. I mean, it wasn't treated like a homicide or even a kidnapping. Between the note, the proof of purchasing the plane ticket, her missing suitcase and clothes and Dad's claims that she'd been having an affair, it was pretty cut and dried. Not a stitch of any of our clothing was missing."

"She'd apparently gotten her own things packed but hadn't gotten to yours and your sisters' before your father caught her."

She drew in a sharp breath, a sudden hollowness in her stomach. "She *did* get our stuff packed, at least Kassie's. The next day, Kassie insisted someone had messed with her clothes. She said the stuff in her dresser drawers had been moved or gone through or something. Kassie was actually picky enough to have noticed something like that. But Alyssa and I thought she was nuts." She shook her head. "Mom didn't walk away from us *or* her faith."

Tony smiled. "She didn't."

"You said I was out for basically three and a half days. That would make today Wednesday, right?"

"Yeah."

"I don't suppose your church streams its midweek services."

"Nope, just Sunday mornings. Why?"

"I have a lot of catching up to do."

A smile spread across his face, even as his eyebrows rose in question.

"You may not have realized it, but you were getting through to me. I was softening. It was just a matter of time until I found my way back to the Lord. But last weekend's events sort of fast-tracked it. When I thought I was staring death in the face, I knew I wasn't ready to meet God. I've remedied that."

"That's awesome. I can't tell you how happy that makes me." He drew in a deep breath. "Recently, I've had some realizations of my own. Ever since the day we got paired up searching for Julia Morris, I've been fighting feelings for you, trying hard to not let what there was between us move beyond friendship."

She could relate. She'd been fighting the same war and had thrown up the white flag of surrender the day he and his family had helped her secure her house. Maybe she was finally ready to admit it.

Her lighthearted tone hid the turmoil inside her. "How has that worked for you?"

"Not too well. It's pretty much been a losing battle." He once again grew serious. "When I discovered you'd been taken, and then hour after hour passed with no leads, I was so afraid I had lost you, and I kept thinking about how I'd never told you how I feel."

He reached across her lap to take her other hand and squeezed them both. "I'm not asking for anything. No decisions. No commitments. And maybe my timing on all this stinks. I mean, a few days after you've had brain surgery probably isn't the best time for me to unload a bunch of heavy stuff, but I just want to let you know that I love you, and not just in a simple friendship way."

As she looked at the affection shining from Tony's eyes, her heart responded. Everything she'd tried to hold back rushed forward, bursting through the floodgates.

And it was okay. Her feelings for Tony no longer felt like they were dishonoring Mark. He'd want her to find love again. She was young and had her whole life ahead of her. He'd also want a good man to be there for their son, to step into the role of father.

And there was the problem. Tony would never be that man, not because he couldn't, but because he wouldn't.

"What about Gavin?"

"I love him, too."

That wasn't what she meant, but his answer was still sweet. "We're a package deal, you know."

"That's a pretty awesome package, I'd say."

Did he really mean it? Loving her little boy and taking responsibility for him were two different things. If he wasn't going to be in it for the long haul, they needed to step right back over the friendship line and forget this conversation ever happened.

"We've discussed your feelings about kids before. What changed?" Or had anything changed?

"My brother gave me a stern talking to at the hospital. It wasn't his first. Like a lot of big brothers, he has a tendency to stick his nose in where it doesn't belong. But this time, I listened. The thing that happened with my niece, he said I need to let it go. Since I'd given someone else the same advice a few hours earlier, I thought it would be best if I listened."

"Funny how that works. So you're not afraid anymore that he's going to snap in two or self-destruct?"

"I'm trusting God to keep him in one piece."

"So am I." And it felt good. She'd been doing life on her own for far too long.

He squeezed her hands. "I would love to kiss you right now, but with what you've been through in the past few days, it probably wouldn't be a pleasant experience."

He was right. It hurt to even try to smile. But how many times as a teenager had she dreamed of a kiss from him? She wasn't about to pass up the opportunity now.

"Stop making excuses and kiss me."

A grin spread across his face, and he leaned toward her. When he was close enough for her to smell his aftershave and feel his breath against her mouth, he hesitated, giving her that three-second pause to change her mind. Then he closed that final distance between them.

His lips met hers, his touch featherlight, and warmth exploded inside of her. He'd been wrong about it not being a pleasant experience. He released her hands to softly cup her face. Even with all the care he was taking, those teenage fantasies hadn't done the real experience justice. Not by a long shot.

All too soon, he pulled away. "I love you, Kris, and I promise there will be more of those to come."

"I love you, too. And I'm going to hold you to it."

"I hope you do."

He released her one hand and leaned back in the chair. "By the way, Kassie's planning a graveside service for next week. She's already contacted Alyssa and says she wants both of your input."

"That sounds good." Her mother was finally getting the burial she deserved, recognition for a life well lived but tragically cut short.

The day would be bittersweet—the public acknowledgment of her love for them, a long overdue goodbye. And Tony would be right by her side.

But she had one more thing to do before paying her final respects to her mother. She had to confront her father.

She'd been hurt and angry before, the hatred for her mother something she'd thought she would carry till her dying day.

She wished she could say that anger was gone. It wasn't. It had only been redirected. Now her father was bearing the full brunt of it.

Killing their mother was unthinkable.

Letting them believe she'd abandoned them was cruel.

Perpetuating that lie for the past ten years, knowing what it was doing to each one of his daughters, was unforgivable.

Chapter Twelve

A steel gray sky hung heavy over the small group of mourners gathered in St. Michael's Cemetery. Concrete monuments topped with crosses rose high above the typical grave markers, and family mausoleums stood stately among graves dating back to the 1700s.

Small cement borders segregated some sections. Others were walled off by fences of wrought iron. In one of those walled-off sections, a funeral tent stood in front of a gold-colored casket, a spray of lilies, carnations and Monte Cassino asters on top.

Kris sat in the front row of cloth-covered chairs, Kassie on one side of her, Tony on the other, his fingers intertwined with hers. Gavin sat in his lap. A monument in the center proclaimed that this section belonged to the Singleton family. Her mother's parents, grandparents and great-grandparents were buried here, as were several aunts, uncles and cousins two and three times removed.

Kassie's pastor stood next to the casket, an open Bible in his hand. Actually, he was Kris's pastor, too, now that she'd returned to her roots. He'd just finished reading Psalm 23 and was currently offering words of comfort to the family and friends.

Jared sat on the other side of Kassie, and Tony's parents were in the row behind them. Nick and Joanne, too. A couple dozen people from their church stood outside the canopy, people who had known and loved their mother.

Alyssa was conspicuously absent. Kris wasn't surprised. Disappointed, yes, but not surprised.

According to Kassie, their younger sister hadn't wanted to be involved in the planning and had told Kassie that she'd be fine with whatever she and Kris did. But they'd both expected her to at least show up.

Kris drew her attention back to the pastor, who looked up from his Bible. "Wherefore comfort one another with these words."

Tony squeezed her hand, offering silent comfort. Someone started singing the first verse of "Amazing Grace," and others joined in. Kris sang along in an undertone, leaving the musical people like Kassie to carry the tune.

A few days ago, she'd gone to visit her father. She'd learned her mother's death was an accident. Her father had come back to the house to get something shortly after leaving for the charter office and walked into their bedroom to find her filled suitcase on the bed. She'd been in the bathroom gathering up her toiletries.

He'd known then that she was leaving and had slapped her hard across the cheek, knocking her to the floor. She'd cracked her head on the edge of the bathtub and lost consciousness immediately. Within minutes, she'd begun to convulse and died. He hadn't meant to kill her.

At least, that was what he'd claimed. She was inclined to believe him. Maybe that was because, although he'd been verbally abusive, he'd never seriously threatened any of them. Or maybe it was because believing her death was an accident was easier than accepting the alternative.

The volume of the voices rose coming into the last verse, and the atmosphere became almost celebratory. *When we've been there ten thousand years...*

Her mother was gone, but Kris had no doubt where she was. She hadn't walked away. Her faith had been as genuine the day she died as it had been throughout their childhood.

She couldn't say where her father's heart was. He'd seemed truly sorry for everything, had even asked for her forgiveness. She hadn't been able to give it. Not yet. Eventually, she'd have to. God would require no less.

The verse ended, and the pastor offered a closing prayer. After lying in a crude grave at the water's edge for ten years, her mother's body would soon be lowered into its final resting place.

She'd asked her father about that, too, how he'd managed to bury her without any of them knowing. He'd said that he'd hid her body in the detached garage until late that night. Then he'd dug the shallow grave, carried her out and covered her up, well before the first hint of daylight.

At the pastor's amen, Tony released Kris's hand to rise and position Gavin on one hip.

Kris stood, too, and held out her hands. "I can carry him."

"I don't mind."

Gavin didn't seem to mind, either. He'd wrapped both arms around Tony's neck.

"Besides, you're in heels."

She was. She was also wearing a dress. It was a rare occasion when she put on either. She'd even applied makeup, equally rare. It had completely hidden the last remnants of bruising. When he'd arrived to pick her up and she'd met him at her front door, his eyes had lit with appreciation. Maybe she should dress up more often.

After the friends attending had offered their condolences, Tony took her hand with his free one and walked her toward the gate where they'd entered the cemetery. Nick and Joanne walked ahead of them, Kassie and Jared beside them. Tony's parents trailed behind.

Kassie released a sigh. "I feel like I can finally shut the door on our troubled past and start fresh."

Kris nodded. "Me, too. It's like a new beginning."

For the first time in months, the future looked bright. She'd been given the opportunity to say goodbye to her mother and remember her with fondness and love. She still had work to do in reconciling with her father, but going to see him was the first step in that process. It wouldn't be her last visit.

Mark was gone, and after a year and a half of almost inconsolable grief, she'd finally begun to heal. It was all because God had put Tony in her life. She couldn't say for sure where things would end up, but she was happy with where they were headed.

Joanne turned around to smile at them. "We're looking forward to a new beginning of our own."

Tony's steps faltered. "Are you saying what I think you are?"

Joanne's smile widened. "We didn't want to say anything until I had passed my first trimester. But everything looks good, and about the middle of next February, we think we'll be welcoming a little boy into our family."

Tony released Kris's hand to wrap Joanne in a one-armed hug. "Congratulations, sis. That's awesome news."

Tony moved to the side to congratulate his brother, and Kris hugged Joanne. "I'm so happy for you. You guys deserve this." She released her and stepped back. "Gavin will have a little playmate." Gentle and sweet, he'd be good with a tiny one.

After all the congratulations had been given, Tony put his arm around her, and they moved toward the arched entry. He squeezed her against his side. "I'm ready for my own new beginning. Today is the first day of the rest of my life, and I want to spend every day of it with you and this sweet little boy of yours."

She craned her neck to look up at him. Her heart began to race. Did he mean...what else could he mean with a statement like that?

"Are you asking me to marry you?"

"I guess I am."

"Then I guess my answer is yes, although I can't believe you actually proposed in a cemetery."

"We're not in the cemetery anymore."

"Okay, we're two feet outside the gate."

He winced. "Really romantic, huh? I guess I didn't plan that very well."

"It's okay. I'll give you a do-over. And you'd better make it good. Candlelight dinner, getting down on one knee, the ring—the whole shebang."

"It's a deal. I'll even get Jared's and Nick's input so I don't blow it." He turned her to face him. "I'll do it right later, but I think even this sorry proposal needs to be sealed with a kiss."

She grinned. "I couldn't agree more."

He leaned toward her, Gavin still propped on one hip, and slid his free hand behind her neck.

When his lips met hers, the warmth that flowed through her had nothing to do with the balmy August afternoon. She wrapped her arms around him, Gavin in the circle. They were a family, permanent and complete.

A horn blew, and they broke the kiss to watch a pickup truck holding a couple of high schoolers drive slowly past, the passenger leaning out the window whooping and hollering.

Tony let out his own whoop. "We just got engaged!"

The truck kept going, and their families moved closer until all nine of them were pressed into a big group hug.

Kris smiled. "If Mom could look down from heaven and see us right now, she'd be happy."

Tony returned her smile. "You think she'd approve?"

"Without a doubt."

As she stood in the small press of bodies, her heart soared. She'd wondered what it would be like to be a part of a family like Tony's.

Now she knew.

She wasn't just part of a family *like* Tony's. She was part of Tony's family, and it was awesome.

She looked over at Kassie and smiled.

Even her own family was turning out to be pretty good.

* * * * *

Romantic Suspense

Danger. Passion. Drama.

Available Next Month

Colton's K-9 Rescue Colleen Thompson
Alaskan Disappearance Karen Whiddon

....

Stranded Jennifer D. Bokal
Bodyguard Rancher Kacy Cross

....

LOVE INSPIRED

Christmas K-9 Guardians Lenora Worth & Katy Lee
Deadly Christmas Inheritance Jessica R. Patch

....

LOVE INSPIRED

Christmas Cold Case Maggie K. Black
Taken At Christmas Jodie Bailey

....

LOVE INSPIRED

Dangerous Christmas Investigation Virginia Vaughan
Colorado Christmas Survival Cate Nolan

Keep reading for an excerpt of a new title
from the Intrigue series,
UNDER LOCK AND KEY by K.D. Richards

Chapter One

Maggie Scott looked around the dimly lit museum gallery, exhausted but content. She'd done it. The donors' open house for the Viperé ruby exhibit had been a rousing success. The classical music that had played softly in the background during the night was silent now, but the air of sophistication and sense of reverence still filled the room. Soft spotlights lit the priceless paintings on the wall while a brighter beam shone down on what was literally the crown jewel of the exhibit. The Viperé ruby glowed under the light like a blood red sun.

Maggie stood in front of the glass case with the almost empty bottle of champagne she'd procured from the caterers before they'd left and a flute. She poured what little was left in the bottle into the flute and toasted herself.

"Congratulations to me." She downed half the liquid in the glass. Her eyes passed over the gallery space with a mixture of awe, satisfaction and pride. The night had been the culmination of a year's worth of labor. A decade of work if she counted undergraduate and graduate school and the handful of jobs she'd held at other museums before joining the Larimer Museum as an assistant curator three years earlier. It had taken a massive amount of work to ensure the success of the display and the open house for the donors and board members, who got a first look at the highly anticipated exhibit. As one of two assistant curators up for a possible promotion to curator and with the director of the British museum who'd loaned the Viperé ruby to the relatively small Larimer Museum watching her, she was under a great deal of pressure from a great many people. But the night had been an unmitigated success, so said her boss, and she was hopeful that she was now a shoo-in for the promotion.

Maggie stepped closer to the jewel, reaching out with her free hand and almost grazing the glass. The spotlight hit the ruby, creating a rainbow of glittering light around her. She raised the champagne flute to her lips and spoke, "To the Viperé ruby and all the other pieces of art that have inspired, challenged and united humanity in ways words cannot express."

She finished the champagne and stood for a moment, taking in the energy and vitality that emanated from the works around her.

Maggie was abruptly yanked from her reverie by the sound of a soft thud. She and Carl Downy were the only two people who were still in the building. Carl was the retired cop who provided security at night for the museum. Mostly, that meant he walked the three floors of the renovated and repurposed Victorian building that was itself a work of art between naps during his nine-hour shift.

A surge of unease traveled through her. She gripped the empty champagne bottle tightly and called out, "Carl, is that you?"

A moment passed without a response.

Unease was replaced with concern. Carl was getting on in years. He could have fallen or had a medical emergency of some type.

Maggie stepped into the even more dimly lit hallway connecting the rooms, the galleries as her boss liked to call them, on the main floor. The thud had sounded as if it had come from the front of the museum, but all she saw was pitch black in that direction. She knew the nooks and crannies of the museum as well as she knew her own house. Normally, she loved wandering through the space, leisurely taking in the pieces. Even though she'd seen each of them dozens of times, she always found herself noticing something new, some aspect or feature of the pieces she'd overlooked. That was one of the reasons she loved art. It was always teaching, always changing, even when it stayed the same.

But she didn't love it at the moment. The museum was eerily still and quiet.

Suddenly, a dark-clad figure stepped out of the shadows. He wore a mask, but she could tell he was a male. That was all she had time to process before the figure charged at her.

Her heartbeat thundered, and a voice in her head told her to run, but her feet felt melted to the floor. The bottle and champagne flute slid from her hands, shattering against the polished wood planks.

The intruder slammed her back into the wall, knocking the breath out of her. Before she had time to recover, he backhanded her across the face with a beefy gloved hand.

Pain exploded on the side of her face.

She slid along the wall, instinct forcing her to try to get away even as her conscious brain still struggled to process what was happening. But her assailant grabbed her arm, stopping her escape.

Her vision was blurred by the blow to her face, and the mask the intruder wore covered all but his dark brown eyes. Still, she was aware of her assailant raising his hand a second time, his fist clenched.

Her limbs felt like they were stuck in molasses, but she tried to raise her arm to deflect the blow.

Too slowly, as it turned out.

The intruder hit her on the side of her head, the impact causing excruciating pain before darkness descended and her world faded to black.

KEVIN LOMBARD'S PHONE RANG, dragging him out of a dreamless sleep at just after one in the morning.

"Lombard."

"Kevin, hey, sorry to wake you." The voice of his new boss, Tess Stenning, flowed over the phone line. "We have a problem. An assault and theft at the Larimer Museum, one of our newer clients. Since you are West Investigation's new director of corporate and institutional accounts, that makes it your problem."

Kevin groaned. He'd only been on the job for three weeks, but Tess was right, his division, his problem. It didn't matter that he hadn't overseen the installation of the security system at the Larimer. He'd looked over the file, as he'd done with all of the security plans that West Security and Investigations' new West Coast office had installed in the six months since they'd been open, so he had an idea of what the gallery security looked like.

West Security and Investigations was one of the premier security and private investigation firms on the East Coast. Run primarily by brothers Ryan and Shawn West, with a little help from their two older brothers, James and Brandon, West Security and Investigations had recently opened a West Coast office in Los Angeles, headed up by Tess Stenning, a long-time West operative and damn good private investigator. If he'd been asked a year ago whether he would ever consider joining a private investigations firm, even one with as sterling a reputation as West Security and Investigations, he'd have laughed.

But staying in Idyllwild had become untenable. A friend of a friend had recommended he reach out to Tess, and after a series of interviews with her and Ryan West, he'd been offered the job. Moving to Los Angeles had been an adjustment, but he was settling in.

He searched his memory for the details of the museum's security. Despite West Security and Investigations' recommendation that the museum update its entire security system, the gallery's board of directors had only approved the security specifications for the Viperé ruby. Shortsighted, he'd noted when he'd read the file, and now he had the feeling that he was about to be proven right.

Tess gave him the sparse details that she'd gotten from her contact on the police force. Someone had broken into the museum, attacked a curator and a guard and made off with the ruby. He ended the call and dragged himself into the bathroom for a quick shower. Ten years on the police force had conditioned him to getting late night— or early morning, as it were—phone calls. The shower helped wake him, and he set his coffee machine to brew while he quickly dressed then pulled up the museum's file on his West-issued tablet. A little more than thirty minutes after he'd gotten the call from Tess, he was headed out.

He arrived at the Larimer Museum twenty minutes later, thankful that most of Los Angeles was still asleep or out partying and not on the roads. He showed his ID to the police officer manning the door and was waved in. Officers milled about in the lobby, but he caught sight of Tess down a short hall toward the back of the Victorian building, talking to a small man in a rumpled suit and haphazardly knotted blue tie. The man waved his hands in obvious distress while it looked like Tess tried to console him.

Kevin made his way toward the pair. In the room twenty feet from where they stood, a police technician worked gathering evidence from the break-in.

"This is going to ruin us. The Larimer Museum will be ruined, and I'll never get another job as curator again." The man wiped the back of his hand over his brow.

Tess gave Kevin a nod. "Mr. Gustev, this is my colleague Kevin Lombard. Kevin, Robert Gustev, managing director and head curator of the Larimer Museum."

Gustev ignored Kevin's outstretched hand. He pointed his index figure at Tess. "This is your fault."

"West Investigations is going to do its best to identify the perpetrators and retrieve the ruby."

Gustev swiped his hand over his brow again. "I can't believe this is happening."

The man looked on the verge of being sick.

"Mr. Gustev—" Tess started.

"You were supposed to protect the ruby."

"If you recall, we did make several recommendations for upgrading the museum's security, which you and the Larimer's board of directors rejected," Tess said pointedly.

Gustev's face reddened, his jowls shaking in anger.

"Mr. Gustev," Kevin said before the curator had a chance to respond to Tess. "We are going to do everything we can to recover the ruby. It would help if you took Tess and I through everything that happened up until the time the intruder assaulted you."

"Me? No, it wasn't me that the thief attacked."

Kevin frowned. On the phone, Tess had said the guard and the curator had been attacked.

"It was my assistant curator who confronted the thief." Gustev frowned. "She's speaking with the police detective in her office right now."

"Oh, well, why don't you tell us what you know, and we'll speak to her once the police have finished."

Gustev ran them through a detailed description of the party that had taken place earlier that night. Kevin pressed the man on whether anything out of the ordinary happened at the party or in the days before, but Gustev swore that nothing of note had occurred.

The curator waved a hand at Tess. "I have to call the board members." He turned and hurried off down the hall, ascending a rear staircase.

Tess's eyes stayed trained on the retreating man's back until he disappeared on the second-floor landing. She let out a labored sigh. "This is going to turn into a you-know-what show if we don't get a handle on it fast."

Kevin's stomach turned over because she was right. "I'm not sure we can avoid that, but I'll do my best to get to the bottom of things as quickly as possible." He turned to look at the activity taking place in the room to the right of where they stood.

Glass sparkled on top of a podium covered with a black velvet blanket. A numbered yellow cone marked the shards as evidence. A crime scene tech made her way around the room, systematically photographing and bagging anything of note.

Tess groaned. "Someone managed to break into the building and steal the Viperé ruby, a ruby the size of your fist and worth more than the gross domestic product of my hometown of Missoula."

His eyebrow quirked up. "Sounds like a lot."

"Try two hundred fifty million a lot."

Kevin gave a low whistle. "That's a lot."

Tess cut him a look. "A lot of problems for us. I'm afraid Gustev—" she nodded toward the staircase that the curator had ascended moments earlier "—is going to throw himself out of a window."

The curator was more than a little bit on edge, but who could blame him. "The thief attacked the assistant curator but left her alive?"

Tess nodded. "The night guard and one of the assistant curators were knocked unconscious by the thief, apparently."

Kevin frowned. "What was an assistant curator still doing here so late?"

"That I don't know." Tess shrugged. "But the museum had a party tonight to kick off the opening of the Viperé ruby exhibit. The board, donors and other muckety mucks, drinking, dancing and, undoubtedly, opening their wallets."

"Undoubtedly," he said, turning his attention back to the crime scene technician at work.

Tess shook her head. "The guard was out cold when the EMTs arrived. They took him to the hospital. He's on the older side, former cop, though, so he's tough. The curator is in her office. Declined transportation to the hospital."

"Sounds like she's pretty tough, too."

Tess shrugged. "Or stupid. Detective Gill Francois is questioning her now."

He frowned. He hadn't had the pleasure of working with Francois yet, but he'd heard of him. The detective was a bulldog.

Tess chuckled. "Don't do that. Gill's good people. I've

already talked to him. He's agreed to let us tag along on the case, as long as we play nice and keep him in the loop regarding anything we find out."

He felt one of his eyebrows arch up. "And he'll do the same?"

Tess rolled her eyes. "You know how it goes. He says he will but..."

"Yeah, *but*." He did know how it went. He'd been one of the boys in blue not so long ago.

"Listen, I made sure West Investigations covered its rear regarding our advice to the board of directors of the museum to upgrade the entire system." Tess waved a hand in the air. "I told them that the security they'd authorized for the Viperé ruby left them open to possible theft, but they didn't want to spend the money and figured the locked and alarmed case along with the on-site twenty-four-hour security guard was enough."

"Didn't want to pony up the money?"

Tess tapped her nose then sighed. "Still, this is going to be a black mark on West Investigations if we don't figure out what happened here quickly. I know you've barely gotten settled in, but do you think you're up for the job?"

"Absolutely," he answered without reservation. "The first thing I want to do is get the security recordings and the alarm logs and get the exact time when the case was broken. We'll also need to figure out what the thief used to break the glass." He pulled the same type of small notebook he'd used when he was a police detective out of his jacket along with the small pen he kept hooked in the spiral. His tablet was in the computer case that hung from his shoulder, but he preferred the old-fashioned methods. Writing out his notes and thoughts helped him remember things better and think things through. "Of course, shatterproof glass isn't invincible, but it would have taken a great deal of force and a strong weapon to do it." He scratched out notes on his thoughts before they got away from him.

Tess cleared her throat. "The alarm went off just after eleven, triggered by the curator after she'd regained consciousness. Getting more specific than that is going to be a problem, at least with regards to the alarm logs."

Kevin looked up from his notebook. "Why?"

Tess looked more than a little green around the gills.

His stomach turned over, anticipating that whatever she was about to say wasn't going to be good.

"Because the alarm didn't go off," she said.

"The alarm didn't go off." Kevin repeated the words back to Tess as if they didn't make any sense to him. Then again, they didn't. "How is that possible?"

"That is a very good question."

He and Tess turned toward the sound of the voice.

A man Kevin would have made as a cop no matter where they'd met descended the back staircase.

Kevin's gaze moved to the woman coming down the stairs next to him, and his world stopped.

The man and woman halted in front of him and Tess.

"Hello, Kevin." The words floated from Maggie's lips on a wisp of a breath.

"Hello, Maggie."

Maggie Scott. His college girlfriend and, at one point, the woman he'd imagined spending his life with.

Subscribe and fall in love with a Mills & Boon series today!

You'll be among the first to read stories delivered to your door monthly and enjoy great savings.

WE
SIMPLY
LOVE
ROMANCE